Praise for the Novels of
#1 *New York Times* Bestselling Author
Nicholas Sparks

TRUE BELIEVER

"Time for a date with Sparks...The slow dance to the couple's first kiss is a two-chapter guilty pleasure." —*People*

"Another winner...a page-turner...has all the things we have come to expect from him: sweet romance and a strong sense of place." —*Charlotte Observer*

THE WISH

"If it's never too early for Christmas in your world, get in the mood with this *awww*-worthy story of first love and its echoes that takes place during the holidays." —*Good Housekeeping*

"Anyone looking for a sweet story will be enchanted." —*Booklist* (Starred Review)

"Sure to top the book lists of romance fans near and far." —CNN Underscored

"With *The Wish*, Sparks reminds us that love...will always move you in ways you can't comprehend." —*BookPage*

"As with all of Sparks's novels, emotions play a huge part. Though a bittersweet story, *The Wish* is a thought-provoking chronicle of a few decades in the protagonist's life. In the course of that life, she unearths her self-worth, self-acceptance, and the magnitude of first love."

—*New York Journal of Books*

"Covers the gamut of emotions from love to loss and will have readers crying gently into a tissue before the end."

—BookReporter.com

"If wishes could come true, this would be the Nicholas Sparks novel you've been asking for... The story of Maggie and Bryce is a timeless, cinematic read traversing both discovery and loss, and above all, the question of what it is we most wish for. Epic is a term bandied about too easily in literary circles, but it applies here."

—*Mountain Times* (NC)

"Beloved author Nicholas Sparks is well-known for his heartfelt, emotional stories—and his newest novel follows suit."

—*Woman's World*

THE RETURN

"As much a family drama as it is a love story... If you, like Trevor, are looking to slow down and focus on what's really important, *The Return* is the heartwarming read you've been waiting for."

—*BookPage*

"A pleasant read that moves like honey."

—BookTrib.com

"Take a trip to rural North Carolina, sit back, and enjoy the lush descriptions of the rambling creek and croaking frogs. Beautiful sunsets, meandering boat trips, exotic wildlife, buzzing bees, and small-town farmers' markets abound. Keep Trevor company as he navigates mysteries and spends time recovering from his personal demons... *The Return* [makes] for a perfect beach read or a fall/winter sitting-by-the-fire read."

—BookReporter.com

"There are few things we love more than a heartwarming Nicholas Sparks book, and his newest novel has definitely satisfied our craving." —*Reader's Digest*

"Will sweep you off your feet... [a] story of secrets, seduction, and forgiveness you'll want to read over and over again."

—CNN Underscored

"Deeply reflective... Sparks's latest novel reminds [us] that we're all human... Will pull you in from the very first page."

—POPSUGAR

"Sparks fans will love it, and readers new to his romantic fiction will be hooked." —*Northern Virginia Magazine*

"*The Return* reads at times like a fine mystery, but with the added benefit of Sparks's mature writing in crafting a love story that will inflame his longtime fans." —*Mountain Times* (NC)

"[Nicholas Sparks's] descriptions of the charms of downtown New Bern and the beauty of Brices Creek made me want to... rush to spend a few days there."

—*Chatham Journal Newspaper*

EVERY BREATH

"Sparks is known for crafting sweeping romances that make readers feel deeply and believe in the power of love...Sparks confirms his gifts...in this thoughtfully researched and spellbinding story of love that defies time, a tale both heartbreaking and heartwarming."
—*Booklist*

"What makes *Every Breath* rise above...is its unpredictability and strong character development."
—*USA Today*

"A heart-wrenching tale of fate and circumstance...an epic romance...Sparks fans will not be disappointed."
—*Publishers Weekly*

TWO BY TWO

"Sparks invites readers to take a journey that stares risks and rewards directly in the face. Whether it's tenderness between a husband and wife or affection between a father and his daughter, Sparks has definitely mastered the art of love."
—*Washington Times*

"Nicholas Sparks creates magic once again with [this] latest emotionally powerful novel."
—*RT Book Reviews*

SEE ME

"Sparks takes readers on a roller-coaster ride of emotion, from the soft tone of a love story to the adrenaline rush of a thriller."
—Associated Press

"*See Me* is not only a tender, engaging, and heartwarming story, but it displays the meshing of two different and opposite lives that come together to prove that love conquers all. Gripping and riveting suspense adds another layer of depth and interest."   —*New York Journal of Books*

"Powerful proof that Nicholas Sparks is a masterful storyteller who remains at the top of his game."
                                    —BookReporter.com

"This deeply emotional book once again proves that Sparks understands human nature and relationships as well as anyone writing today."   —BarnesandNoble.com

THE LONGEST RIDE

"Sparks is a poet...a master."   —*Philadelphia Inquirer*

"*The Longest Ride* is epic Sparks...[It] showcases the author's most accomplished work to date...There are moments of perfection...Reaching not only young and old, the novel is commingled with enough cowboy action, literary flavor, and a maturing gift for dialogue to reach across the sexes."
                                    —*Mountain Times* (NC)

THE BEST OF ME

"A creative genius...his book is great for any love story enthusiast."   —HubPages.com

"Unforgettable...Makes you settle in for another romantic date with this well-respected and talented storyteller."
—*Fredericksburg Free Lance-Star* (VA)

"I could not put it down...a classic Nicholas Sparks tragedy but with a twist of hope...If I can pick my favorites from him, *The Best of Me* will rank with *Message in a Bottle* and *The Notebook*—it was *that* good."   —BookReporter.com

"A beautifully written romance novel that will pull at all the appropriate heartstrings and leave you speechless."
—*The Guardian*

"Sparks's ability to capture the truths of this affair makes the story both heartfelt and heartbreaking. It's quite possibly his best work in years."   —*Publishers Weekly*

SAFE HAVEN

"A compelling love story...a gripping tale of love and survival...a riveting 'read all night' page-turner."   —BookReporter.com

"Sparks has written another wonderful love story that makes you see true love in its simplest form and believe in it...a fantastic book about relationships, love, trust, and friendships."
—BestsellersWorld.com

THE LAST SONG

"Romance, betrayal, and youthful discovery...Fans of *The Notebook*, *Message in a Bottle*, etc., will gobble it up."
—*Entertainment Weekly*

"A very enjoyable read...a plot that allows his characters to learn and grow from their experiences...Sparks is at his best."

—*Greensboro News-Record* (NC)

"Raw emotion, young love, family angst, and—ultimately—sweet resolution."

—*BookPage*

THE LUCKY ONE

"A tale of redemption...holds readers in suspense until the final chapter...It will test readers' beliefs in the power of destiny and fate, and how they relate to choices one makes in life."

—*Chattanooga Times Free Press*

"In true Nicholas Sparks fashion, the reader is engaged from the first to last page. The characters are authentic, and the plot is engrossing and emotionally charged."

—*BookLoons.com*

THE CHOICE

"A tender and moving love story."

—*Publishers Weekly*

"A heartrending love story...will have you entranced. And if *The Notebook* left you teary-eyed, his latest will have the same effect."

—*Myrtle Beach Sun News*

"Provides subtle lessons in love and hope...reinforces the theory that all choices, no matter how seemingly unimportant...often have far-reaching, rippling effects. Sparks has become a favorite storyteller because of his ability to take ordinary people, put them in extraordinary situations, and create unexpected outcomes." —BookReporter.com

DEAR JOHN

"Beautifully moving...Has tremendous emotional depth, revealing the true meaning of unconditional love."
—*RT Book Reviews*

"For Sparks, weighty matters of the day remain set pieces, furniture upon which to hang timeless tales of chaste longing and harsh fate." —*Washington Post Book World*

"Sparks lives up to his reputation...a tribute to courageous and self-sacrificing soldiers." —*Booklist*

AT FIRST SIGHT

"An ending that surprises." —*New York Times Book Review*

"Nicholas Sparks is one of the best-known writers in America and overseas for good reason: He has written stories that reveal the yearning for our most prized possession: love."
—*Mobile Register* (AL)

THE WEDDING

"Sweet but packs a punch...There is a twist that pulls everything together and makes you glad you read this."
—*Charlotte Observer*

"Sparks tells his sweet story... [with] a gasp-inducing twist at the very end. Satisfied female readers will close the covers with a sigh."
                                                        —*Publishers Weekly*

THE GUARDIAN

"An involving love story... an edge-of-your-seat, unpredictable thriller."
                                                        —*Booklist*

"Nicholas Sparks is a top-notch writer. He has created a truly spinetingling thriller exploring love and obsession with a kind of suspense never before experienced in his novels."
                                                        —RedBank.com

NIGHTS IN RODANTHE

"Bittersweet... romance blooms... You'll cry in spite of yourself."
                                                        —*People*

"Passionate and memorable... smooth, sensitive writing... This is a novel that can hold its own."
                                                        —Associated Press

"Extremely hard to put down... a love story, and a good love story at that."
                                                        —*Boston Herald*

A BEND IN THE ROAD

"Sweet, accessible, uplifting."
                                                        —*Publishers Weekly*

"A powerful tale of true love."
                                                        —*Booklist*

"A smoothly written and satisfying novel."

—Romance Reviews Today

THE RESCUE

"A romantic page-turner...Sparks's fans won't be disappointed."

—*Glamour*

"All of Sparks's trademark elements—love, loss, and small-town life—are present in this terrific read." —*Booklist*

A WALK TO REMEMBER

"An extraordinary book...touching, at times riveting...a book you won't soon forget." —*New York Post*

"A sweet tale of young but everlasting love."

—*Chicago Sun-Times*

"Bittersweet...a tragic yet spiritual love story." —*Variety*

MESSAGE IN A BOTTLE

"The novel's unabashed emotion—and an unexpected turn—will put tears in your eyes." —*People*

"Glows with moments of tenderness...delve[s] deeply into the mysteries of eternal love." —*Cleveland Plain Dealer*

"Deeply moving, beautifully written, and extremely romantic."
—*Booklist*

THE NOTEBOOK

"Nicholas Sparks...will not let you go. His novel shines."
—*Dallas Morning News*

"Proves that good things come in small packages...a classic tale of love." —*Christian Science Monitor*

"The lyrical beauty of this touching love story...will captivate the heart of every reader and establish Nicholas Sparks as a gifted novelist." —*Denver Rocky Mountain News*

True Believer

NICHOLAS SPARKS

······◆······

True Believer

GRAND
CENTRAL

NEW YORK   BOSTON

Copyright © 2005 by Nicholas Sparks
Reading group guide copyright © 2011 by Hachette Book Group, Inc.

Cover design by Anna Dorfman. Handlettering by Nick Misani. Cover images from Shutterstock. Cover copyright © 2023 by Hachette Book Group, Inc.

Grand Central Publishing
Hachette Book Group
1290 Avenue of the Americas, New York, NY 10104
grandcentralpublishing.com
twitter.com/grandcentralpub

Originally published in hardcover and ebook by Grand Central Publishing in April 2005
First trade paperback edition: April 2006
Reissued: September 2016, June 2020, May 2023

Grand Central Publishing is a division of Hachette Book Group, Inc. The Grand Central Publishing name and logo is a trademark of Hachette Book Group, Inc.

The publisher is not responsible for websites (or their content) that are not owned by the publisher.

The Hachette Speakers Bureau provides a wide range of authors for speaking events. To find out more, go to hachettespeakersbureau.com or email HachetteSpeakers@hbgusa.com.

Grand Central Publishing books may be purchased in bulk for business, educational, or promotional use. For information, please contact your local bookseller or the Hachette Book Group Special Markets Department at special.markets@hbgusa.com.

The Library of Congress has cataloged the hardcover edition as follows:

Sparks, Nicholas.
     True believer / Nicholas Sparks.—1st ed.
          p. cm.
       ISBN 0-446-53243-6—ISBN 0-446-57829-0 (large print)
       1. Science writers—Fiction. 2. North Carolina—Fiction.
     3. Apparitions—Fiction. 4. Cemeteries—Fiction. I. Title.
     PS3569.P363T78 2005
     813'.54—dc22

                                                    2005000387

ISBNs: 9781538743270 (trade pbk. reissue), 9780759513457 (ebook)

Printed in the United States of America

LSC-C

Printing 4, 2023

For Rhett and Valerie Little,
wonderful people, wonderful friends

Acknowledgments

·····◆·····

As always, I have to thank my wife, Cathy, for her support while writing this novel. All that I'm able to do is because of her.

I also have to thank my children as well: Miles, Ryan, Landon, Lexie, and Savannah. What can I say? I was blessed the moment that each of you came into my life and I'm proud of you all.

Theresa Park, my agent, deserves a long round of applause for all that she does for me. Congrats on your new agency—Park Literary Group (for all you aspiring writers out there). I'm honored to call you my friend.

Jamie Raab, my editor, deserves my thanks, not only for the way she edits my novels, but for all the trust she places in me. I don't know where my career would have ended up without you, and I'm thankful for your generosity and kindness.

Larry Kirshbaum and Maureen Egen are friends and colleagues, and it's been my privilege to work with them. They are simply the best at what they do.

Denise DiNovi also deserves my thanks, not only for the films she's made from my novels, but for those well-timed phone calls, which always brighten my day.

Thanks also to Howie Sanders and Dave Park, my agents at UTA, as well as Richard Green at CAA.

Lynn Harris and Mark Johnson, who helped to make *The Notebook* into the wonderful film that it was, also deserve my gratitude. Thanks for never losing your belief in the novel.

Special thanks to Francis Greenburger as well. He knows why—and I owe him one.

And finally, thanks to those people who work so hard behind the scenes and have become like family to me over the years: Emi Battaglia, Edna Farley, and Jennifer Romanello in the publicity department; Flag, who did another fantastic job with the cover; Scott Schwimer, my attorney; Harvey-Jane Kowal, Shannon O'Keefe, Julie Barer, and Peter McGuigan. I'm fortunate to work with such wonderful people.

True Believer

One

..... ❖ .....

Jeremy Marsh sat with the rest of the live studio audience, feeling unusually conspicuous. He was one of only half a dozen men in attendance on that mid-December afternoon. He'd dressed in black, of course, and with his dark wavy hair, light blue eyes, and fashionable stubble, he looked every bit the New Yorker that he was. While studying the guest onstage, he managed to surreptitiously watch the attractive blonde three rows up. His profession often demanded effective multitasking. He was an investigative journalist in pursuit of a story, and the blonde was just another member of the audience; still, the professional observer in him couldn't help noticing how attractive she looked in her halter top and jeans. Journalistically speaking, that is.

Clearing his mind, he tried to focus his attention on the guest again. This guy was beyond ridiculous. In the glare of television lights, Jeremy thought the spirit guide looked constipated as he claimed to hear voices from beyond the grave. He had assumed a false intimacy, acting as if he were everyone's brother or best friend, and it seemed that the vast majority of the awestruck audience—including the attractive blonde and the woman the guest was addressing—considered him a gift from heaven itself. Which made sense, Jeremy thought, since that was always where the lost loved ones ended up. Spirits from beyond the grave were always surrounded by bright angelic light and enveloped in an aura of peace and tranquillity. Never once had Jeremy heard of a spirit guide channeling from the other, hotter place. A lost loved one never mentioned that he was being roasted on a spit or boiled in a cauldron of motor oil, for instance. But Jeremy knew he was being cynical. And besides, he had to admit, it was a pretty good show. Timothy Clausen was good—far better than most of the quacks Jeremy had written about over the years.

"I know it's hard," Clausen said into the microphone, "but Frank is telling you that it's time to let him go now."

The woman he was addressing with oh-so-much empathy looked as if she was about to faint. Fiftyish, she wore a green-striped blouse, her curly red hair sprouting and spiraling in every direction. Her hands were clasped so tightly at chest level that her fingers were white from the pressure.

Clausen paused and brought his hand to his forehead, drawing once more on "the world beyond," as he put it. In the silence, the crowd collectively leaned forward in their seats. Everyone knew what was coming next; this was the third audience member Clausen had chosen today. Not surprisingly, Clausen was the only featured guest on the popular talk show.

"Do you remember the letter he sent you?" Clausen asked. "Before he died?"

The woman gasped. The crewman beside her held the microphone even closer so that everyone watching on television would be able to hear her clearly.

"Yes, but how could you know about—?" she stammered.

Clausen didn't let her finish. "Do you remember what it said?" he asked.

"Yes," the woman croaked.

Clausen nodded, as if he'd read the letter himself. "It was about forgiveness, wasn't it?"

On the couch, the hostess of the show, the most popular afternoon talk show in America, swiveled her gaze from Clausen to the woman and back again. She looked both amazed and satisfied. Spirit guides were always good for ratings.

As the woman in the audience nodded, Jeremy noticed mascara beginning to stream down her cheeks. The cameras zoomed in to show it more clearly. Daytime television at its dramatic best.

"But how could you . . . ?" the woman repeated.

"He was talking about your sister, too," Clausen murmured. "Not just himself."

The woman stared at Clausen transfixed.

"Your sister Ellen," Clausen added, and with that revelation, the woman finally let loose a raspy cry. Tears burst forth like an automated sprinkler. Clausen—tan and trim in his black suit with nary a hair out of place—continued to nod like one of those bobbing dogs you stick on your dashboard. The audience gazed at the woman in utter silence.

"Frank left something else for you, didn't he? Something from your past."

In spite of the hot studio lights, the woman actually seemed to pale. In the corner of the set, beyond the general viewing area, Jeremy saw the producer rotating an upraised finger in a helicopter pattern. It was getting close to the commercial break. Clausen glanced almost imperceptibly in that direction. No one but Jeremy seemed to notice, and he often wondered why viewers never questioned how channeling from the spirit world could be timed so perfectly to fit with commercial breaks.

Clausen went on. "That no one else could know about. A key of some sort, is that right?"

The sobs continued as the woman nodded.

"You never thought he'd save it, did you?"

Okay, here's the clincher, Jeremy thought. Another true believer on the way.

"It's from the hotel where you stayed on your honeymoon. He put it there so that when you found it, you would remember the happy times you spent together. He doesn't want you to remember him with pain, because he loves you."

"Ooohhhhhhh . . . ," the woman cried.

Or something like that. A moan perhaps. From where he was sitting Jeremy couldn't be certain, because the cry was interrupted by sudden, enthusiastic applause. All at once, the microphone was pulled away. Cameras zoomed out. Her moment in the sun completed, the woman from the audience collapsed in her seat. On cue, the hostess stood from the couch and faced the camera.

"Remember that what you're seeing is real. None of these people have ever met with Timothy Clausen." She smiled. "We'll be back with one more reading after this."

More applause as the show broke for commercials, and Jeremy leaned back in his seat.

As an investigative journalist known for his interest in science, he'd made a career out of writing about people like this. Most of the time, he enjoyed what he did and took pride in his work as a valuable public service, in a profession so special as to have its rights enumerated in the First Amendment of the Constitution of the United States of America. For his regular column in *Scientific American*, he'd interviewed Nobel laureates, explained the theories of Stephen Hawking and Einstein in lay terms, and had once been credited with sparking the groundswell of public opinion that led the FDA to remove a dangerous antidepressant from the market. He'd written extensively about the Cassini project, the faulty mirror on the lens of the Hubble spacecraft, and had been one of the first to publicly decry the Utah cold fusion experiment as a fraud.

Unfortunately, as impressive as it sounded, his column didn't pay much. It was the freelance work that paid most of his bills, and like all freelancers, he was always hustling to come up with stories that would interest magazine or newspaper editors. His niche had broadened to include "anything unusual," and in the past fifteen years, he'd researched and investigated psychics, spirit guides, faith healers, and mediums. He'd exposed frauds, hoaxes, and forgeries. He'd visited haunted houses, searched for mystical creatures, and hunted for the origins of urban legends. Skeptical by nature, he also had the rare ability to explain difficult scientific concepts in a way the average reader could understand, and his articles had appeared in hundreds of newspapers and magazines around the world. Scientific debunking, he felt, was both noble and important, even if the public didn't always appreciate it. Frequently, the mail he received after publishing his freelance articles was peppered with words like "idiot," "moron," and his personal favorite, "government flunky."

Investigative journalism, he'd come to learn, was a thankless business.

Reflecting on this with a frown, he observed the audience chatting eagerly, wondering who would be chosen next. Jeremy stole another glance at the blonde, who was examining her lipstick in a hand mirror.

Jeremy already knew that the people chosen by Clausen weren't officially part of the act, even though Clausen's appearance was announced in advance and people had fought wildly for tickets to the show. Which meant, of course, that the audience was loaded with life-after-death believers. To them, Clausen was legitimate. How else could he know such personal things about strangers, unless he talked to spirits? But like any good magician who had his repertoire down pat, the illusion was still an illusion, and right before the show, Jeremy not only had figured out how he was pulling it off, but had the photographic evidence to prove it.

Bringing down Clausen would be Jeremy's biggest coup to date, and it served the guy right. Clausen was the worst kind of con man. And yet the pragmatic side of Jeremy also realized that this was the kind of story that rarely came along, and he wanted to make the most of it. Clausen, after all, was on the cusp of enormous celebrity, and in America, celebrity was all that mattered. Though he knew the odds were utterly improbable, he fantasized about what would happen if Clausen actually picked *him* next. He didn't expect it; being chosen was akin to winning the trifecta at Santa Anita; and even if it didn't happen, Jeremy knew he'd still have a quality story. But quality and extraordinary were often separated by simple twists of fate, and as the commercial break ended, he felt the slightest twinge of unjustified hope that somehow Clausen would zero in on him.

And, as if God himself wasn't exactly thrilled with what Clausen was doing, either, that was exactly what happened.

Three weeks later, winter in Manhattan was bearing down hard. A front from Canada had moved in, dropping temperatures to nearly zero, and plumes of steam rose steadily from the sewer grates before settling over the icy sidewalks. Not that anyone seemed to mind. New York's hardy citizens displayed their usual indifference to all things weather-related, and Friday nights were not to be wasted under any circumstance. People worked too hard during the week to waste an evening out, especially when there was reason to celebrate. Nate Johnson and Alvin Bernstein had already been celebrating for an hour, as had a couple of dozen friends and journalists—some from *Scientific American*—who'd assembled in Jeremy's honor. Most were well into the buzz phase of the evening and enjoying themselves immensely, mostly because journalists tended to be budget-conscious and Nate was picking up the tab.

Nate was Jeremy's agent. Alvin, a freelance cameraman, was Jeremy's best friend, and they'd gathered at the trendy bar on the Upper West Side to celebrate Jeremy's appearance on ABC's *Primetime Live*. Commercials for *Primetime Live* had been airing that week—most of them featuring Jeremy front and center and the promise of a major exposé—and interview requests were pouring into Nate's office from around the country. Earlier that afternoon, *People* magazine had called, and an interview was scheduled for the following Monday morning.

There hadn't been enough time to organize a private room for the get-together, but no one seemed to mind. With its long granite bar and dramatic lighting, the packed facility was yuppieville. While the journalists from *Scientific American* tended to wear tweed sport jackets with pocket protectors and were crowded into one corner of the room discussing photons, most of the other patrons looked as if they'd dropped by after finishing up at work on Wall Street or Madison Avenue: Italian suit jackets slung over the backs of chairs, Hermès ties loosened, men who seemed to want to do nothing more than to scope out the women in attendance while flashing their Rolexes. Women straight from work in publishing and advertising were dressed in designer skirts and impossibly high heels, sipping flavored martinis while pretending to ignore the men. Jeremy himself had his eye on a tall redhead standing at the other end of the bar who appeared to be glancing his way. He wondered if she recognized him from the television ads, or whether she just wanted some company. She turned away, apparently uninterested, but then looked his way again. With her gaze lingering just a little longer this time, Jeremy raised his glass.

"C'mon, Jeremy, pay attention," Nate said, nudging him with his elbow. "You're on TV! Don't you want to see how you did?"

Jeremy turned from the redhead. Glancing up at the screen, he saw himself sitting opposite Diane Sawyer. Strange, he thought, like being in two places at once. It still didn't seem quite real. Nothing in the past three weeks had seemed real, despite his years in media.

On-screen, Diane was describing him as "America's most esteemed scientific journalist." Not only had the story turned out to be everything he'd wanted, but Nate was even talking to *Primetime Live* about Jeremy doing regular stories for them with a possibility of additional features on *Good Morning America*. Though many journalists believed television was less important than other, more serious forms of reporting, it didn't stop most of them from secretly viewing television as the Holy Grail, by which they meant big money. Despite the congratulations, envy was in the air, a sensation as foreign to Jeremy as space travel.

After all, journalists of his stripe weren't exactly at the top of the media pecking order—until today.

"Did she just call you esteemed?" Alvin asked. "You write about Bigfoot and the legend of Atlantis!"

"Shh," Nate said, his eyes glued to the television. "I'm trying to hear this. It could be important for Jeremy's career." As Jeremy's agent, Nate was forever promoting events that "could be important for Jeremy's career," for the simple reason that freelancing wasn't all that lucrative. Years earlier, when Nate was starting out, Jeremy had pitched a book proposal, and they'd been working together ever since, simply because they'd become friends.

"Whatever," Alvin said, dismissing the scolding.

Meanwhile, flickering on the screen behind Diane Sawyer and Jeremy were the final moments of Jeremy's performance on the day-time television show, in which Jeremy had pretended to be a man grieving the boyhood death of his brother, a boy Clausen claimed to be channeling for Jeremy's benefit.

"He's with me," Clausen could be heard announcing. "He wants you to let him go, Thad." The picture shifted to capture Jeremy's rendition of an anguished guest, his face contorted. Clausen nodded in the background, either oozing sympathy or looking consti-pated, depending on the perspective.

"Your mother never changed his room—the room you shared with him. She insisted that it be kept unchanged, and you still had to sleep there," Clausen went on.

"Yes," Jeremy gasped.

"But you were frightened in there, and in your anger, you took something of his, something very personal, and buried it in the backyard."

"Yes," Jeremy managed again, as if too emotional to say more.

"His retainer!"

"Ooooohhhhhhhhh," Jeremy cried, bringing his hands to his face.

"He loves you, but you have to realize that he's at peace now. He has no anger toward you . . ."

"Ooooohhhhhhh!" Jeremy wailed again, contorting his face even more.

In the bar, Nate watched the clips in silent concentration. Alvin, on the other hand, was laughing as he raised his beer high.

"Give that man an Oscar!" he shouted.

"It was rather impressive, wasn't it?" Jeremy said, grinning.

"I mean it, you two," Nate said, not hiding his irritation. "Talk during the commercials."

"Whatever," Alvin said again. "Whatever" had always been Alvin's favorite word.

On *Primetime Live*, the videotape faded to black and the camera focused on Diane Sawyer and Jeremy, sitting across from each other once again.

"So nothing Timothy Clausen said was true?" Diane asked.

"Not a thing," Jeremy said. "As you already know, my name isn't Thad, and while I do have five brothers, they're all alive and well."

Diane held a pen over a pad of paper, as if she was about to take notes. "So how did Clausen do this?"

"Well, Diane," Jeremy began.

In the bar, Alvin's pierced eyebrow rose. He leaned toward Jeremy. "Did you just call her Diane? Like you're *friends?*"

"Could you please!" Nate said, growing more exasperated by the moment.

On-screen, Jeremy was going on. "What Clausen does is simply a variation on what people have been doing for hundreds of years. First of all, he's good at reading people, and he's an expert at making vague, emotionally charged associations and responding to audience members' cues."

"Yes, but he was so specific. Not only with you, but with the other guests. He had names. How does he do that?"

Jeremy shrugged. "He heard me talking about my brother

Marcus before the show. I simply made up an imaginary life and broadcast it loud and clear."

"How did it actually reach Clausen's ears?"

"Con men like Clausen have been known to use a variety of tricks, including microphones and paid 'listeners' who circulate in the waiting area before the show. Before I was seated, I made sure to move around and strike up conversations with lots of audience members, watching to see if anyone exhibited unusual interest in my story. And sure enough, one man seemed particularly concerned."

Behind them, the videotape was replaced by an enlarged photograph that Jeremy had taken with a small camera hidden in his watch, a high-tech spy toy he'd promptly expensed to *Scientific American*. Jeremy loved high-tech toys almost as much as he loved expensing them to others.

"What are we looking at here?" Diane asked.

Jeremy pointed. "This man was mingling with the studio audience, posing as a visitor from Peoria. I took this photograph right before the show while we were talking. Zoom in further, please."

On-screen, the photograph was enlarged and Jeremy motioned toward it.

"Do you see the small USA pin on his lapel? That's not just for decoration. It's actually a miniature transmitter that broadcasts to a recording device backstage."

Diane frowned. "How do you know this?"

"Because," Jeremy said, raising an eyebrow, "I happen to have one just like it."

On cue, Jeremy reached into his jacket pocket and pulled out what appeared to be the same USA pin, attached to a long, thread-like wire and transmitter.

"This particular model is manufactured in Israel"—Jeremy's voice could be heard over the camera close-up of the gadget—"and it's very high-end. I've heard it's used by the CIA, but, of course, I can't confirm that. What I can tell you is that the technology is very advanced—this little microphone can pick up conversations from across a noisy, crowded room and, with the right filtering systems, can even isolate them."

Diane inspected the pin with apparent fascination. "And you're certain that this was indeed a microphone and not just a pin?"

"Well, as you know, I've been looking into Clausen's past for a long time now, and a week after the show, I managed to obtain some more photographs."

A new photograph flashed on the screen. Though a bit grainy, it was a picture of the same man who'd been wearing the USA pin.

"This photo was taken in Florida, outside Clausen's office. As you can see, the man is heading inside. His name is Rex Moore, and he's actually an employee of Clausen's. He's worked with Clausen for two years."

"Ooohhhhh!" Alvin shouted, and the rest of the broadcast, which was winding down, anyway, was drowned out as others, jealous or not, joined in with hoots and hollers. The free booze had worked its magic, and Jeremy was deluged with congratulations after the show had ended.

"You were fantastic," Nate said. At forty-three, Nate was short and balding and had a tendency to wear suits that were just a bit too tight in the waist. No matter, the man was energy incarnate and, like most agents, positively buzzed with fervent optimism.

"Thanks," Jeremy said, downing the remainder of his beer.

"This is going to be big for your career," Nate went on. "It's your ticket to a regular television gig. No more scrambling for lousy freelance magazine work, no more chasing UFO stories. I've always said that with your looks, you were made for TV."

"You have always said that," Jeremy conceded with the eye-rolling manner of someone reciting an oft-given lecture.

"I mean it. The producers from *Primetime Live* and GMA keep calling, talking about using you as a regular contributor on their shows. You know, 'what this late-breaking science news means for you' and all that. A big leap for a science reporter."

"I'm a journalist," Jeremy sniffed, "not a reporter."

"Whatever," Nate said, making a motion as if brushing away a fly. "Like I've always said, your looks are made for television."

"I'd have to say Nate's right," Alvin added with a wink. "I mean, how else could you be more popular than me with the ladies, despite having zero personality?" For years, Alvin and Jeremy had frequented bars together, trolling for dates.

Jeremy laughed. Alvin Bernstein, whose name conjured up a clean-cut, bespectacled accountant—one of the countless professionals who wore Florsheim shoes and carried a briefcase to work—didn't look like an Alvin Bernstein. As a teenager, he'd seen Eddie Murphy in *Delirious* and had decided to make the full-leather style his own, a wardrobe that horrified his Florsheim-wearing, briefcase-carrying father, Melvin. Fortunately, leather seemed to go well with his tattoos. Alvin considered tattoos to be a reflection of his unique aesthetic, and he was uniquely aesthetic on both his arms, right up to his shoulder blades. All of which complemented Alvin's multiply pierced ears.

"So are you still planning a trip down south to investigate that ghost story?" Nate pressed. Jeremy could fairly see the wheels clicking and clacking away in his brain. "After your interview with *People*, I mean."

Jeremy brushed his dark hair out of his eyes and signaled the bartender for another beer. "Yeah, I guess so. *Primetime* or no *Primetime*, I still have bills to pay, and I was thinking I could use this for my column."

"But you'll be in contact, right? Not like when you went undercover with the Righteous and Holy?" He was referring to a six-thousand-word piece Jeremy had done for *Vanity Fair* about a religious cult; in that instance, Jeremy had essentially severed all communication for a period of three months.

"I'll be in contact," Jeremy said. "This story isn't like that. I should be out of there in less than a week. 'Mysterious lights in the cemetery.' No big deal."

"Hey, you need a cameraman by any chance?" Alvin piped in. Jeremy looked over at him. "Why? Do you want to go?"

"Hell yeah. Head south for the winter, maybe meet me a nice southern belle while you pick up the tab. I hear the women down there will drive you crazy, but in a good way. It'll be like an exotic vacation."

"Aren't you supposed to be shooting something for *Law & Order* next week?"

As strange as Alvin looked, his reputation was impeccable, and his services were usually in high demand.

"Yeah, but I'll be clear toward the end of the week," Alvin said. "And look, if you're serious about this television thing like Nate says you should be, it might be important to get some decent footage of these mysterious lights."

"That's assuming there are even any lights to film."

"You do the advance work and let me know. I'll keep my calendar open."

"Even if there are lights, it's a small story," Jeremy warned. "No one in television will be interested in it."

"Not last month, maybe," Alvin said. "But after seeing you tonight, they'll be interested. You know how it is in television—all those producers chasing their own tails, trying to find the next big thing. If GMA is suddenly hot to trot, then you know the *Today* show will be calling soon and *Dateline* will be knocking at the door. No producer wants to be left out. That's how they get fired. The last thing they want to do is to have to explain to the executives why they missed the boat. Believe me—I work in television. I know these people."

"He's right," Nate said, interrupting them. "You never know what'll happen next, and it might be a good idea to plan ahead. You had definite presence tonight. Don't kid yourself. And if you can get some actual footage of the lights, it might be just the thing that *GMA* or *Primetime* needs to make their decision."

Jeremy squinted at his agent. "You serious about this? It's a *nothing* story. The reason I decided to do it at all was because I needed a break after Clausen. That story took four months of my life."

"And look what it got you," Nate said, putting a hand on Jeremy's shoulder. "This may be a fluff piece, but with sensational footage and a good backstory, who knows what television will think?"

Jeremy was silent for a moment before finally shrugging. "Fine," he said. He glanced at Alvin. "I'm leaving on Tuesday. See if you can get there by next Friday. I'll call you before then with the details."

Alvin reached for his beer and took a drink. "Well, golly," he said, mimicking Gomer Pyle, "I'm off to the land of grits and chitlins. And I promise my bill won't be too high."

Jeremy laughed. "You ever been down south?"

"Nope. You?"

"I've visited New Orleans and Atlanta," Jeremy admitted. "But those are cities, and cities are pretty much the same everywhere. For this story, we're heading to the real South. It's a little town in North Carolina, a place called Boone Creek. You should see the town's Web site. It talks about the azaleas and dogwoods that bloom in April, and proudly displays a picture of the town's most prominent citizen. A guy named Norwood Jefferson."

"Who?" Alvin asked.

"A politician. He served in the North Carolina State Senate from 1907 to 1916."

"Who cares?"

"Exactly," Jeremy said with a nod. Glancing across the bar, he noticed with disappointment that the redhead was gone.

"Where is this place exactly?"

"Right between the *middle of nowhere* and '*where are we exactly?*' I'm staying at a place called Greenleaf Cottages, which the Chamber of Commerce describes as scenic and rustic yet modern. Whatever that means."

Alvin laughed. "Sounds like an adventure."

"Don't worry about it. You'll fit right in down there, I'm sure."

"You think so?"

Jeremy noted the leather, tattoos, and piercings.

"Oh, absolutely," Jeremy said. "They'll probably want to adopt you."

Two

..... ❖ .....

On Tuesday, the day after his interview with *People* magazine, Jeremy arrived in North Carolina. It was just past noon; when he left New York, it had been sleeting and gray, with more snow expected. Here, with an expanse of blue skies stretched out above him, winter seemed a long way off.

According to the map that he'd picked up in the airport gift shop, Boone Creek was in Pamlico County, a hundred miles southeast of Raleigh and—if the drive was any indication—about a zillion miles from what he considered civilization. On either side of him, the landscape was flat and sparse and about as exciting as pancake batter. Farms were separated by thin strands of loblolly pines, and given the sparse traffic, it was everything Jeremy could do to keep from flooring the accelerator out of sheer boredom.

But it wasn't all bad, he had to admit. Well, the actual driving part, anyway. The slight vibration of the wheel, the revving of the engine, and the feeling of acceleration were known to increase adrenaline production, especially in men (he'd once written a column about it). Life in the city made owning a car superfluous, however, and he'd never been able to justify the expense. Instead, he was transported from place to place in crowded subways or whiplash-inducing taxicabs. Travel in the city was noisy, hectic, and, depending on the cabdriver, sometimes life-threatening, but as a born and bred New Yorker, he'd long since come to accept it as just another exciting aspect of living in the place he called home.

His thoughts drifted to his ex-wife. Maria, he reflected, would have loved a drive like this. In the early years of their marriage, they would rent a car and drive to the mountains or the beach, sometimes spending hours on the road. She'd been a publicist at *Elle* magazine when they'd met at a publishing party. When he asked if she'd like to join him at a nearby coffee shop, he had no idea she would end up being the only woman he ever loved. At first, he thought he'd made a mistake in asking her out, simply because they seemed to have nothing in common. She was feisty and emotional, but later, when he kissed her outside her apartment, he was entranced.

He eventually came to appreciate her fiery personality, her unerring instincts about people, and the way she seemed to embrace all of him without judgment, good and bad. A year later, they were married in the church, surrounded by friends and family. He was twenty-six, not yet a columnist for *Scientific American* but steadily building his reputation, and they could barely afford the small apartment they rented in Brooklyn. To his mind, it was young-and-struggling marital bliss. To her mind, he eventually suspected, their marriage was strong in theory but constructed on a shaky foundation. In the beginning, the problem was simple: while her job kept her in the city, Jeremy traveled, pursuing the big story wherever it might be. He was often gone for weeks at a time, and while she'd assured him that she could handle it, she must have realized during his absences that she couldn't. Just after their second anniversary, as he readied himself for yet another trip, Maria sat down beside him on the bed. Clasping her hands together, she raised her brown eyes to meet his.

"This isn't working," she said simply, letting the words hang for a moment. "You're never home anymore and it isn't fair to me. It isn't fair to us."

"You want me to quit?" he asked, feeling a small bubble of panic rise in him.

"No, not quit. But maybe you can find something local. Like at the *Times*. Or the *Post*. Or the *Daily News*."

"It's not going to be like this forever," he pleaded. "It's only for a little while."

"That's what you said six months ago," she said. "It's never going to change."

Looking back, Jeremy knew he should have taken it as the warning that it was, but at the time, he had a story to write, this one concerning Los Alamos. She wore an uncertain smile as he kissed her good-bye, and he thought about her expression briefly as he sat on the plane, but when he returned, she seemed herself again and they spent the weekend curled up in bed. She began to talk about having a baby, and despite the nervousness he felt, he was thrilled at the thought. He assumed he'd been forgiven, but the protective armor of their relationship had been chipped, and imperceptible cracks appeared with every additional absence. The final split came a year later, a month after a visit to a doctor on the Upper East Side, one who presented them with a future that neither of them had ever envisioned. Far more than his traveling, the visit foretold the end of their relationship, and even Jeremy knew it.

"I can't stay," she'd told him afterward. "I want to, and part of me will always love you, but I can't."

She didn't need to say more, and in the quiet, self-pitying moments after the divorce, he sometimes questioned whether she'd ever really loved him. They could have made it, he told himself. But in the end, he understood intuitively why she had left, and he harbored no ill will against her. He even spoke to her on the phone now and then, though he couldn't bring himself to attend her marriage three years later to an attorney who lived in Chappaqua.

The divorce had become final seven years ago, and to be honest, it was the only truly sad thing ever to have happened to him. Not many people could say that, he knew. He'd never been seriously injured, he had an active social life, and he'd emerged from childhood without the sort of psychological trauma that seemed to afflict so many of his age. His brothers and their wives, his parents, and even his grandparents—all four in their nineties—were healthy. They were close, too: a couple of weekends a month, the ever-growing clan would gather at his parents', who still lived in the house in Queens where Jeremy had grown up. He had seventeen nieces and nephews, and though he sometimes felt out of place at family functions, since he was a bachelor again in a family of happily married people, his brothers were respectful enough not to probe the reasons behind the divorce.

And he'd gotten over it. For the most part, anyway. Sometimes, on drives like this, he would feel a pang of yearning for what might have been, but that was rare now, and the divorce hadn't soured him on women in general.

A couple of years back, Jeremy had followed a study about whether the perception of beauty was the product of cultural norms or genetics. For the study, attractive women and less attractive women were asked to hold infants, and the length of eye contact between the women and the infants was compared. The study had shown a direct correlation between beauty and eye contact: the infants stared longer at the attractive women, suggesting that people's perceptions of beauty were instinctive. The study was given prominent play in *Newsweek* and *Time*.

He'd wanted to write a column criticizing the study, partly because it omitted what he felt were some important qualifications. Exterior beauty might catch someone's eye right away—he knew he was just as susceptible as the next guy to a supermodel's appeal—but he'd always found intelligence and passion to be far more attractive and influential over time. Those traits took more than an instant to decipher, and beauty had nothing whatsoever to do with it. Beauty might prevail in the very short term, but in the medium and longer terms, cultural norms—primarily those values and norms influenced by family—were more important. His editor, however, canned the idea as "too subjective" and suggested he write something about the excessive use of antibiotics in chicken feed, which had the potential to turn streptococcus into the next bubonic plague. Which made sense, Jeremy noted with chagrin: the editor was a vegetarian, and his wife was both gorgeous and about as bright as an Alaskan winter sky.

Editors. He'd long ago concluded that most of them were hypocrites. But, as in most professions, he supposed, hypocrites tended to be both passionate and politically savvy—in other words, corporate survivors—which meant they were the ones who not only doled out assignments but ended up paying the expenses.

But maybe, as Nate had suggested, he'd be out of that racket soon. Well, not completely out of it. Alvin was probably right in saying that television producers were no different from editors, but television paid a living wage, which meant he'd be able to pick and choose his projects, instead of having to hustle all the time. Maria had been right to challenge his workload so long ago. In fifteen years, his workload hadn't changed a bit. Oh, the stories might be higher profile, or he might have an easier time placing his freelance pieces because of the relationships he'd built over the years, but neither of those things changed the essential challenge of always coming up with something new and original. He still had to produce a dozen columns for *Scientific American*, at least one or two major investigations, and another fifteen or so smaller articles a year, some in keeping with the theme of the season. Is Christmas coming? Write a story about the real St. Nicholas, who was born in Turkey, became bishop of Myra, and was known for his generosity, love of children, and concern for sailors. Is it summer? How about a story about either (a) global warming and the undeniable 0.8-degree rise in temperature over the last one hundred years, which foretold Sahara-like consequences throughout the

United States, or (b) how global warming might cause the next ice age and turn the United States into an icy tundra. Thanksgiving, on the other hand, was good for the truth about the Pilgrims' lives, which wasn't only about friendly dinners with Native Americans, but instead included the Salem witch hunts, smallpox epidemics, and a nasty tendency toward incest.

Interviews with famous scientists and articles about various satellites or NASA projects were always respected and easy to place no matter what time of year, as were exposés about drugs (legal and illegal), sex, prostitution, gambling, liquor, court cases involving massive settlements, and anything, absolutely anything whatsoever, about the supernatural, most of which had little or nothing to do with science and more to do with quacks like Clausen.

He had to admit the process wasn't anything like he'd imagined a career in journalism would be. At Columbia—he was the only one of his brothers to attend college and became the first in his family ever to graduate, a fact his mother never ceased to point out to strangers—he'd double-majored in physics and chemistry, with the intention of becoming a professor. But a girlfriend who worked at the university paper convinced him to write a story—which relied heavily on the use of statistics—about the bias in SAT scores used in admission. When his article led to a number of student demonstrations, Jeremy realized he had a knack for writing. Still, his career choice didn't change until his father was swindled by a bogus financial planner out of some $40,000, right before Jeremy graduated. With the family home in jeopardy—his father was a bus driver and worked for the Port Authority until retirement—Jeremy bypassed his graduation ceremony to track down the con man. Like a man possessed, he searched court and public records, interviewed associates of the swindler, and produced detailed notes.

As fate would have it, the New York D.A.'s office had bigger fish to fry than a small-time scam artist, so Jeremy double-checked his sources, condensed his notes, and wrote the first exposé of his life. In the end, the house was saved, and New York magazine picked up the piece. The editor there convinced him that life in academia would lead nowhere and, with a subtle blend of flattery and rhetoric about chasing the big dream, suggested that Jeremy write a piece about Leffertex, an antidepressant that was currently undergoing stage III clinical trials and was the subject of intense media speculation.

Jeremy took the suggestion, working two months on the story on his own dime. In the end, his article led the drugmaker to withdraw the drug from FDA consideration. After that, instead of heading to MIT for his master's degree, he traveled to Scotland to follow along with scientists investigating the Loch Ness Monster, the first of his fluff pieces. There, he'd been present for the deathbed confession of a prominent surgeon who admitted that the photograph he'd taken of the monster in 1933—the photograph that brought the legend into the public eye—had been faked by him and a friend one Sunday afternoon as a practical joke. The rest, as they say, was history.

Still, fifteen years of chasing stories was *fifteen years* of chasing stories, and what had he received in exchange? He was thirty-seven years old, single and living in a dingy one-bedroom apartment on the Upper West Side, and heading to Boone Creek, North Carolina, to explain a case of mysterious lights in a cemetery.

He shook his head, perplexed as always at the path his life had taken. The big dream. It was still out there, and he still had the passion to reach it. Only now, he'd begun to wonder if television would be his means.

The story of the mysterious lights originated from a letter Jeremy had received a month earlier. When he'd read it, his first thought was that it would make a good Halloween story. Depending on the angle the story took, *Southern Living* or even *Reader's Digest* might be interested for their October issue; if it ended up being more literary and narrative, maybe *Harper's* or even the *New Yorker*. On the other hand, if the town was trying to cash in like Roswell, New Mexico, with UFOs, the story might be appropriate for one of the major southern newspapers, which might then further syndicate it. Or if he kept it short, he could use it in his column. His editor at *Scientific American*, despite the *seriousness* with which he regarded the contents of the magazine, was also intensely interested in increasing the number of subscribers and talked about it incessantly. He knew full well that the public loved a good ghost story. He might hem and haw while glancing at his wife's picture and pretending to evaluate the merits, but he never passed up a story like this. Editors liked fluff as much as the next guy, since subscribers were the lifeblood of the business. And fluff, sad to say, was becoming a media staple.

In the past, Jeremy had investigated seven different ghostly apparitions; four had ended up in his October column. Some had been fairly ordinary—spectral visions that no one could scientifically document—but three had involved poltergeists, supposedly mischievous spirits that actually move objects or damage the surroundings. According to paranormal investigators—an oxymoron if Jeremy had ever heard one—poltergeists were generally drawn to a particular person instead of a place. In each instance that Jeremy had investigated, including those that were well documented in the media, fraud had been the cause of the mysterious events.

But the lights in Boone Creek were supposed to be different; apparently, they were predictable enough to enable the town to sponsor a Historic Homes and Haunted Cemetery Tour, during which, the brochure promised, people would see not only homes dating back to the mid-1700s but, weather permitting, "the anguished ancestors of our town on their nightly march between the netherworlds."

The brochure, complete with pictures of the tidy town and

melodramatic statements, had been sent to him along with the letter. As he drove, Jeremy recalled the letter.

Dear Mr. Marsh:

My name is Doris McClellan, and two years ago, I read your story in Scientific American about the poltergeist haunting Brenton Manor in Newport, Rhode Island. I thought about writing to you back then, but for whatever reason, I didn't. I suppose it just slipped my mind, but with the way things are going in my town these days, I reckoned that it's high time to tell you about it.

I don't know if you've ever heard about the cemetery in Boone Creek, North Carolina, but legend has it that the cemetery is haunted by spirts of former slaves. In the winter—January through early February—blue lights seem to dance on the headstones whenever the fog rolls in. Some say they're like strobe lights, others swear they're the size of basketballs. I've seen them, too; to me, they look like sparkly disco balls. Anyway, last year, some folks from Duke University came to investigate; I think they were meteorologists or geologists or something. They, too, saw the lights, but they couldn't explain them, and the local paper did a big story on the whole mystery. Maybe if you came down, you could make sense of what the lights really are.

If you need more information, give me a call at Herbs, a restaurant here in town.

The remainder of the letter offered further contact information, and afterward, he flipped through the brochure from the local Historical Society. He read captions describing the various homes on the upcoming tour, skimmed the information concerning the parade and barn dance on Friday night, and found himself raising an eyebrow at the announcement that, for the first time, a visit to the cemetery would be included in the tour on Saturday evening. On the back of the brochure—surrounded by what seemed to be hand-drawn pictures of Casper—were testimonials from people who'd seen the lights and an excerpt from what appeared to be an article in the local newspaper. In the center was a grainy photograph of a bright light in what might, or might not, have been the cemetery (the caption claimed it was).

It wasn't quite the Borely Rectory, a rambling "haunted" Victorian on the north bank of the Stour River in Essex, England, the most famous haunted house in history, where "sightings" included headless horsemen, weird organ chants, and ringing bells, but it was enough to pique his interest.

After failing to find the article mentioned in the letter—there were no archives at the local newspaper's Web site—he contacted various departments at Duke University and eventually found the original research project. It had been written by three graduate students, and though he had their names and phone numbers, he doubted there was any reason to call them. The research report had none of the detail he would have expected. Instead, the entire study had simply documented the existence of the lights and the fact that the students' equipment was functioning properly, which barely scratched the surface of the information he needed. And besides, if he'd learned anything in the past fifteen years, it was to trust no one's work but his own.

See, that was the dirty secret about writing for magazines. While all journalists would claim to do their own research and most did *some*, they still relied heavily on opinions and half-truths that had been published in the past. Thus, they frequently made mistakes, usually small ones, sometimes whoppers. *Every* article in *every* magazine had errors, and two years ago, Jeremy had written a story about it, exposing the less laudable habits of his fellow professionals.

His editor, however, had vetoed publishing it. And no other magazine seemed enthusiastic about the piece, either.

He watched oak trees slide past the windows, wondering if he needed a career change, and he suddenly wished he'd researched the ghost story further. What if there were no lights? What if the letter writer was a quack? What if there wasn't even much of a legend to build an article around? He shook his head. Worrying was pointless, and besides, it was too late now. He was already here, and Nate was busy working the New York phones.

In the trunk, Jeremy had all the necessary items for ghost hunting (as disclosed in *Ghost Busters for Real!*, a book he'd originally bought as a joke after an evening of cocktails). He had a Polaroid camera, 35mm camera, four camcorders and tripods, audio recorder and microphones, microwave radiation detector, electromagnetic detector, compass, night-vision goggles, laptop computer, and other odds and ends.

Had to do this right, after all. Ghostbusting wasn't for amateurs.

As might be expected, his editor had complained about the cost of the most recently purchased gizmos, which always seemed to be required in investigations like this. Technology was moving fast, and yesterday's gizmos were the equivalent of stone tools and flint, Jeremy had explained to his editor, fantasizing about expensing the laser-beam-backpack thing that Bill Murray and Harold Ramis had used in *Ghostbusters*. He would love to have seen his editor's expression with that one. As it was, the guy mowed through celery like a rabbit on amphetamines before finally signing off on the items. He sure would be pissed if the story ended up on television and not in the column.

Grinning at the memory of his editor's expression, Jeremy flipped through various stations—rock, hip-hop, country, gospel—before settling on a local talk show that was interviewing two flounder fishermen who spoke passionately about the need to decrease the weight at which the fish could be harvested. The announcer, who seemed inordinately interested in the topic, spoke with a heavy twang. Commercials advertised the gun and coin show at the Masonic Lodge in Grifton and the latest team changes in NASCAR.

The traffic picked up near Greenville, and he looped around the downtown area near the campus of East Carolina University.

He crossed the wide, brackish waters of the Pamlico River and turned onto a rural highway. The blacktop narrowed as it wound through the country, squeezed on both sides by barren winter fields, denser thickets of trees, and the occasional farmhouse. About thirty minutes later, he found himself approaching Boone Creek.

After the first and only stoplight, the speed limit dropped to twenty-five miles an hour, and slowing the car, Jeremy took in the scene with dismay. In addition to the half dozen mobile homes perched haphazardly off the road and a couple of cross streets, the stretch of blacktop was dominated by two run-down gas stations and Leroy's Tires. Leroy advertised his business with a sign atop a tower of used tires that would be considered a fire hazard in any other jurisdiction. Jeremy reached the other end of town in a minute, at which point the speed limit picked up again. He pulled the car over to the side of the road.

Either the Chamber of Commerce had used photographs of some other town on its Web site or he'd missed something. He pulled over to check the map again, and according to this version of Rand McNally, he was in Boone Creek. He glanced in the rearview mirror wondering where on earth it was. The quiet, treelined streets. The blooming azaleas. The pretty women in dresses.

As he was trying to figure it out, he saw a white church steeple peeking out above the tree line and decided to make his way down one of the cross streets he'd passed. After a serpentine curve, the surroundings suddenly changed, and he soon found himself driving through a town that may once have been gracious and picturesque, but now seemed to be dying of old age. Wraparound porches decorated with hanging flower pots and American flags couldn't hide the peeling paint and mold just below the eaves. Yards were shaded by massive magnolia trees, but the neatly trimmed rhododendron bushes only partially hid cracked foundations. Still, it seemed friendly enough. A few elderly couples in

sweaters who were sitting in rocking chairs on their porches
waved at him as he passed by.

It took more than a few waves before he realized they weren't
waving because they thought they'd recognized him, but because
people here waved to *every*one who drove by. Meandering from
one road to the next, he eventually found the waterfront, recalling that the town had been developed at the confluence of Boone
Creek and the Pamlico River. As he passed through the downtown area, which no doubt once constituted a thriving business
district, he noted how the town seemed to be dying out. Dispersed among the vacant spaces and boarded-up windows were
two antique shops, an old-fashioned diner, a tavern called Lookilu, and a barbershop. Most of the businesses had local-sounding
names and looked as if they'd been in business for decades but
were fighting a losing battle against extinction. The only evidence of modern life was the neon-colored T-shirts emblazoned
with such slogans as *I Survived the Ghosts in Boone Creek!* that
hung in the window of what was probably the rural, southern version of a department store.

Herbs, where Doris McClellan worked, was easy enough to
find. It was located near the end of the block in a restored turn-
of-the-century peach-colored Victorian. Cars were parked out
front and in the small gravel parking lot off to the side, and tables
were visible beyond the curtained windows and on the wraparound porch. From what he could see, every table was occupied,
and Jeremy decided that it might be better if he swung by to talk
to Doris after the crowd had thinned out.

He noted the location of the Chamber of Commerce, a small
nondescript brick building set at the edge of town, and headed
back toward the highway. Impulsively, he pulled into a gas station.

After taking off his sunglasses, Jeremy rolled down the window. The gray-haired proprietor wore dingy coveralls and a Dale
Earnhardt cap. He rose slowly and began strolling toward the car,
gnawing on what Jeremy assumed to be chewing tobacco.

"Can I hep ya?" His accent was unmistakably southern and his teeth were stained brown. His name tag read TULLY.

Jeremy asked for directions to the cemetery, but instead of answering, the proprietor looked Jeremy over carefully.

"Who passed?" he finally asked.

Jeremy blinked. "Excuse me?"

"Headin' to a burial, ain't ya?" the proprietor asked.

"No. I just wanted to see the cemetery."

The man nodded. "Well, you look like you're heading to a burial."

Jeremy glanced at his clothing: black jacket over a black turtleneck, black jeans, black Bruno Magli shoes. The man did have a point.

"I guess I just like wearing black. Anyway, about the directions . . ."

The owner pushed up the brim of his hat and spoke slowly. "I don't like going to burials none. Make me think I ought to be heading to church more often to square things up before it's too late. That ever happen to ya?"

Jeremy wasn't sure exactly what to say. It wasn't a question he typically encountered, especially in response to a question about directions. "I don't think so," he finally ventured.

The proprietor took a rag from his pocket and began to wipe the grease from his hands. "I take it you're not from here. You got a funny accent."

"New York," Jeremy clarified.

"Heard of it, but ain't never been there," he said. He looked over the Taurus. "Is this your car?"

"No, it's a rental."

He nodded, saying nothing for a moment.

"But anyway, about the cemetery," Jeremy prodded. "Can you tell me how to get there?"

"I s'pose. Which one ya lookin' for?"

"It's called Cedar Creek?"

The proprietor looked at him curiously. "Whatcha want to go out there for? Ain't nothin' for anyone to see there. There's nicer cemeteries on the other side of town."

"Actually, I'm interested in just that one."

The man didn't seem to hear him. "You got kin buried there?"

"No."

"You one of them big-shot developers from up north? Maybe thinking of building some condos or one o' them malls on that land out there?"

Jeremy shook his head. "No. Actually, I'm a journalist."

"My wife likes them malls. Condos, too. Might be a good idea."

"Ah," Jeremy said, wondering how long this was going to take. "I wish I could help, but it's not my line of work."

"You need some gas?" he asked, moving toward the rear of the car.

"No, thanks."

He was already unscrewing the cap. "Premium or regular?"

Jeremy shifted in his seat, thinking the man could probably use the business. "Regular, I guess."

After getting the gas going, the man took off his cap and ran his hand through his hair as he made his way back to the window.

"You have any car trouble, don't hesitate to swing by. I can fix both kinds of cars, and do it for the right price, too."

"Both?"

"Foreign *and* domestic," he said. "Whaddya think I was talkin' about?" Without waiting for an answer, the man shook his head, as if Jeremy were a moron. "Name's Tully, by the way. And you are?"

"Jeremy Marsh."

"And you're a urologist?"

"A journalist."

"Don't have any urologists in town. There's a few in Greenville, though."

"Ah," Jeremy said, not bothering to correct him. "But anyway, about the directions to Cedar Creek . . ."

Tully rubbed his nose and glanced up the road before looking at Jeremy again. "Well, you ain't going to see anything now. The ghosts don't come out till nighttime, if that's what you're here for."

"Excuse me?"

"The ghosts. If you ain't got kin buried in the cemetery, then you must be here for the ghosts, right?"

"You've heard about the ghosts?"

"Of course, I have. Seen 'em with my own eyes. But if you want tickets, you'll have to go to the Chamber of Commerce."

"You need tickets?"

"Well, you just can't walk right into someone's home, can you?"

It took a moment to follow the train of thought.

"Oh, that's right," Jeremy said. "The Historic Homes and Haunted Cemetery Tour, right?"

Tully stared at Jeremy, as if he were the densest person ever to walk the face of the earth. "Well, of course, we're talking about the tour," he said. "Whaddya think I was talkin' about?"

"I'm not sure," Jeremy said. "But the directions . . ."

Tully shook his head. "Okay, okay," he said, as if suddenly put out. He pointed toward town.

"What you do is head back to downtown, then follow the main road north until you reach the turn about four miles from where the road used to dead-end. Turn west and keep going until you get to the fork, and follow the road that leads past Wilson Tanner's place. Turn north again where the junked car used to be, go straight for a bit, and the cemetery'll be right there."

Jeremy nodded. "Okay," he said.

"You sure you got it?"

"Fork, Wilson Tanner's place, junked car used to be," he repeated robotically. "Thanks for your help."

"No problem. Glad to be of service. And that'll be seven dollars and forty-nine cents."

"You take credit cards?"

"No. Never liked them things. Don't like the government knowing everything I'm doing. Ain't no one else's business."

"Well," Jeremy said, reaching for his wallet, "it is a problem. I've heard the government has spies everywhere."

Tully nodded knowingly. "I bet it's even worse for you doctor folks. Which reminds me . . ."

Tully kept up a stready stream of talk for the next fifteen minutes. Jeremy learned about the vagaries of the weather, ridiculous government edicts, and how Wyatt—the other gas station owner—would gouge Jeremy if he ever went there for gas, since he fiddled with the calibration on the pumps as soon as the Unocal truck pulled away. But mainly, he heard about Tully's trouble with his prostate, which made it necessary to get out of bed at least five times a night to go to the bathroom. He asked Jeremy's opinion about that, being that he was a urologist. He also asked about Viagra.

After he had replugged his cheek twice with chaw, another car pulled in on the other side of the pump, interrupting their talk. The driver popped his hood up, and Tully peered inside before wiggling some wires and spitting off to the side. Tully promised he could fix it, but being that he was so busy, the man would have to leave his car there for at least a week. The stranger seemed to expect this answer, and a moment later, they were talking about Mrs. Dungeness and the fact that a possum had ended up in her kitchen the night before and eaten from the fruit bowl.

Jeremy used the opportunity to sneak away. He stopped at the department store to buy a map and a packet of postcards featuring the landmarks of Boone Creek, and before long, he was making his way along a winding road that led out of town. He magically found both the turn and the fork, but unfortunately missed Wilson Tanner's place completely. With a bit of backtracking, he finally reached a narrow gravel lane almost hidden by the overgrowth of trees on either side.

Making the turn, he bumped his way through various potholes until the forest began to thin. On the right, he passed a sign that noted he was nearing Riker's Hill—site of a Civil War skirmish— and a few moments later, he pulled to a stop in front of the main gate at Cedar Creek Cemetery. Riker's Hill towered in the background. Of course, "towered" was a relative term, since it seemed to be the only hill in this part of the state. Anything would have towered out here. The place was otherwise as flat as the flounders he'd heard about on the radio.

Surrounded by brick columns and rusting wrought-iron fencing, Cedar Creek Cemetery was set into a slight valley, making it look as if it was slowly sinking. The grounds were shaded with scores of oaks that dripped with Spanish moss, but the massive magnolia tree in the center dominated everything. Roots spread from the trunk and protruded above the earth like arthritic fingers.

Though the cemetery might have once been an orderly, peaceful resting place, it was now neglected. The dirt pathway beyond the main gate was rutted with deep rain grooves and carpeted with decaying leaves. The few patches of dormant grass seemed out of place. Fallen branches were propped here and there, and the undulating terrain reminded Jeremy of waves rolling toward shore. Tall weeds sprouted near the headstones, almost all of which appeared to be broken.

Tully was right. It wasn't much to look at. But for a haunted cemetery, it was perfect. Especially one that might end up on television. Jeremy smiled. The place looked like it had been designed in Hollywood.

Jeremy stepped out of the car and stretched his legs before retrieving his camera from the trunk. The breeze was chilly, but it had none of the arctic bite of New York, and he took a deep breath, enjoying the scent of pine and sweetgrass. Above him, cumulus clouds drifted across the sky and a lone hawk circled in the distance. Riker's Hill was dotted with pines, and in the fields that spread out from the base, he saw an abandoned tobacco barn. Covered in kudzu with half the tin roof missing and one of the walls crumbling, it was tilting to the side, as if any uptick in the breeze would be enough to topple it over. Other than that, there was no sign of civilization.

Jeremy heard the hinge groan as he pushed through the rusting main gate and wandered down the dirt pathway. He glanced at the headstones on either side of him, puzzled by their lack of markings until he realized that the original engravings had largely been erased by weather and the passage of time. The few he could make out dated from the late 1700s. Up ahead, a crypt looked as if it had been invaded. The roof and sides had toppled in, and just beyond that, another monument lay crumbled on the pathway. More damaged crypts and broken monuments followed. Jeremy saw no evidence of purposeful vandalism, only natural, if serious, decay. Nor did he see any evidence that anyone had been buried here within the last thirty years, which would explain why it looked abandoned.

In the shade of the magnolia, he paused, wondering how the place would look on a foggy night. Probably spooky, which could prompt a person's imagination to run wild. But if there were unexplained lights, where were they coming from? He guessed that the "ghosts" were simply reflected light turned into prisms by the water droplets in the fog, but there weren't any streetlamps out here, nor was the cemetery lit. He saw no signs of any dwellings on Riker's Hill that might have been responsible either. He supposed they could come from car headlights, yet he saw only the single road nearby, and people would have noticed the connection long ago.

He'd have to get a good topographical map of the area, in addition to the street map he had just bought. Perhaps the local library would have one. In any case, he'd stop by the library to research the history of the cemetery and the town itself. He needed to know when the lights were first spotted; that might give him an idea as to their cause. Of course, he'd have to spend a couple of nights out here in spookyville as well, if the foggy weather was willing to cooperate.

For a while, he walked around the cemetery taking photographs. These wouldn't be for publication; they would serve as comparison points in case he came across earlier photographs of the cemetery. He wanted to see how it had changed over the years, and it might benefit him to know when—or why—the damage had occurred. He snapped a picture of the magnolia tree as well. It was easily the largest he'd ever seen. Its black trunk was wizened, and the low-hanging branches would have kept him and his brothers occupied for hours when they were boys. If it weren't surrounded by dead people, that is.

As he was flicking through the digital photos to make sure they were sufficient, he saw movement from the corner of his eye.

Glancing up, he saw a woman walking toward him. Dressed in jeans, boots, and a light blue sweater that matched the canvas bag she was carrying, she had brown hair that lightly swept her shoulders. Her skin, with just a hint of olive, made makeup unnecessary, but it was the color of her eyes that caught him: from a distance, they appeared almost violet. Whoever she was, she'd parked her car directly behind his.

For a moment, he wondered whether she was approaching him to ask him to leave. Maybe the cemetery was condemned and now off-limits. Then again, perhaps her visit here was simply a coincidence.

She continued moving toward him.

Come to think of it, a rather *attractive* coincidence. Jeremy straightened as he slipped the camera back into its case. He smiled broadly as she neared.

"Well, hello there," he said.

At his comment, she slowed her gait slightly, as if she hadn't noticed him. Her expression seemed almost amused, and he half expected her to stop. Instead, he thought he caught the sound of her laughter as she walked right by.

With eyebrows raised in appreciation, Jeremy watched her go. She didn't look back. Before he could stop himself, he took a step after her.

"Hey!" he called out.

Instead of stopping, she simply turned and continued walking backward, her head tilted inquisitively. Again, Jeremy saw the same amused expression.

"You know, you really shouldn't stare like that," she called out. "Women like a man who knows how to be subtle."

She turned again, adjusted the canvas bag on her shoulder, and kept on going. In the distance, he heard her laugh again.

Jeremy stood openmouthed, for once at a loss as to how to respond.

Okay, so she wasn't interested. No big deal. Still, most people would have at least said hello in response. Maybe it was a southern thing. Maybe guys hit on her all the time and she was tired of it. Or maybe she simply didn't want to be interrupted while she did . . . did . . .

Did what?

See, that was the problem with journalism, he sighed. It made him too curious. Really, it was none of his business. And besides, he reminded himself, it's a cemetery. She was probably here to visit the departed. People did that all the time, didn't they?

He wrinkled his brow. The only difference was that most cemeteries looked as if someone came by to mow the lawn now and then, while this one looked like San Francisco after the earthquake in 1906. He supposed he could have headed in her direction to see what she was up to, but he'd talked to enough women to realize that spying might come across as far more creepy than staring. And she didn't seem to like his staring.

Jeremy actively tried not to stare as she disappeared behind one of the oak trees, her canvas bag swinging with every graceful stride.

It was only after she'd vanished that he was able to remind himself that pretty girls didn't matter right now. He had a job to do and his future was on the line here. Money, fame, television, yadda yadda yadda. Okay, what next? He'd seen the cemetery . . . he might as well check out some of the surrounding area. Sort of get a feel for the place.

He walked back to his car and hopped in, pleased that he hadn't so much as glanced behind him to see if she was watching him. Two could play that game. Of course, that presupposed that she even cared what he was doing, and he was pretty sure she didn't.

A quick glance now from the driver's seat proved him correct.

He started the engine and accelerated slowly; as he moved farther away from the cemetery, he found it easier to let the woman's image drift from his mind to the task at hand. He drove farther up the road to see if other roads—either gravel or paved—intersected it, and he kept his eye out for windmills or tin-roofed buildings, without luck. Nor did he find something as simple as a farmhouse.

Turning the car around, he started back the way he had come, looking for a road that would lead him to the top of Riker's Hill but finally giving up in frustration. As he neared the cemetery again, he found himself wondering who owned the fields surrounding it and if Riker's Hill was public or private land. The county tax assessor's office would have that information. The sharp-eyed journalist in him also happened to notice that the woman's car was gone, which left him with a slight, though surprising, pang of disappointment, which passed as quickly as it had come.

He checked his watch; it was a little after two, and he figured that the lunch rush at Herbs was probably ending. Might as well talk to Doris. Maybe she could shed some "light" on the subject.

He smiled lamely to himself, wondering if the woman he'd seen at the cemetery would have laughed at that one.

Three

·····❖·····

Only a few tables on the porch were still occupied when Jeremy reached Herbs. As he climbed the steps to the front door, conversations quieted and eyes drifted his way. Only the chewing continued, and Jeremy was reminded of the curious way cows looked at you when you approached the pasture fence. Jeremy nodded and waved, as he'd seen the old folks on the porches doing.

He removed his sunglasses and pushed through the door. The small, square tables were spread through two main rooms on either side of the building, separated by a set of stairs. The peach walls were offset by white trim, giving the place a homey, country feel; toward the rear of the building, he caught a glimpse of the kitchen.

Again, the same cowlike expressions from patrons as he passed. Conversations quieted. Eyes drifted. When he nodded and waved, eyes dropped and the murmur of conversation rose again. This waving thing, he thought, was kind of like having a magic wand.

Jeremy stood fiddling with his sunglasses, hoping Doris was here, when one of the waitresses ambled out from the kitchen. In her late twenties or so, she was tall and reed-thin, with a sunny, open face.

"Just take a seat anywhere, hon," she chirped. "Be with you in a minute."

After making himself comfortable near a window, he watched the waitress approach. Her name tag said RACHEL. Jeremy thought about the name tag phenomenon in town. Did every worker have one? He wondered if it was some sort of rule. Like nodding and waving.

"Can I get you something to drink, darlin'?"

"Do you have cappuccino?" he ventured.

"No, sorry. We have coffee, though."

Jeremy smiled. "Coffee will be fine."

"You got it. Menu's on the table if you want something to eat."

"Actually, I was wondering if Doris McClellan was around."

"Oh, she's in the back," Rachel said, brightening. "Want me to get her?"

"If you wouldn't mind."

She smiled. "No problem at all, darlin'."

He watched her head toward the kitchen and push through the swinging doors. A moment later, a woman whom he assumed was Doris emerged. She was the opposite of Rachel: short and stout, with thinning white hair that was once blond, she was wearing an apron, but no name tag, over a flower-print blouse. She looked to be about sixty. Pausing at the table, she put her hands on her hips before breaking into a smile.

"Well," she said, drawing out the word into two syllables, "you must be Jeremy Marsh."

Jeremy blinked. "You know me?" he asked.

"Of course. I just saw you on *Primetime Live* last Friday. I take it you got my letter."

"I did, thank you."

"And you're here to write a story about the ghosts?"

He raised his hands. "So it seems."

"Well, I'll be." Her accent made it sound like she was pronouncing the letters *L-I-B*. "Why didn't you tell me you were coming?"

"I like to surprise people. Sometimes it makes it a little easier to obtain accurate information."

"L-I-B," she said again. After the surprise had faded, she pulled out a chair. "Mind if I take a seat? I suppose you're here to talk to me."

"I don't want you to get in trouble with your boss if you're supposed to be working."

She glanced over her shoulder and shouted, "Hey, Rachel, do you think the boss would mind if I took a seat? The man here wants to talk to me."

Rachel poked her head out from behind the swinging doors. Jeremy could see her holding a pot of coffee.

"Nah, I don't think the boss would mind at all," Rachel responded. "She loves to talk. Especially when she's with such a handsome fella."

Doris turned around. "See," she said, and nodded. "No problem."

Jeremy smiled. "Seems like a nice place to work."

"It is."

"I take it that you're the boss."

"Guilty as charged," Doris answered. Her eyes flickered with satisfaction.

"How long have you been in business?"

"Almost thirty years now, open for breakfast and lunch. We were doing the healthy food thing long before it was popular, and we have the best omelets this side of Raleigh." She leaned forward. "You hungry? You should try one of our sandwiches for lunch. It's all fresh—we even make the bread daily. You look like you could use a bite, and from the looks of you . . ." She hesitated, looking him over. "I'll bet you'd love the chicken pesto sandwich. It's got sprouts, tomatoes, cucumbers, and I came up with the pesto recipe myself."

"I'm not really that hungry."

Rachel approached with two cups of coffee.

"Well, just to let you know . . . if I'm going to tell a story, I like to do it over a good meal. And I tend to take my time."

Jeremy surrendered. "The chicken pesto sandwich sounds fine."

Doris smiled. "Could you bring us a couple of the Albemarles, Rachel?"

"Sure," Rachel answered. She looked him over with an appreciative eye. "By the way, who's your friend? Haven't seen him around here before."

"This is Jeremy Marsh," Doris answered. "He's a famous journalist here to write a story about our fair town."

"Really?" Rachel said, looking interested.

"Yes," Jeremy answered.

"Oh, thank goodness," Rachel said with a wink. "For a second, I thought you'd just come from a funeral."

Jeremy blinked as Rachel moved away.

Doris laughed at his expression. "Tully stopped in after you swung by for directions," she explained. "I guess he figured I might have had something to do with you coming down, and he wanted to make sure. So anyway, he rehashed the entire conversation, and Rachel probably couldn't resist. We all thought his comment was a hoot."

"Ah," Jeremy said.

Doris leaned forward. "I'll bet he talked your ear off."

"A little."

"He was always a talker. He'd talk to a shoe box if no one else was around, and I swear I don't know how his wife, Bonnie, put up with it for so long. But twelve years ago, she went deaf, and so now he talks to customers. It's all a person can do to get out of there in less time it takes ice cubes to melt in winter. I even had to shoo him out of here today after he came by. Can't get a speck of work done if he's around."

Jeremy reached for his coffee. "His wife went deaf?"

"I think the Good Lord realized she'd sacrificed enough. Bless her heart."

Jeremy laughed before taking a sip. "So why would he think you were the one who contacted me?"

"Every time something unusual happens, I'm always to blame. Comes with the territory, I guess, being the town psychic and all."

Jeremy simply looked at her and Doris smiled.

"I take it you don't believe in psychics," she remarked.

"No, not really," Jeremy admitted.

Doris tugged at her apron. "Well, for the most part, I don't, either. Most of them are kooks. But some people do have the gift."

"Then . . . you can read my mind?"

"No, nothing like that," Doris said, shaking her head. "At least most of the time, anyway. I have a pretty good intuition about people, but reading minds was more my mom's thing. No one could hide a thing from her. She even knew what I planned on buying her for her birthdays, which took a lot of the fun out of it. But my gift is different. I'm a diviner. And I can also tell what sex a baby's going to be before it's born."

"I see."

Doris looked him over. "You don't believe me."

"Well, let's just say you *are* a diviner. That means you can find water and tell me where I should dig a well."

"Of course."

"And if I asked you to do a test, with scientific controls, under strict supervision . . ."

"You could even be the one to supervise me, and if you had to rig me up like a Christmas tree to make sure I wasn't cheating, I'd have no problem with that."

"I see," Jeremy said, thinking of Uri Geller. Geller had been so confident of his powers of telekinesis that he'd gone on British television in 1973, where he'd appeared before scientists and a studio audience. When he balanced a spoon on his finger, both sides began to curve downward before the stupefied observers. Only later did it come out that he'd bent the spoon over and over before the show, producing metal fatigue.

Doris seemed to know just what he was thinking.

"Tell you what . . . you can test me anytime, in any way you'd like. But that's not why you came. You want to hear about the ghosts, right?"

"Sure," Jeremy said, relieved to get straight into it. "Do you mind if I record this?"

"Not at all."

Jeremy reached into his jacket pocket and retrieved the small recorder. He set it between them and pressed the appropriate buttons. Doris took a sip of coffee before beginning.

"Okay, the story goes back to the 1890s or thereabouts. Back then, this town was still segregated, and most of the Negroes lived out in a place called Watts Landing. There's nothing left of the village these days because of Hazel, but back then—"

"Excuse me . . . Hazel?"

"The hurricane? Nineteen fifty-four. Hit the coast near the South Carolina border. It pretty much put most of Boone Creek underwater, and what was left of Watts Landing was washed away."

"Oh, right. Sorry. Go ahead."

"Anyway, like I was saying, you won't find the village now, but back near the turn of the century, I guess about three hundred people lived there. Most of them were descended from the slaves that had come up from South Carolina during the War of Northern Aggression, or what you Yankees call the Civil War."

She winked and Jeremy smiled.

"So Union Pacific came through to set the railroad lines, which, of course, was supposed to turn this place into a big cosmopolitan area. Or so they promised. And the line they proposed ran right through the Negro cemetery. Now, the leader of that town was a woman named Hettie Doubilet. She was from the Caribbean—I don't know which island—but when she found out that they were supposed to dig up all the bodies and transfer them to another place, she got upset and tried to get the county to do something to have the route changed. But the folks that ran the county wouldn't consider it. Wouldn't even grant her the opportunity to make her case."

At that moment, Rachel arrived with the sandwiches. She set both plates on the table.

"Try it," Doris said. "You're skin and bones, anyway."

Jeremy reached for his sandwich and took a bite. He raised his eyebrows and Doris smiled.

"Better than anything you can find in New York, isn't it?"

"Without a doubt. My compliments to the chef."

She looked at him almost coquettishly. "You *are* a charmer, Mr. Marsh," she said, and Jeremy was struck by the thought that in her youth, she must have broken a few hearts. She went on with her story, as if she'd never stopped.

"Back then, a lot of folks were racist. Some of them still are, but they're in the minority now. Being from the North, you probably think I'm lying about that, but I'm not."

"I believe you."

"No, you don't. No one from the North believes it, but that's beside the point. But going on with the story, Hettie Doubilet was enraged by the folks at the county, and legend has it that when they refused her entrance to the mayor's office, she put a curse on us white folk. She said that if graves of her ancestors would be defiled, then ours would be defiled, too. The ancestors of her people would tread the earth in search of their original resting place and would trample through Cedar Creek on their journey, and that in the end, the whole cemetery would be swallowed whole. Of course, no one paid her any attention that day."

Doris took a bite of her sandwich. "And, well, to make a long story short, the Negroes moved the bodies one by one to another cemetery, the railroad went in, and after that, just as Hettie said,

Cedar Creek Cemetery started going bad. Little things at first. A few headstones broken, things like that, like vandals were responsible. The county folks, thinking Hettie's people were responsible, posted guards. But it kept happening, no matter how many guards they put out there. And over the years, it kept getting worse. You went there, right?"

Jeremy nodded.

"So you can see what's happening. Looks like the place is sinking, right, just like Hettie said it would? Anyway, a few years later, the lights started to appear. And ever since then, folks have believed it was the slave spirits marching through."

"So they don't use the cemetery anymore?"

"No, the place was abandoned for good in the late 1970s, but even before that, most people opted to be buried in the other cemeteries around town because of what was happening to that one. The county owns it now, but they don't take care of it. They haven't for the last twenty years."

"Has anyone ever checked into why the cemetery seems to be sinking?"

"I'm not certain, but I'm almost positive that someone has. A lot of powerful folks had ancestors buried in the cemetery, and the last thing they wanted was their grandpa's tomb being broken up. I'm sure they wanted an explanation, and I've heard stories that some folks from Raleigh came to find out what was happening."

"You mean the students from Duke?"

"Oh, no, not them, honey. They were just kids, and they were here last year. No, I'm talking way back. Maybe around the time the damage first started."

"But you don't know what they learned."

"No. Sorry." She paused, and her eyes took on a mischievous gleam. "But I think I have a pretty good idea."

Jeremy raised his eyebrows. "And that is?"

"Water," she said simply.

"Water?"

"I'm a diviner, remember. I know where water is. And I'll tell you straight up that that land is sinking because of the water underneath it. I know it for a fact."

"I see," Jeremy said.

Doris laughed. "You're so cute, Mr. Marsh. Did you know that your face gets all serious-looking when someone tells you something you don't want to believe?"

"No. No one's ever told me that."

"Well, it does. And I think it's darling. My mom would have had a field day with you. You're so easy to read."

"So what am I thinking?"

Doris hesitated. "Well, like I said, my gifts are different than my mother's. She could read you like a book. And besides, I don't want to scare you."

"Go ahead. Scare me."

"All right," she said. She took a long look at him. "Think of something I couldn't possibly know. And remember, my gift isn't reading minds. I just get . . . hints now and then, and only if they're really strong feelings."

"All right," Jeremy said, playing along. "You do realize, however, that you're hedging yourself here."

"Oh, hush, now." Doris reached for his hands. "Let me hold these, okay?"

Jeremy nodded. "Sure."

"Now think of something personal I couldn't possibly know."

"Okay."

She squeezed his hand. "Seriously. Right now you're just playing with me."

"Fine," he said, "I'll think of something."

Jeremy closed his eyes. He thought of the reason Maria had finally left him, and for a long moment, Doris said nothing at all. Instead, she simply looked at him, as if trying to get him to say something.

He'd been through this before. Countless times. He knew

enough to say nothing, and when she remained silent, he knew he had her. She suddenly jerked—unsurprising, Jeremy thought, since it went with the show—and immediately afterward, released his hands.

Jeremy opened his eyes and looked at her.

"And?"

Doris was looking at him strangely. "Nothing," she said.

"Ah," Jeremy added, "I guess it's not in the cards today, huh?"

"Like I said, I'm a diviner." She smiled, almost as if in apology. "But I can definitely say that you're not pregnant."

He chuckled. "I'd have to say that you're right about that."

She smiled at him before glancing toward the table. She brought her eyes up again. "I'm sorry. I shouldn't have done what I did. It was inappropriate."

"No big deal," he said, meaning it.

"No," she insisted. She met his eyes and reached for his hand again. She squeezed it softly. "I'm very sorry."

Jeremy wasn't quite sure how to react when she took his hand again, but he was struck by the compassion in her expression.

And Jeremy had the unnerving feeling that she had guessed more about his personal history than she could possibly know.

Psychic abilities, premonitions, and intuition are simply a product of the interplay among experience, common sense, and accumulated knowledge. Most people greatly underestimate the amount of information they learn in a lifetime, and the human brain is able to instantly correlate the information in a way that no other species—or machine—is capable of doing.

The brain, however, learns to discard the vast majority of information it receives, since, for obvious reasons, it's not critical to remember everything. Of course, some people have better memories than others, a fact that often displays itself in testing scenarios, and the ability to train memories is well documented. But even the worst of students remember 99.99 percent of everything they come across in life. Yet, it's that 0.01 percent that most frequently distinguishes one person from the next. For some people, it manifests itself in the ability to memorize trivia, or excel as doctors, or accurately interpret financial data as a hedge-fund billionaire. For other people, it's an ability to read others, and those people—with an innate ability to draw on memories, common sense, and experience and to codify it quickly and accurately—manifest an ability that strikes others as being supernatural.

But what Doris did was . . . beyond that somehow, Jeremy thought. She knew. Or at least, that was Jeremy's first inclination, until he retreated to the logical explanation of what had happened.

And, in fact, nothing had really happened, he reminded himself. Doris hadn't said anything; it was simply the way she looked at him that made him think she understood those unknowable things. And that belief was coming from *him*, not from Doris.

Science held the real answers, but even so, she seemed like a nice person. And if she believed in her abilities, so what? To her, it probably did seem supernatural.

Again, she seemed to read him almost immediately.

"Well, I suppose I just confirmed that I'm nuts, huh?"

"No, not really," Jeremy said.

She reached for her sandwich. "Well, anyway, since we're supposed to be enjoying this fine meal, maybe it's better if we just visited for a while. Is there anything I can tell you?"

"Tell me about the town of Boone Creek," he said.

"Like what?"

"Oh, anything, really. I figure that since I'm going to be here for a few days, I might as well know a little about the place."

They spent the next half hour discussing . . . well, not much of anything as far as Jeremy was concerned. Even more than Tully, Doris seemed to know everything that was going on in town. Not because of her supposed abilities—and she admitted as much—but because information passed through small towns like prune juice through an infant.

Doris talked almost nonstop. He learned who was seeing whom, who was hard to work with and why, and the fact that the minister at the local Pentecostal Church was having an affair with one of his parishioners. Most important, according to Doris, at least, was that if his car happened to break down, he should never call Trevor's Towing, since Trevor would probably be drunk, no matter what time of day.

"The man is a menace on the roads," Doris declared. "Everyone knows it, but because his father is the sheriff, no one ever does anything about it. But then, I suppose you shouldn't be surprised. Sheriff Wanner has his own problems, what with his gambling debts."

"Ah," Jeremy said in response, as if he were up on all the goings-on in town. "Makes sense."

For a moment, neither of them said anything. In the lull, he glanced at his watch.

"I suppose you need to be going," Doris said.

He reached for the recorder and shut it off before sliding it back into his jacket. "Probably. I wanted to swing by the library before it closes to see what it has to offer."

"Well, lunch was on me. It's not often that we have a famous visitor come by."

"A brief appearance on *Primetime* doesn't make a person famous."

"I know that. But I was talking about your column."

"You've read it?"

"Every month. My husband, bless his heart, used to tinker in the garage and he loved the magazine. And after he passed, I just didn't have the heart to cancel the subscription. I sort of picked up where he left off. You're a pretty smart fellow."

"Thanks," he said.

She stood from the table and began leading him from the restaurant. The remaining patrons, only a few now, looked up to watch them. It went without saying that they'd heard every word, and as soon as Jeremy and Doris had stepped outside, they began to murmur among themselves. This, everyone immediately decided, was exciting stuff.

"Did she say he'd been on television?" one asked.

"I think I've seen him on one of those talk shows."

"He's definitely not a doctor," added another. "I heard him talking about a magazine article."

"Wonder how Doris knows him. Did you happen to catch that?"

"Well, he seemed nice enough."

"I just think he's plain old dreamy," offered Rachel.

Meanwhile, Jeremy and Doris paused on the porch, unaware of the stir they'd caused inside.

"I assume you're staying at Greenleaf?" Doris inquired. When Jeremy nodded, she went on. "Do you know where they are? They're kind of out in the backcountry."

"I have a map," Jeremy said, trying to sound as if he'd been prepared all along. "I'm sure I can find it. But how about directions to the library?"

"Sure," Doris said, "that's just around the corner." She motioned up the road. "Do you see the brick building there? The one with the blue awnings?"

Jeremy nodded.

"Take a left and go through the next stop sign. At the first street after the stop sign, turn right. The library's on the corner just up the way. It's a big white building. Used to be the Middleton House, which belonged to Horace Middleton, before the county bought it."

"They didn't build a new library?"

"It's a small town, Mr. Marsh, and besides, it's plenty big. You'll see."

Jeremy held out his hand. "Thank you. You've been great. And lunch was delicious."

"I do my best."

"Would you mind if I come back with more questions? You seem to have a pretty good handle on things."

"Anytime you want to talk, you just come by. I'm always available. But I will ask that you don't write anything that makes us look like a bunch of bumpkins. A lot of people—me included—love this place."

"All I write is the truth."

"I know," she said. "That's why I contacted you. You have a trustworthy face, and I'm sure you'll put the legend to bed once and for all in the way it should be done."

Jeremy raised his eyebrows. "You don't think there are ghosts out at Cedar Creek?"

"Oh, heavens no. I *know* there's no spirits there. I've been saying that for years, but no one listens to me."

Jeremy looked at her curiously. "Then why did you ask me to come down?"

"Because people don't know what's going on, and they'll keep believing until they find an explanation. You see, ever since that article in the paper about the people from Duke, the mayor has been promoting the idea like crazy, and strangers have been coming from all over hoping to see the lights. To be honest, it's causing a lot of problems—the place is already crumbling and the damage is getting worse."

She trailed off for a moment before continuing. "Of course, the sheriff won't do anything about the teenagers who hang out there or the strangers who traipse through without a thought in their heads. He and the mayor are hunting buddies, and besides, nearly everyone around here except me thinks that promoting the ghosts is a good idea. Ever since the textile mill and the mine closed, the town's been drying up, and I think they think of this idea as some sort of salvation."

Jeremy glanced toward his car, then back to Doris again, thinking about what she'd just said. It made perfect sense, but . . .

"You do realize that you're changing your story from what you wrote in the letter."

"No," she said, "I'm not. All I said was that there were mysterious lights in the cemetery that were credited to an old legend, that most people think ghosts are involved, and that the kids from Duke couldn't figure out what the lights really were. All that's true. Read the letter again if you don't believe me. I don't lie, Mr. Marsh. I may not be perfect, but I don't lie."

"So why do you want me to discredit the story?"

"Because it's not right," she said easily, as if the answer was common sense. "People always traipsing through, tourists coming down to camp out—it's just not very respectful for the departed, even if the cemetery is abandoned. The folks buried out there deserve to rest in peace. And combining it with something worthy like the Historic Homes Tour is just plain old wrong. But I'm a voice in the wilderness these days."

Jeremy thought about what she'd said as he pushed his hands into his pockets. "Can I be frank?" he asked.

She nodded, and Jeremy shifted from one foot to the other. "If you believe your mom was a psychic, and that you can divine water and the sex of babies, it just seems . . ."

When he trailed off, she stared at him.

"Like I'd be the first to believe in ghosts?"

Jeremy nodded.

"Well, actually, I do. I just don't believe they're out there in the cemetery."

"Why not?"

"Because I've been out there and I don't feel the presence of spirits."

"So you can do that, too?"

She shrugged without answering. "Can I be frank now?"

"Sure."

"One day, you're going to learn something that can't be explained with science. And when that happens, your life's going to change in ways you can't imagine."

He smiled. "Is that a promise?"

"Yes," she said, "it is." She paused, looking him in the eye. "And I have to say that I really enjoyed our lunch. It isn't often that I have the company of such a charming young man. It almost makes me feel young again."

"I had a wonderful time, too."

He turned to leave. The clouds had drifted in while they'd been eating. The sky, while not ominous, looked as if winter wanted to settle in, and Jeremy tugged at his collar as he made his way to the car.

"Mr. Marsh?" Doris called out from behind him.

Jeremy turned. "Yes?"

"Say hi to Lex for me."

"Lex?"

"Yeah," she said. "At the reference desk in the library. That's who you should ask for."

Jeremy smiled. "Will do."

Four

..... ❖ .....

The library turned out to be a massive Gothic structure, completely different from any other building in town. To Jeremy, it looked as if it had been plucked from a hillside in Romania and dropped in Boone Creek on a drunken dare.

The building occupied most of the block, and its two stories were adorned with tall, narrow windows, a sharply angled roof, and an arched wooden front door, complete with oversize door knockers. Edgar Allan Poe would have loved the place, but despite the haunted house architecture, the townsfolk had done what they could to make it seem more inviting. The brick exterior—no doubt reddish brown at one point—had been painted white, black shutters had been put up to frame the windows, and beds of pansies lined the walkway out front and circled the flagpole. A friendly, carved sign with italicized gold script welcomed all to BOONE CREEK LIBRARY. Still, the overall appearance was jarring. It was, Jeremy thought, kind of like visiting a rich kid's elegant brownstone in the city, only to have the butler meet you at the door with balloons and a squirt gun.

In the cheerfully lit, pale yellow foyer—at least the building was consistent in its inconsistency—sat an L-shaped desk, the long leg stretching to the rear of the building, where Jeremy saw a large glassed-in room devoted to children. To the left were the bathrooms, and to the right, beyond another glass wall, was what appeared to be the main area. Jeremy nodded and waved to the elderly woman behind the desk. She smiled and waved back before returning to the book she was reading. Jeremy pushed through the heavy glass doors to the main area, proud that he was getting the hang of the way things worked down here.

In the main area, however, he felt a surge of disappointment. Beneath bright fluorescent lights were only six shelves of books, set relatively close together, in a room that wasn't much larger than his apartment. In the nearest two corners were outdated computers, and off to the right was a sitting area that housed a small collection of periodicals. Four small tables were scattered throughout the room, and he saw only three people browsing the shelves, including one elderly man with a hearing aid who was stacking books on the shelves. Looking around, Jeremy had the sinking suspicion that he'd purchased more books in his lifetime than the library had.

He made his way to the reference desk, but not surprisingly, there wasn't anyone behind it. He paused at the desk, waiting for Lex. Turning around to lean against it, he figured that Lex must have been the white-haired man putting the books away, but the man didn't make a move toward him.

He glanced at his watch. Two minutes after that, he glanced at it again.

Another two minutes later, after Jeremy had cleared his throat loudly, the man finally noticed him. Jeremy nodded and waved, making sure the man knew he needed help, but instead of moving toward him, the man waved and nodded before going back to stacking books. No doubt he was trying to stay ahead of the rush. Southern efficiency was legendary, Jeremy observed. Very impressive, this place.

In the small, cluttered office on the upper floor of the library, she stared through the window. She'd known he would be coming.

Doris had called the moment he left Herbs and told her about the man in black from New York City, who was here to write about the ghosts in the cemetery.

She shook her head. Figures that he would have listened to Doris. Once she got an idea about something, she tended to be pretty persuasive, with few concerns about the possible backlash an article like this could cause. She'd read Mr. Marsh's stories before and knew exactly how he operated. It wouldn't be enough to prove that ghosts weren't involved—and she had no doubt about that—but Mr. Marsh wouldn't stop there. He'd interview people in his own charming way, get them to open up, and then he'd pick and choose before twisting the truth in whatever way he wanted. Once he was finished with the hatchet job that would pose as an article, people around the country would assume that everyone who lived here was gullible, foolish, and superstitious.

Oh, no. She didn't like the fact he was here at all.

She closed her eyes, absently twirling strands of her dark hair between her fingers. The thing was, she didn't like people traipsing through the cemetery, either. Doris was right: it was disrespectful, and ever since those kids from Duke came down and the article showed up in the paper, things *had* been getting out of hand. Why couldn't it have just been kept quiet? Those lights had been around for decades, and though everyone knew about them, no one really cared. Sure, once in a while, a few people might head out to take a look—mostly those who'd been drinking at the Lookilu, or teenagers—but T-shirts? Coffee mugs? Cheesy postcards? Combining it with the Historic Homes Tour?

She didn't quite understand the whole reason behind the phenomenon. Why was it so important to increase tourism around here, anyway? Sure, the money was attractive, but people didn't live in Boone Creek because they wanted to get rich. Well, most of them, anyway. There were always a few people out to make a buck, beginning first and foremost with the mayor. But she'd always believed that most people lived here for the same reason she did: because of the awe she felt when the setting sun turned the Pamlico River to a golden yellow ribbon, because she knew and trusted her neighbors, because people could let their kids run around at night without worrying that something bad would happen to them. In a world growing busier by the minute, Boone Creek was a town that hadn't even attempted to keep up with the modern world, and that's what made it special.

That's why she was here, after all. She loved everything about the town: the smell of pine and salt on early spring mornings, the sultry summer evenings that made her skin glisten, the fiery glow of autumn leaves. But most of all, she loved the people and couldn't imagine living anywhere else. She trusted them, she talked to them, she liked them. Of course, a number of her friends hadn't felt the same way, and after heading off to college, they'd never returned. She, too, had moved away for a while, but even then, she'd always known that she would come back; a good thing, it turned out, since she'd been worried about Doris's health for the past two years. And she also knew she would be the librarian, just as her mother had been, in the hope of making the library something that would make the town proud.

No, it wasn't the most glamorous job, nor did it pay much. The library was a work in progress, but first impressions were deceptive. The bottom floor housed contemporary fiction only, while the top floor held classic fiction and nonfiction, additional titles by contemporary authors, and unique collections. She doubted whether Mr. Marsh even realized the library was dispersed through both stories, since the stairs were accessed in the rear of the building, near the children's room. One of the drawbacks to having the library housed in a former residence was that the architecture wasn't designed for public traffic. But the place suited her.

Her office upstairs was almost always quiet, and it was close to her favorite part of the library. A small room next to hers contained the rare titles, books she'd accumulated through estate and garage sales, donations, and visits to bookstores and dealers throughout the state, a project her mother had started. She also had a growing collection of historic manuscripts and maps, some of which dated from before the Revolutionary War. This was her passion. She was always on the lookout for something special, and she wasn't above using charm, guile, or simple pleading to get what she wanted. When that didn't work, she stressed the tax deduction angle, and—because she had worked hard to cultivate contacts with tax and estate lawyers throughout the South—she often received items before other libraries even found out about them. While she didn't have the resources of Duke, Wake Forest, or the University of North Carolina, her library was regarded as one of the best small libraries in the state, if not the country.

And that's how she viewed it now. *Her* library, like this was *her* town. And right now a stranger was waiting for her, a stranger who wanted to write a story that just might not be good for *her* people.

Oh, she'd seen him drive up, all right. Seen him get out of the car and head around front. She'd shaken her head, recognizing the confident city swagger almost immediately. He was just another in a long line of people visiting from someplace more exotic, people who believed they had a deeper understanding of what the real world was like. People who claimed that life could be far more exciting, more fulfilling, if only you moved away. A few years ago, she'd fallen for someone who believed such things, and she refused to be taken in by such ideas again.

A cardinal landed on the outside windowsill. She watched it, clearing her head, and then sighed. Okay, she decided, she should probably go talk to Mr. Marsh from New York. He was, after all, waiting for her. He'd come all this way, and southern hospitality— as well as her job—required her to help him find what he needed. More important, though, she might be able to keep an eye on him. She'd be able to filter the information in a way that he'd understand the good parts about living here, too.

She smiled. Yes, she could handle Mr. Marsh. And besides, she had to admit that he was rather good-looking, even if he couldn't be trusted.

Jeremy Marsh looked almost bored.

He was pacing one of the aisles, his arms crossed, glancing at the contemporary titles. Every now and then he frowned, as if wondering why he couldn't find anything by Dickens, Chaucer, or Austen. If he asked about it, she wondered how he would react if she responded with "Who?" Knowing him—and she readily admitted she didn't know him at all but was simply making an assumption here—he'd probably just stare at her all tongue-tied like he had when she saw him earlier in the cemetery. Men, she thought. Always predictable.

She tugged at her sweater, procrastinating for one last moment before starting toward him. Keep it professional, she reminded herself, you're on a mission here.

"I suppose you're looking for me," she announced, forcing a tight smile.

Jeremy glanced up at the sound of her voice, and for a moment, he seemed frozen in place. Then all at once he smiled as recognition set in. It seemed friendly enough—his dimple was cute—but the smile was a little too practiced and wasn't enough to offset the confidence in his eyes.

"You're Lex?" he asked.

"It's short for 'Lexie.' Lexie Darnell. It's what Doris calls me."

"You're the librarian?"

"When I'm not hanging out in cemeteries and ignoring staring men, I try to be."

"Well, I'll be," he said, trying to drawl the words like Doris had.

She smiled and moved past him to straighten a few books on the shelf that he'd examined.

"Your accent doesn't cut it, Mr. Marsh," she said. "You sound like you're trying out letters for a crossword puzzle."

He laughed easily, unfazed by her comment. "You think so?" he asked.

Definitely a ladies' man, she thought.

"I know so." She continued straightening the books. "Now, what can I help you with, Mr. Marsh? I suppose you're looking for information on the cemetery?"

"My reputation precedes me."

"Doris called to tell me you were on the way."

"Ah," he said. "I should have known. She's an interesting woman."

"She's my grandmother."

Jeremy's eyebrows shot up. L-I-B, he thought, keeping it to himself this time. But wasn't *that* interesting? "Did she tell you about our delightful lunch?" he asked.

"I really didn't ask." She tucked her hair behind her ear, noting that his dimple was the kind that made little kids want to poke their finger in it. Not that she cared one way or the other, of course. She finished with the books and faced him, keeping her tone steady. "Believe it or not, I'm fairly busy at the moment," she asserted. "I've got a load of paperwork that I need to finish today. What type of information were you looking for?"

He shrugged. "Anything that might help me with the history of the cemetery and the town. When the lights started. Any studies that have been done in the past. Any stories that mention the legends. Old maps. Information on Riker's Hill and the topography. Historical records. Things like that." He paused, studying those violet eyes again. They were really quite exotic. And here she was right next to him, instead of walking away. He found that interesting, too.

"I have to say, it's kind of amazing, isn't it?" he asked, leaning against the shelf beside her.

She stared at him. "Excuse me?"

"Seeing you at the cemetery and now here. Your grandmother's letter, which brought me down here. It's quite a coincidence, don't you think?"

"I can't say I've given it much thought."

Jeremy was not to be deterred. He was seldom deterred, especially when things were interesting. "Well, since I'm not from around here, maybe you could tell me what people do for relaxation in these parts. I mean, is there a place to get some coffee? Or a bite to eat?" He paused. "Like maybe a little later, after you're off?"

Wondering if she'd heard him right, she blinked. "Are you asking me out?" she asked.

"Only if you're available."

"I think," she said, regaining her composure, "I'll have to pass. But thank you for the offer."

She held his gaze steady until he finally raised his hands.

"Okay, fair enough," he said, his tone easy. "But you can't blame a guy for trying." He smiled, the dimple flashing again. "Now, would it be possible to get started with the research? If you're not too busy with the paperwork, I mean. I can always come back tomorrow if it's more convenient."

"Is there anything you'd like to start with in particular?"

"I was hoping I might read the article that appeared in the local paper. I haven't had a chance yet. You wouldn't happen to have it around here, would you?"

She nodded. "It'll probably be on the microfiche. We've been working with the paper for the last couple of years, so I shouldn't have any trouble digging it up."

"Great," he said. "And information about the town in general?"

"It's in the same place."

He glanced around for a moment, wondering where to go. She started toward the foyer.

"This way, Mr. Marsh. You'll find what you need is upstairs."

"There's an upstairs?"

She turned, speaking over her shoulder. "If you follow me, I promise to show you."

Jeremy had to step quickly to catch up with her. "Do you mind if I ask you a question?"

She opened the main door and hesitated. "Not at all," she said, her expression unchanged.

"Why were you in the cemetery today?"

Instead of answering, she simply stared at him, her expression the same.

"I mean, I was just wondering," Jeremy continued. "I got the impression that few people head out there these days."

Still she said nothing, and in the silence, Jeremy grew curious, then finally uncomfortable.

"Aren't you going to say anything?" he asked.

She smiled and, surprising him, winked before moving through the open doorway. "I said you could ask, Mr. Marsh. I didn't say that I would answer.

As she strode ahead of him, all Jeremy could do was stare. Oh, she was something, wasn't she? Confident and beautiful and charming all at once, and that was *after* she'd shot down the idea of going on a date.

Maybe Alvin had been right, he thought. Maybe there was something about southern belles that could drive a guy crazy.

They made their way through the foyer, past the children's reading room, and Lexie led him up the stairs. Pausing at the top, Jeremy looked around.

L-I-B, he thought again.

There *was* more to the place than just a few rickety shelves stocked with new books. A lot more. And lots of Gothic feeling, too, right down to the dusty smell and the private-library atmosphere. With oak-paneled walls, mahogany flooring, and burgundy curtains, the cavernous, open room stood in stark contrast to the area downstairs. Overstuffed chairs and imitation Tiffany lamps stood in corners. Along the far wall was a stone fireplace, with a painting hung above it, and the windows, narrow though they were, offered just enough sunlight to give the place an almost homey feel.

"Now I understand," Jeremy observed. "Downstairs was just the appetizer. This is where the real action is."

She nodded. "Most of our daily visitors come in for recent titles by authors they know, so I set up the area downstairs for their convenience. The room downstairs is small because it used to be our offices before we had it converted."

"Where are the offices now?"

"Over there," she said, pointing behind the far shelf. "Next to the rare-book room."

"Wow," he said. "I'm impressed."

She smiled. "Come on—I'll show you around first and tell you about the place."

For the next few minutes, they chatted as they meandered among the shelves. The home, he learned, had been built in 1874 by Horace Middleton, a captain who'd made his fortune shipping timber and tobacco. He'd built the home for his wife and seven children but, sadly, had never lived here. Right before completion, his wife passed away, and he decided to move with his family to Wilmington. The house was empty for years, then occupied by another family until the 1950s, when it was finally sold to the Historical Society, who later sold it to the county for use as the library.

Jeremy listened intently as she talked. They walked slowly, Lexie interrupting her own story to point out some of her favorite books. She was, he soon came to learn, even more well read than he, especially in the classics, but it made sense, now that he thought about it. Why else would you become a librarian if you didn't love books? As if knowing what he was thinking, she paused and motioned to a shelf plaque with her finger.

"This section here is probably more up your alley, Mr. Marsh."

He glanced at the plaque and noted the words SUPERNATURAL/ WITCHCRAFT. He slowed but didn't stop, taking time only to note a few of the titles, including one about the prophecies of Michel de Nostredame. Nostradamus, as he's commonly known, published one hundred exceptionally vague predictions in 1555 in a book called *Centuries*, the first of ten that he wrote in his lifetime. Of the thousand prophecies Nostradamus published, only fifty or so are still quoted today, making for a paltry 5 percent success rate.

Jeremy pushed his hands into his pockets. "I could probably give you some good recommendations, if you'd like."

"By all means. I'm not too proud to admit I need help."

"You ever read this stuff?"

"No. Frankly, I don't find the topic all that interesting. I mean, I'll thumb through these books when they come in, looking at the pictures and skimming some of the conclusions to see if they're appropriate, but that's about it."

"Good idea," he said. "You're probably better off that way."

"It's amazing, though. There are some people in town who don't want me to stock any books on these subjects. Especially the ones on witchcraft. They think they're a bad influence on the young."

"They are. They're all lies."

She smiled. "That may be true, but you're missing the point. They want them removed because they believe that it's really possible to conjure up evil and that kids who read this stuff might accidentally inspire Satan to run amok in our town."

Jeremy nodded. "Impressionable youth in the Bible Belt. Makes sense."

"Don't quote me on that, though. You know we're off the record here, right?"

He raised his fingers. "Scout's honor."

For a few moments, they walked in silence. The winter sun could barely pierce the grayish clouds, and Lexie paused in front of a few lamps to turn them on. A yellowish glow spread through the room. As she leaned over, he caught a flowery trace of the perfume she was wearing.

Jeremy absently motioned toward the portrait above the fireplace. "Who's this?"

Lexie paused, following his gaze. "My mother," she said.

Jeremy looked at her questioningly, and Lexie drew a long breath.

"After the original library burned to the ground in 1964, my mother took it upon herself to find a new building and begin a new collection, since everyone else in town had written off the idea as impossible. She was only twenty-two, but she spent a few years lobbying county and state officials for funds, she held bake sales, and she went door-to-door to the local businesses, pleading with them until they gave in and wrote a check. It took several years, but she finally did it."

As she spoke, Jeremy found himself glancing from Lexie to the portrait and back again. There was, he thought, a resemblance, one that he should have noticed right away. Especially the eyes. While the violet color had struck him immediately, now that he was close, he noticed that Lexie's had a touch of light blue around the rims that somehow reminded him of the color of kindness. Though the portrait had tried to capture the unusual color, it wasn't close to the real thing.

When Lexie finished with her story, she tucked a loose strand of hair behind her ear. She seemed to do that a lot, he noticed. Probably a nervous habit. Which meant, of course, that he was making her nervous. He considered that a good sign.

Jeremy cleared his throat. "She sounds like a fascinating woman," he said. "I'd love to meet her."

Lexie's smile flickered slightly, as if there was more to say, but instead, she shook her head. "I'm sorry," she said. "I suppose I've rambled on long enough. You're here to work and I'm keeping you from it." She nodded toward the rare-book room. "I may as well show you where you'll be cooped up for the next few days."

"You think it'll take that long?"

"You wanted historical references and the article, right? I'd love to tell you that all the information has been indexed, but it hasn't. You have a bit of tedious research ahead of you."

"There aren't that many books to peruse, are there?"

"It's not just books, although we have plenty of those you might find useful. My suspicion is that you'll find some of the information you're looking for in the diaries. I've made it a point to collect as many as I can from people who lived in the area, and there's quite a collection now. I've even got a few dating back to the seventeenth century."

"You wouldn't happen to have Hettie Doubilet's, would you?"

"No. But I do have a couple belonging to people who lived in Watts Landing, and even one by someone who viewed himself as an amateur historian on the local area. You can't check them out of the library, though, and it'll take some time to get through them. They're barely legible."

"I can't wait," he said. "I *live* for tedious research."

She smiled. "I'd be willing to bet you're quite good at it."

He gazed at her archly. "Oh, I am. I'm good at a lot of things."

"I have no doubt about that, Mr. Marsh."

"Jeremy," he said. "Call me Jeremy."

She raised an eyebrow. "I'm not sure that's such a good idea."

"Oh, it's a great idea," he said. "Trust me."

She snorted. Always on the make, this one. "It's a tempting offer," she said. "Really. And I'm flattered. But even so, I don't know you well enough to trust you, Mr. Marsh."

Jeremy watched with amusement as she turned away, thinking that he'd met her type before. Women who used wit to keep men at a distance usually had a sharp edge to them, but somehow with her, it came across as almost . . . well, charming and good-natured. Maybe it was the accent. The way she sang her words, she could probably talk a cat into swimming across the river.

No, he corrected himself, it wasn't just the accent. Or her wit, which he enjoyed. Or even her startling eyes and the way she looked in her jeans. Okay, that was part of it, but there was more. It was . . . what? He didn't know her, didn't know anything about her. Come to think of it, she hadn't said much of anything about herself. She talked a lot about books and her mother, but he knew nothing else about her at all.

He was here to write an article, but with a sudden sinking sensation, he realized that he'd rather spend the next few hours with Lexie. He wanted to walk with her through downtown Boone Creek or, better yet, dine with her in a romantic, out-of-the-way restaurant, where the two of them could be alone and get to know each other. She was mysterious, and he liked mysteries. Mysteries always led to surprises, and as he followed her toward the rare-book room, he couldn't help but think that his trip down south had just become a lot more interesting.

The rare-book room was small, probably a former bedroom, and was further divided by a low wooden wall that ran from one side of the room to the other. The walls had been painted desert beige, the trim was white, and the hardwood floor was scuffed but unwarped. Behind the wall were tall shelves of books; in one corner was a glass-topped case that looked like a treasure chest, with a television and VCR beside it, no doubt for tapes that referenced North Carolina's history. Opposite the door was a window with an antique rolltop desk beneath it. A small table with a microfiche machine stood just off to Jeremy's right, and Lexie motioned toward it. Going to the rolltop desk, she opened the bottom drawer, then returned with a small cardboard box.

Setting the box on the desk, she riffled through the transparent plates and pulled one out. Leaning over him, she turned the machine on and slid the transparency in, moving it around until the article was front and center. Again, he caught a trace of her perfume, and a moment later, the article was in front of him.

"You can start with this," she said. "I'm going to spend a few minutes looking around to see if I can find some more material for you."

"That was fast," he said.

"It wasn't that hard. I remembered the date of the article."

"Impressive."

"Not really. It appeared on my birthday."

"Twenty-six?"

"Somewhere around there. Now, let me see what else I can find." She turned and headed through the swinging doors again.

"Twenty-five?" he called out.

"Nice try, Mr. Marsh. But I'm not playing."

He laughed. This was definitely going to be an interesting week.

Jeremy turned his attention to the article and began to read. It was written just the way he'd expected—heavy on hype and sensationalism, with enough haughtiness to suggest that everyone who lived in Boone Creek always knew the place was extra special.

He learned very little that was new. The article covered the original legend, describing it in much the same way that Doris had, albeit with some minor variation. In the article, Hettie visited the county commissioners, not the mayor, and she was from Louisiana, not the Caribbean. What was interesting was that she supposedly passed the curse outside the doors of the town hall, which caused a riot, and she was brought to the jail. When the guards went to release her the following morning, they discovered that she'd vanished, as if into thin air. After that, the sheriff refused to try to arrest her again, because he feared that she would put a curse on his family as well. But all legends were like that: stories got passed around and altered slightly to make them more compelling. And he had to admit, the part about vanishing was interesting. He'd have to find out if she'd actually been arrested and if she'd really escaped.

Jeremy glanced over his shoulder. No sign of Lexie yet.

Looking back at the screen, he figured he might as well add to what Doris had told him about Boone Creek, and he moved the glass plate housing of the microfiche, watching as other articles popped into view. There was a week's worth of news in a total of four pages—the paper came out every Tuesday—and he quickly learned what the town had to offer. It was scintillating to read, unless you wanted coverage of anything happening anywhere else in the world or anything that might even keep your eyes open. He read about a young man who landscaped the front of the VFW building to earn the right to be an Eagle Scout, a new dry cleaner opening on Main Street, and a recap of a town meeting where the top of the agenda was to decide whether or not to put a stop sign on Leary Point Road. Two days of front-page coverage were devoted to an automobile wreck, in which two local men had sustained minor injuries.

He leaned back in his chair.

So the town was just what he expected. Sleepy and quiet and special in the way that all small communities claimed to be, but nothing more than that. It was the kind of town that continued to exist more as a result of habit than any unique quality and would fade from existence in coming decades as the population aged. There was no future here, not long-term, anyway . . .

"Reading about our exciting town?" she asked.

He jumped, surprised he hadn't heard her come up behind him and feeling strangely sad about the plight of things here. "I am. And it *is* exciting, I must admit. That Eagle Scout was something. Whew."

"Jimmie Telson," she said. "He's actually a great kid. Straight As and a pretty good basketball player. His dad died last year, but he's still volunteering around town, even though he has a part-time job at Pete's Pizza now. We're proud of him."

"I'm sold on the kid."

She smiled, thinking, Sure you are. "Here," she said, setting a stack of books beside him, "these should be enough to get you started."

He scanned the dozen or so titles. "I thought you said that I'd be better off using the diaries. All of these are general history."

"I know. But don't you want to understand the period they were set in first?"

He hesitated. "I suppose," he admitted.

"Good," she said. She absently tugged at the sleeve of her sweater. "And I found a book of ghost stories that you might be interested in. There's a chapter in there that discusses Cedar Creek."

"That's great."

"Well, I'll let you get started, then. I'll be back in a while to see if there's anything else you need."

"You're not going to stay?"

"No. Like I said earlier, I've got quite a bit of work to do. Now, you can stay in here, or you can sit at one of the tables in the main area. But I'd appreciate it if you didn't remove the books from the floor. None of these particular books can be checked out."

"I wouldn't dare," he said.

"Now, if you'll excuse me, Mr. Marsh, I really should go. And keep in mind that even though the library is open until seven, the rare-book room closes at five."

"Even for friends?"

"No. I let them stay as long as they want."

"So I'll see you at seven?"

"No, Mr. Marsh. I'll see you at five."

He laughed. "Maybe tomorrow you'll let me stay late."

She raised her eyebrows without answering, then took a couple of steps toward the door.

"Lexie?"

She turned. "Yes?"

"You've been a great help so far. Thank you."

She gave a lovely, unguarded smile. "You're welcome."

Jeremy spent the next couple of hours perusing information on the town. He thumbed through the books one by one, lingering over the photographs and reading sections he thought appropriate.

Most of the information covered the early history of the town, and he jotted what he thought were relevant notes on the pad beside him. Of course, he wasn't sure what was relevant at this point; it was too early to tell, and thus his notes soon covered a couple of pages.

He'd learned through experience that the best way to approach a story like this was to begin with what he knew, so . . . what did he know for certain? That the cemetery had been used for over a hundred years without any sightings of mysterious lights. That lights first appeared about a hundred years ago and occurred regularly, but only when it was foggy. That many people had seen them, which meant that the lights were unlikely to be simply a figment of the imagination. And, of course, that the cemetery was now sinking.

So even after a couple of hours, he didn't know much more than when he started. Like most mysteries, it was a puzzle with many disparate pieces. The legend, whether or not Hettie cursed the town, was essentially an attempt to link some pieces into an understandable form. But since the legend had as its basis something false, it meant that some pieces—whatever they were— were being either overlooked or ignored. And that meant, of course, that Lexie had been right. He had to read everything so he wouldn't miss anything.

No problem. This was the enjoyable part, actually. The search for the truth was often more fun than writing up the actual conclusion, and he found himself immersed in the subject. He learned that Boone Creek had been founded in 1729, making it one of the oldest towns in the state, and that for a long time, it was nothing more than a tiny trading village on the banks of the Pamlico River and Boone Creek. Later in the century, it became a minor port in the inland waterway system, and the use of steamboats in the mid-1800s accelerated the town's growth. Toward the end of the nineteenth century, the railroad boom hit North Carolina, and forests were leveled while numerous quarries were dug. Again, the town was affected, due to its location as a gateway of sorts to the Outer Banks. After that, the town tended to boom and bust along with the economy of the rest of the state, though the population held steady after around 1930. In the most recent census, the population of the county had actually dropped, which didn't surprise him in the slightest.

He also read the account of the cemetery in the book of ghost stories. In this version, Hettie cursed the town, not because the bodies in the cemetery had been removed, but because she'd refused to step aside and into the road when the wife of one of the commissioners was approaching from the opposite direction. However, because she was regarded as an almost spiritual figure in Watts Landing, she escaped arrest, so a few of the more racist townsfolk took matters into their own hands and caused a great deal of damage in the Negro cemetery. In her anger, Hettie cursed the Cedar Creek Cemetery and swore that her ancestors would tread the cemetery grounds until the earth swallowed it whole.

Jeremy leaned back in his chair, thinking. Three completely different versions of essentially the same legend. He wondered what that meant.

Interestingly, the writer of the book—A. J. Morrison—had added an italicized postscript stating that the Cedar Creek Cemetery had actually begun to sink. According to surveys, the cemetery grounds had sunk by nearly twenty inches; the author offered no explanation.

Jeremy checked the date of publication. The book had been written in 1954, and by the way the cemetery looked now, he figured it had sunk at least another three feet since then. He made a note to see if he could find surveys from that period, as well as any done more recently.

Still, as he absorbed the information, he couldn't help glancing over his shoulder from time to time on the off-chance that Lexie had returned.

Across town, on the fairway of the fourteenth tee and with his cell phone sandwiched against his ear, the mayor snapped to attention as he listened to the caller though the hissing static. Reception was bad in this part of the county, and the mayor wondered if holding his five-iron above his head would help him make sense of what was being said.

"He was at Herbs? Today at lunch? Did you say *Primetime Live?*"

He nodded, pretending not to notice that his golf buddy, who was in turn pretending to see where his most recent shot had landed, had just kicked the ball from behind a tree into a better position.

"Found it!" his buddy yelled, and began setting up for the shot.

The mayor's buddy did things like that all the time, which frankly didn't bother the mayor all that much, since he'd just done the same thing. Maintaining his three handicap would have otherwise been impossible.

Meanwhile, as the caller was finishing up, his buddy launched his shot into the trees again.

"Damnation!" he shouted. The mayor ignored him.

"Well, this is definitely interesting," the mayor said, his mind whirring with possibilities, "and I'm very glad you called. You take care, now. Bye."

He flipped the phone closed, just as his buddy was approaching.

"I hope I get a good lie with that one."

"I wouldn't worry too much," the mayor said, pondering the sudden development in town. "I'm sure it'll end up being right where you want it."

"Who was that on the phone?"

"Fate," he announced. "And if we play this right, just maybe our salvation."

Two hours later, just as the sun was dropping below the treetops and shadows began to stretch through the window, Lexie poked her head into the rare-book room.

"How'd it go?"

Glancing over his shoulder, Jeremy smiled. Pushing back from the desk, he ran his hand through his hair. "Good," he said. "I learned quite a bit."

"Do you have the magic answer yet?"

"No, but I'm getting closer. I can feel it."

She moved into the room. "I'm glad. But as I said earlier, I usually lock up here about five o'clock so I can handle the after-work crowd when they come in."

He stood from the desk. "No problem. I'm getting a little tired, anyway. It's been a long day."

"You'll be in tomorrow morning, right?"

"I was planning on it. Why?"

"Well, normally, I put everything back on the shelves daily."

"Would it be possible to just keep the stack the way it is, for now? I'm sure I'll go through most of the books again."

She thought for a moment. "I suppose that's okay. But I do have to warn you that if you don't show up first thing, I'll think I misjudged you."

He nodded, looking solemn. "I promise I won't stand you up. I'm not that kind of guy."

She rolled her eyes, thinking, Oh, brother. He was persistent, though. She had to give him that. "I'm sure you say that to all the girls, Mr. Marsh."

"No," he said, leaning against the desk. "Actually, I'm very shy. Almost a hermit, really. I hardly ever get out."

She shrugged. "Shows me what I know. Being that you're a journalist from the big city, I had you figured as a ladies' man."

"And that bothers you?"

"No."

"Good. Because, as you know, first impressions can be deceiving."

"Oh, I realized that right away."

"You did?"

"Sure," she said. "When I first bumped into you at the cemetery, I thought you were there for a funeral."

Five

.....❖.....

Fifteen minutes later, after heading down an asphalt road that gave way to yet another gravel road—they sure were fond of gravel around here—Jeremy found himself parking his car in the middle of a swamp, directly in front of a hand-painted sign advertising Greenleaf Cottages. Which reminded him never to trust the promises of the local Chamber of Commerce.

Modern, it definitely wasn't. It wouldn't have been modern thirty years ago. In all, there were six small bungalows set along the river. With peeling paint, plank walls, and tin roofs, they were reached by following small dirt pathways that led from a central bungalow that he assumed to be the main office. It was scenic, he had to admit, but the rustic part probably referred to mosquitoes and alligators, neither of which summoned up a lot of enthusiasm in him for staying there.

As he was debating whether he should even bother checking in—he'd passed some chain hotels in Washington, about forty minutes from Boone Creek—he heard the sound of an engine coming up the road and watched as a maroon Cadillac came rolling toward him, bouncing wildly in the potholes. Surprising him, it pulled into the spot directly beside his own car, spewing up rocks as it slid to a stop.

An overweight, balding man burst from the door, looking frantic. Dressed in green polyester pants and a blue turtleneck sweater, the man looked as if he'd dressed in the dark.

"Mr. Marsh?"

Jeremy was taken aback. "Yes?"

The man scurried around the car. Everything about him seemed to move quickly.

"Well, I'm glad I caught you before you checked in! I wanted to have a chance to speak with you! I can't tell you how excited we all are about your visit here!"

He seemed breathless as he stretched out his hand and shook Jeremy's vigorously.

"Do I know you?" Jeremy asked.

"No, no, of course not." The man laughed. "I'm Mayor Tom Gherkin. Like the pickle, but you can call me Tom." He laughed again. "I just wanted to swing by to welcome you to our fine town. Sorry for my appearance. I would have had you down to the office, but I came straight from the golf course once I learned you were here."

Jeremy looked him over, still a bit in shock. At least it explained the clothes.

"You're the mayor?"

"Have been since '94. It's kind of a family tradition. My daddy, Owen Gherkin, was the mayor here for twenty-four years. Had a big interest in the town, my daddy did. Knew everything there was to know about this place. Of course, being the mayor is only a part-time job here. It's more of an honorary position. I'm more of a businessman, if you want to know the truth. I own the department store and radio station downtown. Oldies. You like oldies?"

"Sure," Jeremy said.

"Good, good. I figured as much from the moment I laid eyes on you. I said to myself, 'That's a man who appreciates good music.' I can't stand most of that new stuff everyone else calls music these days. Gives me a headache. Music should soothe the soul. You know what I mean?"

"Sure," Jeremy repeated, trying to keep up.

He laughed. "I knew you would. Well, like I said, I can't tell you how thrilled we all are that you're here to write a story about our fine town. It's just the thing this town needs. I mean, who doesn't like a good ghost story, right? It's got folks real excited around here, that's for sure. First the folks from Duke, then the local paper. And now a big-city journalist. Word's getting out, and that's good. Why, just last week, we had a call from a group from Alabama that was thinking about spending a few days here this weekend for the Historic Homes Tour."

Jeremy shook his head, trying to slow things down. "How did you know I was even here?"

Mayor Gherkin laid a friendly hand on his shoulder, and almost before Jeremy realized it, they were moving toward the bungalow office. "Word gets around, Mr. Marsh. Passes like wildfire. Always has, always will. Part of the charm of this place. That, and the natural beauty. We've got some of the best fishing and duck hunting in the state, you know. Folks come from all over, even famous ones, and most of 'em stay right here at Greenleaf. This here is a little piece of paradise, if you ask me. Your own quiet bungalow, out here in the middle of nature. Why, you'll be listening to the birds and crickets all night long. I'll bet it makes you see those hotels in New York in a whole new light."

"That it does," Jeremy admitted. The man was definitely a politician.

"And don't you worry none about the snakes."

Jeremy's eyes widened. "Snakes?"

"I'm sure you heard about it, but just keep in mind that the whole situation here last year was just a misunderstanding. Some folks just don't have a speck of common sense. But like I said, don't worry about 'em. The snakes don't normally come out till the summer, anyway. Of course, don't go poking through the brush or anything, lookin' for 'em. Those cottonmouths can be nasty."

"Uh," Jeremy said, trying to summon a response in the midst of the vision that had been conjured up in his mind. He hated snakes. Even more than mosquitoes and alligators. "Actually, I was thinking . . ."

Mayor Gherkin sighed loudly enough to interrupt Jeremy's answer, and looked around, as if making sure Jeremy noticed how much he was enjoying the natural setting. "So tell me, Jeremy . . . you don't mind if I call you Jeremy?"

"No."

"That's mighty kind of you. Mighty kind. So, Jeremy, I was wondering if you think one of those television shows might follow up on your story here."

"I have no idea," he said.

"Well, because if they do, we'd roll out the red carpet. Show 'em some genuine southern hospitality. Why, we'd put 'em up right here at Greenleaf, free of charge. And, of course, they'd have a whale of a story to tell. Much better than what you did on *Primetime*. What we have here is the real thing."

"You do realize that I'm primarily a columnist? Normally, I have nothing to do with television . . ."

"No, of course not." Mayor Gherkin winked, obviously in disbelief. "You just do what you do, and we'll see what happens."

"I'm serious," Jeremy said.

He winked again. "Of course, you are."

Jeremy wasn't quite sure what to say to dissuade him—mainly because the man might be *right*—and a moment later, Mayor Gherkin pushed through the door of the office. If you could call it that.

It looked as if it hadn't been remodeled in a hundred years, and the wood walls reminded him of what he might find in a log cabin. Just beyond the tottering desk was a largemouth bass mounted on the wall; in every corner, along the walls, and atop the file cabinet and desk were stuffed critters: beavers, rabbits, squirrels, opossums, skunks, and a badger. Unlike most of the mounts he'd seen, however, all had been mounted to make them appear as if they'd been cornered and were trying to defend themselves. Mouths were molded into snarls, the bodies arched, teeth and claws exposed. Jeremy was still absorbing the images when he spotted a bear in the corner and jumped in shock. Like the other animals, its paws were outstretched as if attacking. The place was the Museum of Natural History transformed into a horror movie and squeezed into a closet.

Behind the desk, a huge, heavily bearded man sat with his feet propped up, a television in front of him. The picture was fuzzy, with vertical lines passing through the screen every couple of seconds, making it nearly impossible to see what was on.

The man rose from behind the desk and kept on rising until he towered over Jeremy. He had to be at least seven feet tall, and his shoulders were broader than the ones on the stuffed bear in the corner. Dressed in overalls and a plaid shirt, he grabbed a clipboard and set it on the desk.

He pointed to Jeremy and the clipboard. He didn't smile; for all intents and purposes, he looked as if he wanted nothing more than to pull Jeremy's arms from his body so he could use them to beat him, before mounting him on the wall.

Gherkin, not surprisingly, laughed. The man laughed a lot, Jeremy noticed.

"Don't let him worry you none, Jeremy," the mayor offered quickly. "Jed here doesn't talk much to strangers. Just fill out the form, and you'll be on your way to your own little room in paradise."

Jeremy was staring wide-eyed at Jed, thinking the man was the scariest-looking person he'd ever seen in his life.

"Not only does he own Greenleaf and serve on the town council, but he's the local taxidermist," Gherkin went on. "Isn't his work incredible?"

"Incredible," Jeremy said, forcing a smile.

"You shoot anything around here, you come to Jed. He'll do you right."

"I'll try to remember that."

The mayor suddenly brightened. "You hunt, do ya?"

"Not too much, to be honest."

"Well, maybe we'll change that while you're down here. I mentioned that the duck hunting here is spectacular, didn't I?"

As Gherkin spoke, Jed tapped his massive finger on the clipboard again.

"Now, don't try to intimidate the fellow," Mayor Gherkin broke in. "He's from New York. He's a big-city journalist, so you treat him right."

Mayor Gherkin turned his attention to Jeremy again. "And, Jeremy, just so you know, the town will be happy to pay for your accommodations here."

"That's not necessary . . ."

"Not another word," he said, waiving the rebuff off. "The decision's already been made by the higher-ups." He winked. "That's me, by the way. But it's the least we can do for such a distinguished guest."

"Well, thank you."

Jeremy reached for the pen. He began to fill out the registration form, feeling Jed's eyes on him and afraid of what would happen if he changed his mind about staying. Gherkin leaned over his shoulder.

"Did I mention how thrilled we are to have you in town?"

Across town, in a blue-shuttered white bungalow on a quiet street, Doris was sautéing bacon, onions, and garlic as a pot of pasta boiled on a nearby burner. Lexie was dicing tomatoes and carrots over the sink, rinsing as she went along. After finishing at the library, she'd swung by Doris's, as she normally did a few times a week. Though she had her own house nearby, she often had dinner at her grandmother's. Old habits die hard, and all that.

On the windowsill, the radio played jazz, and aside from the perfunctory conversation typical of family members, neither had said much at all. For Doris, the reason was her long day at work. Ever since a heart attack two years ago, she tired more easily, even if she didn't want to admit it. For Lexie, the reason was Jeremy Marsh, though she knew enough not to say anything to Doris about it. Doris had always taken an acute interest in her personal life, and Lexie had learned that it was best to avoid the topic whenever possible.

Lexie knew her grandmother meant no harm. Doris simply didn't understand why someone in her thirties hadn't settled down yet, and she'd reached the point where she frequently wondered aloud why Lexie wasn't married. As sharp as she was, Doris was from the old school; she married at twenty and had spent the next fifty-six years with a man she adored, until he passed away three years ago. Lexie's grandparents had raised her, after all, and Lexie could pretty much condense all of Doris's hemming and hawing into just a few simple thoughts: it was time for her to meet a nice guy, settle down, move into a house with a white picket fence, and have babies.

Doris wasn't so strange in that belief, Lexie knew. Around here, anyway, that's what was expected of women. And when she was honest with herself, Lexie sometimes wished for a life like that as well. In theory, anyway. But she wanted to meet the right guy first, someone who inspired her, the kind of guy she would be proud to call *her man*. That was where she and Doris differed. Doris seemed to think that a decent, moral man with a good job was all a woman should reasonably expect. And maybe in the past, those were all the qualities that someone *could* expect. But Lexie didn't want to settle for someone simply because he was kind and decent and had a good job. Who knows—maybe she had unrealistic expectations, but Lexie wanted to feel passion for him as well. No matter how kind or responsible a man was, if she didn't feel any passion, she couldn't help but think that she'd be "settling" for someone, and she didn't want to settle. That wouldn't be fair to her and it wouldn't be fair to him. She wanted a man who was both sensitive and kind, but at the same time could sweep her off her feet. She wanted someone who would offer to rub her feet after a long day at the library, but also challenge her intellectually. Someone romantic, of course, the kind of guy who would buy her flowers for no reason at all.

It wasn't too much to ask, was it?

According to *Glamour*, *Ladies' Home Journal*, and *Good Housekeeping*—all of which the library received—it was. In those magazines, it seemed that every article stated that it was completely up to the woman to keep the excitement alive in a relationship. But wasn't a relationship supposed to be just that? A *relationship*? Both partners doing everything they could to keep the other satisfied?

See, that was the problem with many of the married couples she knew. In any marriage, there was a fine balance between doing what you wanted and doing what your partner wanted, and as long as both the husband and the wife were doing what the other wanted, there was never any problem. The problems arose when people started doing what they wanted without regard to the other. A husband suddenly decides he needs more sex and looks for it outside of the marriage; a wife decides she needs more affection, which eventually leads to her doing exactly the same thing. A good marriage, like any partnership, meant subordinating one's own needs to that of the other's, in the expectation that the other will do the same. And as long as both partners keep up their end of the bargain, all is well in the world.

But if you didn't feel any passion for your husband, could you really expect that? She wasn't sure. Doris, of course, had a ready answer. "Trust me, honey, that passes after the first couple of years," she would say, despite the fact that, to Lexie's mind, anyway, her grandparents had the kind of relationship that anyone would envy. Her grandfather was one of those naturally romantic men. Until the very end, he would open the car door for Doris and hold her hand when they walked through town. He had been both committed and faithful to her. He clearly adored her and would often comment on how lucky he was to have met a woman like her. After he passed on, part of Doris had begun to die as well. First the heart attack, now worsening arthritis; it was as if they'd always been meant to be together. When coupled with Doris's advice, what did that mean? Did that mean Doris had simply been lucky in meeting a man like him? Or had she seen something in her husband beforehand, something that confirmed he was the right one for her?

More important, why on earth was Lexie even thinking about marriage again?

Probably because she was here at Doris's house, the house she'd grown up in after her parents had died. Cooking with her in the kitchen was comforting in its familiarity, and she remembered growing up thinking that she would one day live in a house like this. Weathered planking; a tin roof that echoed the sound of rain, making it seem that it was raining nowhere else in the world; old-fashioned windows with frames that had been painted so many times that they were almost impossible to open. And she did live in a house like that. Well, sort of, anyway. At first glance, it would seem that Doris's home and hers were similar—they were built in the same era—but she'd never been able to replicate the aromas. The Sunday afternoon stews, the sun-dried scent of sheets on the bed, the slightly stuffy smell of the ancient rocker where her grandfather had relaxed for years. Smells like those reflected a way of life worn smooth with comfort over the years, and whenever she pushed through the door here, she was flooded with vivid childhood memories.

Of course, she'd always imagined that she would have a family of her own by now, maybe even children, but it hadn't worked out. Two relationships had come close: there was the long relationship with Avery, which had begun in college, and after that, another involving a young man from Chicago who was visiting his cousin in Boone Creek one summer. He was the classic Renaissance man: he spoke four languages, spent a year studying at the London School of Economics, and had paid his way through school with a baseball scholarship. Mr. Renaissance was charming and exotic, and she'd fallen for him quickly. She thought he'd stay here, thought he'd grow to love the place as much as she did, but she woke up one Saturday morning to learn that he was on his way back to Chicago. He never even bothered to say good-bye.

And after that? Not much, really. There were a couple of other flings that lasted six months or so, neither of which she thought about much anymore. One had been with a local physician, the other a lawyer; both had proposed to her, but again, she hadn't felt the magic or thrill or whatever it was you were supposed to feel to let you know that you didn't need to look any further. In the last couple of years, the dates had been fewer and further apart, unless you counted Rodney Hopper, a deputy sheriff in town. They'd gone on a dozen or so dates, one every other month or so, whenever there was a local benefit that she was encouraged to attend. Like her, Rodney had been born and raised here, and when they were kids, they used to share the teeter-totter behind the Episcopal Church. Ever since, he'd been pining away for her and had asked her a couple of times to accompany him for drinks at the Lookilu Tavern. Sometimes she wondered whether she should just take him up on his offers to date her regularly, but Rodney . . . well, he was a little too interested in fishing and hunting and lifting weights and not quite interested enough in books or anything going on in the rest of the world. He was a nice guy, though, and she figured he'd make a fine husband. But not for her.

So where did that leave her?

Here at Doris's, three times a week, she thought, waiting for the inevitable questions about her love life.

"So what did you think of him?" Doris asked, right on cue.

Lexie couldn't help smiling. "Who?" she asked, playing innocent.

"Jeremy Marsh. Who did you think I was talking about?"

"I have no idea. That's why I asked the question."

"Quit avoiding the subject. I heard he spent a couple of hours at the library."

Lexie shrugged. "He seemed nice enough. I helped him find a few books to get him started, and that was about it."

"You didn't talk to him?"

"Of course, we talked. Like you said, he was there for a while."

Doris waited for Lexie to add more, but when she didn't, Doris sighed. "Well, I liked him," Doris volunteered. "He seemed like a perfect gentleman."

"Oh, he was," Lexie agreed. "Just perfect."

"You don't sound like you mean that."

"What else do you want me to say?"

"Well, was he charmed by your sparkling personality?"

"Why on earth would that matter? He's only in town for a few days."

"Did I ever tell you about the way I met your grandfather?"

"Many times," Lexie said, remembering the story well. They'd met on a train that was heading to Baltimore; he was from Grifton and on his way to interview for a job, one that he would never take, choosing to be with her instead.

"Then you know that you're most likely to meet someone when you least expect it."

"You always say that."

Doris winked. "That's only because I think you need to keep hearing it."

Lexie brought the salad bowl to the table. "You don't have to worry about me. I'm happy. I love my job, I have good friends, I have time to read and jog and do the things I love."

"And don't forget you're blessed with me, too."

"Of course," Lexie affirmed. "How could I forget that?"

Doris chuckled and went back to sautéing. For a moment, there was silence in the kitchen, and Lexie breathed a sigh of relief. At least that was over, and thankfully, Doris hadn't pushed too hard. Now, she thought, they could have a pleasant dinner.

"I thought he was quite handsome," Doris opined.

Lexie said nothing; instead, she grabbed a couple of plates and utensils before moving to the table. Maybe it was better if she simply pretended not to hear her.

"And just to let you know, there's more to him than you think there is," she went on. "He's not what you imagine him to be."

It was the way she said it that gave Lexie pause. She had heard that tone many times in the past—when she'd wanted to go out with friends in high school, only to have Doris talk her out of going; when she wanted to take a trip to Miami a few years back, only to be talked out of it. In the first instance, the friends she'd wanted to join were involved in a car accident; in the latter, riots had broken out in the city and had spilled into the hotel where she'd been planning to stay.

Doris sometimes sensed things, she knew. Not as much as Doris's own mother had. But even though Doris seldom explained further, Lexie was fully aware that she always sensed the truth.

Completely unaware that phone lines were buzzing all over as people discussed his presence in town, Jeremy was lying in bed under the covers, watching the local news while waiting for the weather report, wishing he had followed his initial impulse and checked into another hotel. He had no doubt that had he done so, he wouldn't have been surrounded by Jed's handiwork, which gave him the willies.

The man obviously had a lot of time on his hands.

And a lot of bullets. Or pellets. Or the front end of a pickup. Or whatever it was he used to kill all these varmints. In his room, there were twelve critters; with the exception of a second stuffed bear, representatives of the entire zoological species of North Carolina would be keeping him company. No doubt Jed would have included a bear as well if he'd had an extra one.

Other than that, the room wasn't too bad, as long as he didn't expect a high-speed connection to the Internet, or to warm the room without use of the fireplace, order room service, watch cable, or even dial out on a push-button phone. He hadn't seen a dial phone in what? Ten years? Even his mother had succumbed to the modern world on that one.

But not Jed. Nope. Good old Jed obviously had his own ideas of what was important in the way of accommodations for his guests.

If there was one decent thing about the room, though, it did have a nice covered porch out back, one that overlooked the river. There was even a rocking chair, and Jeremy considered sitting outside for a while, until he remembered the snakes. Which made him wonder what sort of misunderstanding Gherkin had been talking about. He didn't like the sound of that. He really should have asked more about it, just as he should have asked where he could find some firewood around here. This place was absolutely freezing, but he had the funny suspicion that Jed wouldn't answer the phone if he tried to call the office and ask. And besides, Jed scared him.

Just then the meteorologist appeared on the news. Steeling himself, Jeremy hopped out of bed to turn up the volume. Moving as quickly as he could, he shivered as he adjusted the set, then dove back under the covers.

The meteorologist was immediately replaced by commercials. Figures.

He'd been wondering whether he should head out to the cemetery but wanted to find out if fog was likely. If not, he'd catch up on his rest. It had been a long day; he'd started out in the modern world, went back in time fifty years, and now he was sleeping in the midst of ice and death. It certainly wasn't something that happened to him every day.

And, of course, there was Lexie. Lexie whatever-her-last-name-was. Lexie the mysterious. Lexie who flirted and withdrew and flirted again.

She *had* been flirting, hadn't she? The way she kept calling him Mr. Marsh? The fact that she pretended to have sized him up almost immediately? The funeral comment? Definitely flirting.

Wasn't it?

The meteorologist came on again, looking fresh out of college. The guy couldn't have been more than twenty-three or -four and was no doubt working his first job. He had that deer-in-the-headlights-but-enthusiastic look about him. But at least the guy seemed competent. He didn't stumble over his words, and Jeremy knew almost immediately that he wouldn't be leaving the room. The skies were expected to be clear throughout the evening, and the man mentioned nothing about the possibility of fog tomorrow, either.

Figures, he thought.

Six

.....❖.....

The following morning after showering under a luke-warm trickle of water, Jeremy slipped on a pair of jeans, sweater, and brown leather jacket and made his way to Herbs, which seemed to be the most popular breakfast place in town. At the counter, he noticed Mayor Gherkin talking to a couple of men dressed in suits, and Rachel was busy working the tables. Jed was seated on the far side of the room, looking like the back side of a mountain. Tully was sitting at one of the center tables with three other men and, as could be expected, was doing most of the talk-ing. People nodded and waved as Jeremy wound through the ta-bles, and the mayor raised his coffee cup in salute.

"Well, good morning, Mr. Marsh," Mayor Gherkin called out. "Thinking of positive things to write about our town, I hope?"

"I'm sure he is," Rachel chimed in.

"Hope you found the cemetery," Tully drawled. He leaned toward the others at his table. "That there's the doctor I was telling you about."

Jeremy waved and nodded back, trying to avoid getting cor-ralled into a conversation. He'd never been a morning person, and on top of that, he hadn't slept well. Ice and death, coupled with nightmares about snakes, could do that to a person. He took a seat in the corner booth, and Rachel moved to the table with efficiency, carrying a pot of coffee with her.

"No funeral today?" she teased.

"No. I decided to go with a more casual look," he explained.

"Coffee, darlin'?"

"Please."

After flipping the cup, she filled it to the brim. "Would you like the special this mornin'? People have been ravin' about it."

"What is the special?"

"A Carolina omelet."

"Sure," he said, having no idea what was in a Carolina omelet, but with his stomach growling, anything sounded good.

"With grits and a biscuit?"

"Why not?" he said.

"Be back in a few minutes, darlin'."

Jeremy began nursing his coffee while perusing yesterday's newspaper. All four pages of it, including a big front-page story on a Ms. Judy Roberts, who'd just celebrated her hundredth birthday, a milestone now reached by 1.1 percent of the population. Along with the article was a picture of the staff at the nursing home holding a cupcake with a single lit candle atop it, as Ms. Roberts lay in the bed behind them, looking comatose.

He glanced through the window, wondering why he'd even bothered with the local paper. There was a vending machine out front offering *USA Today*, and he was reaching into his pocket to look for change when a uniformed deputy took a seat directly across the table from him.

The man looked both angry and extremely fit; his biceps swelled the seams of his shirt, and he wore mirrored sunglasses that had gone out of style . . . oh, twenty years ago, Jeremy guessed, right after *CHiPS* went off the air. His hand rested on his holster, right atop a gun. In his mouth was a toothpick, which he moved from one side to the other. He said nothing at all, preferring to simply stare, giving Jeremy plenty of time to study his own reflection.

It was, Jeremy had to admit, sort of intimidating.

"Can I help you?" Jeremy asked.

The toothpick moved from side to side again. Jeremy closed the newspaper, wondering what on earth was going on.

"Jeremy Marsh?" the officer intoned.

"Yes?"

"Thought so," he said.

Above the officer's breast pocket, Jeremy noticed a shiny bar with the name engraved on it. Yet another name tag.

"And you must be Sheriff Hopper?"

"*Deputy* Hopper," he corrected.

"Sorry," Jeremy said. "Have I done something wrong, Officer?"

"I don't know," Hopper said. "Have you?"

"Not that I know of."

Deputy Hopper moved the toothpick again. "You planning to stick around for a while?"

"Just for a week or so. I'm here to write an article—"

"I know why you're here," Hopper interrupted. "I just thought I'd check it out myself. I like to visit with strangers who are planning to hang around for a while."

He put the emphasis on the word "stranger," making Jeremy feel it was some sort of crime. He wasn't quite sure that any response would diffuse the hostility, so he fell back on the obvious.

"Ah," he said.

"I hear you intend to spend a lot of time at the library."

"Well . . . I guess I might—"

"Mmm," the deputy rumbled, cutting him off again.

Jeremy reached for his coffee cup and took a sip, buying time. "I'm sorry, Deputy Hopper, but I'm not exactly sure what's going on here."

"Mmm," Hopper said again.

"Now, you're not hassling our guest, are you, Rodney?" the mayor called out from across the room. "He's a special visitor, here to drum up interest in the local folklore."

Deputy Hopper didn't flinch or turn his gaze away from Jeremy. For whatever reason, he looked downright angry. "Just visiting with him, Mayor."

"Well, let the man enjoy his breakfast," Gherkin chided, moving toward the table. He waved a hand. "Come on over here, Jeremy. I've got a couple of people I'd like you to meet."

Deputy Hopper scowled as Jeremy rose from the table and made his way toward Mayor Gherkin.

When he was close, the mayor introduced him to two people; one was the almost emaciated county lawyer, the other a heavyset physician who worked at the local medical clinic. Both seemed to evaluate him in the same way that Deputy Hopper had. Reserving judgment, as they say. Meanwhile, the mayor was going on about how exciting Jeremy's visit was for the town. Leaning toward the other two, he nodded conspiratorially.

"Might even end up on *Primetime Live*," he whispered.

"Really?" the lawyer said. Jeremy figured the guy could easily pass for a skeleton.

Jeremy shifted his weight from one foot to the other. "Well, as I was trying to explain to the mayor yesterday—"

Mayor Gherkin slapped him on the back, cutting him off.

"Very exciting," Mayor Gherkin added. "Major television exposure."

The others nodded, their faces solemn.

"And speaking of the town," the mayor suddenly added, "I'd like to invite you to a little get-together dinner this evening with a few close friends. Nothing too extravagant, of course, but since you'll be here for a few days, I'd like to give you the chance to get to know some of the folks around here."

Jeremy held up his hands. "That's not really necessary . . ."

"Nonsense," Mayor Gherkin said. "It's the least we can do.

And, remember, some of these people I'm inviting have seen those ghosts, and you'll have the chance to pick their collective brains. Their stories might even give you nightmares."

He raised his eyebrows; the lawyer and the physician waited expectantly. When Jeremy hesitated, it was all the mayor needed to conclude.

"Say about seven o'clock?" he said.

"Yeah . . . sure. I guess that's fine," Jeremy agreed. "Where's the dinner going to be?"

"I'll let you know a little later. I assume you'll be at the library, right?"

"Probably."

The mayor raised his eyebrows. "So I take it you've already met our fine librarian, Miss Lexie?"

"I have, yes."

"She's quite impressive, isn't she?"

There was just a hint of other possibilities in the way he phrased it, something akin to locker-room talk.

"She's been very helpful," Jeremy said.

The lawyer and the physician smiled, but before the conversation went any further, Rachel came slithering by, just a little too close. Holding a plate, she nudged Jeremy.

"Come on, darlin'. I've got your breakfast right here."

Jeremy glanced at the mayor.

"By all means," Mayor Gherkin said, waving his hands.

Jeremy followed her back to the table. Thankfully, Deputy Hopper was gone by then, and Jeremy slid back into his seat. Rachel set the plate in front of him.

"You just enjoy that. I told 'em to make it extra special, since you're visiting from New York City. I absolutely love that place!"

"Oh, you've been there?"

"Well, no. But I've always wanted to go. It seems so . . . glamorous and exciting."

"You should go. It's like nowhere else in the world."

She smiled, looking coy. "Why, Mr. Marsh . . . is that an invitation?"

Jeremy's jaw dropped. Huh?

Rachel, on the other hand, didn't seem to notice his expression. "Well, I just might want to take you up on that," she twittered. "And I'd be glad to show you 'round the cemetery, any night you'd like to go. I'm usually finished here by three o'clock."

"I'll keep that in mind," Jeremy mumbled.

Over the next twenty minutes, as Jeremy ate, Rachel came by a dozen times, refilling his coffee cup a quarter inch each time, smiling at him unrelentingly.

Jeremy made his way to his car, recovering from what was supposed to have been a leisurely breakfast.

Deputy Hopper. Mayor Gherkin. Tully. Rachel. Jed.

Small-town USA was way too much to deal with before coffee.

Tomorrow he'd just grab a cup of coffee somewhere else. He wasn't sure eating at Herbs was worth it, even if the food was great. And, he had to admit, it was even better than he'd thought it would be. As Doris had said yesterday, it tasted fresh, like the ingredients had been gathered from the farm that morning.

Still, tomorrow would be coffee elsewhere. And not from Tully's gas station, either, assuming he even had coffee. He didn't want to get stuck in a conversation when he had other things to do.

He paused in midstep, amazed. Good Lord, he thought, I'm already thinking like a local.

He shook his head and retrieved his keys from his pocket as he walked toward the car. At least breakfast was over. Checking his watch, he saw that it was coming up on nine o'clock. Good.

Lexie found herself glancing out the window of her office the exact moment Jeremy Marsh pulled into the library parking lot.

Jeremy Marsh. Who'd continued to creep into her thoughts, even though she was trying to work. And just look at him now.

Trying to dress more casually to blend with folks around here, she supposed. And somehow he'd almost pulled it off.

But enough of that. She had work to do. Her office was lined with bookcases crammed from top to bottom: books piled every which way, vertical and horizontal. A steel-gray filing cabinet stood in the corner, and her desk and chair were typically functional. There was little in the office that was decorative, simply for lack of space, and paperwork was piled everywhere: in corners, beneath the window, on the extra chair perched in a corner. Large stacks were also present on her desk, which held everything she considered urgent.

The budget was due at the end of the month, and she had a stack of publishers' catalogs to go through before placing her weekly order. Add to the list finding a speaker for the Friends of the Library luncheon in April and getting everything set for the Historic Homes Tour—of which the library was part, since at one point it was a historic home—and she barely had enough time to breathe. She had two full-time employees, but she'd learned that things worked best if she didn't delegate. The employees were fine for recommending recent titles and helping students find what they were looking for, but the last time she'd let one of them decide what books to order, she'd ended up with six different titles about orchids, since that happened to be the employee's favorite flower. Earlier, after taking a seat in front of her computer, she'd tried to lay out a plan for organizing her schedule, but she hadn't gotten anywhere. No matter how hard she'd tried to squelch it, her mind kept wandering back to Jeremy Marsh. She didn't want to think about him, but Doris had said just enough to pique her curiosity.

He's not what you imagine him to be.

What was that supposed to mean? Last night, when she'd pressed, Doris had clammed up, as if she hadn't said anything in the first place. She didn't mention Lexie's love life again, or Jeremy Marsh, either. Instead, they circled the topic: what happened at work, what was going on with people they knew, how the Historic Homes Tour was shaping up for the weekend. Doris was the chair of the Historical Society, and the tour was one of the big events of the year, not that it took a lot of planning. For the most part, the same dozen homes were chosen every year, in addition to four churches and the library. As her grandmother rambled on, Lexie kept thinking about her pronouncement.

He's not what you imagine him to be.

And what might that be? A big-city type? A ladies' man? Someone in search of a quick fling? Someone who would make fun of the town the moment he left? Someone out for a story and willing to find one any way he could, even if it ended up hurting someone in the process?

And why on earth did she even care? He was here for a few days, and then he'd be gone and everything would return to normal again. Thank goodness.

Oh, she'd already heard the gossip this morning. At the bakery, where she'd stopped in for a muffin, she'd heard a couple of women talking about him. How he was going to make the town famous, how things might get a little better around here business-wise. The moment they saw her, they peppered her with questions about him and offered their own opinions as to whether he'd find the source of the mysterious lights.

Some people here, after all, actually believed they were caused by ghosts. But others clearly didn't. Mayor Gherkin, for instance. No, he had a different angle, one that regarded Jeremy's investigation as a wager of sorts. If Jeremy Marsh couldn't find the cause, it would be good for the town's economy, and that's what the mayor was betting on. After all, Mayor Gherkin knew something that only a few others knew.

People had been studying the mystery for years. Not just the students from Duke. Aside from the local historian—who seemed to have fathomed a plausible explanation, in Lexie's opinion—at least two other outside groups or individuals had investigated the claim in the past without success. Mayor Gherkin had actually invited the students from Duke to pay the cemetery a visit, in the hope that they wouldn't figure it out, either. And sure enough, tourist traffic had been picking up ever since.

She supposed she could have mentioned that to Mr. Marsh yesterday. But since he hadn't asked, she hadn't offered. She was too busy trying to ward off his advances and make it clear she wasn't interested in him. Oh, he'd tried to be charming . . . well, okay, he *was* sort of charming in his own way, but that didn't change the fact that she had no intention of letting her emotions get the better of her. She'd even been sort of relieved when he left last night.

And then Doris made that ridiculous comment, which essentially meant that she thought Lexie *should* get to know him better. But what really burned her was that she knew Doris wouldn't have said anything unless she was certain. For whatever reason, she saw something special in Jeremy.

Sometimes she hated Doris's premonitions.

Of course, she didn't have to listen to Doris. After all, she'd already done the "visiting stranger" thing, and she wasn't about to go down that road again. Despite her resolution, she had to admit that the whole thing left her feeling a little off-balance. As she pondered it, she heard her office door open with a squeak.

"Good morning," Jeremy said, poking his head in. "I thought I saw a light on in here."

Swiveling in her chair, she noticed he'd draped his jacket over his shoulder.

"Hey there." She nodded politely. "I was just trying to get caught up on some work."

He held up his jacket. "Do you have a place I can put this? There's not much room at the desk in the rare-book room."

"Here, I'll take it. The coat hanger's behind the door."

Entering the office, he handed Lexie the jacket. She hung it next to hers on the rack behind the door. Jeremy looked around the office.

"So this is mission control, huh? Where it all happens?"

"This is it," she confirmed. "It's not too roomy, but it's enough to get the job done."

"I like your filing system," he said, gesturing at the piles of paperwork on the desk. "I've got one just like it at home."

A smile escaped her lips as he took a step toward her desk and peeked out the window.

"Nice view, too. Why, you can see all the way to the next house. And the parking lot, too."

"Well, you seem to be in a spunky mood this morning."

"How can I not be? I slept in a freezing room filled with dead animals. Or rather, barely slept at all. I kept hearing all these strange noises coming from the woods."

"I wondered how you'd like Greenleaf. I hear it's rustic."

"The word 'rustic' doesn't quite do the place justice. And then this morning. Half the town was at breakfast."

"I take it you went to Herbs," she remarked.

"I did," he said. "I noticed you weren't there."

"No. It's too busy. I like a little quiet time to start the day."

"You should have warned me."

She smiled. "You should have asked."

He laughed, and Lexie motioned toward the door with her hand.

Walking to the rare-book room with him, she sensed he was in a good mood despite his exhaustion, but it still wasn't enough to make her trust him.

"Would you happen to know a Deputy Hopper?" he asked.

She looked over in surprise. "Rodney?"

"I think that was his name. What's his deal, anyway? He seemed a little perturbed by my presence here in town."

"Oh, he's harmless."

"He didn't seem harmless."

She shrugged. "He probably heard that you'd be spending time at the library. He's kind of protective when it comes to things like that. He's been sweet on me for years."

"Put in a good word for me, will you?"

"I suppose I could do that."

Half expecting another witty comeback, he raised his eyebrow in pleasant surprise.

"Thanks," he said.

"No problem. Just don't do anything to make me take it back."

They continued in silence to the rare-book room. She led the way inside, flicking on the light.

"I've been thinking about your project, and there's something you should probably know."

"What's that?"

She told him about the two previous investigations into the cemetery before adding, "If you give me a few minutes, I can dig them up for you."

"I'd appreciate that," he said. "But why didn't you mention them yesterday?"

She smiled without answering.

"Let me guess," he said. "Because I didn't ask?"

"I'm only a librarian, not a mind reader."

"Like your grandmother? Oh, wait, she's a diviner, right?"

"Actually, she is. And she can tell the sex of babies before they're born, too."

"So I've heard," Jeremy said.

Her eyes flashed. "It's true, Jeremy. Whether or not you want to believe it, she can do those things."

He grinned at her. "Did you just call me Jeremy?"

"Yes. But don't make a big deal out of it. You did ask me to, remember?"

"I remember," he said, *"Lexie."*

"Don't push it," she said, but even as she spoke, Jeremy noticed that she held his gaze just a little longer than usual, and he liked that.

He liked that a lot.

Seven

······❖······

Jeremy spent the rest of the morning hunched over a stack of books and the two articles Lexie had found. The first, written in 1958 by a folklore professor at the University of North Carolina and published in the *Journal of the South*, seemed to have been intended as a response to A. J. Morrison's account of the legend. The article pulled a few quotes from Morrison's work, summarized the legend, and recounted the professor's stay in the cemetery over a one-week period. On four of those evenings, he witnessed the lights. He seemed to have made at least a preliminary attempt to find the cause: he counted the number of homes in the surrounding area (there were eighteen within one mile of the cemetery and, interestingly, none on Riker's Hill), and also noted the number of cars that passed within two minutes of the lights' appearance. In two instances, the span of time was less than a minute. In the other two instances, however, there were no passing cars at all, which seemed to eliminate the possibility that headlights were the source of the "ghosts."

The second article was only a bit more informative. Published in a 1969 issue of *Coastal Carolina*, a small magazine that went belly-up in 1980, the article reported the fact that the cemetery was sinking and the damage that had been caused as a result. The author also mentioned the legend and the proximity of Riker's Hill, and while he hadn't seen the lights (he'd visited during the summer months), he drew heavily on eyewitness accounts before speculating on a number of possibilities, all of which Jeremy was already aware.

The first was rotting vegetation that sometimes bursts into flames, giving off vapors known as swamp gas. In a coastal area like this, Jeremy knew the idea couldn't be completely discounted, though he did think it unlikely, since the lights occurred on cold and foggy nights. They could also be "earthquake lights," which are electrical atmospheric charges generated by the shifting and grinding of rocks deep below the earth's crust. The automobile headlights theory was again advanced, as was the idea of refracted starlight and fox fire, which is a phosphorescent glow emitted by certain fungi on rotting wood. Algae, it was noted, could also glow phosphorescently. The author even mentioned the possibility of the Novaya Zemlya effect, in which light beams are bent by adjacent layers of air at different temperatures, thus seeming to glow. And, in offering a final possibility, the author concluded that it might be St. Elmo's fire, which is created by electrical discharges from sharp-pointed objects that occur during thunderstorms.

In other words, the author had said it could be anything.

However inconclusive, the articles did help Jeremy clarify his own thoughts. In his opinion, the lights had everything to do with geography. The hill behind the cemetery seemed to be the highest point in any direction, and the sinking cemetery made the fog more dense in that particular area. All of which meant refracted or reflected light.

He just had to pinpoint the source, and for that, he needed to find the first time the lights had ever been noted. Not something general, but an actual date, so he could then determine what was happening in the town at that time. If the town was undergoing a dramatic change around then—a new construction project, a new factory, or something along those lines—he just might find the cause. Or if he did see the lights—and he wasn't counting on it—his job would be even simpler. If they occurred at midnight, for instance, and he saw no passing cars, he could then survey the area, noting the location of occupied houses with lamps blazing in the window, the proximity of the highway, or possibly even river traffic. Boats, he suspected, were a possibility, if they were large enough.

Going through the stack of books a second time, he made additional notes regarding the changes in the town over the years, with special emphasis on changes around the turn of the century.

As the hours rolled on, the list grew. In the early twentieth century, there was a mini–housing boom that lasted from 1907 to 1914, during which the north side of the town grew. The small port was widened in 1910, again in 1916, and once more in 1922; combined with the quarries and phosphorous mines, excavation was extensive. The railroad was started in 1898, and spurs continued to be built in various areas of the county until 1912. A trestle over the river was completed in 1904, and from 1908 to 1915 three major factories were constructed: a textile mill, a phosphorous mine, and a paper mill. Of the three, only the paper mill was still in operation—the textile mill had closed four years ago, the mine in 1987—so that seemed to eliminate the other two as possibilities.

He checked his facts again, made sure they were correct, and restacked the books so Lexie could shelve them. He leaned back in his chair, stretched the stiffness from his body, and glanced at the clock. Already, it was coming up on noon. All in all, he thought it was a few hours well spent, and he glanced over his shoulder at the open door behind him.

Lexie hadn't returned to check on him. He sort of liked the fact that he couldn't read her, and for a moment, he wished she lived in the city, or even someplace near the city. It would have been interesting to see the way things might have developed between them. A moment later, she pushed through the door.

"Hey there," Lexie greeted him. "How's it going?"

Jeremy turned. "Good. Thanks."

She slipped into her jacket. "Listen, I was thinking about running out to grab lunch, and I was wondering if you wanted me to bring you something back."

"Are you going to Herbs?" he asked.

"No. If you thought breakfast was busy, you should see the place at lunch. But I'd be happy to pick up a to-go order on my way back."

He hesitated for only an instant.

"Well, would it be all right if I came with you to wherever it is you're going? I should probably stretch my legs. I've been sitting here all morning, and I'd love to see someplace new. Maybe you could even show me around a bit." He paused. "If that's okay, I mean."

She almost said no, but again, she heard Doris's words, and her thoughts became muddled. Should I or shouldn't I? Despite her better judgment—thank you very much for that, Doris—she said, "Sure. But I've only got an hour or so before I have to get back, so I don't know how much help I can be."

He seemed almost as surprised as she did, and he stood, then followed her out the door. "Anything at all is fine," he said. "Helps me fill in the blanks, you know. It's important to know what goes on in a place like this."

"In our little hick town, you mean?"

"I didn't say it was a hick town. Those are your words."

"Yeah. But they're your thoughts, not mine. I love this place."

"I'm sure," he agreed. "Why else would you live here?"

"Because it's not New York City, for one thing."

"You've been there?"

"I used to live in Manhattan. On West Sixty-ninth."

He almost stumbled in midstep. "That's just a few blocks from where I live."

She smiled. "Small world, isn't it?"

Walking quickly, Jeremy struggled to keep up with her as she approached the stairs. "You're kidding, right?"

"Nope," she said. "Lived there with my boyfriend for almost a year. He worked for Morgan Stanley while I interned in the NYU library."

"I can't believe this . . ."

"What? That I lived in New York and left? Or that I lived near you? Or that I lived with my boyfriend?"

"All of it," he said. "Or none of it. I'm not sure." He was trying to fathom the thought of this small-town librarian living in his neighborhood. Noticing his expression, she had to laugh. "You're all alike, you know that?" she said.

"Who?"

"People who live in the city. You live your life thinking that there's no place in the world as special as New York and that no place else has anything to offer."

"You're right," Jeremy admitted. "But that's only because the rest of the world pales in comparison."

Glancing over at him, she made a face that clearly telegraphed, *You didn't just say what I think you said, did you?*

He shrugged, acting innocent. "I mean, come on . . . Greenleaf Cottages can't exactly compare to the Four Seasons or the Plaza, can it? I mean, even you've got to admit that."

She bristled at his smug attitude and began to walk even faster. She decided then and there that Doris didn't know what she was talking about.

Jeremy, however, wouldn't let it go. "Come on . . . admit it. You know I'm right, don't you?"

By that point, they'd reached the front door of the library, and he held it open for her. Behind them, the elderly woman who worked in the lobby was watching them intently. Lexie held her tongue until she was just outside the door, then she turned on him.

"People don't live in hotels," she snapped. "They live in communities. And that's what we have here. A community. Where people know and care about each other. Where kids can play at night and not worry about strangers."

He raised his hands. "Hey," he said, "don't get me wrong. I love communities. I lived in one growing up. I knew every family in my neighborhood by name, because they'd lived there for years. Some of them still do, so believe me, I know exactly how important it is to get to know your neighbors, and how important it is for parents to know what their kids are doing and who they're hanging out with. That's the way it was for me. Even when I was off and about, neighbors would keep tabs on us. My point is that New York City has that, too, depending on where you live. Sure, if you live in my neighborhood, it's filled with a lot of young career people on the move. But visit Park Slope in Brooklyn or Astoria in Queens, and you'll see kids hanging out in the parks, playing basketball and soccer, and pretty much doing the same thing that kids are doing here."

"Like you've ever thought about things like that."

She regretted the sharpness in her tone the moment she lashed out at Jeremy. He, however, seemed unfazed.

"I have," he said. "And believe me, if I had kids, I wouldn't live where I do. I have a ton of nephews and nieces who live in the city, and every one of them lives in a neighborhood with lots of other kids and people watching out for them. In many ways, it's a lot like this place."

She said nothing, wondering if he was telling the truth.

"Look," he offered, "I'm not trying to pick a fight here. My point is simply that kids turn out okay as long as the parents are involved, no matter where they live. It's not like small towns have a monopoly on values. I mean, I'm sure if I did some digging, I'd find lots of kids that were in trouble here, too. Kids are kids, no matter where they live." He smiled, trying to signal that he didn't take what she'd said personally. "And besides, I'm not exactly sure how we got on the subject of kids, anyway. From this point on, I promise not to mention it again. All I was trying to say was that I was surprised that you lived in New York and only a couple of blocks from me." He paused. "Truce?"

She stared at him before finally releasing her breath. Maybe he was right. No, she knew he was right. And, she admitted, she'd been the one who escalated the whole thing. Muddled thoughts can do that to a person. What on earth was she getting herself into here?

"Truce," she finally agreed. "On one condition."

"What's that?"

"You have to do the driving. I didn't bring a car."

He looked relieved. "Let me find my keys."

Neither was particularly hungry, so Lexie directed Jeremy to a small grocery store, and they emerged a few minutes later with a box of crackers, some fresh fruit, various kinds of cheese, and two bottles of Snapple.

In the car, Lexie set the food at her feet. "Is there anything in particular you'd like to see?" Lexie asked.

"Riker's Hill. Is there a road that leads to the top?"

She nodded. "It's not much of a road. It was originally used for logging, but now it's mainly deer hunters. It's rough, though—I don't know if you want to bring your car up there."

"No big deal. It's a rental. And besides, I'm getting used to bad roads around here."

"Okay," she said, "but don't say I didn't warn you."

Neither said much as they headed out of town, past Cedar Creek Cemetery and over a small bridge. The road was soon lined with ever-thickening groves of trees on both sides. The blue sky had given way to an expanse of gray, reminding Jeremy of winter afternoons much farther north. Occasionally, flocks of starlings broke into flight as the car passed, moving in unison as if tethered together by string.

Lexie was uneasy in the silence, and so she began describing the area: real estate projects that had never come to fruition, the names of trees, Cedar Creek when it could be seen through the thicket. Riker's Hill loomed off to the left, looking gloomy and forbidding in the muted light.

Jeremy had driven this way after leaving the cemetery the first time and had turned around about here. It had been just a minute or so too soon, he learned, because she told him to turn at the next intersection, which seemed to loop around toward the rear of Riker's Hill. Leaning forward in her seat, she peered out the windshield.

"The turn is just up ahead," she said. "You might want to slow down."

Jeremy did, and as she continued to stare, he glanced over at her, noting the slight indentation of a frown line between her eyebrows.

"Okay . . . there," she said, pointing.

She was right: it wasn't much of a road. Gravel and rutted, kind of like the entrance to Greenleaf, but worse. Exiting the main road, the car began to lurch and bounce. Jeremy slowed even more.

"Is Riker's Hill state property?"

She nodded. "The state bought it from one of the big timber companies—Weyerhaeuser or Georgia-Pacific or something like that—when I was a little girl. Part of our local history, you know. But it's not a park or anything. I think there were plans to make it into a campground at one time or another, but the state's never gotten around to it."

Loblolly pines closed in as the road narrowed, but the road itself seemed to improve as they moved higher, following an almost zigzag pattern to the top. Every now and then, a trail could be spotted, which he assumed was used by hunters.

In time, the trees began to thin and the sky became more

noticeable; as they neared the crest, the vegetation looked more weathered, then almost devastated. Dozens of trees had snapped in half; less than a third still seemed to be standing upright. The incline grew less steep, then flattened out as they neared the top. Jeremy pulled over to the side. Lexie motioned for him to turn off the engine, and they stepped out of the car.

Lexie crossed her arms as they walked. The air seemed colder up here, the breeze wintry and stinging. The sky seemed closer as well; clouds were no longer featureless, but twisting and curling into distinctive shapes. Down below, they could see the town, rooftops clustered together and perched along straight roads, one of which led to Cedar Creek Cemetery. Just beyond the town, the ancient, brackish river looked like flowing iron. He spotted both the highway bridge and a picturesque railroad trestle that rose high behind it as a red-tailed hawk circled overhead. Looking closely, Jeremy could just make out the tiny shape of the library and could even spot where Greenleaf was, though the cottages were lost in their surroundings.

"The view is amazing," he finally said.

Lexie pointed toward the edge of town and helped him zero in on where to look. "See that little house over there? Kind of off to the side, near the pond? That's where I live now. And over there? That's Doris's place. It's where I grew up. Sometimes when I was little, I'd stare toward the hill imagining that I could see myself staring down from up here."

He smiled. The breeze tossed her hair as she went on.

"As teenagers, my friends and I would sometimes come up here, and we'd stay for hours. During the summer, the heat makes the house lights twinkle, almost like stars. And the lightning bugs—well, there are so many in June that it almost looks like there's another town in the sky. Even though everyone knew about this place, it wasn't ever too crowded up here. It was always like a secret place that my friends and I could share."

She paused, realizing that she felt strangely nervous. Though why she should be nervous was beyond her.

"I remember this one time when a big thunderstorm was expected. My friends and I got one of the boys to drive us up here in his truck. You know, one of those big-tired things that could make it down the Grand Canyon, if need be. So we all came up here to watch the lightning, expecting to see it flickering in the sky. We didn't stop to consider that we'd put ourselves at the highest spot in any direction. When the lightning started, it was beautiful at first. It would light up the sky, sometimes with a jagged flash, other times almost like a strobe light, and we'd count out loud until the thunder boomed. You know, to see how far away the lightning was. But the next thing we knew, the storm was on us. I mean, the wind was blowing so hard that the truck was actually rocking, and the rain made it impossible to see anything. Then the lightning started striking the trees around us. Gigantic bolts came down from the sky so close that the ground would tremble, and then the tops of pines would just explode into sparks."

As she spoke, Jeremy studied her. It was the most she'd said about herself since they'd met, and he tried to imagine what her life was like back then. Who was she in high school? One of the popular cheerleaders? Or one of the bookish girls, who spent her lunches in the library? Granted, it was ancient history—I mean, who cared about high school?—but even now, when she was lost in the memories, he wasn't quite able to put his finger on who she'd been.

"I'll bet you were terrified," he said. "Lightning bolts can reach fifty thousand degrees, you know." He glanced at her. "That's ten times hotter than the surface of the sun."

She smiled, amused. "I didn't know that. But you're right—I don't think I've ever been so terrified in my entire life."

"So what happened?"

"The storm passed as they always do. And once we collected

ourselves, we drove back home. But I remember Rachel was holding my hand so hard that she left fingernail marks in my skin."

"Rachel? That wouldn't happen to be the waitress at Herbs,
would it?"

"Yeah, that's the one." Crossing her arms, she looked over
at him. "Why? Did she put the move on you at breakfast this
morning?"

He shifted from one foot to the other. "Well, I wouldn't call it
that. She just seemed a little . . . forward is all."

Lexie laughed. "It doesn't surprise me. She's . . . well, she's
Rachel. She and I were best friends growing up, and I still think of
her as a sister of sorts. I suppose I always will. But after I went off to
college and New York . . . well, it wasn't the same after I got back.
It just changed, for lack of a better word. Don't get me wrong—
she's a sweet girl and she's a lot of fun to spend time with and she
hasn't got a mean bone in her body, but . . ."

She trailed off. Jeremy looked at her closely.

"You see the world differently these days?" he suggested.

She sighed. "Yeah, I suppose that's it."

"I think it happens to everyone as they grow up," Jeremy responded. "You find out who you are and what you want, and then
you realize that people you've known forever don't see things the
way you do. And so you keep the wonderful memories, but find
yourself moving on. It's perfectly normal."

"I know. But in a town this size, it's a little harder to do. There
are only so many people in their thirties here, and even fewer
who are still single. It's kind of a small world down here."

He nodded before breaking into a smile. "Thirties?"

She suddenly remembered that he'd been trying to guess her
age yesterday.

"Yep," she said with a shrug. "Getting old, I guess."

"Or staying young," he countered. "That's how I think of myself, by the way. Whenever I get worried about aging, I just start

wearing my pants lower, flash the waistband of my boxers, wear my ball cap backward, and walk around the mall listening to rap."

She gave an involuntary giggle at the image. Despite the chill in the air, she felt warm with the recognition, unexpected and yet strangely inevitable, that she was enjoying his company. She wasn't sure she liked him yet—in fact, she was pretty sure she didn't—and for a moment, she struggled to reconcile the two feelings. Which meant, of course, that the whole subject should best be avoided. She brought a finger to her chin. "Yes, I can see that. You do seem to regard personal style as important."

"Without a doubt. Why, just yesterday, in fact, people were particularly impressed with my wardrobe, including you."

She laughed, and in the ensuing silence, she glanced at him. "I'll bet you travel a lot for your job, don't you?" she asked.

"Maybe four or five trips a year, each lasting a couple of weeks."

"Have you ever been in a town like this?"

"No," he said, "not really. Every place I go has its own charms, but I can say with all honesty that I've never been to a place like this. How about you? Other than New York, I mean."

"I've been to UNC, in Chapel Hill, and spent a lot of time in Raleigh. And I've been to Charlotte, too, when I was in high school. Our football team made the state championship my senior year, so pretty much everyone in town made the road trip. Our convoy stretched four miles down the highway. And Washington, D.C., on a field trip when I was little. But I've never been overseas or anything like that."

Even as she spoke, she knew how small her life would seem to him. Jeremy, as if reading her mind, flashed a hint of a smile.

"You'd like Europe. The cathedrals, the gorgeous countryside, the bistros and city squares. The relaxed lifestyle . . . you'd fit right in."

Lexie dipped her eyes. It was a nice thought, but . . .

And that was the thing. The *but*. There was always a *but*. Life had a nasty tendency to make exotic opportunities few and far between. It simply wasn't a reality for most folks. Like her. It wasn't as if she could take Doris or take off much time from the library. And why on earth was he telling her all this, anyway? To show her that he was more cosmopolitan than she was? Well, I hate to break it to you, she thought, but I already know that.

And yet, even as she digested those thoughts, another voice piped in, telling her that he was trying to flatter her. He seemed to be saying that he knew she was different, more worldly, than he'd expected her to be. That she could fit in anywhere.

"I've always wanted to travel," she admitted, sort of hedging the conflicting voices in her head. "It must be nice, having that chance."

"It is, at times. But believe it or not, what I most enjoy is meeting new people. And when I look back on the places I've gone, more often than not I see faces, not things."

"Now you're sounding like a romantic," she said. Oh, he was difficult to resist, this Mr. Jeremy Marsh. First the ladies' man and now the great altruist; well traveled but still grounded; worldly but still cognizant of the things that really mattered. No matter whom he met or where he was, she had no doubt that he had an innate ability to make others—especially women—feel as if he was in kinship with them. Which, of course, led directly back to her first impression of him.

"Maybe I am a romantic," he said, glancing over at her.

"You know what I liked about New York?" she asked, changing the subject.

He watched her expectantly.

"I liked the fact that there was always something happening. There were always people hurrying down the sidewalks and cabs buzzing by, no matter what time it was. There was always someplace to go, something to see, a new restaurant to try. It was exciting, especially to someone who'd grown up here. Like going to Mars, almost."

"Why didn't you stay?"

"I suppose I could have. But it wasn't the place for me. I guess you might say that my reason for going there at all kind of changed. I went to be with someone."

"Ah," Jeremy said. "So you'd followed him up there?"

She nodded. "We met in college. He seemed so . . . I don't know . . . perfect, I guess. He'd grown up in Greensboro, came from a good family, was intelligent. And really handsome, too. Handsome enough to make any woman ignore her best instincts. He looked my way, and the next thing I knew I was following him up to the city. Couldn't help myself."

Jeremy squirmed. "Is that right?"

She smiled inwardly. Men never wanted to hear how handsome other men were, especially if the relationship had been serious.

"Everything was great for a year or so. We were even engaged." She seemed lost in thought before she let out a deep breath. "I took an internship at the NYU library, Avery went to work on Wall Street, and then one day I found him in bed with one of his co-workers. It kind of made me realize that he wasn't the right guy, so I packed up that night and came back here. After that, I never saw him again."

The breeze picked up, sounding almost like a whistle as it rushed up the slopes, and smelling faintly of the earth.

"Are you hungry?" she asked, wanting to change the subject again. "I mean, it's nice visiting with you out here, but if I don't get some nourishment, I tend to get grumpy."

"I'm starved," he said.

They made their way back to the car and divided up the lunch. Jeremy opened the box of crackers on the front seat. Noticing that the view wasn't much, he started the car, maneuvered around the crest, then—angling the car just right—reparked with a view of the town again.

"So you came back here and began working at the library, and . . ."

"That's it," she said. "That's what I've been doing for the last seven years."

He did the math, figuring she was about thirty-one.

"Any other boyfriends since then?" he asked.

With her fruit cup wedged between her legs, she broke off a piece of cheese and put it on a cracker. She wondered if she should answer, then decided, What the hell, he's leaving, anyway.

"Oh, sure. There were a few here and there." She told him about the lawyer, the doctor, and—lately—Rodney Hopper. She didn't mention Mr. Renaissance.

"Well . . . good. You sound like you're happy," he said.

"I am," she was quick to agree. "Aren't you?"

"Most of the time. Every now and then, I go nuts, but I think that's normal."

"And that's when you start wearing your pants low?"

"Exactly," he said with a smile. He grabbed a handful of crackers, balanced a couple on his leg, and began stacking some cheese. He glanced up, looking serious. "Would you mind if I asked a personal question? You don't have to answer, of course. I won't take it the wrong way, believe me. I'm just curious."

"You mean, more personal than telling you about my previous boyfriends?"

He gave a sheepish shrug, and she had a sudden vision of what he must have looked like as a small boy: a narrow, unlined face, bangs cut straight, shirt and jeans dirty from playing outside.

"Go ahead," she said. "Ask away."

He focused on the lid of his fruit cup as he spoke, suddenly reluctant to meet her gaze. "When we first got here, you pointed out your grandmother's house. And you said you'd grown up there."

She nodded. She'd wondered when he would ask about that.

"I did," she said.

"Why?"

She looked out the window; habit made her search out the highway that led out of town. When she spotted it, she spoke slowly.

"My parents were coming back from Buxton, out on the Outer Banks. That was where they got married, and they owned a small beach cottage there. It's kind of hard to get to from here, but my mom swore that it was the most beautiful place in the world, so my dad bought a small boat so they wouldn't have to use the ferry to get there. It was their little escape, the two of them sneaking away, you know. There's a beautiful lighthouse that you can see from the porch, and every now and then, I head out there, too, just like they used to, just to get away from it all."

Her lips formed the tiniest of half-smiles before she went on. "But anyway, on their way back that night, my parents were tired. It still takes a couple of hours to get there even without the ferry, and the best guess is that on the way home, my dad fell asleep at the wheel and the car went off the bridge. By the time the police found the car and dredged it out the following morning, they were both dead."

Jeremy was quiet for a long moment. "That's terrible," he finally said. "How old were you?"

"Three. I was staying with Doris that night, and the next day, she headed off to the hospital with my granddad. When they got back, they told me that I'd be living with them from now on. And so I did. But it's strange; I mean, I know what happened, but it's never seemed particularly real. I didn't feel like I was missing anything when I was growing up. To me, my grandparents seemed like everyone else's parents, except that I called them by their first names." She smiled. "That was their idea, by the way. I guess they didn't want me to think of them as grandparents anymore since they were raising me, but they weren't my parents, either."

When she finished, she looked over at him, noticing the way his shoulders seemed to fill out his sweater, and eyeing that dimple again.

"Now it's my turn to ask questions," she said. "I've talked too much, and I know that my life must be boring compared to yours. Not so much about my parents, of course, but living here, I mean."

"No, it's not boring at all. It's interesting. Kind of like . . . reading a new book when you turn the pages and experience something unexpected."

"Nice metaphor."

"I thought you might appreciate that."

"So what about you? What made you want to become a journalist?"

For the next few minutes, he told her about his college years, his plans to become a professor, and the turn of events that had brought him to this point.

"And you said that you have five brothers?"

He nodded. "Five older brothers. I'm the baby of the family."

"For some reason, I just can't see you with brothers."

"Why?"

"You strike me as more the only-child type."

He shook his head. "It's a shame you didn't inherit the psychic abilities of the rest of your family."

She smiled before glancing away. In the distance, red-tailed hawks circled above the town. She put her hand to the window, feeling the cold press of glass against her skin. "Two hundred forty-seven," she said.

He looked over at her. "Excuse me?"

"That's how many women visited Doris to find out the sex of their babies. Growing up, I'd see them sitting in the kitchen visiting with my grandmother. And it's funny, even now I can remember thinking that they all had this look about them: the sparkle in their eyes, the fresh glow to their skin, and their genuine excitement. There is truth to the old wives' tale that women who are pregnant glow, and I remember thinking that I wanted to look just like them when I grew up. Doris would talk to them for a while to make sure they were sure they wanted to know, and then she'd take their hand and get really quiet all of a sudden.

Hardly any of them were even showing, and a few seconds after that, she'd make her pronouncement." Lexie let out a soft breath. "She was right every time. Two hundred forty-seven women came by, and she was right two hundred and forty-seven times. Doris kept their names in a book and wrote everything down, including the dates of the visits. You can check it out if you'd like. She still has the book in her kitchen."

Jeremy simply stared at her. Impossible, he thought, a statistical fluke. One that pressed the limits of believability, but a fluke nonetheless. And her notebook, no doubt, would only show the guesses that had been right.

"I know what you're thinking," she said, "but you can check it out with the hospital, too. Or the women. And you can ask anyone you want, to see if she was ever mistaken. But she wasn't. Even the doctors around town will tell you straight up that she had a gift."

"Did you ever think that maybe she knew someone who did the ultrasounds?"

"That wasn't it," she insisted.

"How can you know for sure?"

"Because that's when she stopped. When the technology finally arrived in town. There was no reason for people to come to her anymore, once they could see the picture of the baby themselves. The women visitors began slowing after that, then turned into a trickle. Now it's maybe one or two people a year, usually folks from out in the country who don't have medical insurance. I guess you could say her abilities aren't in too much demand these days."

"And the divining?"

"Same thing," she said. "There isn't much demand around here for someone with her skills. The entire eastern section of the state sits over a vast reservoir. You can sink a well anywhere and find water around here. But when she was growing up in Cobb County, Georgia, farmers would come to the house begging for her help, especially during the droughts. And even though she wasn't more than eight or nine, she'd find the water every time."

"Interesting," Jeremy said.

"I take it you still don't believe it."

He shifted in his seat. "There's an explanation somewhere. There always is."

"You don't believe in magic of any kind?"

"No," he said.

"That's sad," she said. "Because sometimes it's real."

He smiled. "Well, maybe I'll find something that changes my mind while I'm down here."

She smiled, too. "You already have. You're just too stubborn to believe it."

After finishing their makeshift lunch, Jeremy slid the car into gear, and they bounced back down Riker's Hill, the front wheels seemingly drawn to every deep rut. The shocks squeaked and groaned, and by the time they reached the bottom, Jeremy's knuckles were white on the wheel.

They followed the same roads back. Passing Cedar Creek Cemetery, Jeremy found his eyes drawn to the top of Riker's Hill; despite the distance, he could pick out the spot where they'd parked.

"Do we have time to see a couple of other places? I'd love to swing by the marina, the paper mill, and maybe the railroad trestle."

"We have time," she said. "As long as we don't stay too long. They're pretty much all in the same area."

Ten minutes later, following her directions, he parked again. They were at the far edge of downtown, a few blocks from Herbs, near the boardwalk that stretched along the riverfront. The Pamlico River was nearly a mile wide and flowed angrily, the currents rippling to form tiny whitecaps as they rushed downstream. On the far side of the river, near the railroad trestle, the paper mill— a huge structure—spewed clouds from the dueling smokestacks.

Jeremy stretched as he stepped out of the car, and Lexie crossed her arms. Her cheeks began to redden in the chill.

"Is it getting colder, or is it just my imagination?" she asked.

"It's pretty cold," he agreed. "Seems colder than it was up top, but maybe we just got used to the heater in the car."

Jeremy struggled to catch up to her as she set off for the board-walk. Lexie finally slowed and then stopped to lean against the railing as Jeremy gazed up at the railroad trestle. Perched high above the river to let large boats pass, it was crisscrossed with beams, resembling a suspension bridge.

"I didn't know how close you wanted to get," she said. "If we had more time, I would have taken you across the river to the mill, but you probably get a better view from here." She motioned toward the other end of town. "The marina is over there, near the highway. Can you see where all those sailboats are docked?"

Jeremy nodded. For some reason, he'd expected something grander.

"Can big boats dock there?"

"I think so. Some big yachts from New Bern sometimes stop over for a couple of days."

"How about barges?"

"I suppose they could. The river is dredged to allow for some of the logging barges, but they usually stop on the far side. Over there"—she pointed to what seemed to be a small cove—"you can see a couple there now, all loaded up."

He followed her gaze, then turned around, coordinating locations. With Riker's Hill in the distance, the trestle and the factory seemed perfectly aligned. Coincidence? Or completely unimportant? He stared in the direction of the paper mill, trying to figure out whether the tops of the smokestacks were lit at night. He'd have to check on that.

"Do they ship all the logs by barge, or do you know if they use the railroad, too?"

"I've never noticed, to tell you the truth. I'm sure it would be easy to find out, though."

"Do you know how many trains use the trestle?"

"Again, I'm not sure. Sometimes I hear the whistle at night, and I've had to stop more than once in town at the crossing to let the train pass, but it's not as if I could tell you for certain. I do know they make a lot of shipments from the mill, though. That's where the train actually stops."

Jeremy nodded as he stared at the trestle.

Lexie smiled and went on. "I know what you're thinking. You're thinking that maybe the light from the train shines as it goes over the trestle and that's what's causing the lights, right?"

"It did cross my mind."

"That's not it," she said, shaking her head.

"You're sure?"

"At night, the trains pull into the yard at the paper mill so they can be loaded the following day. So the light on the locomotive is shining in the opposite direction, *away* from Riker's Hill."

He considered that as he joined her at the railing. The wind whipped her hair, making it look wild. She tucked her hands into her jacket pockets.

"I can see why you liked growing up here," he commented.

She turned so that she could lean back against the railing, and stared toward the downtown area—the neat little shops festooned with American flags, a barbershop pole, a small park nestled at the edge of the boardwalk. On the sidewalk, passersby moved in and out of the establishments, carrying bags. Despite the chill, no one seemed to be rushing at all.

"Well, it is a lot like New York, I have to admit."

He laughed. "That's not what I meant. I meant that my parents probably would have loved to raise their kids in a place like this. With big green lawns and forests to play in. Even a river where you could go swimming when it gets hot. It must have been . . . idyllic."

"It still is. And that's what people say about living here."

"You seem to have thrived here."

For an instant, she seemed almost sad. "Yeah, but I went off to college. A lot of people around here never do. It's a poor county, and the town has been struggling ever since the textile mill and phosphorous mine closed, and a lot of parents don't put much stock into getting a good education. That's what's hard some-times—trying to convince some kids that there's more to life than working in the paper mill across the river. I live here because I want to live here. I made the choice. But for a lot of these peo-ple, they simply stay because it's impossible for them to leave."

"That happens everywhere. None of my brothers went to col-lege, either, so I was sort of the oddball, in that learning came easy for me. My parents are working-class folks and lived in Queens their whole life. My dad was a bus driver for the city. Spent forty years of his life sitting behind the wheel until he finally retired."

She seemed amused. "That's funny. Yesterday I had you pegged as an Upper East Sider. You know, doorman greeting you by name, prep schools, five-course meals for dinner, a butler who an-nounces guests."

He recoiled in mock horror. "First an only child and now this? I'm beginning to think that you perceive me as spoiled."

"No, not spoiled . . . just . . ."

"Don't say it," he said, raising his hand. "I'd rather not know. Especially since it isn't true."

"How do you know what I was going to say?"

"Because you're currently oh for two, and neither was particu-larly flattering."

The corners of her mouth turned up slightly. "I'm sorry. I didn't mean it."

"Yes, you did," he said with a grin. He turned around and leaned his back against the rail as well. The breeze stung his face. "But don't worry, I won't take it personally. Since I'm not some spoiled rich kid, I mean."

"No. You're an objective journalist."

"Exactly."

"Even though you refuse to have an open mind about anything mysterious."

"Exactly."

She laughed. "What about the supposed mysteriousness of women? Don't you believe in that?"

"Oh, I know that's true," he said, thinking of her in particular. "But it's different than believing the possibility of cold fusion."

"Why?"

"Because women are a subjective mystery, not an objective one. You can't measure anything about them scientifically, although, of course, there are genetic differences between the genders. Women only strike men as being mysterious because they don't realize that men and women see the world differently."

"They do, huh?"

"Sure. It goes back to evolution and the best ways to preserve the species."

"And you're an expert on that?"

"I have a bit of knowledge in that area, yes."

"And so you consider yourself an expert on women, too?"

"No, not really. I'm shy, remember?"

"Uh-huh, I remember. I just don't believe it."

He crossed his arms. "Let me guess . . . you think I have a problem with commitment?"

She looked him over. "I think that about sums it up."

He laughed. "What can I say? Investigative journalism is a glamorous world, and there are legions of women who yearn to be part of it."

She rolled her eyes. "Puh-lease," she said. "It's not like you're a movie star or sing in a rock band. You write for *Scientific American*."

"And?"

"Well, I may be from the South, but even so, I can't imagine your magazine is deluged with groupies."

He gazed at her triumphantly. "I think you just contradicted yourself."

She raised an eyebrow. "You think you're very clever, Mr. Marsh, don't you?"

"Oh, so we're back to 'Mr. Marsh' now?"

"Maybe. I haven't decided yet." She tucked a blowing strand of hair behind her ear. "But you missed the fact that you don't have to have groupies to . . . get around. All you need is to hang out in the right kind of places and pour on the charm."

"And you think I'm charming?"

"I would say some women would find you charming."

"But not you."

"We're not talking about me. We're talking about you, and right now you're doing your best to change the subject. Which probably means that I'm right but that you don't want to admit it."

He stared at her admiringly. "You're very clever, Ms. Darnell." She nodded. "I've heard that."

"And charming," he added for good measure.

She smiled at him, then glanced away. She looked down the boardwalk, then across the street toward the town, then up at the sky before she sighed. She wasn't going to respond to his flattery, she decided. Nonetheless, she felt herself blushing.

As if reading her mind, Jeremy changed the subject. "So this weekend," he started. "What's it like?"

"Won't you be here?" she asked.

"Probably. For part of it, anyway. But I was just curious how you felt about it."

"Aside from making a lot of people's lives crazy for a few days?" she asked. "It's . . . needed at this time of year. You go through

Thanksgiving and Christmas in a rush, and then nothing is on the schedule until spring. And meanwhile, it's cold and gray and rainy . . . so years ago, the town council decided to do the Historic Homes Tour. And ever since then, they've just added more festivities to it in the hope of making for a special weekend. This year it's the cemetery, last year the parade, the year before that, they added a Friday night barn dance. Now it's becoming part of the tradition of the town, so most of the folks who live here look forward to it." She glanced at him. "As small-town forgettable as it sounds, it's actually sort of fun."

Watching her, Jeremy raised his eyebrows, remembering the barn dance from the brochure. "They have a dance?" he asked, feigning ignorance.

She nodded. "On Friday night. In Meyer's tobacco barn downtown. It's quite the shindig, with a live band and everything. It's the only night of the year that the Lookilu Tavern is pretty much empty."

"Well, if I happen to go, maybe you'll dance with me."

She smiled before finally eyeing him with an almost seductive look. "I'll tell you what. If you solve the mystery by then, I'll dance with you."

"You promise?"

"I promise," she said. "But our deal is that you have to solve the mystery first."

"Fair enough," he said. "I can't wait. And when it comes to the Lindy or the fox-trot . . ." He shook his head, drawing a long breath. "Well, all I can say is that I hope you can keep up."

She laughed. "I'll do my best."

Crossing her arms, Lexie watched the sun trying and failing to break through the gloom. "Tonight," she said.

He frowned. "Tonight?"

"You'll see the lights tonight. If you go to the cemetery."

"How do you know?"

"The fog is coming in."

He followed her gaze. "How can you tell? It doesn't seem any different to me."

"Look across the river behind me," she said. "The tops of the smokestacks on the paper mill are already hidden by clouds."

"Yeah, sure . . . ," he said, trailing off.

"Turn around and look. You'll see."

He looked over his shoulder and back, then looked once more, studying the outlines of the paper mill. "You're right," he said.

"Of course, I am."

"I guess you peeked when I wasn't looking, huh?"

"No," she said. "I just knew."

"Ah," he said. "One of those pesky mysteries again?"

She pushed herself from the railing. "If that's what you want to call it," she said. "But c'mon. It's getting a little late, and I have to get back to the library. I have to read to the children in fifteen minutes."

As they made their way back to the car, Jeremy noticed that the top of Riker's Hill had become hidden as well. He smiled, thinking, So that's how she did it. See it over there, figure it must be happening across the river, too. Tricky.

"Well, tell me," he said, doing his best to hide his smirk, "since you seem to have hidden talents, how can you be so sure the lights will be out tonight?"

It took a moment for her to answer.

"I just am," she said.

"Well, I guess it's settled, then. I should probably head out there, shouldn't I?" As soon as he spoke the words, he remembered the dinner he was supposed to attend and he suddenly winced.

"What?" she asked, puzzled.

"Oh, the mayor is setting up a dinner with a few people he thought I should meet," he said. "A little get-together or something."

"For you?"

He smiled. "What? You're impressed by that?"

"No, just surprised."

"Why?"

"Because I hadn't heard about it."

"I only found out this morning."

"Still, it's surprising. But I wouldn't worry about not seeing the lights, even if you do go to dinner with the mayor. The lights don't usually come out until late, anyway. You'll have plenty of time."

"Are you sure?"

"That's when *I* saw them. It was a little before midnight."

He stopped in his tracks. "Wait—you've seen them? You didn't mention that."

She smiled. "You didn't ask."

"You keep saying that."

"Well, Mr. Journalist, that's only because you keep forgetting to ask."

Eight

· · · · · ❖ · · · ·

Across town at Herbs, Deputy Rodney Hopper was stewing over his cup of coffee, wondering where on earth Lexie and that . . . city boy had gone off to.

He'd wanted to surprise Lexie at the library and take her out to lunch so City Boy would know exactly where things stood. Maybe she would have even let him escort her to the car while City Boy watched with envy.

Oh, he knew exactly what City Boy saw in Lexie. And he had to be seeing it. Hell, it was impossible not to notice, Rodney thought. She was the prettiest woman in the county, probably the state. Maybe even the whole wide world, for that matter.

Usually, he wouldn't have worried about any guy doing research at the library, and he wasn't worried when he first heard about it. But then he started hearing all those folks whispering about the new stranger in town, so he'd wanted to check it out. And they were right: all it took was one look at City Boy to figure out that he had that *city* look about him. People who researched at the library were supposed to be older and look like absentminded professors, complete with reading glasses, poor posture, and coffee breath. But not this guy; no, this guy looked like he'd just strolled out of Della's Beauty Parlor. But even that wouldn't have bothered him so much except for the fact that right now they were off gallivanting around town, just the two of them.

Rodney scowled. Just where were they, anyway?

Not at Herbs. And not at Pike's Diner, either. No, he'd scanned their parking lots and come up empty. He supposed he could have gone in and asked around, but word would probably have spread, and he wasn't sure that would have been such a good idea. All his buddies teased him about Lexie as it was, especially whenever he mentioned that they were going out on a date again. They'd tell him to get over her, that she was just spending time with him to be nice, but he knew better. She always said yes when he asked, didn't she? He thought about it. Well, most of the time, anyway. She never kissed him afterward, but that was beside the point. He was patient and the time was coming. Every time they went out, they edged a little closer to something more serious. He knew it. He could *feel* it. His buddies, he knew, were just jealous.

He'd hoped that Doris would have some insight, but it just so happened that she wasn't around, either. Off at the accountant's, they said, but she'd be back in a little while. Which, of course, didn't help him at all, since his lunch break was almost over, and he couldn't exactly wait around for her. And besides, she'd probably deny knowing anything about it. He'd heard she actually liked City Boy, and well . . . wasn't that special?

"Scuse me, darlin'?" Rachel said. "You okay?"

Rodney looked up and saw her standing at the table with the coffeepot.

"Nothing, Rachel," he said. "Just one of those days."

"Bad guys getting you down again?"

Rodney nodded. "You could say that."

She smiled, looking pretty, though Rodney didn't seem to notice. He'd long since come to view her as something of a sister.

"Well, it'll get better," she reassured him.

He nodded. "You're probably right."

Her lips went together. Sometimes she worried about Rodney.

"Are you sure you can't squeeze in a quick bite to eat? I know you're in a hurry and I can tell 'em to make it quick."

"No. I'm not all that hungry. And I've got some protein powder in the car for later. I'll be fine." He extended his cup. "A refill might be nice, though."

"You got it," she said, pouring.

"Hey, would you happen to have noticed whether Lexie came through here? Maybe for a to-go order?"

She shook her head. "I haven't seen her all day. Have you checked at the library? I can call over there if it's important."

"No, it's not that important."

She hovered over the table, as if debating what to say next. "I saw you sitting with Jeremy Marsh this morning."

"Who?" Rodney asked, trying to appear innocent.

"The journalist from New York. Don't you remember?"

"Oh, yeah. I just thought I should introduce myself."

"He's a handsome fella, isn't he?"

"I don't notice whether other men are handsome," he growled.

"Well, he is. I could look at him all day. I mean, that hair. Just makes me want to run my fingers through it. Everyone's talking about him."

"Great," Rodney mumbled, feeling worse.

"He invited me to New York," she boasted.

At this, Rodney perked up, wondering if he'd heard her right. "He did?"

"Well, sort of, anyway. He said I should visit, and even though he didn't put it in so many words, I think he kind of wanted me to visit *him*."

"Really?" he asked. "That's great, Rachel."

"What did you think of him?"

Rodney shifted in his seat. "We didn't really talk that much."

"Oh, you should. He's really interesting and very smart. And that hair. Did I mention his hair?"

"Yes," Rodney said. He took another gulp of his coffee, trying to stall until he figured things out. Did he really invite Rachel to New York? Or did Rachel invite herself? He wasn't quite sure. He could see how City Boy might find her attractive, and he was definitely the type who'd make his move on a woman, but . . . but . . . Rachel tended to exaggerate and Lexie and City Boy were out and about and nowhere to be found. Something here didn't quite add up, did it?

He began sliding from the booth. "Well, listen, if you see Lexie, tell her I stopped by, okay?"

"Sure thing. You want me to put your coffee in a Styrofoam cup to go?"

"No, thanks. My stomach's feeling a little green already."

"Oh, you poor thing. I think we have some Pepto-Bismol in the back. Do you want me to get some for you?"

"To be honest, Rach," he said, puffing his chest out and trying to look official again, "I don't think it's going to help."

Across town, just outside the accountant's office, Mayor Gherkin hustled to catch up to Doris.

"Just the woman I wanted to see," he called out.

Doris turned to watch the mayor approach; in his red jacket and checkered pants, she couldn't help but wonder whether the man was color-blind. More often than not, he looked ridiculous.

"What can I do for you, Tom?"

"Well, as you may or may not have heard, we're arranging a special evening for our guest, Jeremy Marsh," he said. "He's writing a big story, you know, and . . ."

Doris mentally finished the story, mouthing the words along with him.

". . . you know how important this could be for the town."

"I've heard," she said. "And it's especially good for your businesses."

"I'm thinking of the whole community here," he said, ignoring her comment. "I've spent all morning trying to set things up so it'll be just right. But I was hoping you'd be willing to help us out with something to eat."

"You want me to be the caterer?"

"Not for charity, mind you. The town would be happy to reimburse you for expenses. We're planning to hold it at the old Lawson Plantation just outside town. I've already talked to the folks there, and they said that they'd be happy to let us use the premises. I figure we'd have a little get-together, and we could sort of use it as a kickoff to the Historic Homes Tour. I've already talked to the newspaper, and a reporter plans to swing by—"

"When are you planning to have this little get-together?" she asked, cutting him off.

He looked momentarily baffled by the interruption. "Well, tonight, of course . . . but like I was saying—"

"Tonight?" she interrupted again. "You want me to prepare for one of your little get-togethers *tonight?*"

"It's for a good cause, Doris. I know it's inconsiderate of me to drop this on you like this, but big things might be happening, and we have to move fast to take advantage of it. You and I both know you're the only one who could handle something like this. Nothing fancy, of course. I was thinking that maybe you could do your special chicken pesto but without the sandwiches . . ."

"Does Jeremy Marsh even know about this?"

"Of course, he does. Why, I spoke to him about it this morning, and he seemed genuinely excited by the possibility."

"Really?" she asked, leaning back, doubting it.

"And I was hoping that Lexie might come as well. You know how important she is to folks in this town."

"I doubt if she would. She hates doing these types of things any more than absolutely necessary. And this doesn't strike me as absolutely necessary."

"You might be right. But anyway, like I was saying, I'd like to use this evening to help us kick off the weekend."

"Aren't you forgetting that I'm against the whole idea of using the cemetery as a tourist attraction?"

"Not at all," he said. "I remember what you told me exactly. But you do want your voice heard, don't you? If you don't show up, there's going to be no one there to represent your side of things."

Doris stared at Mayor Gherkin for a long moment. The man certainly knew what buttons to press. And besides, he had a point. If she didn't go, she could imagine what Jeremy would end up writing if all he had to go on was the mayor and the town council. Tom was right: she was the only one who could handle something like this on such short notice. They both knew she'd been preparing for the tour this weekend and had plenty of food on hand in the kitchen already.

"All right," she capitulated, "I'll take care of it. But don't think for a second I'm going to serve all those people. It'll be a buffet, and I'm going to sit at the tables like the rest of you."

Mayor Gherkin smiled. "I wouldn't have it any other way, Doris."

Deputy Rodney Hopper was sitting in his car across the street from the library, wondering whether or not to go inside and talk to Lexie. He could see City Boy's car parked in the lot, which meant that they'd returned from wherever they'd gone, and he could see lights from Lexie's office glowing through the window.

He could imagine Lexie sitting at her desk reading, her legs propped up on the chair with knees bent, twirling those strands of hair as she thumbed through the pages of a book. He wanted to talk to her, but the thing was, he knew he didn't have a good reason. He never dropped by the library just to chat because, honestly, he wasn't all that sure that she wanted him to. She had never casually suggested that he stop by to see her, and whenever he veered the conversation in that direction, she would change the subject. On one level, it made sense, since she was supposed to be working, but at the same time, he knew that encouraging him to visit would have been another small step in the progress of their relationship.

He saw a figure pass by the window, and he wondered if City Boy was in the office with her.

He scowled. That would take the cake, wouldn't it? First a lunch date—something he and Lexie had never done—and now a friendly visit at work. He scowled just thinking about it. In less than a day, City Boy had moved right in, hadn't he? Well, maybe he'd just have to have another little talk with him about the situation. Spell things out for him, so that City Boy would understand exactly where things stood.

Of course, that would mean that things with Lexie stood *some-where*, and right now he wasn't exactly sure they did. Yesterday he'd been content with the status of the relationship. Well, okay, maybe not completely content. He would have preferred things to be moving just a little faster, but that was beside the point. The point was, yesterday he knew there was no competition, but today the two of them were sitting up there, probably laughing and joking, having a grand old time. And here he was, sitting in an idling car, staring at them from the outside.

Then again, maybe Lexie and City Boy weren't in the office together. Maybe Lexie was doing . . . well, librarian stuff while City Boy was hunched in the corner, reading some moldy book. Maybe Lexie was just being friendly, since the guy was a visitor in town. He wondered about it, before deciding it made sense. Hell, everybody was going out of their way to make the guy feel welcome, right? And the mayor was leading the charge. This morning, when he had City Boy right where he wanted him, just when he was going to set the boundaries, the mayor (the mayor!) helped the guy slink away to safety. And bam! City Boy and Lexie are picking flowers and watching rainbows together.

Then again, maybe not.

He hated not knowing what was going on, and just as he was

getting ready to head inside, his thoughts were interrupted by a tapping on the glass. It took an instant for the face to come into focus.

The mayor. Mr. *Interrupt at the Wrong Moment.* Twice now.

Rodney rolled down his window and the chill swept into the car. Mayor Gherkin leaned over, using his hands as support.

"Just the man I was looking for," Mayor Gherkin said. "I happened to be driving by, and when I saw you, I was struck by the thought that we're going to need a representative from law enforcement this evening."

"What for?"

"The little get-together, of course. For Jeremy Marsh, our distinguished visitor. Tonight at the Lawson Plantation."

Rodney blinked. "You're kidding, right?"

"No, not at all. In fact, I've got Gary making him up a key to the city right now."

"A key to the city," Rodney repeated.

"Of course, don't tell anyone about that. It's supposed to be a surprise. But since this is becoming more official, I sure would appreciate your presence tonight. It would make the evening seem a bit more . . . ceremonious. I was hoping that you'd stand by my side as I presented the key to him."

Rodney puffed his chest out just a bit, flattered. Still, there wasn't a chance he'd even consider doing something like that. "I think that's more my boss's duty, don't you?"

"Well, sure. But you and I both know he's hunting in the mountains right now. And since you're in charge while he's gone, it's one of those things that falls in your lap."

"I don't know, Tom. I'd have to call someone in to cover for me. It's a shame, but I really don't think I'm going to be able to make it."

"That is a shame. But I understand. Duty is duty."

Rodney breathed a sigh of relief. "Thanks."

"I'm sure Lexie would love to have seen you, though."

"Lexie?"

"Well, of course. She runs the library, so that makes her one of the dignitaries that will attend. Why, I was just coming by to tell her about it. But I'm sure she'll enjoy visiting with our guest, even if you're not there." The mayor straightened up. "But all right, like I said, I understand."

"Wait!" Rodney said, his mind moving quickly, trying to recover. "You said it's tonight, right?"

The mayor nodded.

"I don't know what I was thinking, but I think Bruce is already scheduled, so I just might be able to work something out."

The mayor smiled. "Glad to hear it," he said. "Now, let me head inside so I can talk to Ms. Darnell. You weren't planning to head inside and talk to her yourself, were you? I mean, I'd be happy to wait."

"No," Rodney said. "Just tell her I'll see her later."

"Will do, Deputy."

After retrieving some additional information for Jeremy and making a quick stop in her office, Lexie found herself surrounded by twenty children, some nestled in their mothers' laps. Lexie was sitting on the floor, reading her third book. The room was boisterous, as it always was. On a low table off to the side, cookies and punch had been set out; in the far corner, a few of the less engaged children were playing with some of the many toys she kept on the shelves. Still others were finger-painting on a makeshift table she'd designed. The room was decorated in bright colors—the shelves were like crayons, with no apparent theme other than vividness. Despite the protests of some of the senior volunteers and employees—who wanted children to sit quietly as they were being read to, as had always been done—Lexie wanted children to have fun in the library. She wanted them to be excited about coming, even if that required toys, games, and a room that was less than quiet. Over the years, she could remember dozens of kids who played for a year or more before discovering the joy of stories, but that was fine by her. As long as they kept coming in.

But today, as she was reading, she felt her mind wandering back to the lunch she'd shared with Jeremy. Though it couldn't be described as a date, it almost had that feeling, which made it a little disconcerting. Thinking back on it, she realized that she'd revealed far more about herself than she'd intended, and she kept trying to remember how that had happened. It wasn't as if he'd pried. Instead, it had just happened. But why on earth was she still dwelling on it?

She didn't like to think of herself as neurotic, but this endless analysis wasn't like her. And besides, she told herself, it hadn't even been a date as much as a guided tour. But no matter how much she tried to stop it, Jeremy's image kept popping up unexpectedly: the slightly crooked smile, his expression of amusement at things she said. She couldn't help wondering what he had thought about her life here, not to mention what he'd thought about her. She'd even blushed when he said he'd found her charming. What was that all about? Maybe, she thought, it was because I spilled my guts about my past and left myself vulnerable.

She made a note not to do it again. And yet . . .

It hadn't been so bad, she admitted. Just talking to someone new, someone who didn't already know everyone and everything going on in town, was refreshing. She'd almost forgotten how special that could be. And he'd surprised her. Doris had been right, at least in part. He wasn't what she thought he'd be. He was smarter than she'd first assumed, and even if he held his mind closed to the possibility of mystery, he made up for it by being good-humored about their differing beliefs and way of life. He poked fun at himself, too, which was also appealing.

As she continued to read to the children—thank goodness, it wasn't a complicated book—her mind refused to stop whirling.

Okay, so she liked him. She admitted that. And if truth be told, she wanted to spend more time with him. But even that realization didn't change the little voice in her head warning her not to get hurt. She had to tread carefully here, for—as much as they seemed to get along—Jeremy Marsh would indeed hurt her if she allowed it to happen.

Jeremy was hunched over a series of street maps of Boone Creek, dating back to the 1850s. The older they were, the more written detail they seemed to have, and as he watched how the town had changed decade by decade, he jotted additional notes. From a sleepy village nestled along a dozen roads, the town had continued to expand outward.

The cemetery, as he already knew, sat between the river and Riker's Hill; more important, he realized that a line drawn between Riker's Hill and the paper mill would pass directly through the cemetery. The total distance was a little more than three miles, and he knew that it was possible for light to be refracted that far, even on foggy nights. He wondered if the factory had a third shift, which would necessitate keeping the place brightly lit, even at night. With the right layering of the fog and enough brightness, everything could be explained in one fell swoop.

Upon reflection, he realized he should have noticed the straight-line relationship between the paper mill and Riker's Hill when he was up there. Instead, he'd been caught up in enjoying the view, looking over the town, and spending time with Lexie.

He was still trying to figure out the sudden change in her behavior. Yesterday she wanted nothing to do with him, and today . . . well, today was a new day, wasn't it? And damned if he couldn't stop thinking about her, and not just in the usual, clothes-heaped-at-the-foot-of-the-bed sort of way. He couldn't remember the last time that had happened. Maria, probably, but that was a long time ago. A lifetime ago, when he was someone else entirely. But today the conversation had been so natural, so comfortable, that despite the fact he should finish studying the maps, all he really wanted to do was get to know her even better.

Strange, he thought, and before he realized what was happening, he stood from his desk and began making his way to the stairs. He knew she was reading to the children, and he had no intention of disturbing her, but he suddenly wanted to see her.

He walked down the steps, rounded the corner, and moved to one of the glass walls. It took only a moment for him to spot Lexie sitting on the floor, surrounded by children.

She read in an animated way, and he smiled at her expressions: the wide eyes, the "O" she made with her mouth, the way she leaned forward to emphasize something that was happening in the story. The mothers sat with smiles on their faces. A couple of the kids were abolutely still; the others looked as if they'd taken wiggle pills.

"She's really something, isn't she?"

Jeremy turned in surprise. "Mayor Gherkin. What are you doing here?"

"Why, I came to see you, of course. And Miss Lexie, too. About the dinner tonight. We've got everything just about set up. I think you'll be quite impressed."

"I'm sure I will," Jeremy said.

"But like I was saying, she's really something, isn't she?"

Jeremy said nothing, and the mayor winked before going on. "I saw the way you were looking at her. A man's eyes give him away. The eyes always tell the truth."

"What's that supposed to mean?"

The mayor grinned. "Well, I don't know. Why don't you tell me?"

"There's nothing to tell."

"Of course not," he said.

Jeremy shook his head. "Look, Mr. Mayor . . . Tom—"

"Oh, never mind. I was just teasing. But let me tell you a bit about our little get-together this evening."

Mayor Gherkin told Jeremy the location, then offered directions that, somewhat unsurprisingly, were heavy on local landmarks. No doubt Tully taught him everything he knew, Jeremy thought.

"Do you think you'll be able to find it?" the mayor asked when he was finished.

"I've got a map," Jeremy said.

"That might help, but keep in mind that those back roads can get kind of dark. It's easy to get lost if you're not careful. You might consider coming with someone who knows where it is."

When Jeremy looked at him curiously, Gherkin glanced knowingly through the window.

"You think I should ask Lexie?" Jeremy asked.

The mayor's eyes twinkled. "That's up to you. If you think she'd agree. A lot of men consider her the prize of the county."

"She'd say yes," Jeremy said, feeling more hopeful than certain.

The mayor looked doubtful. "I think you may be overestimating your own abilities. But if you're so sure, then I suppose my business is through here. You see, I came to invite her myself, but since you're going to take care of it, I'll just see you tonight."

The mayor turned to leave, and a few minutes later, Jeremy watched Lexie finish up. She closed the book, and as the parents rose, he felt a jolt of nervous adrenaline. The sensation amazed him. When was the last time that had happened?

A few mothers called to those kids who hadn't been listening, and a moment later, Lexie was following the group out of the children's room. When she saw Jeremy, she headed over.

"I take it you're ready to start looking through the diaries," she surmised.

"If you have time to get them," he said. "I still have a way to go with the maps. But actually, there's something else, too."

"Oh?" She tilted her head slightly.

As he spoke, he noticed the butterflies in his stomach. Weird.

"The mayor came by to tell me about the dinner tonight at the Lawson Plantation, and he's not sure if I can find the place on my own, so he suggested that I bring someone who knows where it is. And, well, since you're pretty much the only one I know in town, I was wondering if you'd be willing to accompany me."

For a long moment, Lexie said nothing.

"Figures," she finally said.

Her response caught Jeremy off-guard.

"Excuse me?"

"Oh, it's not you. It's the mayor and the way he does things. He knows I try to avoid events like this whenever possible, unless it has to do with the library. He figured that I'd say no if he asked, so he finagled a way to get you to ask me instead. And here you are. And here I am."

Jeremy blinked at the thought, trying to remember the exact exchange, but only coming up with bits and pieces. Who had suggested he go with Lexie? He or the mayor?

"Why do I suddenly feel like I'm in the middle of a soap opera?"

"Because you are. It's called living in a small southern town."

Jeremy paused, looking uncertain. "You really think the mayor had all this planned?"

"I know he had it planned. He might come across like he's no smarter than a sack of grass, but he has a funny knack of getting people to do exactly what he wants and making them think it was their idea all along. Why on earth do you think you're still staying at Greenleaf?"

Jeremy pushed his hands into his pockets, considering it. "Well, just so you know, you don't have to come. I'm sure I can find the place on my own."

She put her hands on her hips and looked at him. "Are you backing out on me?"

Jeremy froze, unsure how to respond. "Well, I just thought that since the mayor . . ."

"Do you want me to come with you or not?" she asked.

"I do, but if you're not—"

"Then ask me again."

"Excuse me?"

"Ask me to come with you tonight. For yourself this time, and don't use the excuse about needing directions. Say something like, 'I'd really like to bring you to the dinner tonight. Can I pick you up later?'"

He looked at her, trying to decide if she was serious. "You want me to say those words?"

"If you don't, it'll still be the mayor's idea and I won't go. But if you ask me, you have to mean it, so use the right tone."

Jeremy fidgeted like a nervous schoolboy. "I'd really like to bring you to the dinner tonight. May I pick you up later?"

She smiled and placed her hand on his arm.

"Why, Mr. Marsh," she drawled, "I'd be delighted."

Minutes later, Jeremy was watching Lexie retrieve the diaries from a locked case in the rare-book room, his head still spinning. Women in New York simply didn't talk to him the way Lexie did. He wasn't sure if she'd been reasonable or unreasonable or somewhere in between. *Ask me again and use the right tone.* What kind of woman did that? And why on earth did he find it so . . . compelling?

He wasn't sure, and all of a sudden, the story and the opportunity for television were nothing more than minor details. Instead, as he watched Lexie, all he could think about was how warm her hand felt when she'd laid it ever so gently on his arm.

Nine

......❖......

Later that evening, as the fog thickened into a soupy mess, Rodney Hopper decided that the Lawson Plantation looked like it was about to host a Barry Manilow concert.

For the last twenty minutes, he'd been directing the traffic into parking spots and watching in disbelief at the procession excitedly making its way toward the door. To this point, he'd seen Drs. Benson and Tricket, Albert the dentist, all eight members of the town council, including Tully and Jed, the mayor and the staff from the Chamber of Commerce, the entire school board, all nine county commissioners, the volunteers from the Historical Society, three accountants, the entire crew from Herbs, the bartender from Lookilu, the barber, and even Toby, who emptied septic tanks for a living but looked remarkably spiffy nonetheless. Lawson Plantation wasn't even this crowded during the Christmas season, when the place was decorated to the nines and free to the public on the first Friday in December.

Tonight wasn't the same. This wasn't a celebration where friends and acquaintances got together to enjoy each other's company before the hectic holiday rush. This was a party meant to honor someone who had nothing to do with the town and didn't give a damn about this place. Even worse, though Rodney was here on official business, he suddenly knew he shouldn't have bothered ironing his shirt and polishing his shoes, since he doubted that Lexie would even notice.

He knew all about it. After Doris had gone back to Herbs to get the cooking under way, the mayor had rolled in and mentioned the awful news about Jeremy and Lexie, and Rachel had called him straightaway. Rachel, he thought, was sweet in that way and always had been. She knew how he felt about Lexie and didn't tease him like a lot of other folks did. Anyway, he got the impression that she wasn't all that thrilled, either, with the idea of them showing up together. But Rachel was better at hiding her feelings than he was, and right now he wished he were somewhere else. Everything about tonight left him feeling lousy.

Especially the way the whole town was acting. By his reckoning, folks around here hadn't been this excited about the town's prospects since the *Raleigh News & Observer* had sent a reporter to do a story about Jumpy Walton, who was attempting to build a replica of the Wright Brothers' plane, one he planned to fly in commemoration of the hundredth anniversary of aviation at Kitty Hawk. Jumpy, who'd always had a couple of screws loose, had long claimed to be nearly finished with the replica, but when he opened the barn doors to proudly show how far he'd gotten, the reporter realized that Jumpy didn't have the slightest clue about what he was doing. In the barn, the replica looked like a giant, crooked version of a barbed-wire and plywood chicken.

And now the town was placing its bets on the existence of ghosts in the cemetery and that the city boy would bring the world to their doorstep because of them. Rodney strongly doubted it. And besides, he didn't honestly care if the world came or not, as long as Lexie stayed part of *his* world.

Across town and at about the same time, Lexie stepped onto her porch just as Jeremy was coming up the walkway with a small bouquet of wildflowers in hand. Nice touch, she thought, and she suddenly hoped he couldn't tell how frazzled she'd been until just a few minutes ago.

Being a woman was challenging sometimes, and tonight had been rougher than most. First, of course, there was the question of whether this was even an actual date. Granted, it was closer to a date than what had gone on at lunch, but it wasn't exactly a romantic dinner for two, and she wasn't sure whether she would have even consented to something like that. Then there was the whole image question and how she wanted to be perceived, not only by Jeremy but by everyone else who would see them together. Add the fact that she was most comfortable when she wore jeans and had no intention of showing any cleavage, and the whole thing became so confusing that she'd finally just thrown in the towel. In the end, she'd decided to go with a professional look: brown pantsuit with an ivory blouse.

But here he comes waltzing up in his Johnny Cash look, as if he hadn't given the evening a second thought.

"You found the place," Lexie observed.

"It wasn't too hard," Jeremy said. "You showed me where you lived when we were on Riker's Hill, remember?" He offered the flowers. "Here. These are for you."

She smiled as she took them, looking absolutely lovely. Sexy, too, of course. But "lovely" seemed more appropriate.

"Thank you," she said. "How'd the diary search go?"

"Okay," he said. "Nothing too spectacular in the ones I've looked through so far."

"Just give it a chance," she said with a smile. "Who knows what you'll find?" She raised the bouquet to her nose. "These are beautiful, by the way. Give me a second to put them in a vase, grab a long coat, and then I'll be ready."

He opened his palms. "I'll wait here."

A couple of minutes later in the car, they were driving through town in the opposite direction from the cemetery. As the fog continued to thicken, Lexie directed Jeremy along the back roads until they came to a long winding drive, bordered on both sides by oaks that looked as if they'd been planted a hundred years ago. Though he couldn't see the house, he slowed the car as he approached a towering hedge that he assumed lined a circular drive. He leaned over the steering wheel, wondering which way to turn.

"You might want to consider parking here," Lexie suggested. "I doubt if you'll find something any closer, and besides, you'll want to be able to get out of here later when you need to."

"Are you sure? We can't even see the house yet."

"Trust me," she said. "Why do you think I brought the long coat?"

He debated only for an instant before deciding, Why not? And a moment later, they were walking up the drive, Lexie doing her best to keep the jacket pinched together. They followed the curve of the drive near the hedge, and all at once, the old Georgian mansion stood in blazing glory before them.

The house, however, wasn't the first thing Jeremy noticed. What he saw first were the cars. Scores of cars, parked haphazardly, noses pointing in every direction as if planning a fast getaway. Numerous others were either circling the mayhem and flashing their brake lights or trying to squeeze into improbably tiny spaces.

Jeremy halted, staring at the scene.

"I thought this was supposed to be a little get-together with friends."

Lexie nodded. "This is the mayor's version of a little get-together. You have to remember, he knows practically everyone in the county."

"And you knew this was coming?"

"Of course."

"Why didn't you tell me it would be like this?"

"Like I keep telling you, you keep forgetting to ask. And besides, I thought you knew."

"How could I have known he was planning something like this?"

She smiled, looking toward the house. "It is kind of impressive, isn't it? Not that I think you necessarily deserve it."

He grunted in amusement. "You know, I've really come to appreciate your southern charm."

"Thank you. And don't worry about tonight. It's not going to be as stressful as you think. Everyone's friendly, and when in doubt, just remember that you're the guest of honor."

Doris had to be the single most organized and efficient caterer in the world, Rachel thought, since this whole thing had been pulled off without a hitch and with plenty of time to spare. Instead of having to dish up food all night, Rachel was wiggling through the crowds in her best imitation Chanel party dress when she spotted Rodney walking up to the porch.

With his neatly pressed uniform, she thought he looked quite official, like a marine in one of those old World War II posters in the VFW building on Main Street. Most of the other deputies carried a few too many chicken wings and Budweisers around the midsection, but in his off-hours, Rodney pumped iron in his garage gym. He kept the garage door open, and sometimes on her way home from work, she'd stop and visit with him for a while, like the old friends that they were. As little kids, they'd been neighbors, and her mother had pictures of them bathing in the tub together. Most old friends couldn't say that.

She took a tube of lipstick from her purse and dabbed at her lips, conscious of the soft spot she had for him. Oh, they'd gone their separate ways for a while, but in the last couple of years, things had been changing. Two summers ago, they'd ended up sitting near each other at the Lookilu, and she'd seen his expression as he watched a newscast about a young boy who had died in a tragic fire in Raleigh. Seeing his eyes well up over the loss of a stranger had affected her in a way she hadn't expected. She'd noticed it a second time last Easter, when the Sheriff's Department sponsored the town's official egg hunt at the Masonic Lodge and he'd pulled her aside to tell her some of the trickier places in which he'd hidden the goodies. He'd looked more excited than the children, which made for a funny contrast with his bulging biceps, and she remembered thinking to herself that he'd be the kind of father who would make any wife proud.

Looking back, she supposed that was the moment she realized that her feelings for Rodney had changed. It wasn't that she fell in love with him right then and there, but it was the moment when she realized that she'd stopped believing the possibility to be nil. Not that it was likely, though. Rodney was over the moon for Lexie. Always had been, always would be, and Rachel had long since come to the conclusion that nothing would ever change the way he felt about her. There were times when it wasn't easy, and there were times when it didn't bother her at all, but lately, she admitted that the times it didn't bother her were fewer and further between.

Pushing through the crowd, she wished she hadn't brought up the subject of Jeremy Marsh at lunch. She should have known what was bothering Rodney. By now, it seemed, the entire town was talking about Lexie and Jeremy, starting with the grocer who had sold them their lunch and spreading like fire once the mayor made his announcement. She would still like to go to New York, but as she'd mentally replayed her conversation with Jeremy, she'd gradually come to the realization that he might have simply been making conversation and not extending an invitation. Sometimes she read too much into situations like that.

But Jeremy Marsh was just so . . . perfect.

Cultured, intelligent, charming, famous, and, best of all, not from here. There was no way Rodney could compete with that, and she had the sinking suspicion that Rodney knew it, too. But Rodney, on the other hand, *was* here and didn't plan to leave, which was a different sort of an advantage, if one chose to see it that way. And, she had to admit, he was responsible and good-looking, too, in his own way.

"Hey, Rodney," she said, smiling.

Rodney glanced over his shoulder. "Oh, hey, Rach. How are you?"

"Good, thanks. Some party, huh?"

"It's great," he said, not hiding the sarcasm in his voice. "How's it going inside?"

"Pretty good. They just got the banner up."

"Banner?"

"Sure. The one welcoming him to town. His name is in big blue letters and everything."

Rodney exhaled, his chest collapsing slightly. "Great," he said again.

"You should see what else the mayor has in store for him. Not only the banner and the food, but he had a key to the city made."

"I heard," Rodney said.

"And the Mahi-Mahis are here, too," she continued, referring to a barbershop quartet. Local citizens, they'd been singing together for forty-three years, and even though two of the members had to use walkers and one had a nervous twitch that forced him to sing with his eyes closed, they were nonetheless the most famous entertainers within a hundred miles.

"Swell," Rodney said again.

His tone gave her pause for the first time. "I guess you don't want to hear about any of that, though, huh?"

"No, not really."

"Why did you come, then?"

"Tom talked me into it. One day I'm going to figure out where he's coming from before he opens his mouth."

"It won't be so bad," she said. "I mean, you've seen how people are tonight. Everyone wants to talk to him. It's not like he and Lexie can hole up in some corner somewhere. I'll bet you ten to one they won't even be able to say more than ten words to each other all night. And, just to let you know, I saved a plate of food for you, if you don't have a chance to get anything to eat."

Rodney hesitated for a moment before smiling. Rachel always looked out for him.

"Thanks, Rach." For the first time, he noticed what she was wearing, his eyes alighting on the little gold hoops in her ears. He added, "You look nice tonight."

"Thank you."

"You want to keep me company for a while?"

She smiled. "I'd like that."

Jeremy and Lexie wove through the mass of parked cars, their breaths coming out in little puffs as they neared the mansion. On the steps up ahead, Jeremy saw one couple after another pausing at the door before going inside, and it took just an instant to recognize Rodney Hopper standing near the door. Rodney saw Jeremy at the same time, and his smile immediately changed into a scowl. Even from a distance, he looked large, jealous, and, most important, armed, none of which made Jeremy feel particularly comfortable.

Lexie followed his gaze. "Oh, don't worry about Rodney," she said. "You're with me."

"That's what I'm worried about," he said. "I kind of get the feeling he isn't all that happy that we showed up together."

She knew Jeremy was right, although she was thankful that Rachel was beside the deputy. Rachel always had a way of keeping Rodney calm, and Lexie had long thought that she'd be perfect for him. She hadn't, however, figured out a way of spelling it out for him without hurting his feelings. It wasn't the sort of thing she could bring up while they were dancing at the Shriners' Benefit Ball, was it?

"If it'll make you feel better, just let me do the talking," she said.

"I was planning on it."

Rachel brightened when she saw them coming up the steps.

"Hey, you two!" she said. When they were close, she reached out to tug on Lexie's jacket. "I love your outfit, Lex."

"Thanks, Rachel," Lexie said. "And you look like a million bucks, too."

Jeremy said nothing, preferring to examine his fingernails as he tried to avoid the evil eye that Rodney was sending his way. In the sudden silence, Rachel and Lexie glanced at each other. Reading Lexie's clues, Rachel stepped forward.

"And look at you, Mr. Famous Journalist," she sang out. "Why, one look at you, and women's hearts will be fluttering all night." She flashed a broad smile. "I almost hate to ask, Lexie, but would you mind if I escorted him inside? I just know the mayor is waiting for him."

"Not at all," Lexie said, knowing she needed a minute alone with Rodney. She nodded to Jeremy. "Go ahead, I'll catch up in a minute."

Rachel clamped onto Jeremy's arm, and before he realized it, he was being led away. "Now, have you ever been to a southern plantation as fine as this one?" Rachel asked.

"I can't say that I have," Jeremy answered, wondering if he was being thrown to the wolves. As they passed, Lexie mouthed a silent thank-you and Rachel winked.

Lexie turned toward Rodney.

"It's not what you think," she began, and Rodney raised his hands to stop her from continuing.

"Look," he said, "you don't have to explain. I've seen it before, remember?"

She knew he was referring to Mr. Renaissance, and her first instinct was to tell him that he was wrong. She wanted to tell him that she wasn't going to let her feelings run wild this time, but she knew she'd made that promise before. That was what she said to Rodney, after all, when he'd tried to gently warn her that Mr. Renaissance had no intention of staying.

"I wish I knew what to say," she said, hating the guilty note in her voice.

"You don't have to say anything."

She knew she didn't. It wasn't as if they were a couple or had ever been a couple, but she had the strange sensation of confronting an ex-spouse after a recent divorce, when the wounds were still fresh. Again, she wished he would simply move on, but a little voice reminded her that she'd played a role in keeping the spark alive these last couple of years, even if it had more to do with security and comfort on her part than with anything romantic.

"Well, just so you know, I'm actually looking forward to things getting back to normal around here," she volunteered.

"Me, too," he said.

Neither said anything for a moment. In the silence, Lexie glanced off to the side, wishing that Rodney wore his feelings with a bit more subtlety.

"Rachel sure looks nice, doesn't she?" she said.

Rodney's chin dropped to his chest before he looked at Lexie again. For the first time, she saw the tiniest of smiles.

"Yeah," he said, "she does."

"Is she still seeing Jim?" she asked, referring to the Terminix man. Lexie had seen them together in the green truck mounted with a giant bug on their way to Greenville for dinner during the holidays.

"No, that's over," he said. "They only went out once. She said his car smelled like disinfectant, and she sneezed like crazy the whole night."

Despite the tension, Lexie laughed. "That sounds like something that could only happen to Rachel."

"She got over it. And it's not like it made her bitter or anything. She keeps getting back on the horse, you know."

"Sometimes I think she needs to pick better horses. Or at least ones without giant bugs on the car."

He chuckled, as if thinking the same thing. Their eyes met for an instant, then Lexie turned away. She tucked a strand of hair behind her ear.

"Well, listen, I should probably head inside," she said.

"I know," he said.

"Are you coming in?"

"I'm not sure yet. I wasn't planning on staying that long. And besides, I'm still on call. The county is pretty big for one person, and Bruce is the only one in the field right now."

She nodded. "Well, if I don't see you again tonight, keep safe, okay?"

"I will. See you later."

She began moving toward the door.

"Hey, Lexie?"

She turned. "Yes?"

He swallowed. "You look nice, too, by the way."

The sad way he said it nearly broke her heart, and her eyes dipped for an instant. "Thank you," she said.

Rachel and Jeremy kept a low profile, moving around the edges of the crowd, as Rachel showed him the paintings of various members of the Lawson family who shared a striking resemblance not only from one generation to the next but, strangely, across genders as well. The men had effeminate qualities, and the women tended to be masculine, thus making it seem as if every artist had used the same androgynous model.

But he appreciated the fact that Rachel was keeping him occupied and out of harm's way, even if she refused to release his arm. He could hear people talking about him but wasn't quite ready to mingle yet, even if the whole thing did leave him feeling just a bit flattered. Nate hadn't been able to rustle up a tenth of this number of people to watch his television appearance, and he'd had to offer free booze as an enticement to get even that many to show.

Not here, though. Not in small-town America, where people played bingo, went bowling, and watched reruns of *Matlock* on TNT. He hadn't seen so much blue hair and polyester since . . . well, since ever, and as he was pondering the whole situation, Rachel squeezed his arm to get his attention.

"Get ready, darlin'. It's showtime."

"Excuse me?"

She looked past him, toward the rising commotion behind them.

"Well, Mayor Tom, how are you?" Rachel asked, beaming that Hollywood smile again.

Mayor Gherkin seemed to be the only person in the room who was perspiring. His bald head was shiny in the light, and if he seemed surprised that Jeremy was with Rachel, he didn't show it.

"Rachel! You are looking lovely as always, and I see you've been sharing the illustrious past of this fine home with our guest here."

"Doing my best," she said.

"Good, good. I'm glad to hear it." They engaged in more small talk before Gherkin got to the point.

"And I hate to ask you this, being that you've been kind enough to tell him about this fine establishment, but would you mind?" he said, motioning to Jeremy. "People are excited to get this fine event started."

"Not at all," she answered, and in the next instant, the mayor had replaced Rachel's hand with his own and began leading Jeremy through the crowd.

As they walked, people quieted and moved off to the side, like the Red Sea parting for Moses. Others stared with wide eyes or craned their necks to get a better view. People oohed and aahed, whispering aloud that it must be *him*.

"I can't tell you how glad we are that you finally made it," Mayor Gherkin said, speaking from the corner of his mouth and continuing to smile to the crowd. "For a minute there, I was beginning to worry."

"Maybe we should wait for Lexie," Jeremy answered, trying to keep his cheeks from turning red. This whole thing, especially being escorted by the mayor like a prom queen, was just a little bit *too* small-town America, not to mention a little on the weird side.

"I've already spoken to her, and she'll meet us there."

"And where's that?"

"Why, you're going to meet the rest of the town council, of course. You've already met Jed and Tully and the folks I introduced you to this morning, but there are a few others. And the county commissioners, too. Like me, they're mighty impressed with your visit here. Mighty impressed. And don't worry—they've got all their ghost stories ready. You brought your tape recorder, right?"

"It's in my pocket."

"Good, good. Glad to hear it. And . . ." For the first time, he turned from the crowd to look at Jeremy. "I take it you are heading out to the cemetery tonight . . ."

"I was, and speaking of that, I wanted to make sure—"

The mayor kept on going as if he hadn't heard him, while nodding and waving to the crowd. "Well, as the mayor, I feel it's my obligation to tell you not to worry none about meeting those ghosts. Oh, they're a sight, of course. Enough to startle an elephant into fainting. But so far, no one's ever been hurt, except for Bobby Lee Howard, and ramming into that road sign afterward had less to do with what he saw than the fact that he'd finished a twelve-pack of Pabst before he got behind the wheel."

"Ah," Jeremy said, beginning to mimic the mayor by nodding and waving. "I'll try to keep that in mind."

Lexie was waiting for him when he met the town council, and he breathed a sigh of relief when she moved to his side as he was introduced to the town's power elite. Most were friendly enough—although Jed stood frowning with his arms crossed—but he couldn't help watching Lexie from the corner of his eye. She seemed distracted, and he wondered what had happened between her and Rodney.

Jeremy didn't have a chance to find out, or even relax, for the next three hours, as the rest of the evening was akin to an old-fashioned political convention. After his meeting with the council—each and every one of them, Jed excluded, seemed to have been prepped by the mayor and promised "it could be the biggest story ever" and reminded him that "tourism is important to the town"—Jeremy was brought to the stage, which had been festooned with a banner proclaiming, WELCOME JEREMY MARSH!

Technically, it wasn't a stage, but a long wooden table topped with a shiny purple tablecloth. Jeremy had to use a chair to step up onto it, as did Gherkin, only to confront a sea of strange faces gazing up at him. Once the crowd quieted, the mayor made a long-winded speech praising Jeremy for his professionalism and honesty as if they'd known each other for years. Additionally, Gherkin not only mentioned the *Primetime Live* appearance— which elicited the familiar smiles and nods, as well as a few more oohs and aahs—but a number of well-received articles he'd written, including a piece he'd done for the *Atlantic Monthly* concerning biological weapons research at Fort Detrick. As much as he sometimes came off as a goofball, Jeremy thought, the man had done his homework and definitely knew how to flatter. At the end of the speech, Jeremy was presented with a key to the city, and the Mahi-Mahis—who were standing on another table along an adjacent wall—broke in and sang three songs: "Carolina in My Mind," "New York, New York," and, perhaps most appropriate, the theme from *Ghostbusters*.

Surprisingly, the Mahi-Mahis weren't half-bad, even though he had no idea how they managed to get up on the table. The crowd loved them, and for an instant, Jeremy found himself smiling and actually enjoying himself. As he stood onstage, Lexie winked at him, which only made the whole thing seem more surreal.

From there, the mayor led him off to the corner, where he was seated in a comfortable antique chair set in front of an antique table. With his tape recorder running, Jeremy spent the rest of the evening listening to one story after another about encounters with the ghosts. The mayor had people line up, and they chatted excitedly while waiting their turn to meet him, as if he were giving autographs.

Unfortunately, most of the stories he heard began to run together. Everyone in line claimed to have seen the lights, but each one of them had a different description. Some swore they looked like people, others like strobe lights. One man said they looked exactly like a Halloween costume, right down to the sheet. The most original was from a guy named Joe, who said he'd seen the lights more than half a dozen times, and he spoke with authority when he said they looked exactly like the glowing Piggly Wiggly sign on Route 54 near Vanceboro.

At the same time, Lexie was always in the area talking to various people, and every now and then, their eyes would meet while both she and he were engaged in conversation with others. As if they were sharing a private joke, she would smile with raised eyebrows, her expression seeming to ask him, *See what you've gotten yourself into?*

Lexie, Jeremy reflected, wasn't like any of the women he'd recently dated. She didn't hide what she was thinking, she didn't try to impress him, nor was she swayed by anything he'd accomplished in the past. Instead, she seemed to evaluate him as he was today, right now, without holding either the past or the future against him.

It was, he realized, one of the reasons he'd married Maria. It wasn't simply the heady flush of emotions he'd felt when they first made love that had enthralled him—rather, it was the simple things that convinced him that she was the one. Her lack of pretense around others, the steely way she confronted him when he did something wrong, the patience with which she would listen to him as he paced around, struggling with a vexing problem. And though he and Lexie hadn't shared any of the daily nitty-gritty of life, he couldn't shake the thought that she'd be good at dealing with it, if that was what she wanted.

Jeremy realized she had a genuine affection for the people here, and she seemed to be truly interested in whatever it was they were saying. Her behavior suggested that she had no reason to rush or cut someone's conversation short, and she had no inhibitions about laughing aloud when something amused her. Every now and then, she'd lean in to hug someone, and pulling back, she'd reach for the person's hands and murmur something along the lines of "I'm so glad to see you again." That she didn't seem to think of herself as different, or even notice the fact that others obviously did, reminded Jeremy of an aunt who had always been the most popular person at holiday dinners, simply because she focused her attention so completely on others.

A few minutes later when he rose from the table to stretch his legs, Jeremy saw Lexie moving toward him, with just a trace of seduction in the gentle sway of her hips. And as he watched her, there was a moment, just a moment, when the scene seemed as if it weren't happening now, but taking place in the future, just another little get-together in a long procession of get-togethers in a tiny southern town in the middle of nowhere.

Ten

..... ❖ .....

As the evening drew to a close, Jeremy stood with Mayor Gherkin on the porch while Lexie and Doris stood off to the side.

"I sure do hope this evening met with your approval," Mayor Gherkin said, "and that you were able to see for yourself what a wonderful opportunity you have when it comes to this story."

"I did, thank you. But you didn't have to go to all this trouble," Jeremy protested.

"Nonsense," Gherkin replied. "Why, it's the least we can do. And besides, I wanted you to see what this town is capable of when it sets its mind to something. You can only imagine what we'd do for those television folks. Of course, you'll get a little bit more of the town's flavor this weekend, too. The small-town atmosphere, the feeling of traveling back in time as you walk through the homes. It's like nothing you can imagine."

"I have no doubt about that," Jeremy said.

Gherkin smiled. "Well, listen, I have a few things to take care of inside. A mayor's duty never ends, you know."

"I understand," he said. "And thanks for this, by the way," Jeremy said, raising the key to the city.

"Oh, you're very welcome. You deserve it." He reached for

Jeremy's hand. "But don't get any funny ideas. It's not like you can open the bank vault with it. It's more of a symbolic gesture."

Jeremy smiled as Gherkin pumped his hand. After Gherkin vanished inside, Doris and Lexie approached Jeremy, smirks on their faces. Despite that, Jeremy couldn't help but notice that Doris looked exhausted.

"L-I-B," Doris said.

"What?" Jeremy asked.

"You and your city slicker ways."

"Excuse me?"

"It's just that you should have heard the way some of these folks were talking about you," Doris teased. "I just feel lucky that I can say I knew you way back when."

Jeremy smiled, looking sheepish. "It was a little crazy, wasn't it?"

"I'll say," Doris said. "My Bible study group talked all night about how handsome you are. A couple of them wanted to bring you home, but fortunately, I was able to talk them out of it. And besides, I don't think their husbands would have been too thrilled."

"I appreciate that."

"Did you get enough to eat? I think I can rustle up some food if you're hungry."

"No, I'm fine. Thanks."

"You sure? Your night's really just beginning, isn't it?"

"I'll be okay," he assured her. In the silence, he looked around, noting that the fog had become even thicker. "But on that note, I suppose I should probably be going. I'd hate to miss my big chance at getting a whiff of the supernatural."

"Don't worry. You won't miss the lights," Doris said. "They don't come out until later, so you've still got a couple of hours." Surprising Jeremy, she leaned in and gave him a tired hug. "I just wanted to thank you for taking the time to meet everyone. It's not every stranger who's as good at listening as you are."

"No problem. I enjoyed it."

After Doris had released him, Jeremy turned his attention to Lexie, thinking that growing up with Doris must have been a lot like growing up with his own mother.

"You ready to go?"

Lexie nodded, but still hadn't said a word to him. Instead, she kissed Doris on the cheek, said she'd see her tomorrow, and a moment later, Jeremy and Lexie were walking to the car, the gravel crunching softly beneath their feet. She seemed to be staring into the distance but seeing nothing at all. After a few steps in silence, Jeremy gently nudged her shoulder with his.

"You okay? You're sort of quiet."

She shook her head, coming back to him. "I'm just thinking about Doris. Tonight really tired her out, and even though I probably shouldn't, I worry about her."

"She seemed fine."

"Yeah, she puts up a good front. But she's got to learn to take it easier. She had a heart attack a couple of years ago, but she likes to pretend it never happened. And after this, she has a big weekend, too."

Jeremy wasn't quite sure what to say; the thought that Doris was anything but healthy had never entered his mind.

Lexie noticed his discomfort and smiled. "But she did enjoy herself, that's for sure. We both had the chance to talk to a lot of people that we haven't seen in a while."

"I thought everyone here saw everyone else all the time."

"We do. But people are busy, and it's not often that you have more than a few minutes to chat between errands. Tonight was nice, though." She glanced toward him. "And Doris was right. People *loved* you."

She sounded almost shocked by the admission, and Jeremy pushed his hands into his pockets.

"Well, you shouldn't have been surprised. I am very lovable, you know."

She rolled her eyes, looking more playful than annoyed. Behind them, the house was receding into the distance as they rounded the hedge.

"Hey, I know it's none of my business, but how did it go with Rodney?"

She hesitated before finally shrugging. "You're right. It is none of your business."

He looked for a smile but saw none. "Well, the only reason I asked was because I was wondering whether you think it might be a good idea if I sneak out of town under the cover of darkness so he doesn't have the chance to crush my head with his bare hands."

That brought a smile. "You'll be fine. And besides, you'd break the mayor's heart if you left. Not every visitor gets a party like this or a key to the city."

"It's the first one I've ever received. Usually, I just get hate mail."

She laughed, the sound melodic. In the moonlight, her features were unreadable, and he thought back to how animated she had been among the townspeople.

Reaching the car, he opened the door for her. As she climbed in, she brushed against him slightly, and he wondered if she did so in response to the way he'd nudged her, or if she even noticed. After rounding the car, he slid behind the wheel, slipping the keys into the ignition but hesitating before starting the engine.

"What?" she asked.

"I was just thinking . . . ," he said, trailing off.

The words seemed to hang in the car and she nodded. "I thought I heard some squeaking."

"Funny. I was trying to say, I know it's getting late, but would you like to come with me to the cemetery?"

"In case you get scared?"

"Something like that."

She peeked at her watch, thinking, Oh, boy . . .

She shouldn't go. She really shouldn't. She'd already opened the door by coming with him tonight, and to spend the next couple of hours alone with him would open the door even further. She knew that nothing good could come of that, and there wasn't a single reason to say yes. But before she could stop herself, the words were already coming.

"I'd have to swing by the house first to change into something more comfortable."

"That's fine," he said. "I'm all for you changing into something more comfortable."

"I'll bet you are," she said knowingly.

"Now, don't start getting fresh," he said, feigning offense. "I don't think we know each other well enough for that."

"That's my line," she said.

"I thought I'd heard it somewhere."

"Well, get your own material next time. And just so you know, I don't want you getting any funny ideas about tonight, either."

"I have no funny ideas. I'm completely devoid of humor."

"You know what I meant."

"No," he said, trying to look innocent. "What did you mean?"

"Just drive, will you? Or I'll change my mind."

"Okay, okay," he said, turning the key. "Gee, you can be pushy sometimes."

"Thank you. I've been told it's one of my better qualities."

"By whom?"

"Wouldn't you like to know?"

The Taurus rolled along the foggy streets, the yellow streetlamps only making the night seem murkier. As soon as they pulled into her drive, she opened her door.

"Wait here," she said, tucking a strand of hair behind her ear. "I'll only be a few minutes."

He smiled, liking the fact she was nervous.

"Do you need my key to the city to open your door? I'd be happy to lend it to you."

"Now, don't start thinking you're special, Mr. Marsh. My mother got a key to the city, too."

"Are we back to 'Mr. Marsh' again? And here I thought we were getting along just fine."

"And I'm beginning to think this evening has gone to your head."

She stepped out of the car and closed the door behind her in an attempt to have the last word. Jeremy laughed, thinking she was a lot like he was. Unable to resist, he pressed the button on his door to lower her window. He leaned across the seat.

"Hey, Lexie?"

She turned. "Yes?"

"Since it might be chilly tonight, feel free to grab a bottle of wine."

She put her hands on her hips. "Why? So you can ply me with liquor?"

He grinned. "Only if you're okay with that."

Her eyes narrowed, but like before, she looked more playful than offended. "Not only do I not keep any wine in the house, Mr. Marsh, but I'd say no, anyway."

"You don't drink?"

"Not too much," she said. "Now, wait there," she warned, pointing toward the drive. "I'm going to throw on a pair of jeans."

"I promise not to even *try* to peek in the window."

"Good idea. I'd definitely have to tell Rodney if you did something that stupid."

"That doesn't sound good."

"Trust me," she said, trying to muster a severe look, "it wouldn't be."

Jeremy watched her move up the walkway, certain that he'd never met anyone quite like her.

Fifteen minutes later, they pulled to a stop in front of Cedar Creek Cemetery. He'd angled the car so the headlights shone into the cemetery, and his first thought was that even the fog looked different here. It was dense and impenetrable in places while thin in others, and the slight breeze made discrete tendrils curve and twist, almost as if alive. The low-hanging branches of the magnolia tree were nothing but darkened shadows, and the crumbling tombs added to the eerie effect. It was so dark that Jeremy was unable to discern even the faintest sliver of the moon in the sky.

Leaving the car idling, he popped the trunk. As she peered in, Lexie's eyes widened.

"It looks like you've got the makings to build a bomb in there."

"Nah," he said. "Just a bunch of cool things. Guys love their toys, you know."

"I thought you'd just have a video camera or something like that."

"I do. I have four of them."

"Why do you need four?"

"To film every angle, of course. For instance, what if the ghosts are walking in the wrong direction? I might not get their faces."

She ignored the comment. "And what's this thing?" she asked, pointing to an electronic box.

"A microwave radiation detector. And this over here," he said, gesturing at another item, "sort of goes with it. It detects electromagnetic activity."

"You're kidding."

"No," he said. "It's in the official ghostbuster's handbook. You'll often find increased spiritual activity in areas where there are high concentrations of energy, and this will help detect an abnormal energy field."

"Have you ever recorded an abnormal energy field?"

"As a matter of fact, I have. In a supposedly haunted house, no less. Unfortunately, it had nothing to do with ghosts. The owner's microwave oven wasn't working properly."

"Ah," she said.

He looked at her. "Now you're stealing my lines."

"It's all I could come up with. Sorry."

"It's okay. I'll share."

"Why do you have all this stuff?"

"Because," he said, "when I debunk the possibility of ghosts, I have to use everything that paranormal investigators use. I don't want to be accused of missing anything, and these people have their rules. Besides, it seems more impressive when someone reads that you've used an electromagnetic detector. They think you know what you're doing."

"And do you?"

"Sure. I told you, I have the official handbook."

She laughed. "So what can I help you with? Do you need me to help carry any of this stuff?"

"We'll be using all of it. But if you consider this to be manly work, I'm sure I can handle it on my own while you do your nails or something."

She pulled out one of the camcorders, slung it over her shoulder, and grabbed another one.

"Okay, Mr. Manly, which way?"

"That depends. Where do you think we should set up? Since you've seen the lights, maybe you have some ideas."

She nodded in the direction of the magnolia tree, where she'd been heading when he'd first seen her in the cemetery.

"Over there," she said. "That's where you'll see the lights."

It was the spot directly in front of Riker's Hill, though the hill was hidden in the fog.

"Do they always appear in the same spot?"

"I have no idea. But that's where they were when I saw them."

Over the next hour, as Lexie filmed him with one of the camcorders, Jeremy set everything up. He arranged the other three video recorders in a large triangular pattern, mounting them on tripods, attaching special filtering lenses to two of them, and adjusting the zoom until the entire area was overlapped. He tested the laser remotes, then began setting up the audio equipment. Four microphones were attached to nearby trees, and a fifth was placed near the center, which was where he'd set the electromagnetic and radiation detectors, as well as the central recorder.

As he was making sure everything worked properly, he heard Lexie calling out to him.

"Hey, how do I look?"

He turned and saw her wearing the night-vision goggles and looking something like a bug.

"Very sexy," he said. "I think you've definitely found your style."

"These things are neat. I can see everything out here."

"Anything I should be worried about?"

"Aside from a couple of hungry cougars and bears, you seem to be alone."

"Well, I'm almost done here. All I still have to do is spread some flour and unwind the thread."

"Flour? Like baking flour?"

"It's to make sure no one tampers with the equipment. The flour is so I can check for footprints, and the thread will let me know if anyone else approaches."

"That's very clever. But you know we're alone out here, right?"

"You can never be certain," he said.

"Oh, I'm certain. But you just do your thing, and I'll keep the camera pointed in the right direction. You're doing great, by the way."

He laughed as he opened the bag of flour and began pouring, circling the cameras with a thin white layer. He did the same around the microphones and other equipment, then tied the thread to a branch and formed a large square around the whole area as if closing off a crime scene. He ran a second thread about two feet lower and then hung small bells on the thread. When he finally finished, he made his way back to Lexie.

"I didn't know there was so much to do," she said.

"I guess you're developing a whole new level of respect for me, huh?"

"Not really. I was actually just trying to make conversation."

He smiled before nodding toward the car. "I'm going to go hit the lights on the car. And hopefully, none of this will have been in vain."

When he shut off the engine, the cemetery turned black and he waited for his eyes to adjust. Unfortunately, they didn't, the cemetery proving to be darker than a cave. After feeling his way back to the gate like a blind spelunker, he stumbled on an exposed root just inside the entrance and nearly fell.

"Can I have my night-vision goggles?" he shouted.

"No," he heard her respond. "Like I said, these things are neat. And besides, you're doing fine."

"But I can't see anything."

"You're clear for the next few steps. Just walk forward."

He moved forward slowly with his arms outstretched before stopping.

"Now what?"

"You're in front of a crypt, so move to your left." She sounded way too amused by this, Jeremy thought.

"You forgot to say 'Simon says.'"

"Do you want my help or not?"

"I really want my goggles," he almost pleaded.

"You'll have to come and get them."

"You could always come and get me instead."

"I could, but I won't. It's much more fun to see you wandering around like a zombie. Now move to your left. I'll tell you when to stop."

The game proceeded this way until he finally found his way back to her side. As he took a seat, she slipped the goggles off, grinning.

"Here you go," she said.

"Gee, thanks."

"No problem. I'm glad I could help."

For the next half hour or so, Lexie and Jeremy rehashed the events of the party. It was too dark for Jeremy to read Lexie's face, but he liked how close she felt in the enveloping darkness.

Changing the topic of conversation, he said, "Tell me about the time that you saw the lights. I heard everyone else's story tonight."

Though her features were nothing but shadows, Jeremy had the impression that she was being drawn back in time to something she wasn't sure she wanted to remember.

"I was eight years old," she said, her voice soft. "For whatever reason, I'd started having nightmares about my parents. Doris kept their wedding picture on the wall, and that was the way they always looked in the dream: Mom in her wedding dress and Dad in his tuxedo. Only this time, they were trapped in their car after it had fallen in the river. It was like I was looking at them from outside the car, and I could see the panic and fear on both their faces as water slowly filled the car. And my mom would get this real sad expression on her face, like she knew it was the end, and all of a sudden, the car would start sinking faster, and I'd be watching it descend from above."

Her voice was strangely devoid of emotion, and she sighed.

"I'd wake up screaming. I don't know how many times it happened—it just sort of blurs together now in one big memory—but it must have gone on long enough for Doris to realize it wasn't just a phase. I suppose other parents might have taken me to a therapist, but Doris . . . well, she just woke me up late one night and told me to get dressed and put on a warm jacket, and the next thing I knew she'd brought me here. She told me she was going to show me something wonderful . . .

"I remember it was a night like tonight, so Doris held my hand to keep me from stumbling. We wound our way among the tombstones and then sat for a while until the lights came. They looked almost alive—everything got really bright . . . until the lights just faded away. And then we went home."

He could almost hear her shrug. "Even though I was young, I knew then what had happened, and when I got back home, I couldn't sleep, because I'd just seen the ghosts of my parents. It was like they'd come to visit me. After that, I stopped having the nightmares."

Jeremy was silent.

She leaned closer. "Do you believe me?"

"Yes," he said, "actually, I do. Your story would have been the one that I remembered from tonight, even if I didn't know you."

"Well, just so you know, I'd rather my experience not end up in your article."

"Are you sure? You can be famous."

"I'll pass. I'm witnessing firsthand how a little fame can ruin a person."

He laughed. "Since this is off the record, then, can I ask if your memories were part of the reason you agreed to come out here tonight? Or was it because you wanted to enjoy my scintillating company?"

"Well, it definitely wasn't the latter," she said, but even as she said it, she knew it was. She thought he realized it as well, but in the brief pause that followed her remark, she sensed that her words had stung.

"I'm sorry," she said.

"It's okay," he said, waiving it off. "Remember, I had five older brothers. Insults were mandatory in a family like ours, so I'm used to it."

She straightened up. "Okay, to answer your question . . . maybe I did want to see the lights again. To me, they've always been a source of comfort."

Jeremy picked up a twig from the ground and tossed it aside.

"Your grandmother was a smart lady. Doing what she did, I mean."

"She *is* a smart lady."

"I stand corrected," he said, and just then Lexie shifted beside him, as if straining to see into the distance.

"I think you may want to turn your equipment on," she said.

"Why?"

"Because they're coming. Can't you tell?"

He was about to make a crack about being "ghostproof" when he realized that he could see not only Lexie but the cameras in the distance. And, he noticed, the route to the car. It *was* getting lighter out here, wasn't it?

"Hello," she prompted. "You're missing your big chance here."

He squinted, trying to make sure his eyes weren't playing tricks on him, then aimed the remote at each of the three cameras. In the distance, the red power lights switched on. Still, it was all he could do to process the fact that something actually seemed to be happening.

He glanced around, looking for passing cars or illuminated houses, and when he looked toward the cameras again, he decided that he definitely wasn't seeing things. Not only were the cameras visible, but he could see the electromagnetic detector in the center of his triangle as well. He reached for his night-vision goggles.

"You won't need those," she said.

He put them on, anyway, and the world took on a greenish phosphorescent glow. As the light grew in intensity, the fog began to curve and swirl, assuming different shapes.

He glanced at his watch: it was 11:44:10 p.m., and he made a note to remember it. He wondered if the moon had suddenly risen—he doubted it, but he would check on the phase when he got back to his room at Greenleaf.

But these were secondary thoughts. The fog, as Lexie had predicted, continued to brighten, and he lowered the goggles for a moment, noting the difference between the images. It was still growing brighter outside, but the change seemed more significant with the goggles. He couldn't wait to compare the videotaped images side by side. But right now all he could do was stare straight ahead, this time without the goggles.

Holding his breath, he watched as the fog in front of them grew more silver by the moment, before changing to a pale yellow, then an opaque white, and finally an almost blinding brightness. For a moment, just a moment, most of the cemetery was visible—like a football field illuminated before the big game—and portions of the foggy light began to churn in a small circle before suddenly spreading outward from the cluster, like an exploding star. For an instant, Jeremy imagined that he saw the shapes of people or things, but just then the light began to recede, as if being pulled on a string, back toward the center, and even before he realized the lights had vanished, the cemetery had turned black once more.

He blinked, as if to reassure himself that it had really happened, then checked his watch again. The whole event had taken twenty-two seconds from start to finish. Though he knew he should get up to check the equipment, there was a brief instant in which all he could do was stare at the spot where the ghosts of Cedar Creek had made their appearance.

Fraud, honest mistakes, and coincidence were the most common explanations for events regarded as supernatural, and up to this point, every one of Jeremy's investigations into such events had fallen into one of these three categories. The first tended to be the most prevalent explanation in situations where someone stood to profit somehow. William Newell, for instance, who claimed to find the petrified remains of a giant on his farm in New York in 1869, a statue known as the Cardiff Giant, fell into this category. Timothy Clausen, the spirit guide, was another example.

But fraud also encompassed those who simply wanted to see how many people they could fool, not for money, but just to see if it was possible. Doug Bower and Dave Chorley, the English farmers who created the phenomenon known as crop circles, were one such example; the surgeon who photographed the Loch Ness Monster in 1933 was another. In both cases, the hoax was originally perpetrated as a practical joke, but public interest escalated so quickly that confessions were rendered difficult.

Honest mistakes, on the other hand, were simply that. A weather balloon is mistaken for a flying saucer, a bear is mistaken for Bigfoot, an archaeological find is discovered to have been moved to its current location hundreds or thousands of years after its original deposition. In cases like these, the witness has seen something, but the mind extrapolates the vision into something else entirely.

Coincidence accounted for nearly everything else and was simply a function of mathematical probability. As unlikely as an event might seem, as long as it is theoretically possible, it more than likely would happen sometime, somewhere, to someone. Take, for instance, Robert Morgan's novel *Futility*, published in 1898—fourteen years before the *Titanic* sailed—which told the story of the largest and grandest passenger liner in existence that sailed on its maiden voyage from Southampton, only to be ripped apart by an iceberg, and whose rich and famous passengers were largely doomed in the icy North Atlantic because of a lack of lifeboats. The name of the ship, ironically, was *Titan*.

But what happened here didn't fall neatly into any of those categories. The lights struck Jeremy as neither fraud nor coincidence, and yet it wasn't an honest mistake, either. There was a ready explanation somewhere, but as he sat in the cemetery in the rush of the moment, he had no idea what it could be.

Through it all, Lexie had remained seated and hadn't said a word. "Well?" she finally asked. "What do you think?"

"I don't know yet," Jeremy admitted. "I saw something, that's for sure."

"Have you ever seen anything like it?"

"No," he said. "Actually, this is the first time I've ever seen anything that even remotely struck me as mysterious."

"It is amazing, isn't it?" she said, her voice soft. "I'd almost forgotten how pretty it could be. I've heard about the aurora borealis, and I've often wondered whether it looked like this."

Jeremy didn't respond. In his mind's eye, he re-created the lights, thinking that the way they'd risen in intensity reminded him of headlights of oncoming cars as they rounded a curve. They simply had to be caused by a moving vehicle of some sort, he thought. He looked toward the road, waiting for passing cars, but not completely surprised at their absence.

Lexie let him sit in silence for a minute and could almost see the wheels turning. Finally, she leaned forward and poked him in the arm to get his attention again.

"Well?" she asked. "What do we do next?"

Jeremy shook his head, coming back to her.

"Is there a highway around here? Or another major road?"

"Just the one you came in on that runs through town."

"Huh," he said, frowning.

"What? No 'ah' this time?"

"Not yet," he said. "I'm getting there, though." Despite the inky darkness, he thought he could see her smirking. "Why do I get the impression that you already know what's causing them?"

"I don't know," she said, playing coy. "Why do you?"

"It's just a feeling I get. I'm good at reading people. A guy named Clausen taught me his secrets."

She laughed. "Well, then, you already know what I think."

She gave him a moment to figure it out before she leaned forward. Her eyes looked darkly seductive, and though his mind should have been elsewhere, he again flashed on an image of her at the party and how beautiful she had been.

"Don't you remember my story?" she whispered. "It was my parents. They probably wanted to meet you."

Perhaps it was the orphaned tone she used when she said it—simultaneously sad and resilient—but as a tiny lump formed in his throat, it was all he could do not to take her in his arms right then and there, in the hope of holding her close forever.

Half an hour later, after loading up the equipment, they arrived back at her house.

Neither of them had said much on the way home, and when they reached her door, Jeremy realized that he'd spent far more time thinking about Lexie as he drove than he had about the lights. He didn't want the evening to end, not yet.

Hesitating before the door, Lexie brought a hand to her mouth, stifling a yawn before breaking into an embarrassed laugh.

"Sorry about that," she said. "I'm not normally up this late."

"It's okay," he said, meeting her gaze. "I had a great time tonight."

"So did I," she said, meaning it.

He took a small step forward, and when she realized he was thinking of trying to kiss her, she pretended to fiddle with something on her jacket.

"I suppose I should call it a night, then," she said, hoping he took the hint.

"Are you sure?" he asked. "We could watch the tapes inside, if you'd like. Maybe you could help me figure out what the lights really are."

She looked away, her expression wistful.

"Please don't ruin this for me, okay?" she whispered.

"Ruin what?"

"This . . . everything . . ." She closed her eyes, trying to collect her thoughts. "Both you and I know why you want to come inside, but even if I wanted you to, I wouldn't let you. So please don't ask."

"Did I do something wrong?"

"No. You didn't do anything wrong. I had a great day, a wonderful day. Actually, it's the best day I've had in a long time."

"Then what is it?"

"You've been giving me the full-court press since you got here, and we know what'll happen if I let you through that door. But you're leaving. And when you do, I'll be the one who's hurt afterward. So why start something you have no intention of finishing?"

With someone else, with anyone else, he would have said something flippant or changed the subject until he figured out another way to get through her door. But as he looked at her on the porch, he couldn't form the words. Nor, strangely, did he want to.

"You're right," he admitted. He forced a smile. "Let's call it a night. I should probably go find out where those lights are coming from, anyway."

For a moment, she wasn't sure she'd heard him correctly, but when he took a small step backward, she caught his eye.

"Thank you," she said.

"Good night, Lexie."

She nodded, and after an awkward pause, she turned toward the door. Jeremy took that as his signal to leave, and he stepped off the porch as Lexie took her keys from her jacket pocket. She was sliding the key into the door when she heard his voice behind her.

"Hey, Lexie?" he called out.

In the fog, he was nothing but a blur.

"Yes?"

"I know you may not believe it, but the last thing I want to do is hurt you or do anything that would make you regret that we've met."

Though she smiled briefly at his comment, she turned away without a word. The lack of response spoke volumes, and for the first time in his life, Jeremy was not only disappointed in himself but suddenly wished he were someone else entirely.

Eleven

· · · · ❖ · · · ·

Birds were chirping, the fog had begun to thin, and a raccoon scurried across the bungalow porch when Jeremy's cell phone rang. The harsh gray light of early morning passed through the torn curtains, smacking him in the eye like a prizefighter's punch.

A quick glance at the clock showed it was 8:00 a.m., way too early to talk to anyone, especially after pulling an all-nighter. He was getting too old for nights like that, and he winced before groping for the phone.

"This better be important," he grumbled.

"Jeremy? Is that you? Where have you been? Why haven't you called? I've been trying to reach you!"

Nate, Jeremy thought, closing his eyes again. Good God, Nate.

Meanwhile, Nate was going on. He had to be a long-lost relative of the mayor, Jeremy thought. Put these two in a room, hook them up to a generator while they talked, and they could power Brooklyn for a month.

"You said you were going to keep in touch!"

Jeremy forced himself to sit upright on the side of his bed, though his body was aching.

"Sorry, Nate," he said. "I've just been tied up, and the reception isn't too good down here."

"You've got to keep me filled in! I tried calling you all day yesterday, but I kept getting put through to your voice mail. You can't imagine what's going on. I've got producers hounding me left and right, coming to me for ideas about what you might want to discuss. And things are really moving. One of them suggested that you do a piece on these high-protein diets. You know, the ones that tell you that it's okay to eat all the bacon and steaks you want and still lose weight."

Jeremy shook his head, trying to keep up.

"Wait? What are you talking about? Who wants me to talk about what diet?"

"GMA. Who did you think I was talking about? Of course, I said I'd have to get back to them, but I think you'd be a natural at this."

The man sometimes gave Jeremy a headache, and he rubbed his forehead.

"I have no interest in talking about a new diet, Nate. I'm a science journalist, not Oprah."

"So you put your own spin on it. That's what you do, right? And diets have something to do with chemistry and science. Am I right or am I right? Hell, you know I'm right, and you know me—when I'm right, I'm right. And besides, I'm just tossing out ideas here—"

"I saw the lights," Jeremy interrupted.

"I mean, if you have something better, then we can talk. But I'm flying blind here, and this diet thing might be a way to get your foot—"

"I saw the lights," Jeremy said again, raising his voice.

This time Nate heard him. "You mean the lights in the cemetery?" he asked.

Jeremy continued to rub his temples. "Yeah, those lights."

"When? Why didn't you call me? This gives me something to run with. Oh, *please* tell me you got it on film."

"I did, but I haven't seen the tapes yet, so I don't know how they turned out."

"So the lights are for real?"

"Yeah. But I think I found out where they're coming from, too."

"So it's not real . . ."

"Listen, Nate, I'm tired, so listen for a second, will you? I went to the cemetery last night and saw the lights. And to be honest, I can see why some people consider them to be ghosts, because of the way they appear. There's a pretty interesting legend attached to them, and the town even has a tour planned for the weekend to capitalize on it. But after I left the cemetery, I went looking for the source and I'm pretty sure I found it. All I have to do is figure out how and why it happens when it does, but I have some ideas about that, too, and hopefully, I'll have it figured out by later today."

Nate, for a rare moment, had nothing to say. Like the trained professional he was, however, he recovered quickly.

"Okay, okay, give me a second to figure out the best way to play this. I'm thinking of the television folks here . . ."

Who else would he be thinking of? Jeremy wondered.

"Okay, how's this?" Nate was going on. "We open with the legend itself, sort of setting the scene. Misty cemetery, a close-up on some of the graves, maybe a quick shot of a black raven looking ominous, you talking in voice-over . . ."

The man was the master of Hollywood clichés, and Jeremy glanced at the clock again, thinking it was way too early for this.

"I'm tired, Nate. How about this? You think about it and let me know later, okay?"

"Yeah, yeah. I can do that. That's what I'm here for, right? To make your life easier. Hey, do you think I should call Alvin?"

"I'm not sure yet. Let me see the tapes first, and then I'll talk to Alvin, and we'll see what he thinks."

"Right," he said, his voice rising in enthusiasm. "Good plan, good idea! And this is great news! A genuine ghost story! They're going to love this! I told you they were hot and heavy about the idea, didn't I? Believe me, I told them you'd come through with this story and that you wouldn't be interested in talking about the latest diet fad. But now that we have a bargaining chip, they're going to go crazy. I can't wait to tell them, and listen, I'll be calling you in just a couple of hours, so make sure you keep your phone on. Things could be moving quickly . . ."

"Good-bye, Nate. I'll talk to you later."

Jeremy rolled back onto the bed and pulled the pillow over his head, but finding it impossible to fall back to sleep, he groaned as he got up and made his way to the bathroom, doing his best to ignore the stuffed creatures that seemed to be watching his every move. Still, he was getting used to them, and as he undressed, he hung his towel on the outstretched paws of a badger, thinking he might as well take advantage of the animal's convenient pose.

Hopping into the shower, he turned the water as far as it would go and stayed under the single jet for twenty minutes, until his skin was pruned. Only then did he begin to feel alive again. Sleeping less than two hours would do that to a person.

After throwing on his jeans, he grabbed the tapes and got in his car. The fog hung over the road like evaporating dry ice on a concert stage, and the sky had the same ugly tones as it had the day before, making him suspect that the lights would appear again tonight, which not only boded well for the tourists this weekend but also meant that he should probably call Alvin. Even if the tapes were okay, Alvin was magic with a camera, and he'd capture images that would no doubt make Nate's finger swell up from making frantic calls.

His first step, though, was to see what he'd caught on camera, if only to see that he'd captured *something*. Not surprisingly, Greenleaf didn't have a VCR, but he'd seen one in the rare-book room, and as he drove along the quiet road that led toward town, he wondered how Lexie would behave toward him when he got there. Would she go back to being distant and professional? Would the good feelings from their day together linger? Or would she simply remember their final moments on the porch, when he'd pushed too hard? He had no idea what was going to happen, even though he'd devoted much of the night to trying to figure it out.

Sure, he'd found the source of the light. Like most mysteries, it wasn't that hard to solve if you knew what to look for, and a quick check of a Web site sponsored by NASA eliminated the only other possibility. The moon, he'd learned, couldn't have been responsible for the lights. It was, in fact, a new moon, when the moon was hidden by the earth's shadow, and he had a sneaking suspicion that the mysterious lights only occurred in this particular phase. It would make sense: without moonlight, even the faintest traces of other light would become that much more obvious, especially when reflected in the water droplets of the fog.

But as he'd stood in the chilly air with the answer within reach, all he could think about was Lexie. It seemed impossible that he'd only met her two days earlier. It made no sense. Of course, Einstein had postulated that time was relative, and he supposed that could explain it. How did the old saying about relativity go? A minute with a beautiful woman would pass in an instant, while a minute with your hand placed against a hot burner would feel like an eternity? Yeah, he thought, that was it. Or close, anyway.

He again regretted his behavior on the porch, wishing for the hundredth time that he had taken her hint when he'd been thinking about kissing her. She'd made her feelings obvious and he'd ignored them. The regular Jeremy would have forgotten all about it already, shrugging the whole thing off as inconsequential. For some reason, this time it wasn't so easy.

Though he'd dated a lot and hadn't exactly become a hermit after Maria had left him, he had seldom done the spend-the-

whole-day-talking-with-someone thing. Usually, it was just dinner or drinks and enough flirtatious conversation to loosen the
inhibitions before the good part. Part of him knew it was time to
grow up when it came to dating, maybe even try to settle down
and live the sort of life his brothers did. His brothers readily con-
curred, and so, of course, did their wives. They were of the widely
shared opinion that he should get to know women before trying
to sleep with them, and one had gone so far as to set him up on a
date with a divorced neighbor who believed the same. Of course,
she'd declined a second date, in large part because of the pass he'd
made at her on the first. In the past few years, it just seemed easier to not get to know women too well, to keep them in the realm
of perpetual strangers, when they could still project hope and potential on him.

And that was the thing. There wasn't hope or potential. At
least, not for the sort of life his brothers and sisters-in-law believed in, or even, he suspected, the kind Lexie wanted. His divorce from Maria had proved that. Lexie was a small-town girl
with small-town dreams, and it wouldn't be enough to be faithful and responsible and to have things in common. Most women
wanted something else, a way of life he couldn't give them. Not
because he didn't want to, not because he was enamored of the
bachelor scene, but simply because it was impossible. Science
could answer a lot of questions, science could solve a lot of problems, but it couldn't change his particular reality. And the reality was that Maria had left him because he hadn't been, nor ever
could be, the kind of husband she'd wanted.

He admitted this painful truth to no one, of course. Not to his
brothers, not to his parents, not to Lexie. And usually, even in
quiet moments, not even to himself.

Though the library was open by the time he got there, Lexie
wasn't in yet, and he felt a pang of disappointment when he
pushed open the office door only to find the room empty. She'd

been in earlier, though: the rare-book room had been left unlocked, and when he turned on the light, he saw a note on the
desk, along with the topography maps he'd mentioned. The note
took only an instant to read:

I'm taking care of some personal things. Feel free to use the VCR.

Lexie

No mention of yesterday or last night, no mention of wanting to make arrangements to see him again. Not even an ac-
knowledgment above the signature. It wasn't exactly chilly as
far as notes went, but it didn't leave him with the warm fuzzies,
either.

Then again, he was probably reading too much into it. She
might have been in a rush this morning, or she might have kept
it short because she planned to be back soon. She did mention it
was personal, and with women, that could mean anything from a
doctor's appointment to shopping for a friend's birthday. There
was just no way to tell.

And besides, he had work to do, he told himself. Nate was
waiting and his career was on the line. Jeremy forced himself to
focus on chasing the tail end of the story.

The audio recorders had picked up no unusual sounds, and neither the microwave nor the electromagnetic detector had registered the slightest energy variances. The videotapes, however,
had picked up everything he'd seen the night before, and he
watched the images half a dozen times from every different angle.
The cameras with the special light-filtering capacity showed the
glowing fog most vividly. Though the tapes might have been
good enough to provide a small still to accompany his column,
they were far from television quality. When viewed in real time,
they had a sort of home-video feel to them, one that reminded
him of cheesy tapes offered in proof of other supernatural events.

He made a note to purchase a real camera, no matter how much celery his editor would eat because of it.

But even if the tapes weren't of the quality he'd hoped they would be, observing the way in which the lights had changed during the twenty-two seconds they were visible assured him again that he'd indeed found the answer. He popped the tapes out, perused the topography maps, and calculated the distance from Riker's Hill to the river. He compared the earlier photographs he'd taken of the cemetery to photos of the cemetery he found in books about the town's history, and came up with what he assumed to be a fairly accurate estimate regarding the rate that the cemetery was sinking. Though he wasn't able to find any more information on the legend of Hettie Doubilet—the records from that period shed no light on the subject—he made a call to the state water bureau concerning the underground reservoir in this part of the state, and one to the department of mines, which had information on the quarries that had been dug earlier in the century. After that, he tapped a few words into a search engine of the Internet looking for the timetables he needed, and finally, after being put on hold for ten minutes, he spoke to a Mr. Larsen at the paper mill, who was eager to help in any way he could.

And with that, all the pieces had finally come together in a way that he could definitively prove.

The truth had been in front of everyone all along. Like most mysteries, the solution had been simple, and it made him wonder why no one had realized it before. Unless, of course, someone had, which opened the door to another angle on the story.

Nate, no doubt, would be thrilled, but despite the morning's success, Jeremy felt little sense of accomplishment. Instead, all he thought about was the fact that Lexie wasn't around to either congratulate or tease him about it. Honestly, he didn't care how she'd react as long as she was here to react, and he rose from his seat to check her office again.

For the most part, it looked the same as it had the day before. Stacks of documents were still piled on her desk, books were scattered haphazardly, and the screen saver on her computer was etching and erasing colorful drawings. The answering machine, flashing with messages, sat next to a small potted plant.

Still, he couldn't shake the feeling that without Lexie, the room may as well have been completely empty.

Twelve

· · · · ❖ · · · ·

M y main man!" Alvin shouted into the receiver. "Life treating you good down south?"

Despite the static on Jeremy's cell phone, Alvin sounded remarkably chipper.

"I'm fine. I was calling to see if you'd still like to come on down and help me."

"I'm already gathering my gear," he answered, sounding out of breath. "Nate called me an hour ago and told me all about it. I'll meet you at Greenleaf later tonight—Nate made the reservation. But, anyway, my flight leaves in a couple of hours. And believe me, I can't wait. Another few days in this stuff, and I'll go crazy."

"What are you talking about?"

"Haven't you been reading the papers or watching the news?"

"Of course. I've yet to miss an issue of the *Boone Creek Weekly*."

"Huh?"

"Never mind," Jeremy said. "It's not important."

"Well, anyway, it's been an absolute blizzard since you left," Alvin informed him. "And I mean North Pole stuff, where even Rudolph's nose is worthless. Manhattan is practically buried. You got out of here just in time. Since you've left, this is the first day that flights are even close to being on schedule. I had to pull a few strings to even get the flight I did. How can you not know about this?"

As Alvin explained, Jeremy tapped his computer keys, calling up the Weather Channel on the Internet. On the national map, the Northeast was a blanket of white.

L-I-B, he thought. Who could have guessed?

"I guess I've been busy," he said.

"Hiding's more like it," Alvin said. "But I hope she's worth it."

"What are you talking about?"

"Don't bother pulling my chain. We're friends, remember? Nate's been in a panic because he can't reach you, you haven't been reading the papers, and you haven't been watching the news. We both know what that means. You always get like this when you meet someone new."

"Look, Alvin . . ."

"Is she pretty? I'll bet she's beautiful, right? You always strike gold. Makes me sick."

Jeremy hesitated before answering, then finally gave in. If Alvin was coming down, he'd learn soon enough, anyway.

"Yeah, she's pretty. But it's not what you think. We're just friends."

"I'm sure," he said, laughing. "But what you consider friends and what I consider friends are just a little different."

"Not this time," Jeremy said.

"Does she have a sister?" Alvin asked, ignoring the comment. "No."

"But she has friends, right? And I'm not interested in the ugly one, remember . . ."

Jeremy felt his headache coming on again, and his tone took on an edge. "I'm not in the mood for this, okay?"

Alvin paused on the other end. "Hey, what's going on here?" he asked. "I'm just joking around."

"Some of your jokes aren't funny."

"You like her, don't you? I mean, you like her a lot."

"I told you that we're just friends."

"I can't believe this. You're falling in love."

"No," Jeremy said.

"Hey, pal, I know you, so don't try to deny it. And I think that's great. Weird but great. But unfortunately, I have to cut this short if I'm going to catch my flight. Traffic is miserable, as you can probably imagine. But I can't wait to see the woman who finally tamed you."

"She didn't tame me," Jeremy protested. "Why aren't you listening to me?"

"I am listening," he said. "I just hear the things you're not saying."

"Yeah, whatever. When will you be here?"

"I'm guessing around seven tonight. I'll see you then. And, by the way, say hello from me, okay? Tell her I'm dying to meet her *and* her friend . . ."

Jeremy ended the call before Alvin had a chance to finish, and, as if to underscore the point, he shoved his phone back into his pocket.

No wonder he'd been keeping it turned off. It must have been a subconscious decision, one based on the fact that both his friends had a tendency to be irritating at times. First, there was Nate the Energizer Bunny and his never-ending search for fame. And now this.

Alvin didn't have a clue as to what he was talking about. They may have been friends, they may have spent a lot of Friday nights staring at women over beers, they may have talked about life for hours, and deep down, Alvin may have honestly believed that he was right. But he wasn't, simply because he couldn't be.

The facts, after all, spoke for themselves. For one thing, Jeremy hadn't loved a woman in years, and though it had been a long time, he could still remember how he'd felt back then. He was certain that he would have recognized the feeling again, and frankly, he didn't. And in light of the fact that he'd just met the woman, the whole idea seemed preposterous. Even his highly emotional Italian mother didn't believe that true love could blossom overnight. Like his brothers and sisters-in-law, she wanted nothing more for him than to marry and start a family, but if he showed up at her doorstep and said that he'd met someone two days ago and knew she was the one for him, his mother would smack him with a broom, curse in Italian, and drag him to church, sure that he had some serious sins that needed confessing.

His mother knew men. She'd married one, raised six boys, and was sure she'd seen it all. She knew exactly how men tended to think when it came to women, and although she relied on common sense instead of science, she was completely accurate in her judgment that love wasn't possible in just a couple of days. Love could be *set in motion* quickly, but true love needed time to grow into something strong and enduring. Love was, above all, about commitment and dedication and a belief that spending years with a certain person would create something greater than the sum of what the two could accomplish separately. Only time, however, could show whether you'd been accurate in your judgment.

Lust, meanwhile, could happen almost instantly, and that's why his mother would have smacked him. To her, the description of lust was simple: two people learn they're compatible, attraction grows, and the ancient instinct to preserve the species kicks in. All of which meant that while lust was a possibility, he couldn't *love* Lexie.

So there it was. Case closed. Alvin was wrong, Jeremy was right, and once again, the truth had set him free.

He smiled with satisfaction for a moment before his brow began to wrinkle.

And yet . . .

Well, the thing was, it didn't quite feel like lust, either. Not this morning, anyway. Because even more than wanting to hold her or kiss her, he simply ached to see her again. To spend time with her. To talk to her. He wanted to watch her roll her eyes when he said something ridiculous, he wanted to feel her hand on his arm like the day before. He wanted to watch her nervously tuck strands of hair behind her ear, and listen as she told him about her childhood. He wanted to ask her about her dreams and hopes for the future, to know her secrets.

But that wasn't the strange part. The strange part was that he couldn't perceive an ulterior motive for his impulses. Granted, he wouldn't say no if she wanted to sleep with him, but even if she didn't, just spending time with her would be enough for now.

Deep down, he simply lacked an ulterior motive. He'd already made the decision that he would never again put Lexie in the position he had the night before. It had taken a lot of courage, he thought, to say what she had. More courage than he had. After all, in the two days they'd seen each other, he hadn't even been able to tell her that he'd been married before.

But if it couldn't be love and it didn't feel like lust, what was it? Like? Did he *like* her? Of course, he did, but that word didn't quite capture his feelings, either. It was a little too . . . vague and soft around the edges. People *liked* ice cream. People *liked* to watch television. It meant nothing, and it didn't come close to explaining why, for the first time, he felt the urge to tell someone else the truth about his divorce. His brothers didn't know the truth, nor did his parents. But, for whatever reason, he couldn't shake the realization that he wanted Lexie to know; and right now she was nowhere to be found.

Two minutes later, Jeremy's phone rang, and he recognized the number on the screen of his cell phone. Though not in the mood, he knew he had to answer, or the man would probably burst an artery.

"Hey there," Jeremy said. "What's happening?"

"Jeremy!" Nate shouted. Through the static, Jeremy could barely hear him. "Great news! You can't believe how busy I've been.

It's been a madhouse! We've got a conference call with ABC at two o'clock!"

"Great," he said.

"Hold on. I can't hear you. This reception is terrible."

"Sorry . . ."

"Jeremy! Are you still there? You're breaking up!"

"Yeah, Nate, I'm here . . ."

"Jeremy?" Nate shouted, oblivious to his answer. "Listen, if you can still hear me, you've got to use a public phone and call me here. At two o'clock! Your career depends on this! Your entire future depends on this!"

"Yeah, I got it."

"Oh, this is ridiculous," he said, almost as if talking to himself. "I can't hear a thing you're saying. Hit a button if you caught everything I'm saying."

Jeremy pressed the 6.

"Great! Fantastic! Two o'clock! And be yourself! Except for the sarcastic part, I mean. These people seem pretty uptight . . ."

Jeremy hung up the phone, wondering how long it would take for Nate to realize that he wasn't on the line anymore.

Jeremy waited. Then waited some more.

He paced the library, he wandered past Lexie's office, he peeked out the window for signs of her car, feeling a growing sense of uneasiness as the minutes ticked by. It was just a hunch, but nothing about her absence this morning seemed right. Nonetheless, he did his best to convince himself otherwise. He told himself that she would come in eventually, and later he'd probably laugh about his ridiculous feelings. Still, now that he was finished with his research—other than possibly finding anecdotes in some of the diaries, which he hadn't finished going through yet—he wasn't sure what to do next.

Greenleaf was out—he didn't want to spend any more time there than he had to, even though he was beginning to like the towel hangers. Alvin wouldn't be here until the evening, and the last thing he wanted was to wander around town, where he might be corralled by Mayor Gherkin. Nor did he want to hang around the library all day.

He really wished Lexie had been a bit more specific in her note about when she might show up. Or even where she'd gone. He couldn't make sense of the note even after reading it a third time. Had the lack of detail been inadvertent or something she'd done on purpose? Neither possibility made him feel any better. He had to get out of here; it was hard not to think the worst.

After gathering his things, he went downstairs and paused at the reception desk. The elderly volunteer was buried in a book. Standing before her, he cleared his throat. When she looked up, she beamed. "Well, Mr. Marsh!" she said. "I saw you come in earlier, but you looked preoccupied, so I just let you go. What can I do for you?"

Jeremy adjusted the notes beneath his arm, attempting to sound as casual as he could.

"Do you know where Ms. Darnell is? I got a note that said that she was out, and I was just wondering when she might be coming in."

"That's funny," she said, "she was here when I came in." She checked the calendar on her desk. "She doesn't have any meetings scheduled and I don't see any other appointments. Have you checked her office? Maybe she's locked herself in. She does that quite a bit when the work starts piling up."

"I have," he said. "Would you know if she happens to have a cell phone where I can reach her?"

"She doesn't—that I know for sure. She's told me that when she's off and about, the last thing she wants is for someone to find her."

"Well . . . thanks, anyway."

"Is there anything I could help you with?"

"No," he said, "I just needed her help on my story."

"I'm sorry I can't be more help to you."

"That's okay."

"Have you thought about checking Herbs? She might be helping Doris get things ready for the weekend. Or maybe she went home. The thing about Lexie is that you can never predict anything about her. I've learned not to be surprised by anything she does."

"Thanks, anyway. But if she comes in, will you tell her that I was looking for her?"

Feeling more agitated than ever, Jeremy left the library.

Before heading to Herbs, Jeremy swung by Lexie's house, noting the drawn curtains in the window and the fact that her car was gone. Although there was nothing out of the ordinary about the scene before him, it again struck him as *wrong* somehow, and the uneasiness only deepened as he retraced the roads back to town.

The morning rush at Herbs had died down, and the restaurant was in the twilight period between breakfast and lunch, when things were cleaned up from the last rush and preparations were being made for the next. The staff outnumbered the remaining patrons four to one, and it took only a moment to see that Lexie wasn't here, either. Rachel was wiping a table and waved a towel when she saw him.

"Morning, darlin'," she said, approaching. "It's a little late, but I'm sure we can whip up some breakfast if you're hungry."

Jeremy slipped his keys into his pocket. "No, thanks," he said. "I'm not that hungry. But would you happen to know if Doris is around? I'd love to talk to her if she has a moment."

"Back for her again, huh?" She smiled and nodded over her shoulder. "She's in the back. I'll tell her you're here. And by the way, that was quite a party last night. People were talking about you all morning, and the mayor dropped by to see if you'd recovered. I think he was disappointed you weren't here."

"I enjoyed it."

"Do you want some coffee or tea while you're waiting?"

"No, thanks," he answered.

She disappeared into the back, and a minute later, Doris emerged, wiping her hands on her apron. Her cheek was smudged with dough, but even from a distance, he could see the bags under her eyes, and she seemed to be moving more slowly than usual.

"Sorry about looking like this," she said, gesturing at herself. "You caught me mixing dough. Last night set me back a little for the weekend, and it's going to take a bit to catch up before the crowds tomorrow."

Remembering what Lexie had told him, he asked, "How many people are you expecting this weekend?"

"Who knows?" she said. "Usually, a couple of hundred come in for the tour, sometimes a bit more. The mayor was hoping for close to a thousand for the tour this year, but it's always a wild guess for me to figure out how many will come in for breakfast and lunch."

"If the mayor's right, that's quite a jump this year."

"Well, take his estimate for what it's worth. Tom has a tendency to be overly optimistic, but he's got to create a sense of urgency to get everything ready in time. And besides, even if people don't do the tour, folks still like to come to the parade on Saturday. The Shriners will be here zooming around with their cars, you know, and kids love to see them. And there'll be a petting zoo, too, this year, which is new."

"Sounds great."

"It would be better if it wasn't in the middle of winter. The Pamlico Festival always draws the biggest crowds, but that's in June, and we usually have one of those traveling carnivals set up shop that weekend. Now, those are weekends that can make or break a business. Talk about stress. It's about ten times what I'm going through now."

He smiled. "Life here never ceases to amaze me."

"Don't knock it till you try it. I have a funny feeling you'd love it here."

She sounded almost as if she was testing him, and he wasn't quite sure how to respond. Behind them, Rachel cleared a table while jawing with the cook, who was half a room away. Both were laughing at something one or the other had said.

"But, anyway," Doris said, letting him off the hook, "I'm glad you came by. Lexie mentioned that she told you about my notebook. She warned me that you probably wouldn't believe a word of it, but you're welcome to look through it if you'd like. It's in my office in the back."

"I'd like that," he said. "She told me you kept quite a record."

"I did my best. It's probably not up to your standards, but then again, I never thought anyone but me would read it."

"I'm sure I'll be amazed. But speaking of Lexie, that's part of the reason I came by. Have you seen her around? She wasn't at the library today."

She nodded. "She came by the house this morning. That's how I knew to bring my book. She told me you two saw the lights last night."

"We did."

"And?"

"They were amazing, but like you said, they weren't ghosts."

She looked at him, satisfied. "And I take it that you've already figured everything out, or you wouldn't be here otherwise."

"I think so."

"Good for you," she said. She motioned over her shoulder. "I'm sorry I can't chat more now, but I'm kind of busy, so let me get my notebook for you. Who knows, maybe you'll want to do a story about my amazing powers next."

"You never know," he said. "I just might."

As Jeremy watched her vanish into the kitchen, he wondered about their conversation. It had been perfectly pleasant but curiously impersonal. And he noticed that Doris hadn't really responded to his question about Lexie's whereabouts. Nor had she even ventured a guess, which seemed to suggest that—for whatever reason—she viewed the subject of Lexie as suddenly off-limits. Which wasn't good. He looked up to see her approaching again. She wore the same pleasant smile as she had before, but this time it gave him a sinking feeling in his stomach.

"Now, if you have any questions about this," she said, handing the notebook over, "don't hesitate to call. And feel free to make copies if you want, but bring this back before you leave. It's pretty special to me."

"I'll do that," he promised.

She remained standing silently before him, and Jeremy got the impression that it was her way of telling him their conversation was at an end. He, on the other hand, wasn't about to give up so easily.

"Oh, one more thing," he said.

"Yes?"

"Would it be okay if I return the notebook to Lexie? If I happen to see her today?"

"That's fine," she said. "But I'll be here, too, just in case."

As he caught her obvious meaning, he felt his stomach sink even more.

"Did she say anything about me?" he asked. "When you saw her this morning?"

"Not much. However, she did say that you'd probably be coming by."

"Did she seem okay?"

"Lexie," she began slowly, as if choosing her words carefully, "is hard to read sometimes, so I'm not sure I can answer that. But I'm sure she'll be okay, if that's what you're asking."

"Was she angry with me?"

"No, that I can tell you. She definitely wasn't angry."

Waiting for more, Jeremy said nothing. In the silence Doris took a long breath. For the first time since they'd met, he noticed her age in the lines around her eyes.

"I like you, Jeremy, you know that," she said, her voice soft. "But you're putting me on the spot. What you have to understand is that I have certain loyalties, and Lexie is one of them."

"Which means what?" he asked, feeling his throat go dry.

"It means that I know what you want and what you're asking, but I can't answer your questions. What I can say is that if Lexie wanted you to know where she is, she would have told you."

"Will I see her again? Before I leave?"

"I don't know," she said. "I suppose that's up to her."

With that comment, his mind began to absorb the fact that she was really gone.

"I don't understand why she'd do something like this," he said. She gave a sad smile. "Yes," she said, "I think you do."

She was gone.

Like an echo, the words kept repeating themselves. Behind the wheel on the way to Greenleaf, Jeremy tried to analyze the facts with cool remove. He didn't panic. He never panicked. No matter how wild he'd felt, no matter how much he wanted to press Doris for information about Lexie's whereabouts or state of mind, he'd simply thanked her for her help and headed out to the car, as if he'd expected nothing different.

And besides, he reminded himself, there was no reason to panic. It wasn't as if something terrible had happened to her. It simply boiled down to the fact that she didn't want to see him again. Perhaps he should have seen it coming. He'd expected too much from her, even when she'd made it perfectly clear from the very beginning that she wasn't interested.

He shook his head, thinking it was no wonder that she'd left.

As modern as she was in some ways, she was traditional in others, and she was probably tired of having to deal with his transparent ploys. It was probably easier for her to simply leave town than to explain her reasoning to someone like him.

So where did that leave him? Either she would come back or she wouldn't. If she came back, no problem. But if she didn't . . . well, that's where reality started getting complicated. He could sit back and accept her decision, or he could try to track her down. If there was one thing he was good at, it was finding people. Using public records, friendly conversations, and the right sites on the Web, he'd learned how to follow a trail of bread crumbs to anyone's doorstep. He doubted, however, that any of that would be necessary. After all, she'd already given him the answer he needed, and he was sure he knew exactly where she'd gone. Which meant that he *could* handle this any way he wanted.

His thoughts stopped again.

The thing was, it didn't quite help him with the idea of what he *should* do. He reminded himself that he had a conference call in just a few hours, one with important ramifications for his career, and if he headed off to look for Lexie now, he doubted he'd be able to find a pay phone when he needed one. Alvin would be arriving later this evening—possibly the last of the foggy evenings—and though Alvin could handle the filming on his own tonight, they had to work together tomorrow. Not to mention that he needed a nap—he had another long night ahead, and even his bones were tired.

On the other hand, he didn't want everything to end like this. He wanted to see Lexie, he needed to see her. A voice in his head warned him not to let his emotions govern his actions, and rationally, he couldn't see how anything good could come of him traipsing off in search of her. Even if he found her, she'd probably ignore him or, worse, find it creepy. And in the meantime, Nate would probably have a stroke, Alvin would be stranded and furious, and his story and future career might just go down the tubes.

In the end, the decision was simple. Pulling his car into the spot in front of his cottage at Greenleaf, he nodded to himself. Putting it in those terms made his choice clear. After all, he hadn't spent the last fifteen years using logic and science without learning something along the way.

Now, he thought to himself, all he had to do was pack.

Thirteen

.....❖.....

Okay, she admitted, she was a coward.

It wasn't the easiest thing for her to own up to the fact that she'd run away, but hey, she wasn't exactly thinking clearly these past couple of days, and she could forgive herself for not being perfect. The truth was, if she had stayed around, things would have become even more complicated. It didn't matter that she liked him and that he liked her; she woke up this morning knowing that she had to end things before they went too far, and when she pulled in the sandy driveway out front, she knew she'd done the right thing by coming here.

The place wasn't much to look at. The old cottage was weathered and blended into the sea oats that surrounded it. The small, rectangular white-curtained windows were coated with salted mist, and the siding had streaks of gray, remnants from the fury of a dozen hurricanes. In some ways, she'd always considered the cottage a time capsule of sorts; most of the furniture was over twenty years old, the pipes groaned when she turned on the shower, and she had to light the stove burners with a match. But the memories of spending parts of her youth here never ceased to calm her, and after storing her bags and the groceries she'd picked up for the weekend, she'd opened the windows to air out the place. Then, grabbing a blanket, she settled into a rocker on the back porch, wanting nothing more than to watch the ocean. The steady roar of the waves was soothing, almost hypnotic, and when the sun broke through the clouds and beams of light stretched toward the water like individual fingers from above, she found herself holding her breath.

She did that every time she came here. The first time she'd seen the light breaking through this way was soon after her visit to the cemetery with Doris, when she was still a little girl, and she remembered thinking that her parents had found another way to make their presence known in her life. Like heaven-sent angels, she believed they were watching out for her, always present but never intervening, as if they felt that she would always make the right decisions.

For a long time, she'd needed to believe in such things, simply because she'd often felt alone. Her grandparents had been kind and wonderful, but as much as she loved them for their care and sacrifice, she'd never quite gotten used to the feeling of being different from her peers. Her friends' parents played softball on the weekends and looked youthful even in the soft morning light of church, an observation that made her wonder what, if anything, she was missing.

She couldn't talk to Doris about these things. Nor could she talk to Doris about the guilt she felt as a result. No matter how she phrased it, Doris's feelings would have been hurt, and even as a young girl, she'd known that.

But still, that feeling of being different had left its mark. Not only on her but on Doris as well, and it began to manifest itself during her teenage years. When Lexie would push the limits, Doris would frequently give in to avoid an argument, leaving Lexie with the belief that she could establish her own rules. She'd been a bit on the wild side when she was young, made mistakes and had too many regrets, but somehow turned serious during college. In her new, more mature incarnation, she embraced the idea that maturity meant thinking about risk long before you pondered the reward, and that success and happiness in life were as much about avoiding mistakes as making your mark in the world.

Last night, she knew, she'd almost made a mistake. She'd expected him to try to kiss her, and she was pleased by how resolute she'd been when he wanted to come inside.

She knew she'd hurt his feelings, and she was sorry for that. But what he probably didn't realize was that it wasn't until after he'd driven off that her heart had stopped pounding, because part of her *had* wanted to let him inside, no matter what it might have led to. She knew better, but she couldn't help it. Even worse, as she tossed and turned in her bed last night, she realized she might not have the strength to do the right thing again.

In all honesty, she should have seen it coming. As the evening had worn on, she found herself comparing Jeremy to both Avery and Mr. Renaissance, and to her surprise, Jeremy more than held his own. He had Avery's wit and sense of humor and Mr. Renaissance's intelligence and charm, but Jeremy seemed more comfortable with himself than either of them. Perhaps she should just chalk it up to the wonderful day she'd had, something that hadn't happened in a long time. When was the last time she'd had a spontaneous lunch? Or sat up on Riker's Hill? Or visited the cemetery after a party, when normally she would have gone straight to bed? No doubt the excitement and unpredictability had reminded her of how happy she'd been when she still believed that Avery and Mr. Renaissance were the men of her dreams.

But she'd been wrong then, just as she was wrong now. She knew Jeremy would solve the mystery today—okay, maybe it was just a *feeling*, but she was sure of it, since the answer was in one of the diaries and all he had to do was find it—and she had no doubt that he would have asked her to celebrate the solution with him. Had she been in town, the two of them would have spent most of the day together, and she didn't want that. Then again, deep down, it was exactly what she wanted, leaving her feeling more confused than she'd been in years.

Doris had intuited every bit of it this morning when Lexie stopped by, but that wasn't surprising. Lexie could feel the exhaustion around her own eyes and knew she looked like a wreck when she showed up out of the blue. After throwing a few days' worth of clothes into the suitcase, she'd left her house without showering; she didn't even attempt to explain what she was feeling. Even so, Doris had simply nodded when Lexie told her she had to go. Doris, tired though she was, seemed to understand that while she'd set the whole thing in motion, she hadn't anticipated what might happen as a result. That was the thing about premonitions; while they might be accurate in the short term, anything beyond that was impossible to know.

So she'd come here because she had to, if only to preserve her sanity, and she'd return to Boone Creek when things were back to normal. It wouldn't take long. In a couple of days, people would have stopped talking about the ghosts and the historic homes and the stranger in town, and the visiting tourists would be nothing but a memory. The mayor would be back on the golf course, Rachel would date the wrong sorts of men, and Rodney would probably find a way to accidentally bump into Lexie near the library, no doubt breathing a sigh of relief when he realized their relationship could go back to the way it once was.

Maybe it wasn't an exciting life, but it was her life, and she wasn't about to let anyone or anything upset the balance. In another place and time, she might have felt differently, but thinking along those lines was pointless now. As she continued to stare out over the water, she forced herself not to imagine what might have been.

On the porch, Lexie tugged the blanket tighter around her shoulders. She was a big girl and she'd get over him, just as she'd gotten over the others. She was certain about it. But even with the comfort of that realization, the roiling sea reminded her again of her feelings for Jeremy, and it took everything she had to keep her tears in check.

It had seemed relatively simple when Jeremy set out, and he'd rushed through his room at Greenleaf, making the necessary plans as he did so. Grab the map and his wallet, just in case. Leave the computer because he didn't need it. Ditto his notes. Put Doris's book in his leather satchel and bring it along. Write a note for Alvin and leave it at the front desk, despite the fact that Jed didn't seem too pleased about it. Make sure he had the recharger for his phone—and go.

He was in and out in less than ten minutes, on his way to Swan Quarter, where the ferry would take him to Ocracoke, a village in the Outer Banks. From there, he'd head north on Highway 12 to Buxton. He figured it was the route she would have taken, and all he had to do was follow the same path and he'd reach the place in just a couple of hours.

But while the drive to Swan Quarter had been an easy one on straight and empty roads, he'd found himself thinking about Lexie and pressed the accelerator harder, trying to ward off the jitters. But jitters were just another word for panic, and he didn't panic. He prided himself on that. Nonetheless, whenever he was forced to slow the car—in places like Belhaven and Leechville— he found himself tapping the wheel with his fingers and muttering under his breath.

It was an odd feeling for him, one that only grew stronger as he drew nearer to his destination. He couldn't explain it, but somehow he didn't want to analyze it. For one of the few times in his life, he was moving on autopilot, doing exactly the opposite of what logic demanded, thinking only about how she'd react when she saw him.

Just when he thought he was beginning to understand the reason for his odd behavior, Jeremy found himself at the ferry station staring at a thin, uniformed man who barely looked up from the magazine he was reading. The ferry to Ocracoke, he learned, didn't run with the same regularity as the one from Staten Island to Manhattan, and he'd missed the last departure of the day, which meant he could either come back tomorrow or cancel his plan altogether, neither of which he was willing to consider.

"Are you sure there's no other way that I can get to Hatteras Lighthouse?" he asked, feeling his heart pick up speed. "This is important."

"You could drive it, I suppose."

"How long would that take?"

"Depends on how fast you drive."

Obviously, Jeremy thought. "Let's say I drove fast."

The man shrugged, as if the whole topic bored him. "Five or six hours maybe. You'd have to head north till you get to Plymouth, then take 64 over Roanoke Island, then into Whalebone. From there, you head south into Buxton. The lighthouse is right there."

Jeremy checked his watch; it was already coming up on one o'clock; by the time he got there, Alvin would probably be pulling into Boone Creek. No good.

"Is there another place to catch the ferry?"

"There's one out of Cedar Island."

"Great. Where's that?"

"It's about three hours in the other direction. But again, you'd have to wait until tomorrow morning."

Over the man's shoulder, he saw a poster displaying the various lighthouses of North Carolina. Hatteras, the grandest of them all, was in the center.

"What if I told you this was an emergency?" he asked.

For the first time, the man looked up.

"Is it an emergency?"

"Let's just say that it is."

"Then I'd call the Coast Guard. Or maybe the sheriff."

"Ah," Jeremy said, trying to remain patient. "But what you're telling me is that there's no way for me to get out there right now? From here, I mean."

The man brought a finger to his chin. "I suppose you could take a boat, if you're in such a hurry."

Now we're getting somewhere, Jeremy thought. "And how would I arrange that?"

"I don't know. No one's ever asked."

Jeremy hopped back into his car, finally admitting that he was beginning to panic.

Maybe it was because he'd already come this far, or maybe it was because he realized his final words to Lexie the night before had signaled a deeper truth, but something else had taken hold of him and he wasn't going back. He refused to go back, not after getting this close.

Nate would be expecting his call, but suddenly, that didn't seem as important to him as it once was. Nor did the fact that Alvin would be arriving; if all went well, they could still film both this evening and tomorrow evening. He had ten hours until the lights would appear; in a fast boat, he figured that he could reach Hatteras in two. It gave him plenty of time to get there, talk to Lexie, and come back, assuming he could find someone to take him there.

Anything could go wrong, of course. He might not be able to hire a boat, but if that happened, he'd drive to Buxton if he had to. Once there, however, he couldn't even be sure that he'd find her.

Nothing about this entire scenario made sense. But who cared? Once in a while, everyone was entitled to be a bit flaky, and now it was his turn. He had cash in his wallet, and he'd find a way to get there. He'd take the risk and see how things turned out with her, if only to prove to himself that he could leave her and never think about her again.

That's what this was all about, he knew. When Doris intimated that he might never see her again, his thoughts about her had gone into overdrive. Sure, he was leaving in a couple of days, but that didn't mean this had to be over. Not yet, anyway. He could visit down here, she could come up to New York and if it was meant to be, they'd somehow work it out. People did that all the time, right? But even if that wasn't possible, even if she was resolute in her determination to end things completely, he wanted to hear her say it. Only then could he return to New York knowing he'd had no other choice.

And yet, as he came to a sliding stop at the first marina he saw, he realized he didn't want her to speak those words. He wasn't going to Buxton to say good-bye or to hear her say that she never wanted to see him again. In fact, he thought with amazement, he knew that he was going there to find out if Alvin had been right all along.

Late afternoon was Lexie's favorite time of day. The soft winter sunlight, combined with the austere natural beauty of the landscape, made the world appear dreamlike.

Even the lighthouse, with its black and white candy-cane pattern, seemed like a mirage from here, and as she walked the length of the beach, she tried to imagine how difficult it had been for the sailors and fishermen to navigate the point before it had been built. The waters just offshore, with their shallow seabed and shifting shoals, were nicknamed the Graveyard of the Atlantic, and a thousand wrecks dotted the seafloor. The *Monitor*, which engaged in the first battle between ironclads during the Civil War, had been lost here. So had the *Central America*, laden with California gold, whose sinking helped cause the financial panic of 1857. Blackbeard's ship, *Queen Anne's Revenge*, had supposedly been found in the Beaufort Inlet, and half a dozen German U-boats sunk during World War II were now visited almost daily by scuba divers.

Her grandfather had been a history buff, and every time they walked the beach holding hands, he told her stories about the ships that had been lost over the centuries. She learned about hurricanes and dangerous surf and faulty navigation that stranded boats until they were torn apart by the raging surf. Though she wasn't particularly interested and was sometimes even frightened by the images conjured up, his slow, melodic drawl was strangely soothing, and she never tried to change the subject. Even though she was young at the time, she sensed that talking to her about these things meant a lot to him. Years later, she would learn that his ship had been torpedoed in World War II and that he'd barely survived.

Recalling those walks made her miss her grandfather with sudden intensity. The strolls had been part of their daily routine, something for just the two of them, and they usually went out in the hour just before dinner, when Doris was cooking. More often than not, he'd be reading in the chair with his glasses propped on his nose, and he'd close the book with a sigh and set it aside. Rising from his seat, he'd ask if she'd like to take a walk to see the wild horses.

The thought of seeing the horses always thrilled her. She wasn't quite sure why; she'd never ridden a horse, nor did she particularly want to, but she remembered how she would jump up and run to the door as soon as her grandfather mentioned it. Usually, the horses kept themselves at a distance from people and darted away whenever someone approached, but at dusk, they liked to graze, lowering their defenses, if only for a few minutes. It was often possible to get close enough to see their distinctive markings and, if you were lucky, to hear them snorting and whinnying a warning not to come any closer.

The horses were descended from the Spanish mustangs, and their presence on the Outer Banks dated from 1523. These days, there were all sorts of government regulations that ensured their survival, and they were as much a part of the surroundings as deer were in Pennsylvania, with the only problem being occasional overpopulation. People who lived here largely ignored them unless they became a nuisance, but for many vacationers, seeing them was one of the highlights of their visit. Lexie considered herself something of a local, but watching them always made her feel as if she were young again, with all of life's pleasures and expectations ahead of her.

She wanted to feel that way now, if only to escape the pressures of her adult life. Doris had called to tell her that Jeremy had come in looking for her. It hadn't surprised her. Though she'd assumed he would wonder what he'd done wrong or why she'd left, she also felt he'd get over it quickly. Jeremy was just one of those blessed people who were confident in everything they did, forever moving forward without a regret or backward glance.

Avery had been that way, and even now she still remembered how hurt she'd been by his sense of entitlement, his indifference to her pain. Looking back, she knew she should have seen his character flaws for what they were, but at the time, she hadn't seen the warning signs: the way his stare lingered just a bit too long when he was looking at other women, or the way he'd squeeze just a bit too hard when he hugged women he swore were only friends. In the beginning, she'd wanted to believe him when he said he'd only been unfaithful once, but bits and pieces of forgotten conversations had resurfaced: a friend from college had long ago confessed that she'd heard rumors about Avery and a particular sorority sister; one of his co-workers mentioned a few too many unexplained absences from work. She hated to think of herself as naive, but she had been, and even more than being disappointed in him, she'd long since realized that she was disappointed in herself. She'd told herself she would get over it, that she would meet someone better . . . someone like Mr. Renaissance, who proved once and for all that she wasn't a good judge of men. Nor, it seemed, could she keep one.

It wasn't easy to admit that, and there were moments when she wondered whether she might have done something to drive both men off. Okay, maybe not Mr. Renaissance, since theirs was less a relationship than a fling, but what about Avery? She'd loved him and thought he loved her. Sure, it was easy to say that Avery was a cad and that the demise of their relationship had been all his fault, but at the same time, he must have felt that the relationship was lacking somehow. That *she* was lacking somehow. But in what way? Had she been too pushy? Was she boring? Was he unsatisfied in the bedroom? Why didn't he run out afterward, looking for her and begging forgiveness? These were the quesions she'd never been able to answer. Her friends, of course, assured her that she didn't know what she was talking about, and Doris had said the same thing. Even so, it wasn't entirely clear to her what had happened. There were, after all, two sides to every story, and even now she sometimes fantasized about calling him to ask if there was anything she could have done differently.

As one of her friends pointed out, it was typical of women to worry about such things. Men seemed immune to these sorts of insecurities. Even if they weren't, they'd learned to either disguise their feelings or bury them deep enough so as not to be crippled by them. Usually, she tried to do the same, and usually, it worked. Usually.

In the distance, with the sun sinking into the waters of the

Pamlico Sound, the town of Buxton, with its white clapboard houses, looked like a postcard. She was staring toward the lighthouse, and just as she'd hoped, she saw a small herd of horses grazing in the sea oats around the base. There were maybe a dozen in total—tans and browns, mainly—and their coats were rough and wild, grown thick for the winter. Two foals stood together near the center, their tails swishing in unison.

Lexie stopped to watch them, tucking her hands in her jacket pockets. It was getting cold now that the evening was coming, and she could feel the sting on her cheeks and nose. The air was bracing, and though she would have liked to stay longer, she was tired. It had been a long day, and felt even longer.

Despite herself, she wondered what Jeremy was doing. Was he preparing to film again? Or deciding where to eat? Was he packing? And why did her thoughts constantly turn to him?

She sighed, already knowing the answer. As much as she'd wanted to see the horses, the sight of them reminded her less of new beginnings than the simple fact that she was lonely. As much as she thought of herself as independent, as much as she tried to downplay Doris's constant remarks, she couldn't help but feel a yearning for companionship, for intimacy. It didn't even have to be marriage; sometimes all she wanted was to look forward to Friday or Saturday night. She yearned to spend a leisurely morning lounging in bed with someone she cared about, and as impossible as the idea seemed, Jeremy was the one she kept picturing beside her.

Lexie shook her head, forcing the thought away. In coming here, she had hoped to find relief from her thoughts, but as she stood near the lighthouse and watched the horses grazing, she felt the world bearing down hard. She was thirty-one, alone and living in a place without any prospects. Her grandfather and parents were nothing but memories, the state of Doris's health was a source of constant worry to her, and the one man she'd found even remotely interesting in recent years would be gone forever by the time she returned home.

That was when she started to cry, and for a long time, she found it difficult to stop. But just as she was finally beginning to collect herself, she saw someone approaching, and all she could do was stare when she realized who it was.

Fourteen

····❖····

Lexie blinked, trying to make sure that what she was seeing was real. It couldn't be *him*, because he couldn't be *here*. The whole idea was so foreign, so unexpected, that she felt as if she were watching the scene through someone else's eyes.

Jeremy smiled as he set his satchel down. "You know, you really shouldn't stare like that," he said. "Men like women who know how to be subtle."

Lexie continued to watch him. "You," she replied.

"Me," he agreed with a nod.

"You're . . . here."

"I am here," he agreed again.

She squinted at him in the waning light, and it occurred to Jeremy that she was even prettier than he remembered.

"What are you . . . ?" She hesitated, trying to make sense of his appearance. "I mean, how did you . . . ?"

"It's kind of a long story," he admitted. When she made no move toward him, he nodded at the lighthouse. "And this is the lighthouse where your parents were married?"

"You remembered that?"

"I remember everything," he said, tapping his temple. "Little gray cells and all that. Where exactly were they married?"

He spoke casually, as if this were the most ordinary of con-versations, which only made everything feel even more surreal to her.

"Over there," she said, pointing. "On the ocean side, near the waterline."

"It must have been beautiful," he said, gazing in that direction. "This whole place is beautiful. I can see why you love it here."

Instead of responding, Lexie took a long breath, trying to settle her turbulent emotions. "What are you doing here, Jeremy?"

It was a moment before he answered. "I wasn't sure you were coming back," he said. "And I realized that if I wanted to see you again, the best option was to come to you."

"But why?"

Jeremy continued staring toward the lighthouse. "It felt like I didn't have a choice."

"I'm not sure what that means," she said.

Jeremy studied his feet, then looked up and smiled as if in apol-ogy. "To be honest, I've spent most of the day trying to figure it out, too."

As they stood near the lighthouse, the sun began to sink below the horizon, turning the sky a forbidding gray. The breeze, damp and cold, skimmed the surface of the sand, whipping up foam at the water's edge.

In the distance, a figure in a dark heavy jacket was feeding the seagulls, tossing scraps of bread into the air. As Lexie watched him, she could feel the shock of Jeremy's appearance beginning to wear off. Part of her wanted to be angry that he'd ignored her desire to be alone, and yet another part, the greater part, was flattered that he'd come to find her. Avery had never bothered to come after her, nor had Mr. Renaissance. Even Rodney would never have thought of coming here, and until a few minutes ago, if someone had suggested that Jeremy would do such a thing, she would have laughed at the very notion. But it was beginning to dawn on her that Jeremy was different from anyone she'd met before, and that she shouldn't be surprised by anything he did.

The horses in the distance had begun to wander off, nibbling here and there as they moved back over the dune. The coastal mist was rolling in, merging sea and sky. Terns bobbed at the sand near the water's edge, their long strawlike legs moving quickly as they searched for tiny crustaceans.

In the silence, Jeremy cupped his hands and blew into them, trying to stop them from aching. "Are you angry that I came?" he finally asked.

"No," she admitted. "Surprised, but not angry."

He smiled, and she returned it with a flicker of her own.

"How did you get here?" she asked.

He motioned over his shoulder toward Buxton. "I got a ride from a couple of fishermen who were heading this way," he said. "They dropped me off at the marina."

"They gave you a ride just like that?"

"Just like that."

"You were lucky. Most fishermen are pretty tough characters."

"That may be true, but people are people," he said. "While I'm not an expert in psychology, I'm of the opinion that anyone—even strangers—can sense the urgency of a request, and most people will usually do the right thing." He stood straighter, clearing his throat. "But when that didn't work, I offered to pay them."

She giggled at his admission.

"Let me guess," she said. "They took you to the cleaners, didn't they?"

He gave a sheepish shrug. "I suppose that depends on the perspective. It did seem like a lot of money for a boat ride."

"Naturally. That's quite a trip. Just the gas alone would have been expensive. And then there's the wear and tear on the boat . . ."

"They mentioned that."

"And, of course, their time and the fact that they'll be working tomorrow before dawn."

"They mentioned that, too."

In the distance, the last of the horses vanished over the dune.

"But you came, anyway."

He nodded, as amazed as she was. "But they did make sure I understood it was a one-way trip. They didn't intend to wait for me, so I guess I'm stuck here."

She raised an eyebrow. "Oh, really? How did you plan on getting back?"

He gave an impish grin. "Well, I happen to know someone who's staying out here, and I was planning on using my dazzling charm to convince her to give me a ride back home."

"And what if I'm not leaving for a while? Or if I just said you're on your own?"

"I didn't figure that part out yet."

"And where did you intend to stay while you were out here?"

"I haven't figured that part out yet, either."

"At least you're honest about it," she said, smiling. "But tell me, what would you have done if I wasn't here?"

"Where else would you have gone?"

She glanced away, liking the fact that he'd remembered this about her. In the distance, she saw the lights of a shrimp trawler moving so slowly it almost seemed stationary.

"Are you hungry?" she asked.

"I'm starved. I haven't eaten anything all day."

"Would you like to have dinner?"

"Do you know a nice place?"

"I have a pretty good place in mind."

"Do they take credit cards?" he asked. "I used all my cash to get here."

"I'm sure," she said, "that we'll be able to work something out."

* * *

Turning from the lighthouse, they made their way back down the beach, walking along the compact sand near the water's edge. There was a space between them that neither seemed willing to cross. Instead, with their noses turning red in the chill, they moved steadily forward, as if pulled toward the place that both were meant to be.

In the silence, Jeremy mentally replayed his journey here, feeling a pang of guilt about Nate and Alvin. He'd missed the conference call—there had been no reception at all as he was crossing the Pamlico Sound—and figured that he should probably call from the landline as soon as he was able, though he wasn't looking forward to it. Nate, he suspected, had been revving up for hours and was waiting for Jeremy's call so he could finally go ballistic, but Jeremy planned to suggest a meeting with the producers next week, complete with the footage and the outlines of the story, an idea that he suspected had been the whole point of the call, anyway. If that wasn't enough to appease them, if missing a single call could end his career before it started, then he wasn't sure he wanted to work in television.

And Alvin . . . well, that was a little easier. There was no way Jeremy could get back to Boone Creek to meet Alvin tonight— he'd come to that realization by the time the boat had dropped him off—but Alvin had a cell phone, and he'd explain what was going on. Alvin wouldn't be happy about having to work alone tonight, but he'd recover by tomorrow. Alvin was one of those rare people who never let anything bother them for more than a day.

Yet, being honest with himself, Jeremy admitted that he didn't really care about any of that now. Instead, all that seemed to matter was that he was walking with Lexie on a quiet beach in the middle of nowhere and that as they trudged into the salty breeze, she quietly looped her arm through his.

* * *

Lexie led the way up the warped wooden steps of the old buga-low and hung her jacket on the rack beside the door. Jeremy hung his as well, along with his satchel. As she walked ahead of him through the living room, Jeremy watched her, thinking again that she was beautiful.

"Do you like pasta?" she asked, breaking into his thoughts.

"Are you kidding? I grew up on pasta. My mother happens to be Italian."

"Good," she said. "Because that's what I planned on making."

"We're eating here?"

"I guess we have to," she said over her shoulder. "You're out of cash, remember?"

The kitchen was small, with fading yellow paint, flowery wall-paper that was peeling in the corners, scuffed cabinets, and a small painted table set beneath the window. On the counters were the groceries she'd picked up earlier. Reaching into the first bag, she pulled out a box of Cheerios and a loaf of bread. From his spot near the sink, Jeremy saw a flash of her skin when she stood on her toes to put them in the cupboard.

"Do you need a hand?" he asked.

"No, I've got it, thanks," she said, turning around. After straight-ening her shirt, she reached into another bag and set two onions off to the side, along with two large cans of San Marzano tomatoes. "But while I'm doing this, do you want something to drink? I have a six-pack of beer in the refrigerator if you're interested."

He widened his eyes, feigning shock. "You have beer? I thought you didn't drink much."

"I don't."

"For someone who doesn't drink, though, a six-pack can do a lot of damage." He shook his head before going on. "If I didn't know you better, I'd think you were planning to go on a bender this weekend."

She shot him a withering look, but, like yesterday, there was something playful in it. "It's more than enough to get me through the month, thank you very much. Now, would you like one or not?"

He smiled, relieved at their familiar exchange. "I'd love one, thanks."

"Would you mind getting it, though? I've got to get the sauce going."

Jeremy moved to the refrigerator and pulled two bottles of Coors Light from the six-pack. He twisted one cap off and then the other before setting a bottle before her. When she saw it, he shrugged. "I hate to drink alone," he said.

He raised his bottle in toast and she lifted hers as well. They clinked bottles without a word. Leaning against the counter beside her, he crossed one leg over the other. "Just to let you know, I'm pretty good at chopping if you need help."

"I'll keep that in mind," she said.

He smiled. "How long has your family owned this place?"

"My grandparents bought it in the early forties. Back then, there wasn't even a road on the island. You had to drive across the sand to get here. There are some pictures in the living room of how this place looked back then."

"Would you mind if I took a look?"

"Go ahead. I'm still getting things ready. There's a bathroom down the hall if you want to wash up before dinner. In the guest bedroom on the right."

Moving to the living room, Jeremy examined the pictures of rustic shore life, then noticed Lexie's suitcase near the couch. After debating for an instant, he grabbed it and headed down the hall. On the left, he saw an airy room with a large pedestal bed topped by a seashell-patterned comforter. The walls were decorated with additional photos portraying the Outer Banks. Assuming this was her room, he set her suitcase just inside the door.

Crossing the hall, he entered the other room. It was nautical in theme, and the navy curtains provided a nice contrast to the wooden end tables and dresser. As he slipped off his shoes and socks at the foot of the bed, he wondered what it would be like to sleep in here while knowing Lexie was alone across the hall.

At the bathroom sink, he peeked at himself in the mirror and used his hands in an attempt to get a semblance of control over his hair again. His skin was coated with a thin layer of salt, and after washing his hands, he splashed water on his face as well. Feeling somewhat better, he went back to the kitchen and heard the melancholy notes of the Beatles' "Yesterday" coming from a small radio on the windowsill.

"Ready for some help yet?" he asked. Beside her, he saw a medium-size salad bowl; in it were small chunks of tomatoes and olives.

While rinsing the lettuce, Lexie nodded toward the onions. "I'm almost done with the salad, but would you mind taking the skin off those?"

"Sure. Do you need me to dice them, too?"

"No, that's okay. Just take off the skins. The knife is in the drawer there."

Jeremy pulled out a steak knife, and reached for the onions on the counter. For a moment, they worked without speaking, listening to the music. As she finished with the lettuce and set it off to the side, Lexie tried to ignore how close they were standing together. But from the corner of her eye, she couldn't help admiring Jeremy's casual grace, along with the plane of his hips and legs, the broad shoulders, the high cheekbones.

Jeremy held up a bald onion, oblivious to what she'd been thinking. "Like this?"

"Just like that," she said.

"Are you sure you don't want me to dice it?"

"No. If you do, you'll ruin the sauce, and I'll never forgive you."

"Everyone dices the onions. My *Italian mother* dices the onions."

"Not me."

"So you're just going to put these big round onions in the sauce?"

"No. I'll cut them in half first."

"Can I at least do that?"

"No, thanks. I'd hate to put you out." She smiled. "And besides, I'm the cook, remember? You just watch and learn. Right now think of yourself as . . . the prep boy."

He glanced at her. Since they'd come in from the cold, the rosiness in her cheeks had faded, leaving her skin with a fresh, natural glow.

"The prep boy?"

She shrugged. "What can I say? Your mom might have been Italian, but I grew up with a grandmother who tried just about every recipe out there."

"And that makes you an expert?"

"No, but it made Doris one, and for a long time, I was the prep girl. I learned through osmosis and now it's your turn."

He reached for the second onion. "Tell me, then, what's so special about your recipe? Aside from having onions the size of baseballs, I mean."

She took the skinned onion and sliced it in half. "Well, since your mother was Italian, I'm sure you've heard of San Marzano tomatoes."

"Of course," he said. "They're tomatoes. From San Marzano."

"Ha, ha," she said. "Actually, they're the sweetest and most flavorful of all tomatoes, especially in sauces. Now, watch and learn."

She pulled out a pot from beneath the stove and set it off to the side, then turned on the gas and lit the fumes under the burner. The blue flame whooshed to life, and she set the empty pot on top of it.

"I'm impressed so far," he said, finishing the second onion and setting it aside. He picked up his beer and leaned against the counter again. "You should get your own cooking show."

Ignoring him, she poured both cans of tomatoes into the pot, then added a whole stick of butter to the sauce. Jeremy peeked over her shoulder, watching as the butter began to melt.

"Looks healthy," he said. "My doctor always told me I needed extra cholesterol in my diet."

"Did you know you have a tendency toward sarcasm?"

"I've heard that," he said, raising his bottle. "But thanks for noticing."

"Are you done with the other onion yet?"

"I am the prep boy, aren't I?" he said, handing it over.

She split that one as well before adding all four halves to the sauce. Stirring for a moment with a long wooden spoon, she let it come to a boil, then set the heat on low.

"Okay, then," she said, satisfied, returning to the sink, "we're done for now. It'll be ready in an hour and a half."

As she washed her hands, Jeremy peeked into the saucepan, frowning. "That's it? No garlic? No salt and pepper? No sausage? No meatballs?"

She shook her head. "Three ingredients only. Of course, we'll pour it over linguine and top it with some fresh-grated Parmesan cheese."

"This isn't very Italian."

"Actually, it is. It's the way they've made it in San Marzano for hundreds of years. That's in Italy, by the way." She turned the faucet off, shook her hands over the sink, and dried them on a dish towel. "But since we've got some time, I'm going to clean up before dinner," she said. "Which means you'll be on your own for a bit."

"Don't worry about me. I'll figure out something."

"If you'd like, you can take a shower," she said. "I'll set some towels out for you."

Still feeling the salt on his neck and arms, it took only an instant for him to agree. "Thanks. That would be great."

"Give me just a minute to set things up for you, okay?"

She smiled and grabbed her beer as she squeezed past him, feeling his eyes on her hips. She wondered whether he was feeling as self-conscious as she was.

At the end of the hall, she opened the closet door, grabbed a couple of towels, and put them on his bed. Beneath the sink in his bathroom were asssorted shampoos and a new bar of soap, and she set those out as well. As she did, she caught a reflection of herself in the mirror and had the sudden image of Jeremy wrapped in a towel after showering. The image made something jump inside. She drew a long breath, feeling like a teenager again.

"Hello?" she heard him call. "Where are you?"

"I'm in the bathroom," she answered, amazed by how calm her voice sounded. "Just making sure you have everything you need."

He came up behind her. "You wouldn't happen to have a disposable razor in any of those drawers, would you?"

"No, sorry," she said. "I'll look in my bathroom, too, but . . ."

"No big deal," he said, running his hand over his whiskers. "I'll just go with the scruffy look tonight."

Scruffy would be just fine, she decided, feeling herself blush. Turning away so he wouldn't notice, she motioned to the shampoos. "Use whichever one you want," she said. "And keep in mind that it takes a while for the hot water to come out, so just be patient."

"Will do," he said. "But I did want to ask if it's okay to use your phone. I have to make a couple of calls."

She nodded. "The phone's in the kitchen."

Edging past him, she sensed him watching her again, though she didn't turn around to check. Instead, she went to her room, closed the door behind her, and leaned against it, embarrassed at the foolish way she'd been feeling. Nothing had happened, nothing would happen, she told herself again. She locked the door, hoping it would be enough to block out her thoughts. And it worked, at least for a moment, until she noticed that he'd placed her suitcase in her room.

Knowing that he'd been in here moments before gave her such a rush of forbidden anticipation that, even though she willed her mind blank, she had to admit that she'd been lying to herself all along.

By the time Jeremy returned to the kitchen after his shower, he could smell the sauce as it simmered on the stove. He finished his beer, found the garbage can below the sink, and threw the bottle away, then got another from the fridge. On the shelf below, he saw a fresh block of Parmesan cheese and an unopened jar of Amfiso olives; he debated sneaking one before deciding against it.

Locating the phone, he dialed Nate's office number and was put through immediately. For the first twenty seconds, he held the receiver away from his ear while Nate went off the deep end, but when he finally calmed down, he reacted positively to Jeremy's suggestion about the meeting next week. Jeremy ended the call with a promise to talk to him again tomorrow morning.

Alvin, on the other hand, was impossible to reach. After dialing the number and getting his voice mail, Jeremy waited for a minute and tried again with the same result. The clock in the kitchen showed that it was almost six, and Jeremy figured that Alvin was somewhere on the highway. Hopefully, they'd have a chance to talk before he went out tonight.

With nothing else to do and Lexie still nowhere in sight, Jeremy slipped out the back door and stood on the porch. The chill had deepened. The ever-increasing wind was cold and sharp, and though he couldn't see the ocean, the waves rolled continuously, the sound rhythmic, lulling him into an almost trancelike state.

In time, he headed back into the darkened living room. Peeking down the hall, he noted a sliver of light beneath Lexie's closed door. Unsure of what to do next, he turned on a small reading lamp near the fireplace. With just enough light to spill shadows through the room, he perused the books that had been stacked on top of the mantel before remembering the satchel. In his haste to get here, he hadn't looked at Doris's notebook yet, and after pulling it out of the satchel, he carried it with him back to the easy chair. As he took his seat, he felt the tension in his shoulders begin to ease for the first time in hours.

Now, this, he thought, was nice. No, change that. This felt like the way things always should be.

Earlier, as she heard Jeremy close the door to his room, Lexie stood near the window and took a pull of her beer, glad she had something to calm her nerves.

Both of them had kept their kitchen conversation superficial, keeping their distance until things were sorted out. She knew she should stay the course when she headed back out there, but as she set her beer aside, she realized that she didn't want to keep her distance. Not anymore.

Despite the knowledge of the risks, everything about him had drawn her closer—the surprise at seeing him walking toward her on the beach, his easy smile and tousled hair, the nervous, boylike gaze—and in that instant, he'd been both the man she knew and the man she didn't. Though she hadn't admitted it to herself then, she realized now that she wanted to know the part of him he'd kept hidden from her, whatever that might be and wherever it might lead.

Two days ago, she would never have imagined something like this was possible, especially with a man she barely knew. She'd been hurt before, and she realized now that she'd reacted to the hurt by retreating into the safety of solitude. But a risk-free life wasn't much of a life, really, and if she was going to change, she might as well start now.

After showering, she sat on the edge of the bed as she unzipped the top pocket of her suitcase and retrieved a bottle of lotion. She applied some to her legs and arms, smoothing it over her breasts and belly, relishing the vibrant way it made her skin feel.

She hadn't brought anything fancy to wear; in her rush to get out in the morning, she'd grabbed the first things she could find, and she sorted through the suitcase until she found her favorite pair of jeans. Deeply faded, they were ripped at the knees and the cuffs were frayed. But the endless washing had softened and thinned the denim, and she was aware of how they accentuated her figure. She felt a secret thrill at her certainty that Jeremy would notice.

She slipped into a long-sleeved white shirt, which she didn't bother to tuck in, and rolled the sleeves up to her elbows. Standing in front of the mirror, she buttoned the front, stopping one button lower than she normally would, revealing the briefest glimpse of her cleavage.

She dried her hair with a blow-dryer and ran a brush through it. For makeup, she did the best with what she had, applying a touch of blush to her cheeks, eyeliner, and lipstick. She wished she had some perfume, but there wasn't anything she could do about that now.

When she was ready, she tugged at her shirt in the mirror in an attempt to make it look just right, pleased with how she looked. Smiling, she tried to remember the last time looking good had really mattered to her.

Jeremy was sitting in the chair with his feet propped up when she came into the room. He looked up at her, and for a moment, it seemed as if he wanted to say something, but no words came out. Instead, he just stared.

Unable to look away from Lexie, he suddenly knew why it had been so important to find her again. He'd had no choice, for he knew then that he was in love with her.

"You look . . . incredible," he finally whispered.

"Thank you," she said, hearing the raw emotion in his voice and reveling in the way it made her feel. Their eyes met and held, and in that instant, she understood that the message in his gaze was mirroring her own.

Fifteen

······❖······

For a moment, neither of them seemed able to move, until Lexie drew a long breath and glanced away. Still shaken, she raised her bottle slightly.

"I think I need another one of these," she said with a tentative smile. "Would you like one?"

Jeremy cleared his throat. "I already got one. Thanks."

"I'll be back in a minute. I should check on the sauce, too."

Lexie headed for the kitchen on unsteady legs, and she stopped before the stove. The wooden spoon had left a smudge of tomato sauce on the counter after she had picked it up to stir, and she put it in the same spot when she was finished. Then, opening the refrigerator, she took out another beer and set it on the counter, along with the olives. She tried to open the jar, but because her hands were trembling, she couldn't get the grip she needed.

"Need a hand with that?" Jeremy asked.

She looked up, surprised. She hadn't heard him come in, and wondered if her feelings were as obvious as they felt.

"If you wouldn't mind," she said.

Jeremy took the olives from her. She watched the sinewy muscles of his forearms as he twisted the cap off. Then, eyeing her beer, he opened that as well and handed it to her.

He wouldn't meet her eyes, nor did he seem to want to say anything more. In the stillness of the room, she watched him lean against the counter. The overhead light was on, but without the fading light of dusk streaming through the windows, it seemed softer than it had when they started cooking.

Lexie took a mouthful of beer, savoring the taste, savoring everything about the evening: the way she looked and felt and the way he'd stared at her. She was close enough to reach out and touch Jeremy and for a fleeting moment almost did, but instead, she turned away and went to the cupboard.

She took out some olive oil and balsamic vinegar and put some of each in a small bowl, along with salt and pepper.

"Everything smells delicious," he said.

Finished with the dressing, she reached for the olives and put them into another small bowl. "We still have an hour before dinner," she said. Talking seemed to keep her steadier. "Since I didn't plan on having company, these will have to do for an appetizer. If it was summer, I'd say we could wait on the porch outside, but I tried that earlier and it's freezing. And I should warn you that the chairs in the kitchen aren't too comfortable."

"Which means?"

"Would you like to go sit in the living room again?"

He led the way, paused at the easy chair to pick up Doris's book, then watched as Lexie took a seat on the couch. She put the olives on the coffee table, then shifted slightly trying to get comfortable. When he took a seat beside her, he could smell the sweet, floral scent of the shampoo she'd used. From the kitchen, he heard the faintest strains of the radio.

"I see you have Doris's notebook," she said.

He nodded. "She let me borrow it."

"And?"

"I just had a chance to look over the first few pages. But it has a lot more detail than I thought it would."

"Now do you believe that she predicted the sex of all those babies?"

"No," he said. "Like I said, she might have recorded only the ones she was right about."

Lexie smiled. "And the different way the entries look? Sometimes pens, sometimes pencils, sometimes it looks like she was in a rush, sometimes she took her time."

"I'm not saying the book doesn't look convincing," he said. "I'm just saying that she can't predict the sex of babies by holding someone's hand."

"Because you say so."

"No. Because it's impossible."

"Don't you mean statistically improbable?"

"No," he said, "impossible."

"Fair enough, Mr. Skeptic. But how's your story going?"

Jeremy began picking at the label of his beer with his thumb. "Good," he said. "If I can, I'd still like to finish looking through some of the diaries at the library, though. Maybe find something to spice up the story."

"Have you figured it out?"

"Yes," he said. "Now all I have to do is prove it. Hopefully, the weather will cooperate."

"It will," she said. "It's supposed to be foggy all weekend. I heard it on the radio earlier."

"Good," he said. "But the bad part is that the solution isn't nearly as much fun as the legend."

"Was it worth coming down, then?"

He nodded. "Without a doubt," he said, his voice quiet. "I wouldn't have missed this trip for the world."

Hearing his tone, she knew exactly what he meant, and she turned toward him. Propping her chin on her hand, she put a leg on the couch, liking how intimate it felt, how desirable he made her feel.

"So what is it?" she asked, leaning forward slightly. "Can you tell me the answer?"

The lamplight behind her gave her the faintest halo, and her eyes glowed violet beneath dark lashes.

"I'd rather show you," he said.

She smiled. "Since I'm bringing you back, anyway, you mean. Right?"

"Right."

"And you want to go back . . . ?"

"Tomorrow, if we can." He shook his head, trying to regain control of his feelings, not wanting to ruin this, not wanting to push too hard, but wanting nothing more than to take her in his arms. "I've got to meet Alvin. He's a friend of mine—a cameraman from New York. He's coming to get some professional footage."

"He's coming to Boone Creek?"

"Actually, he's probably arriving in town as we speak."

"Right now? Shouldn't you be there?"

"Probably," he admitted.

She thought about what he'd said, touched by the effort he had made to come today.

"Okay," she said. "There's an early ferry we can catch. We can be back in town around ten."

"Thanks," he said.

"And you're going to film tomorrow night?"

He nodded. "I left a note telling Alvin to go to the cemetery tonight, but we have to film elsewhere, too. And tomorrow's going to be a full day, anyway. There are some loose ends I have to tie up."

"What about the barn dance? I thought we had a deal that if you solved the mystery, I'd dance with you."

Jeremy lowered his head. "If I can make it, I will. Believe me. There's nothing I want more."

Silence filled the room.

"When are you going back to New York?" she finally asked.

"Saturday," he said. "I have to be in New York for a meeting next week."

Her heart sank at his words. Though she already knew it was coming, it still ached to hear him say it. "Back to the exciting life, huh?"

He shook his head. "My life in New York isn't all that glamorous. For the most part, it's about work. I spend most of my time either researching or writing, and those are solitary endeavors. Actually, it can get pretty lonely at times."

She raised a brow. "Don't try to make me feel sorry for you, because I'm not buying it."

He glanced at her. "What if I mentioned my creepy neighbors? Would you feel sorry for me then?"

"No."

He laughed. "I don't live in New York for the excitement, no matter what you might think. I live there because my family's there, because I'm comfortable there. Because it's home to me. Just like Boone Creek is home to you."

"I take it your family is close."

"Yeah," he said, "we are. We get together almost every weekend at my mom and dad's in Queens for these great big dinners. My dad had a heart attack a few years back and it's tough on him, but he loves those weekends. It's always a real zoo: a bunch of kids running around, Mom cooking in the kitchen, my brothers and their wives standing around in the backyard. Of course, they all live nearby, so they're over there even more often than I am."

She took another drink, trying to picture the scene. "Sounds nice."

"It is. But it's hard sometimes."

She looked at him. "I don't understand."

He was quiet as he rotated the bottle in his hands. "Sometimes I don't, either," he said.

Perhaps it was the way he said it that kept her from saying

anything; in the silence, she watched him closely, waiting for him to continue.

"Did you ever have a dream?" he asked. "Something you wanted so badly and just when you think you're about to reach out and grab it, something else takes it away?"

"Everyone has dreams that don't come true," she answered, her voice guarded.

His shoulders slumped. "Yeah," he said, "I guess you're right."

"I'm not sure what you're trying to tell me," she said.

"There's something you don't know about me," he said, turning to face her again. "Actually, it's something I've never told anyone."

At his words, she felt her shoulders tense. "You're married," she said, leaning back.

He shook his head. "No."

"Then you're seeing someone in New York and it's serious."

"No, that's not it, either."

When he said no more, she thought she saw a shadow of doubt cross his face.

"It's okay," she offered. "It's none of my business, anyway."

He shook his head and forced a smile. "You were close the first time," he said. "I was married. And divorced."

Expecting far worse, she almost laughed aloud in relief, but his somber expression restrained her.

"Her name was Maria. We were fire and ice at first, and no one could understand what we saw in each other. But once you got past the surface, we shared the same values and beliefs about all the big things in life. Including our desire for children. She wanted four, I wanted five." He hesitated when he saw her expression. "I know that's a lot of kids these days, but it was something we were both used to. Like me, she'd come from a large family." He paused. "We didn't know there was a problem right away, but after six months, she still wasn't pregnant, and we went in for some routine tests. She turned out to be fine, but for whatever reason, it turned out that I wasn't. No reason given, no answer possible. Just one of those things that sometimes happen to people. When she found out, she decided she didn't want to stay in the marriage anymore. And now . . . I mean, I love my family, I love spending time with them, but when I'm there, I'm always reminded of the family that I'll never be able to have. I know that sounds strange, but I guess you'd have to be me to understand how much I wanted kids."

When he finished, Lexie simply stared at him, trying to make sense of what he'd just told her. "Your wife left you because you found out that you couldn't have kids?" she asked.

"Not right away. But in the end, yes."

"And there was nothing the doctors could do?"

"No." He seemed almost embarrassed. "I mean, they didn't say it was utterly impossible for me to have a child, but they made it clear that it would most likely *never* happen. And that was enough for her."

"What about adoption? Or finding a donor? Or . . ."

Jeremy shook his head. "I know it's easy to think she was heartless, but it wasn't like that," he said. "You had to know her to fully understand. She grew up thinking that she'd be a mother. After all, her sisters were all becoming mothers, and she would have been a mother, too, if it wasn't for me." He glanced up toward the ceiling. "For a long time, I didn't want to believe it. I didn't want to think I was defective, but I was. And I know it sounds ridiculous, but after that, I just felt like less of a man. Like I wasn't worthy enough for anyone."

He shrugged, his voice growing more matter-of-fact as he went on. "Yeah, we could have adopted; yeah, we could have found a donor. I suggested all of that. But her heart wasn't in it. She wanted to be pregnant, she wanted to experience childbirth, and it went without saying that she wanted it to be her husband's. After that, things started going downhill. But it wasn't just her. I changed, too. I was moody . . . I started traveling even more for my work . . . I don't know . . . maybe I drove her away."

Lexie studied him for a long moment. "Why are you telling me all this?"

He took a sip of his beer and scratched at the label on the bottle again. "Maybe it's because I want you to know what you're getting into with someone like me."

At his words, Lexie felt the blood rush to her cheeks. She shook her head and turned away.

"Don't say things you don't mean."

"What makes you think I don't mean them?"

Outside, the wind began to pick up, and she heard the faint tones of the wind chime near the door.

"Because you don't. Because you can't. Because it's not who you are, and it has nothing to do with what you just told me," she said. "You and I . . . we're not the same, as much as you want to think we are. You're there, I'm here. You have a big family that you see frequently, I only have Doris, and she needs me here, especially now, considering her health. You like cities, I like small towns. You have a career you love, and I . . . well, I have the library and I love that, too. If one of us is forced to change what we have, what we've chosen to make of our lives . . ." She closed her eyes briefly. "I know that's possible for some people to do, but it's a hard row to hoe when it comes to building a relationship. You said yourself that the reason you fell in love with Maria was because you shared the same values. But with us, one of us would have to sacrifice. And if I don't want to have to sacrifice, I don't think it's fair to expect you to sacrifice, either."

She lowered her gaze, and in the ensuing stillness, he could hear the clock above the fireplace ticking. Her lovely face was clouded with sadness, and he was suddenly gripped by the fear that he might be losing any chance he had with her. Reaching over, he used his finger to turn her cheek toward him.

"What if I don't think it's a sacrifice?" he said. "What if I tell you that I'd rather be with you than go back to my old life?"

His finger felt electric against her skin. Trying to ignore the sensation, she held her voice steady.

"Then I would tell you that I've had a wonderful time in the last couple of days, too. That meeting you has been . . . well, amazing. And that yes, I'd like to think that there was some way to make this work. And that I'm flattered."

"But you don't want to try to make this work."

Lexie shook her head. "Jeremy . . . I . . ."

"It's okay," he said, "I understand."

"No," she said, "you don't. Because you heard what I said, but you didn't listen. It means that, of course, I'd like it to work between us. You're intelligent and kind and charming . . ." She broke off, hesitating. "Okay, maybe you're a little too forward at times . . ."

Despite the tension, he couldn't help laughing. She went on, choosing her words carefully.

"The reason I'm saying this is that the last two days have been incredible, but I have things in my past that left me wounded, too," she said. Quickly and calmly, she told him about Mr. Renaissance. When she finished, she looked almost guilty. "Maybe that's why I'm trying to be practical about this. I'm not saying that you'll disappear like he did, but can you honestly say that we'll feel the same way about each other if we have to travel to spend time together?"

"Yes," he said, his voice firm. "I can."

She looked almost sad at his answer. "You can say that now, but what about tomorrow? What about a month from now?"

Outside, the wind made a whistling sound as it moved around the cottage. Sand blew against the windows, and the curtains swayed as the air forced its way through the old panes.

Jeremy stared at Lexie, realizing once again that he loved her.

"Lexie," he said, his mouth going dry. "I . . ."

Knowing what he was going to say, she raised her hands to stop him. "Please," she said. "Don't. I'm not ready for that yet, okay? For now, let's just enjoy dinner. Can we do that?" She hesitated before gently setting her bottle of beer on the table. "I should probably go check on it and get the linguine going."

With a sinking feeling, Jeremy watched as she rose from the couch. Pausing in the doorway of the kitchen, she turned around to face him.

"And just so you know, I think what your ex-wife did was terrible and she's nowhere near as great as you tried to make her out to be. You don't leave your husband for something like that, and the fact that you can say anything kind about her at all says that she's the one who made the mistake. Believe me—I've seen what it takes to be a good parent. Having kids means taking care of them, raising them, loving and supporting them, and none of those things have anything to do with who makes them one night in the bedroom or the experience of being pregnant."

She turned in the direction of the kitchen, vanishing from sight. He could hear Billie Holiday singing "I'll Be Seeing You" on the radio. With his throat tightening, Jeremy rose to follow her, knowing that if he didn't seize the moment, it might never come again. Lexie, he suddenly understood, was the reason he'd come to Boone Creek; Lexie was the answer he'd been looking for all along.

He leaned against the doorway of the kitchen, watching as she set another pot on the stove.

"Thank you for saying what you said," he said.

"You're welcome," she responded, refusing to meet his eyes. He knew she was trying to remain strong in the face of the same emotions he was experiencing, and he admired both her passion and her reserve. Yet he took a step toward her, knowing he had to take a chance.

"Will you do me a favor?" he asked. "Since I might not make it tomorrow night," he said, reaching out his hand, "would you mind dancing with me?"

"Here?" She looked up, startled, her heart racing. "Now?"

Without another word, he moved closer, taking her hand in his. He smiled as he raised her hand to his mouth and kissed her fingers before lowering it into position. Then, with his eyes locked on hers, he slipped his other arm around her back and gently pulled her toward him. As his thumb began to gently trace the skin of her hand and he whispered her name, she found herself beginning to follow his lead.

The melody played softly in the background as they began to rotate in slow circles, and though she felt embarrassed at first, she finally leaned into him, relaxing into the warmth of his body. His breath warmed her neck, and as his hand tenderly skimmed her back, she closed her eyes and leaned further into him, dropping her head onto his shoulder and feeling the last of her resolve slip away. This, she realized, was what she had wanted all along, and in the tiny kitchen, they moved in rhythm to the gentle music, each of them lost in the other.

Beyond the windows, the waves continued to roll, washing toward the dune. The cold wind whistled around the cottage, vanishing into the ever-blackening evening. Dinner simmered quietly on the stove.

When at last she lifted her head to meet his eyes, he wrapped his arms around her. He brushed his lips against hers once, and then twice, before pressing them close. After pulling back slightly to make sure she was okay, he kissed her again, and she kissed him back, reveling in the strength of his arms. She felt his tongue against hers, the moisture intoxicating, and brought a hand to his face, tracing the stubble on his cheek. He responded to her touch by kissing her cheek and neck, his tongue hot against her skin.

They kissed in the kitchen for a long time, both of them savoring the other without hurry or urgency, until Lexie finally pulled back. She turned off the burner behind her, then, taking his hand again, she led him back to her bedroom.

They made love slowly. As he moved above her, he whispered how much he loved her and breathed her name like a prayer. His hands never stopped moving, as if proving to himself that she was real. They stayed in bed for hours, making love and laughing quietly, savoring each other's touch.

Hours later, Lexie rose from the bed and slipped into a bathrobe. Jeremy put on his jeans, and joining her in the kitchen, they finished cooking dinner. After Lexie had lit a candle, he stared at her over the small flame, marveling at the lingering flush of her cheeks, as he devoured the most delicious meal he'd ever tasted. For some reason, the act of eating together in the kitchen, him shirtless and her naked beneath the thin robe, seemed almost more intimate than anything else that had happened that night.

Afterward, they went back to bed, and he pulled her close, content to simply hold her. When Lexie eventually fell asleep in his arms, Jeremy watched her sleep. Every now and then, he brushed the hair from her eyes, reliving the evening, remembering it all, and knowing in his heart that he'd met the woman with whom he wanted to spend the rest of his life.

Just before dawn, Jeremy woke and realized that Lexie was gone. He sat up in bed, patted the covers as if to make sure, then hopped out of bed and put on his jeans. Her clothes were still on the floor, but the bathrobe she'd worn during dinner was gone. Snapping his jeans, he shivered slightly in the chill and crossed his arms as he made his way down the hall.

He found her in the easy chair near the fireplace, a cup of milk on the small table beside her. In her lap was Doris's notebook, opened near the beginning, but she wasn't looking at it. Instead, she was gazing out the dark window toward nothing at all.

He took another step toward her, the floorboards squeaking underfoot, and she started at the sound. When she saw him, she smiled.

"Hey there," she said.

In the dim light, Jeremy sensed that something was wrong. He sat on the armrest beside her and slipped his arm around her.

"Are you okay?" he murmured.

"Yeah," she said, "I'm okay."

"What are you doing? It's the middle of the night."

"I couldn't sleep," she said. "And besides, we have to be up in a little while to catch the ferry."

He nodded, though he wasn't completely satisfied by her answer. "Are you mad at me?"

"No," she said.

"Are you sorry about what happened?"

"No," she said, "it's not that, either." She didn't, however, add anything else, and Jeremy pulled her closer, trying to believe her.

"It's an interesting book," he said, not wanting to press her. "I hope to spend a bit of time with it later."

Lexie smiled. "It's been a while since I've looked through it. Seeing it here brings back memories."

"How so?"

She hesitated, then pointed down at the open page in her lap. "When you were reading it earlier, did you get to this entry?"

"No," he answered.

"Read it," she said.

Jeremy read the entry quickly; in many ways, it seemed identical to the others. The first names of the parents, the age, how far along the woman was in her pregnancy. And the fact that the woman would have a girl. When he finished, he looked at her.

"Does it mean anything to you?" she asked.

"I'm not sure what you're asking," he admitted.

"The names Jim and Claire don't mean anything to you?"

"No." He scrutinized her face. "Should they?"

Lexie lowered her eyes. "They were my parents," she said, her voice quiet. "This is the entry that predicted I would be a girl."

Jeremy raised his eyebrows quizzically.

"That's what I was thinking about," she said. "We think we

know each other, but you didn't even know the names of my parents. And I don't know the names of your parents."

Jeremy felt a knot beginning to form in his stomach. "And that bothers you? That you don't think we know each other that well?"

"No," she said. "What bothers me is that I don't know if we ever will."

Then, with a tenderness that made his heart ache, she wrapped her arms around him. For a long time, they sat in the chair holding each other, both of them wishing they could stay in that moment forever.

Sixteen

......❖......

"So this is your friend, huh?" Lexie asked.

She gestured discreetly to the holding cell. Although Lexie had lived in Boone Creek all her life, she'd never had the privilege of visiting the county jail—until today.

Jeremy nodded. "He's not normally like this," he whispered back.

Earlier in the morning, they had packed their belongings and closed up the beach cottage, each reluctant to leave it behind. But when they drove off the ferry in Swan Quarter, Jeremy's cell phone picked up enough signal strength to retrieve his messages. Nate had left four of them about the upcoming meeting; Alvin, on the other hand, had left a frantic one saying that he'd been arrested.

Lexie had dropped Jeremy off at his car, and he'd followed her back to Boone Creek, worried about Alvin, but worried about Lexie as well. Lexie's disconcerting mood, which had started in the predawn darkness, had continued for the next few hours. Though she hadn't pulled away when he slipped his arm around her on the ferry, she'd been quiet, gazing at the waters of the Pamlico Sound. When she smiled, it was only a flicker, and when he took her hand, she didn't squeeze his. Nor would she talk about what she'd said to him earlier; strangely, she spoke instead about the numerous shipwrecks off the coast, and when he did try to steer the conversation toward more serious issues, she either changed the subject or didn't answer at all.

Meanwhile, Alvin was languishing in the county jail, looking—to Lexie's eyes, at least—like he belonged there. Dressed in a black Metallica T-shirt, leather pants and jacket, and a studded wristband, Alvin was staring at them with wild eyes, his face flushed. "I mean, what the hell kind of a cracker town is this? Does anything normal ever happen here?" He'd been going on in this vein from the moment Lexie and Jeremy arrived, and his knuckles were white as he squeezed the iron bars. "Now, can you *please* get me out of here?"

Behind them, Rodney stood scowling, his arms crossed, ignoring Alvin as he had been for the last eight hours. The guy whined way too much, and besides, Rodney was far more interested in Jeremy and Lexie. According to Jed, Jeremy hadn't come back to his room last night, and Lexie hadn't been at home, either. It could have been a coincidence, but he strongly doubted that, which meant they'd most likely spent the night together. Which wasn't good at all.

"I'm sure we'll figure something out," Jeremy said, not wanting to rile Rodney any further. He'd seemed downright angry when Jeremy and Lexie showed up. "Tell me what happened."

"What happened?" Alvin repeated, his voice rising. His eyes took on a crazed look. "You want to know what happened? I'll tell you what happened! This whole place is nuts, that's what happened! First, I get lost trying to find this stupid town. I mean, I'm driving down the highway, pass a couple of gas stations, and keep going, right? Since there doesn't seem to be a town? And the next thing you know, I'm lost in the middle of a swamp for hours. I don't find the town until almost nine o'clock. And then you'd think someone could give me directions to Greenleaf, right? I mean, how hard could it be? Small town, the only place to stay?

Well, I get lost again! And that's after some guy at the gas station talks my ear off for half an hour—"

"Tully," Jeremy said, nodding.

"What?"

"The guy you talked to."

"Yeah, whatever . . . so I finally get to Greenleaf, right? And the gigantic hairy guy there isn't exactly friendly and sort of gives me the evil eye, hands me your note, and sticks me in this room with all these dead animals—"

"All the rooms are like that."

"Whatever!" Alvin grunted. "And, of course, you're not even around—"

"Sorry about that."

"Would you let me finish?" Alvin hollered. "So, okay, I got your note and follow your directions to the cemetery, right? And I get there just in time to see the lights, and it's fantastic, you know. Like for the first time in hours, I'm not pissed, right? So I head down to this place called Lookilu for a nightcap, which seems to be the only place in town open at that hour. And there's only a couple of people in the whole place, so I get to talking to this gal named Rachel. And it's going great. We're really hitting it off, and then this guy walks in, looking like he just swallowed a porcupine . . ." He nodded toward Rodney. Rodney smiled without showing his teeth.

"So, anyway, a little while later, I go out to my car, and the next thing I know this guy is tapping on my window with his flashlight and asking me to step out of the car. So I ask why, and he tells me again to get out. And then he starts asking me how much I've had to drink and that maybe I shouldn't be driving. So I tell him I'm fine and that I'm here working with you, and the next thing I know I'm locked up for the night! Now, *get me out of here!*"

Lexie looked over her shoulder. "Is that what happened, Rodney?"

Rodney cleared his throat. "To a point. But he forgot the part where he called me a big dumb Barney Fife and said that he'd have me brought up on charges for harassment if I didn't let him go. He seemed so irrational that I thought he might be on drugs or get violent, so I brought him in for his own safety. Oh, and he called me a stupid musclehead, too."

"You were harassing me! I didn't do anything!"

"You were drinking and driving."

"Two beers! I had two beers!" Alvin was looking maniacal again. "Check with the bartender! He'll tell you!"

"I already did," Rodney said, "and he told me you had seven drinks."

"He's lying!" Alvin shouted, his eyes swiveling to Jeremy. He looked through the bars, his face panicked between his hands. "I had two drinks! I swear, Jeremy! I would never drive if I had too much. I swear on my mother's Bible!"

Jeremy and Lexie looked over at Rodney. He shrugged. "I was just doing my job. "

"Your job! Your job!" Alvin shouted. "Arresting innocent people! This is America and you can't do that here! And this isn't ending! When I get through with you, you won't even be able to work security at Wal-Mart! Do you hear me, Barney! Wal-Mart!"

It was clear that the two of them had been going on like this most of the night.

"Let me talk to Rodney," Lexie finally whispered.

When she left with the deputy, Alvin fell silent.

"We'll get you out of here," Jeremy reassured him.

"I don't belong in here in the first place!"

"I know that. But you're not helping yourself."

"He's harassing me!"

"I know that. But let Lexie handle it. She'll take care of it."

Out in the hallway, Lexie looked up at Rodney. "What's really going on?" she asked.

Rodney wouldn't meet her eyes; instead, he continued to look in the direction of the holding cell.

"Where were you last night?" he asked.

She crossed her arms. "I was at the cottage at the beach."

"With him?"

Lexie hesitated, wondering about the best way to answer. "I didn't go with him, if that's what you're asking."

Rodney nodded, knowing she hadn't answered completely, but suddenly realizing he didn't want to know any more.

"Why did you arrest him? Honestly."

"I wasn't planning to. He brought it on himself."

"Rodney . . ."

He turned around, lowering his head to his chest.

"He was hitting on Rachel, and you know how she can get when she drinks: all flirty and without a speck of common sense. I mean, I know it's none of my business, but someone has to watch out for her." He paused. "Anyway, when he was leaving, I went over to talk to this guy to see if he was planning to head over to her place and what kind of guy he was and he starts insulting me. And I wasn't in the best of moods, anyway . . ."

Lexie knew the reason for that, and when Rodney trailed off, she said nothing. In time, Rodney shook his head, as if he were still trying to justify it to himself. "But the fact is, he was drinking and planning on driving. And that's illegal."

"Was he over the legal limit?"

"I don't know. I never bothered to check."

"Rodney!" she whispered loudly.

"He made me angry, Lexie. He's rude and weird-looking and hitting on Rachel and calling me names, then he says he's working with this guy . . ." He motioned with his head toward Jeremy.

Lexie laid a hand on his shoulder. "Listen to me, okay? You know that you will get in trouble if you keep him in here for no reason. Especially with the mayor. If he finds out what you did to the cameraman—especially after he's gone through all this trouble to make sure the story turns out okay—he'll cause trouble for you." She let that sink in for a moment before going on. "And besides, you and I both know that the sooner you let him out, the sooner the both of them can leave."

"You really think he'll leave?"

Lexie looked Rodney in the eye. "His flight is tomorrow."

For the first time, Rodney held her gaze. "Are you going with him?"

It took a moment for her to answer the question she'd been asking herself all morning. "No," she whispered. "Boone Creek is my home. And this is where I'm staying."

Ten minutes later, Alvin was walking out to the parking lot beside Jeremy and Lexie. Rodney was standing in the doorway of the county jail, watching them go.

"Don't say anything," Jeremy warned again, keeping hold of Alvin's arm. "Just keep walking."

"He's a hick with a gun and a badge!"

"No, he isn't," Lexie said, her voice firm. "He's a good guy no matter what you might think."

"He arrested me for no reason!"

"And he also watches out for people who live here."

They reached the car, and Jeremy motioned for Alvin to get in the backseat.

"This isn't the end of this," Alvin grumbled, crawling in. "I'm calling the D.A. That guy should be fired."

"The best thing you can do is forget about it," Lexie said, looking through the open car door at him.

"Forget about it? Are you insane? He was wrong and you know it!"

"Yes, he was. But since no charges were filed, you'll let it go, anyway."

"Who are you to tell me what to do?"

"I'm Lexie Darnell," she said, drawling out her name. "And

not only am I a friend of Jeremy's, but I have to live here with Rodney, and I'm not lying when I say that I feel a lot safer with him around. Everyone in town feels safer because of him. You, on the other hand, are leaving tomorrow, and he's not going to bother you again." She smiled. "And c'mon, you have to admit that this will make one heck of a story when you get back to New York."

He stared at her in disbelief before glancing at Jeremy. "She's the one?" he asked.

Jeremy nodded.

"She's pretty," Alvin commented. "Maybe a little on the pushy side, but pretty."

"Better yet, she cooks like an Italian."

"As good as your mom?"

"Maybe better."

Alvin nodded, silent for a moment. "I take it you think she's right about dropping this whole thing."

"I do. She understands this place better than you or me, and she hasn't led me wrong yet."

"So she's smart, too, huh?"

"Very," Jeremy said.

Alvin broke into a wolfish grin. "I take it you two were together last night."

Jeremy said nothing.

"She must be really something . . ."

"I'm right here, you guys!" Lexie finally interjected. "You do realize that I can hear everything you're saying."

"Sorry," Jeremy said. "Old habits and all that."

"Can we go now?" Lexie asked.

Jeremy looked at Alvin, who seemed to be considering his options.

"Sure," he said with a shrug. "And not only that, I'll forget any of this ever happened. On one condition."

"What's that?" Jeremy asked.

"All this talk about Italian food has made me hungry, and I haven't eaten since yesterday. Buy me lunch, and not only will I drop the whole thing, but I'll tell you how the filming came out last night, too."

Rodney watched them go before heading back inside, tired from lack of sleep. He knew he shouldn't have arrested the guy, but even so, he didn't feel too bad about it. All he'd wanted to do was exert a little pressure, and the guy starts running his mouth and acting all uppity . . .

He rubbed the top of his head, not wanting to think about it. It was over now. What wasn't over was the fact that Lexie and Jeremy had spent the night together. Suspicions were one thing, but proof was another, and he saw the way they were acting this morning. It was different somehow from the way they'd been acting at the party the other night, which meant something had changed between them. Still, he hadn't been completely certain about them until he heard the tricky way she'd tried to answer without answering. *I didn't go with him, if that's what you're asking.* No, he'd wanted to say, he hadn't asked her that. He'd asked if she'd been at the beach with Jeremy last night. But her vague response was enough, and it didn't take a rocket scientist to figure out what happened.

The realization nearly broke his heart, and he wished again that he understood her better. There'd been times in the past when he thought he was getting closer to knowing what made her tick, but this . . . well, this just proved otherwise, didn't it? Why on earth would she let it happen again? Why hadn't she learned from the first traveling stranger who'd passed through town? Didn't she remember how depressed she'd been afterward? Didn't she know she was only going to be hurt again?

She had to know those things, he thought, but she must have decided—at least for an evening, anyway—that she didn't care. It made no sense at all, and Rodney was getting tired of caring about it. He was tired of being hurt by her. Yeah, he still loved her, but he'd given her more than enough time to figure out her own feelings for him. It was time, he thought, for Lexie to make a decision one way or the other.

His anger fading, Alvin paused in the doorway of Herbs when he saw Jed sitting at one of the tables. Jed scowled and crossed his arms as soon as he saw Alvin, Jeremy, and Lexie take their seats at a booth near the front windows.

"Our friendly concierge doesn't seem too pleased to see us," Alvin whispered across the table.

Jeremy stole a glance at him. Jed's eyes became little slits. "Gee, that's strange. He's always seemed so friendly before. You must have done something to upset him."

"I didn't do anything. I just checked in."

"Maybe he doesn't like the way you look."

"What's wrong with the way I look?"

Lexie raised her eyebrows as if to say, *You've got to be kidding*.

"I don't know," Jeremy pondered out loud. "Maybe he doesn't like Metallica."

Alvin glanced at his shirt and shook his head. "Whatever," he said.

Jeremy winked at Lexie; while she smiled in return, her expression was distant, as if her mind was elsewhere.

"The filming went great last night," Alvin said, reaching for a menu. "Caught it all from two angles and watched it on playback last night. Amazing stuff. The networks are going to love it. Which reminds me, I've got to call Nate. Since he couldn't reach you, he kept calling me all afternoon instead. I have no idea how you put up with that guy."

When Lexie looked perplexed, Jeremy leaned toward her. "He's talking about my agent," he said.

"Is he coming down, too?"

"No. He's too busy dreaming up my future career. And besides, he wouldn't know what to do outside the city. He's the kind of guy who thinks Central Park should be developed into condos and retail outlets."

She flashed a quick smile.

"So what's with you two?" Alvin demanded. "How did you meet?"

When Lexie showed no inclination to answer, Jeremy shifted in his seat.

"She's a librarian and she's been helping me research the story," he said vaguely.

"And you two have been spending quite a bit of time together, huh?"

From the corner of his eye, Jeremy saw Lexie glance away.

"There's been a lot to research," he said.

Alvin looked at his friend, sensing that something was off. It seemed almost as if they'd had a lovers' quarrel and gotten over it but were still licking their wounds. Which was a lot to have happen in a single morning.

"Well . . . good," he said, deciding to drop it for now. Instead, he looked over the entries as Rachel came sauntering toward the table.

"Hey, Lex, hey, Jeremy," she said as she approached. "Hey, Alvin."

Alvin looked up. "Rachel!" he said.

"I thought you told me you were coming in for breakfast," she said. "I'd just about given up on you."

"I'm sorry about that," he said. He glanced at Jeremy and Lexie. "I guess I slept in."

Reaching into her apron, Rachel pulled out a small pad and retrieved the pencil she kept behind her ear. She dabbed the tip with her tongue. "Now, what can I get y'all?"

Jeremy ordered a sandwich; Alvin asked for the lobster bisque and a sandwich as well. Lexie shook her head. "I'm not that hungry," she said. "But is Doris around?"

"No, she didn't come in today. She was tired and decided to take the day off. She worked late last night getting things ready for the weekend."

Lexie tried to read her expression.

"Really, Lex," Rachel added, her voice serious. "There's nothing to worry about. She sounded fine on the phone."

"Maybe I should go check on her, anyway," Lexie said. She looked around the table for confirmation before rising. Rachel moved aside to make room.

"Would you like me to come with you?" Jeremy asked.

"No, that's okay," she said. "You've got work to do, and I've got things to do, too. Would you like to meet up at the library later? You wanted to finish looking through the diaries, didn't you?"

"If that's okay," he said, stung by the nonchalance in her tone. He would rather have spent the rest of the afternoon with her.

"How about if I meet you there at four?" she suggested.

"That's fine," he said. "But let me know what's going on, okay?"

"Like Rachel said, I'm sure she's fine. But I'm going to grab her notebook from the backseat, if that's okay."

"Yeah, of course."

She looked at Alvin. "Nice meeting you, Alvin."

"You, too."

A moment later, Lexie was gone and Rachel was on her way back to the kitchen. As soon as they were out of earshot, Alvin leaned across the table.

"Okay, my friend, spill it."

"What do you mean?"

"You know exactly what I'm talking about. First you fall for her. Then you spend the night together. But when you show up at the jail, you both act like you barely know each other. And just now she makes the first excuse she can to get out of here."

"Doris is her grandmother," Jeremy explained, "and Lexie worries about her. She's not in the best of health."

"Whatever," Alvin said, clearly skeptical. "My point is, you've been staring at her like a lonely puppy dog, and she's been doing her best to pretend you aren't. Did you two have a fight or something?"

"No," he said. He paused, glancing around the restaurant. At the corner table, he saw three members of the town council, as well as the elderly volunteer from the library. They all waved at him. "Actually, I don't know what it was. One minute everything was great, and then later . . ."

When he didn't continue, Alvin leaned back in the booth. "Yeah, well, it wasn't going to last, anyway."

"It might have," Jeremy insisted.

"Oh, yeah? What? Were you planning to move down here to the Twilight Zone? Or is she coming to New York?"

Jeremy folded and refolded his napkin without answering, not wanting to be reminded of the obvious.

In the silence, Alvin raised his eyebrows. "I definitely have to spend more time with this lady," he said. "I haven't seen someone get under your skin like this since Maria."

Jeremy looked up wordlessly, knowing that his friend was right.

Doris was lying propped up in bed, looking over her reading glasses when Lexie peeked in her bedroom door.

"Doris?" Lexie asked.

"Lexie," she cried, "what are you doing here? Come in, come in . . ."

Doris set aside the open book in her lap. She was still in her pajamas, and though her skin had a slightly grayish cast, she looked otherwise okay.

Lexie crossed the room. "Rachel said you stayed home today, and I just wanted to check on you."

"Oh, I'm fine. Just a little off today, that's all. But I thought you were supposed to be at the beach."

"I was," she said, taking a seat on the edge of the bed. "But I had to come back."

"Oh?"

"Jeremy showed up," she said.

Doris raised her hands as if in surrender. "Don't blame me. I didn't tell him where you were. And I didn't tell him to go looking for you, either."

"I know." Lexie gave Doris's arm a reassuring squeeze.

"Then how did he know where to find you?"

Lexie brought her hands together in her lap. "I told him the other day about the cottage, and he put two and two together. You can't believe how surprised I was when I saw him walking up the beach."

Doris eyed Lexie carefully before sitting up a little straighter. "So . . . you two were at the beach house last night?"

Lexie nodded.

"And?"

Lexie didn't answer right away, but after a moment, her lips formed a small smile. "I made him your famous tomato sauce."

"Oh?"

"He was impressed," she said. Lexie ran her hand through her hair. "I brought your notebook back, by the way. It's in the living room."

Doris slipped off her reading glasses and began wiping the lenses with the corner of her sheet. "None of this explains why you're back, though."

"Jeremy needed a ride. A friend from New York—a cameraman—came down to film the lights. They're going to film tonight, too."

"What's his friend like?"

Lexie hesitated, thinking about it. "He looks like a cross between a punk rocker and a motorcycle gang member, but other than that . . . he's okay."

When she grew silent, Doris reached over and took Lexie's hand. Squeezing it gently, she studied her granddaughter.

"Do you want to talk about why you're really here?"

"No," Lexie answered, tracing the seams of Doris's quilt with her finger. "Not really. This is something I have to figure out on my own."

Doris nodded. Lexie always put on a brave front. At times, she knew it was best to say nothing at all.

Seventeen

······❖······

Jeremy glanced at his watch as he stood on the porch at Herbs, waiting for Alvin to finish his conversation with Rachel. Alvin was giving it his best shot, and Rachel seemed to be in no rush to say good-bye, which normally would have been considered a good omen. Yet, to Jeremy's eye, Rachel seemed less interested in Alvin than in simply being polite, and Alvin wasn't reading her cues. Then again, Alvin always had trouble reading cues.

When Alvin and Rachel finally parted, Alvin joined Jeremy, a big grin on his face, as if he'd already forgotten about the events of last night. Which he probably had.

"Did you see that?" he whispered when he was close. "I think she likes me."

"What's not to like?"

"Exactly my point," he agreed. "Man, she's something. I love the way she talks. It's so . . . sexy."

"You think everything is sexy," Jeremy observed.

"That's not true," he protested. "Only most things."

Jeremy smiled. "Well, maybe you'll see her tonight at the dance. We might be able to drop in before we head out to film again."

"There's a dance tonight?"

"At the old tobacco barn. I hear the whole town turns out. I'm sure she'll be there."

"Good," Alvin said, stepping off the porch. But then, almost to himself, he added, "I wonder why she didn't mention it."

Rachel absently leafed through her order tickets, as she watched Alvin leave the restaurant with Jeremy.

She'd been a little standoffish when he first took a seat beside her at Lookilu, but once he mentioned what he was doing in town and that he knew Jeremy, they struck up a conversation, and he spent most of the next hour telling her about New York. He made it sound like paradise itself, and when she mentioned that she hoped to take a trip there someday, he'd scribbled his phone number on the cover of her notepad and said to give him a call. He'd even promised to get her tickets to the *Regis and Kelly* show if she wanted.

As flattering as the gesture was, she knew she wouldn't call. She'd never been too keen on tattoos, and though she hadn't had much luck with men over the years, she had long made it a point never to date someone who had more piercings in his ear than she did. But that wasn't her only reason for her lack of interest, she had to admit; Rodney also had something to do with it.

Rodney often visited the Lookilu to make sure that no one would try to drive while inebriated, and pretty much everyone who spent any time there knew there was a chance that he'd be dropping in sometime during the night. He'd move around the bar, say hello to various folks, and if he got the feeling that you were too far gone, he'd let you know what he was thinking and mention that he'd be watching for your car later. While it sounded intimidating—and probably was if you were drinking too much—he'd also add that he'd be happy to drive you home. It was his way of keeping drunks off the road, and in the past four years, he hadn't needed to make a single arrest. Even the owner of the Lookilu didn't mind him coming in anymore; oh, he'd moaned about the thought of a deputy patrolling the lounge in the beginning, but since no one seemed to mind, he'd gradually come to accept it, and he'd even begun calling Rodney when he thought there was someone in the bar who needed a ride.

Last night, Rodney had come in like he always did, and it didn't take long for him to spot Rachel sitting at the bar. In the past, he usually smiled and would come over to visit, but this time, when he saw her with Alvin, there was a moment when she thought he looked almost hurt. It was an unexpected reaction, but almost as quickly as it appeared, it passed, and all of a sudden, he looked angry. In a way, it seemed almost as if he were jealous, and she supposed that was the reason she left the bar right after he did. During the ride home, she kept replaying the scene, trying to figure out if she'd really seen what she had, or whether she'd simply been imagining it. Later, when she was lying in bed, she concluded that she wouldn't have been upset at all if Rodney had been jealous.

Maybe, she thought, there was hope for them yet.

After picking up Alvin's car, which had remained parked on the street near Lookilu, Jeremy and Alvin drove to Greenleaf. Alvin took a quick shower, Jeremy threw on a change of clothes, and the two of them spent the next couple of hours going over what Jeremy had learned. For Jeremy, it was a method of escape; concentrating on work was the only way he knew to keep himself from worrying about Lexie.

Alvin's tapes were as extraordinary as he'd promised, especially when compared with the ones Jeremy had shot. Their clarity and crispness, combined with slow-motion playback, made it easy to pick out details that Jeremy had missed in the rush of the moment. Even better, there were a few frames that Jeremy could isolate and freeze, which he knew would help viewers understand what was actually being shown.

From there, Jeremy walked Alvin through the historic time line using the references he'd found to interpret what was being seen. But as Jeremy continued to lay out the proof in intricate detail—all three versions of the legend; maps, notes on quarries, water tables, and schedules; various construction projects; and the detailed aspects of refracted light—Alvin began to yawn. He'd never been interested in the nitty-gritty of Jeremy's work, and he finally convinced Jeremy to drive him across the bridge to the paper mill so he could see the place himself. They spent a few minutes looking around the yard, watching timber being loaded onto platforms, and on their way back through town, Jeremy pointed out where they'd be filming later. From there, they headed to the cemetery so Alvin could get some footage during the daytime.

Alvin set up the camera in various locations while Jeremy paced on his own, the stillness of the cemetery forcing his thoughts back to Lexie and his worries about her. He remembered their night together and tried once again to understand what had made her rise from the bed in the middle of the night. Despite her denials, he knew she was feeling regret, maybe even remorse, about what had happened, but even that didn't make sense to him.

Yes, he was leaving, but he'd told her repeatedly that they would find a way to make it work. And yes, it was true that they didn't know each other well, but considering the short time they'd been together, he'd learned enough to know that he could love her forever. All they needed was a chance.

But Alvin, he thought, had been right. Whatever her concerns about Doris, her behavior this morning suggested that she'd been looking for an excuse to get away from him. What he wasn't sure of, however, was whether it was because she loved him and thought it would be easier to distance herself from him now, or because she didn't love him and didn't want to spend more time with him.

Last night, he'd been sure that she felt the same way that he did. But now . . .

He wished they could have spent the afternoon together. He

wanted to hear her concerns and alleviate them; he wanted to hold her and kiss her and convince her that he would find a way to make their relationship work, no matter how hard that might be. He wanted to make her hear his words: that he couldn't imagine a life without her, that his feelings for her were real. But most of all, he wanted to reassure himself that she felt the same way about him.

In the distance, Alvin was hauling the camera and tripod to another location, lost in his own world and oblivious to Jeremy's worries. Jeremy sighed before realizing that he'd drifted to the part of the cemetery where Lexie had vanished from sight the first time he saw her here.

He hesitated for a moment, a hunch taking root in his mind, then began searching the grounds, pausing every few steps. It took only a few minutes until he spotted the obvious. Making his way over a small ridge, he stopped at the foot of an untamed azalea bush. Twigs and branches surrounded it, but the area in front seemed to have been tended to. Squatting down, he reset the flowers she must have been carrying in her bag, and he suddenly understood why neither Doris nor Lexie wanted people trampling through the cemetery.

In the gray light, he stared at the graves of Claire and James Darnell, wondering why he hadn't figured it out before.

On the way back from the cemetery, Jeremy dropped Alvin off at Greenleaf for a nap, then returned to the library, rehearsing what he wanted to say to Lexie.

He noticed the library was more crowded than usual, at least on the outside. People were milling on the sidewalk in groups of two or three, pointing upward and gazing at the architecture, as if getting an early jump on the Historic Homes Tour. Most seemed to be holding the same brochure that Doris had sent Jeremy and were reading aloud from the captions highlighting the unique properties of the building.

Inside, the staff seemed to be preparing as well. A number of volunteers were sweeping and dusting; two others were setting out additional Tiffany lamps, and Jeremy assumed that once the official tour began, the overhead lights would be dimmed to give the library a more historic atmosphere.

Jeremy walked past the children's room, noting that it looked far less cluttered than it had the other day, and continued up the stairs. Lexie's office door was open, and he paused for a moment to collect himself before entering. Lexie was bending down near the desk, which had been nearly cleared. Like everyone else in the library, she was doing her best to get rid of clutter, stacking various piles under the desk.

"Hey," he said.

Lexie looked up. "Oh, hey," she said, standing. She smoothed her blouse. "I guess you caught me making the place look presentable."

"You do have a big weekend on tap."

"Yeah, I suppose I should have taken care of this earlier," she said, motioning around the room, "but I guess I've picked up a nasty case of procrastination."

She smiled, beautiful even in her slight dishevelment.

"It happens to the best of us," he said.

"Yeah, well, not usually to me." Instead of moving toward him, she reached for another pile, then ducked her head beneath the desk again.

"How's Doris doing?" he inquired.

"Fine," she said, speaking from below the desk. "Like Rachel said, she's just a little under the weather, but she'll be up and about tomorrow." Lexie reappeared, reaching for another stack of papers. "If you get the chance, you might swing by before you head out. I'm sure she'd appreciate that."

For a moment, he simply watched her, but when he realized the implication of what she was saying, he took a step toward her.

As he did, Lexie moved around the desk, acting as if she hadn't noticed, but making sure to keep the desk between them.

"What's going on?" he asked.

She shuffled a few more items on her desk. "I'm just busy," she answered.

"I meant what's going on with us," he said.

"Nothing," she said. Her voice was neutral, as if discussing the weather.

"You won't even look at me," he said.

With that, she finally looked up, meeting his eyes for the first time. He could sense her simmering hostility, though he wasn't sure whether she was mad at him or mad at herself. "I don't know what you want me to say. I've already explained that I've got things to do. Believe it or not, I am in sort of a rush here."

Jeremy stared without moving, suddenly sensing that she was looking for any excuse to start an argument.

"Is there anything I can do to help?" he asked.

"No, thanks. I've got it." Lexie slipped another stack under the desk. "How was Alvin?" she asked, her voice rising from below.

Jeremy scratched the back of his head. "He's not mad anymore, if that's what you're asking."

"Good," she said. "Did you two get your work done?"

"For the most part," he said.

She popped up again, trying to appear rushed. "I pulled the diaries out for you again. They're on the desk in the rare-book room."

Jeremy gave a weak smile. "Thanks," he said.

"And if you can think of anything else that you might need before you leave," she added, "I'll be here for at least another hour or so. The tour starts at seven, though, so you should plan on being out of here no later than six-thirty, since that's when we turn off the overhead lights."

"I thought the rare-book room closed at five."

"Since you're leaving tomorrow, I figured I could relax the rules just this once."

"And because we're friends, right?"

"Sure," she said. She smiled automatically. "Because we're friends."

Jeremy left the office and made his way to the rare-book room, replaying the conversation in his head and trying to make sense of it. Their meeting hadn't gone as he'd hoped. Despite the flippancy of her final comment, he hoped that she would follow him, but somehow knew she wouldn't. The afternoon apart hadn't helped to mend things between them; if anything, they'd gotten worse. If she seemed distant before, she now seemed to view him as radioactive.

As much as her behavior bothered him, on some level he knew it made sense. Maybe she shouldn't have been quite so . . . cold about it, but everything came back to the fact that he lived in New York and she lived here. Yesterday at the beach, it had been easy to fool himself with the belief that things would magically work out between them. And he *had* believed it. That was the thing. When people cared about each other, they always found a way to make it work.

He realized he was getting ahead of himself, but that's what he did when confronted with a problem. He looked for solutions, he made suppositions, he tried to analyze long-term scenarios, in order to carefully assess the potential outcomes. And, he supposed, that's what he expected of her as well.

What he didn't expect was to be treated like a pariah. Or for her to act as if nothing had happened between them at all. Or to act as if she believed that last night had been a mistake.

He glanced at the stack of diaries on the desk as he took his seat. He began separating the ones that he'd already skimmed from the ones that he hadn't, leaving four to go. To this point, none of the other seven had been particularly helpful—two had mentioned family funerals taking place at Cedar Creek—so he reached for one that he hadn't examined. Instead of reading from the first entry, he leaned back in his chair and skimmed passages at random, trying to determine whether the diarist typically wrote about herself or the town she lived in. It was written from 1912 to 1915 by a young teenager named Anne Dempsey, and for the most part, it was a personal account of the day-to-day events in her life over that period. Whom she liked, what she ate, her thoughts about her parents and friends, and the fact that no one seemed to understand her. If there was anything remarkable about Anne, it was that her angst and worries were the same ones characteristic of young people today. While interesting, he set it aside, along with the others he'd rejected.

The next two diaries he perused—both written during the 1920s—were largely personal accounts as well. A fisherman wrote of tides and catches in almost minute detail; the second, by a chatty schoolteacher named Glenara, described her budding relationship with a young visiting doctor over an eight-month period, as well as her thoughts about her students and people she knew in town. In addition, there were a couple of entries concerning the town's social events, which seemed to consist largely of watching sailboats on the Pamlico River, going to church, playing bridge, and promenading along Main Street on Saturday afternoons. He saw no mention of Cedar Creek at all.

He expected the last diary to be another waste of time, but calling it quits would mean leaving, and he couldn't imagine doing so without trying to talk to Lexie again, if only to keep the lines of communication open. Yesterday he could have strolled right in and said the first thing that came to mind, but the recent zig and zag of their relationship, combined with her clearly agitated state, made it impossible to figure out exactly what he should say or how he should act.

Should he be distant? Should he try to talk to her, even knowing that she was itching for a fight? Or should he pretend he hadn't even noticed her attitude and just assume that she still wanted to see how the mysterious lights really came about? Should he ask her out to dinner? Or just take her in his arms?

See, that was the problem in relationships when emotion began muddying the waters. It was as if Lexie expected him to do or say exactly the right thing at exactly the right time, whatever that was. And that, he decided, wasn't fair.

Yeah, he loved her. And yeah, he, too, was concerned about their future. But where *he* wanted to try to figure things out, *she* was acting as if she was willing to throw in the towel already. He thought again about their conversation.

If you get the chance, you might swing by before you head out . . .

Not, "if *we* get the chance." If *you* . . .

And what about her final comment? *Sure,* she'd said, *because we're friends.* It had been all he could do to bite his tongue at that. *Friends?* he should have said. *After last night, all you can say is that we're friends? Is that all I mean to you?*

It wasn't the way you talked to someone you cared about. It wasn't the way you treated someone you hoped to see again, and the more he thought about it, the more he wanted to respond in kind. You're pulling back? *I can do that, too.* You want to have an argument? *Here I am.* He hadn't done anything wrong, after all. What happened the night before had as much to do with her as it had with him. He'd been trying to tell her how he felt; she hadn't seemed to want to hear it. He'd been promising to try to make it work; she'd been dismissive of the idea all along. And in the end, she'd led him to the bedroom, not the other way around.

He stared out the window, his lips pressed together. No, he thought, he wasn't going to play her game anymore. If she wanted to talk to him, fine. But if not . . . well, then, that was the way it was going to be, and honestly, he couldn't really do anything about it. He wasn't about to go crawling back to beg and plead with her, so whatever happened next was in her hands. She knew where he was. He decided that he'd leave the library as soon as he was finished and head back to Greenleaf. Maybe it would give her the chance to figure out what she really wanted while letting her know he wasn't prepared to stick around and be mistreated.

As soon as he left, Lexie cursed herself, wishing she had handled things better. She'd thought that spending time with Doris would have clarified things, but all it had done was to postpone the inevitable. The next thing she knew, Jeremy came waltzing in, acting as if nothing had changed. As if nothing were changing tomorrow. As if he wouldn't be gone.

Yes, she had known he would be going back, that he would leave her behind just like Mr. Renaissance, but the fairy tale he'd started the night before nonetheless continued to linger, fueling fantasies in which people lived happily ever after. If he could find her at the beach, if he had enough courage to say the things he'd said to her, couldn't he also find a reason to stay?

Deep down, she knew he was nurturing the hope that she would come with him to New York, but she couldn't figure out why. Didn't he understand that she cared nothing about money or fame? Or about shopping or going to shows or being able to buy Thai food in the middle of the night? Life wasn't about those things. Life was about spending time together, about having the time to walk together holding hands, talking quietly as they watched the sun go down. It wasn't glamorous, but it was, in many ways, the best that life had to offer. Wasn't that how the old saying went? Who, on their deathbed, ever said they wished they had worked harder? Or spent less time enjoying a quiet afternoon? Or spent less time with their family?

She wasn't naive enough to deny that modern culture had its own seductions. Be famous and rich and beautiful and go to exclusive parties: *only then will you be happy.* It was, in her opinion, a bunch of hogwash, the song of the desperate. If it wasn't, why were so many rich, famous, and beautiful people taking drugs? Why couldn't they seem to hold a marriage together? Why were they always getting arrested? Why did they seem so unhappy when removed from the spotlight?

Jeremy, she suspected, was seduced by this particular world, as much as he didn't want to admit it. She had guessed this about him from the moment they'd met and had warned herself not to get emotionally involved. Nonetheless, she regretted the way she'd behaved just now. She hadn't been ready to deal with him when he showed up at her office, but she supposed she should have simply said as much, instead of keeping the desk between them and denying that anything was wrong.

Yes, she should have handled it better. Whatever their differences, Jeremy deserved at least that much.

Friends, he thought again. *Because we're friends.*

The way she said it still galled him, and absently tapping his pen against his notebook, Jeremy shook his head. He had to finish up here. Rolling his shoulders to ease the tension, he reached for the final diary and scooted his seat forward. After opening it, it took only a few seconds for him to realize that this one was different from all of the others.

Instead of short, personal passages, the diary was a collection of dated and titled essays written from 1955 to 1962. The first had to do with the building of St. Richard's Episcopal Church in 1859 and—while the site was being excavated—the discovery of what appeared to be an ancient Lumbee Indian settlement. The essay covered three pages and was followed by an essay on the fate of Mc-Tauten's Tannery, built on the shores of Boone Creek in 1794. The third essay, prompting Jeremy to raise his eyebrows, presented the writer's opinion as to what had really happened to the settlers on Roanoke Island in 1587.

Jeremy, vaguely recalling that one of the diaries belonged to an amateur historian, began flipping through the pages more quickly . . . scanning the headings, looking through the articles for anything obvious . . . turning the pages fast . . . skimming . . . stopping suddenly when he realized he had seen something and flipping the pages back, only to freeze when he realized that what he'd seen . . .

He leaned back in his chair, blinking as he moved his fingers down the page.

Solving the Mystery of the Lights
in Cedar Creek Cemetery

Over the years, some residents of our town have made the claim that ghosts are present in Cedar Creek Cemetery, and three years ago, an article was published regarding the phenomenon in Journal of the South. *Though no solution was offered, after conducting my own investigation, I believe I have solved the riddle of why the lights seem to appear at certain times while not at others.*

I will say definitively that ghosts are not present. Instead, the lights are actually those of the Henrickson Paper Mill and are influenced by the train as it crosses the trestle, the location of Riker's Hill, and the phases of the moon.

As Jeremy continued reading, he found himself holding his breath. Though the writer hadn't attempted an explanation as to why the cemetery was sinking—without which the lights would probably not be visible at all—his conclusion was otherwise essentially the same as Jeremy's.

The writer, whoever it was, had nailed it almost forty years ago. *Forty years . . .*

He marked the page with a piece of scratch paper and flipped the book to the front cover, looking for the name of the author, his mind flashing to the first conversation he'd had with the mayor. And with that, he felt his suspicions come together like pieces in a puzzle.

Owen Gherkin.

The journal had been written by the mayor's father. Who, according to Mayor Gherkin, "knew everything there was to know about this place." Who understood what was causing the lights. Who had undoubtedly told his son. Who then knew there had never been anything supernatural at all about the lights, but had nonetheless pretended otherwise. Which meant that Mayor Gherkin had been lying all along, in the hope of using Jeremy to help make a buck from unsuspecting visitors.

And Lexie . . .

The librarian. The woman who'd hinted that he might find the answers he was looking for in the diaries. Which meant that she'd read Owen Gherkin's account. Which meant that she, too, had been lying, preferring to play along with the mayor.

He wondered how many others in town had known the answer. Doris? Maybe, he thought. No, change that, he quickly decided. She *had* to have known. In their first conversation, she'd come right and out and said what the lights weren't. But like the mayor and Lexie, she hadn't said what they really were, even though she probably knew, too.

And that meant . . . this whole thing had been a joke all along. The letter. The investigation. The party. The joke, however, was on him.

And now Lexie was pulling away, but not until *after* she'd told him that story about Doris bringing her to the cemetery to see the spirit of her parents. And that sweet story about how her parents had wanted her to meet him.

Coincidence? Or planned all along? And now the way she was acting . . .

As if she wanted him to leave. As if she didn't feel anything for him. As if she had known what would happen . . .

Had *everything* been planned? And if so, why?

Jeremy grabbed the diary and headed to Lexie's office, determined to get some answers. He barely noticed that he slammed the door on the way out; nor did he notice the faces of the volunteers who turned to watch him. Lexie's door was cracked open, and he pushed it wider as he stepped into her office.

With the piles of clutter now hidden, Lexie was holding a can of furniture polish and wiping the top of the desk with a cloth, bringing the wood to a shine. She looked up as Jeremy raised the diary.

"Oh, hey," she said, looking up. She forced a smile. "I'm just about finished up here."

Jeremy stared at her. "You can quit the act," he announced.

Even from across the room, she sensed his anger, and she instinctively tucked a strand of hair behind her ear.

"What are you talking about?"

"This," he said, holding up the diary. "You have read this, haven't you?"

"Yes," she said simply, recognizing it as Owen Gherkin's. "I've read it."

"Did you know there's a passage that talks about the lights at Cedar Creek?"

"Yes," she said again.

"Why didn't you tell me about it?"

"I did," she said. "I told you about the diaries when you first came to the library. And if I remember right, I said you might find the answers you were looking for, remember?"

"Don't play games," Jeremy said, his eyes narrowing. "You knew what I was looking for."

"And you found it," she countered, her voice rising. "I don't see what the problem is."

"The problem is that I've been wasting my time. This diary had the answer all along. There is no mystery here. There never was. And you've been in on this little charade all along."

"What charade?"

"Don't bother trying to deny it," he said, cutting her off. He held up the diary. "I've got the proof right here, remember? You lied to me. You lied right to my face."

Lexie stared at him, feeling the heat of his anger, feeling her own rise in response. "Is this the reason you came to my office? To start firing accusations at me?"

"You knew!" he shouted.

She put her hands on her hips. "No," she said. "I didn't."

"But you read it!"

"So what?" she shot back. "I read the article in the paper, too. And I read the articles by those other people. How on earth was I supposed to know that Owen Gherkin got it right? For all I knew, he was guessing like the others were. And that's assuming I even cared about the subject. Do you honestly think I've ever spent more than a minute thinking about it until you got here? I don't care! I never cared! You're the one down here investigating. And if you'd read the diary two days ago, you wouldn't have been sure, either. We both know you would have done your own investigation, anyway."

"That's not the point," he said, dismissing the likelihood that she was right. "The point is that this whole thing has been a scam. The tour, the ghosts, the legend—it's a con, plain and simple."

"What are you talking about? The tour is about historic homes, and yeah, they added the cemetery to it. Whoop-de-do. All it is, is a nice weekend in the middle of a dreary season. No one's being conned, no one's being hurt. And come on, do you really think that most people actually think they're ghosts? Most people just like to say they do because it's fun."

"Did Doris know?" he demanded, cutting her off again.

"About Owen Gherkin's diary?" She shook her head, furious at his refusal to listen. "How would she know about it?"

"See," he said, raising his finger, like a teacher emphasizing a point to a student. "That's the part that I don't understand. If you didn't want the cemetery as part of the tour, and Doris didn't want it as part of the tour, then why didn't you just go to the newspaper with the truth? Why did you want to involve me in your little game?"

"*I* didn't want to involve you. And it's not a game. It's a harmless weekend that you're blowing completely out of proportion."

"I didn't blow it out of proportion. You and the mayor did that."

"So I'm one of the bad guys now?"

When Jeremy said nothing, her eyes narrowed. "Then why did I give you the diary in the first place? Why didn't I just keep it hidden from you?"

"I don't know. Maybe it has something to do with Doris's notebook. You two have been pushing that on me since I got here. Maybe you figured that I wouldn't come down for that, so you concocted this whole thing."

"Can you even hear how ridiculous you sound?" She leaned over the desk, face flushed.

"Hey, I'm just trying to figure out why I was brought down here in the first place."

She raised her hands, as if trying to stop him. "I don't want to hear this."

"I'll bet you don't."

"Just get out," she said, shoving the can of furniture polish into her desk drawer. "You don't belong here and I don't want to talk to you anymore. Go back to where you came from."

He crossed his arms. "At least you finally admitted what you've been thinking all day."

"Oh, now you're a mind reader?"

"No. But I don't have to read minds to understand why you've been acting the way you are."

"Well, then, let me read your mind, okay?" she hissed, tired of his superior attitude, tired of him. "Let me tell you what I see, okay?" She knew her voice was loud enough for the entire library to hear, but she didn't care. "I see someone who's really good at saying the right things, but when push comes to shove, doesn't mean a thing he says."

"And what's that supposed to mean?"

She started across the room, anger stiffening every muscle in her body.

"What? You don't think I know how you really feel about our town? That it's nothing more than a stop on the highway? Or that deep down, you can't understand why anyone would live here? And that, no matter what you said last night, the thought that you might live here is ridiculous?"

"I didn't say that."

"You didn't have to!" she shouted, hating the smug way he sounded. "That's the point. When I was talking about sacrifice, I knew full well that you thought I should be the one to uproot. That I should leave my family, my friends, my home, because New York is so much better. That I should be the good little woman who follows her man wherever he thinks we should be. The thought never even crossed your mind that you'd be the one to leave."

"You're exaggerating."

"I am, huh? About what? Expecting me to be the one to leave? Or were you planning to pick up a real estate guide on your way out of town tomorrow? Here, let me make it easier for you," she said, reaching for the phone. "Mrs. Reynolds has her office across the street, and I'm sure she'd be delighted to walk you through a couple of houses tonight if you're in the market for something."

Jeremy simply stared at her, unable to deny her accusations.

"Nothing to say?" she demanded, slamming the phone back down. "Cat got your tongue? Then tell me this instead. What did you mean exactly when you said that we'd find a way to make it work? Did you think I was interested in waiting around for you to visit every now and then for a quick roll in the sack, without the possibility of a future together? Or were you thinking of using those visits to convince me of the error of my ways, since you think I'm wasting my life here and would be so much happier tagging along in your life?"

The anger and pain in her voice were unmistakable; so was the meaning behind what she was saying. For a long time, neither of them said anything.

"Why didn't you say any of this last night?" he asked, his voice dropping an octave.

"I tried," she said. "It's just that you didn't want to listen."

"Then why . . . ?"

He let the question hang, the implication clear.

"I don't know." She looked away. "You're a nice guy, we had a couple of good days. Maybe I was just in the mood."

He stared at her. "Is that all it meant to you?" he asked.

"No," she admitted, seeing the pain in his expression. "Not last night. But it doesn't change the fact that it's over, does it?"

"So you're pulling away?"

"No," she said. To her dismay, she felt tears begin to well in her eyes. "Don't put this on me. You're the one who's leaving. You came into my world. It wasn't the other way around. I was content until you arrived. Maybe not perfectly happy, maybe a little lonely, but content. I like my life here. I like being able to check on Doris if she isn't having a good day. I like reading to the children at story hour. And I even like our little Historic Homes Tour, even if you're intent to turn it into something ugly so you can make a big impression on television."

They stood facing each other, frozen and finally wordless. With everything out in the open, with all the words spoken, both of them felt drained.

"Don't be like this," he said at last.

"Like what? Like someone who tells the truth?"

Instead of waiting for him to respond, Lexie reached for her jacket and purse. Slinging them over her arm, she headed for the door. Jeremy moved aside to allow her to pass, and she brushed by him without another word. She was a few steps away from the office when Jeremy finally summoned the will to speak again.

"Where are you going?"

Lexie took another step before stopping. With a sigh, she turned around. "I'm going home," she said. She brushed away a tear on her cheek and stood straighter. "Just like you will."

Eighteen

.....◆.....

Later that night, Alvin and Jeremy set up the cameras near the boardwalk on the Pamlico River. In the distance, the sounds of music drifted from Meyer's tobacco barn as the dance got under way. The rest of the shops downtown had closed up for the night; even Lookilu had been abandoned. Bundled in their jackets, they seemed to be alone.

"And then what?" Alvin asked.

"That's it," Jeremy said. "She left."

"You didn't follow her?"

"She didn't want me to," he said.

"How do you know?"

Jeremy rubbed his eyes, replaying the argument for the umpteenth time. The last few hours had passed in a haze. He vaguely remembered heading back to the rare-book room before putting the stack of diaries on the shelf and locking the door behind him. On the drive back, he'd brooded over what she'd said, his feelings of anger and betrayal mingling with those of sadness and regret. He spent the next four hours lying on the bed at Greenleaf, trying to figure out how he could have handled it better. He shouldn't have stormed into her office the way he had. Had he really been so angry about the diary? About the thought that he'd been duped? Or was it simply that he was angry at Lexie and, like her, looking for any excuse to start an argument?

He wasn't sure, and Alvin didn't have any answers, either, after he'd related the day's events. All Jeremy knew was that he was exhausted, and despite the fact he had to film, he was fighting the urge to go to Lexie's house and see if he could mend things. Assuming she was even there. For all he knew, she was at the dance with everyone else.

Jeremy sighed, his thoughts going back to their final moment in the library. "I could see it in the way she looked at me," he said.

"So it's over?"

"Yeah," Jeremy said, "it's over."

In the darkness, Alvin shook his head and turned away. How his friend had become so attached in such a short period of time was beyond him. She hadn't been that charming, and she didn't fit the deferential image he'd had of southern women.

But whatever. This was a fling, Alvin knew, and he had little doubt that Jeremy would get over it as soon as he boarded the flight back home.

Jeremy always got over everyone.

At the dance, Mayor Gherkin sat alone at a table in the corner, his hand on his chin.

He'd hoped that Jeremy would swing by, preferably with Lexie, but as soon as he'd arrived, he heard the chatter from the library volunteers about the argument in the library. According to those folks, it had been a big one, and had something to do with one of the diaries and some sort of scam.

Thinking about it now, he decided he shouldn't have donated his father's journal to the library, but at the time, it hadn't seemed all that important, and it was a fairly accurate record of the town's history. The library was the obvious place to donate it. But who could have guessed what would happen in the next fifteen years? Who knew the textile mill would be closed or the mine abandoned? Who knew that hundreds of people would find themselves out of work? Who knew that a number of young families would leave and never return? Who knew the town would end up fighting a battle of survival? Maybe he shouldn't have added the cemetery to the tour. Maybe he shouldn't have publicized ghosts when he knew they were simply the lights from the night shift at the paper mill. But the simple fact was that the town needed something to build on, something to get people to visit, something to make them spend a couple of days in town so they could experience how wonderful this place was. With enough people passing through, maybe they could eventually become a retirement mecca like Oriental or Washington or New Bern. It was, he thought, the town's only hope. Retirees wanted hospitable places to eat and bank, they wanted places to shop. It wouldn't happen right away, but it was the only plan he had, and it had to start somewhere. Thanks to the addition of the cemetery and its mysterious lights, they'd sold a few hundred extra tickets to the tour, and Jeremy's presence had offered them the opportunity to get the word out nationally.

Oh, he'd always figured that Jeremy was smart enough to figure it out on his own. That part didn't bother him. So what if Jeremy exposed the truth on national television? Or even in his column? People around the country would still hear about Boone Creek, and some might seek it out. Any publicity was better than no publicity. Unless, of course, he used the word "scam."

It was such a nasty-sounding word, and not in keeping with what was happening. Sure, he knew what the lights were, but hardly anyone else did, and what was the harm, anyway? The simple fact was that there was a legend, there were lights, and some people did believe that they were ghosts. Others simply played along, thinking it made the town seem different and special. People needed that now, more than ever.

Jeremy Marsh with fond memories of the town would understand that. Jeremy Marsh without them might not. And right now

Mayor Gherkin wasn't sure which impression Jeremy would be leaving with tomorrow.

"The mayor looks sort of worried, don't you think?" Rodney remarked.

Rachel looked over, feeling rather proud that they'd been standing together most of the night. Even the fact that he sometimes glanced toward the door and seemed to scan the crowd for Lexie did nothing to diminish the feeling, for the simple reason that he seemed happy to be with her as well.

"Sort of. But he always looks that way."

"No," Rodney said, "it's not the same. He's got something serious on his mind."

"Do you want to talk to him?"

Rodney thought about it. Like the mayor—like everyone else, it seemed—he'd heard about the argument at the library, but unlike most of them, he figured he had a pretty good handle on what was going on. He was able to put the bits and pieces together, especially after seeing the mayor's expression. The mayor, he suddenly knew, was worried about the way Jeremy was going to present their little mystery to the world.

As for the argument, he'd tried to warn Lexie it was coming. It had been inevitable. She was just about the most hardheaded woman he'd ever met, someone who always stood her ground. She could be volatile, and Jeremy had finally gotten a taste of it. Though Rodney wished she wouldn't have put herself through the wringer again, he was relieved to know the affair was just about over.

"No," Rodney said, "there's not much I can tell him. It's out of his hands now."

Rachel furrowed her brow. "What's out of his hands?"

"Nothing." He waived the subject off with a smile. "It's not important."

Rachel studied him for a moment before shrugging. They stood together as one song ended and the band began a new one. As more people took to the dance floor, Rachel began tapping her foot to the beat.

Rodney didn't seem to notice the dancers, preoccupied as he was. He wanted to talk to Lexie. On his way here, he'd driven past her house and seen her lights on and the car in the driveway. Earlier, he'd also received a report from another deputy, noting that City Boy and his cartoon character friend were setting up their camera on the boardwalk. Which meant that the argument had yet to be resolved.

If Lexie's lights were still on after the dance had ended, he supposed he could drop by on his way home, like he'd done the night after Mr. Renaissance had left. He had a feeling she wouldn't be entirely surprised to see him. He figured she'd probably stare at him for a moment before opening the door. She'd brew some decaf, and just like the last time, he'd sit on the couch and listen for hours as she berated herself for being so foolish.

He nodded to himself. He knew her better than he knew himself.

Even so, he wasn't ready to do that just yet. For one thing, she needed a bit more time alone so she could sort things out. And he had to admit he was a little tired of being viewed as the big-brother type, and he wasn't sure he was in the mood to listen to her. He was feeling pretty good, after all, and right now he wasn't anxious to end the evening on a downer.

Besides, the band wasn't half-bad. It was a lot better than the one they'd had last year. From the corner of his eye, he watched Rachel swaying in time to the music, pleased that she'd sought him out for company, just as she had the other night at the party. She had always been easy to be around, but the strange thing was that lately, every time he saw her, she seemed just a bit prettier than he remembered. No doubt it was just his imagination, but he couldn't help thinking that she looked especially nice tonight.

Rachel noticed him watching her and grinned in embarrassment. "Sorry," she said, "I like this song."

Rodney cleared his throat. "Would you like to dance?" he asked.

Her eyebrows shot up. "Really?"

"I'm not much of a dancer, though—"

"I'd love to," she interrupted, reaching for his hand.

Following her to the floor, he decided then and there that he'd figure out what to do about Lexie later.

Doris sat in the rocker in the living room, staring absently in the direction of the window and wondering if Lexie would drop by. Her intuition led her to doubt it, but it was one of those moments when she wished she was wrong. She knew that Lexie was upset— this was less a premonition than a reading of the obvious—and it had everything to do with Jeremy leaving.

In some ways, she wished she hadn't pushed Lexie toward him. Looking back, she knew now that she should have suspected it might end this way, so why had she done everything she could to set their affair in motion? Because Lexie was lonely? Because Lexie was stuck in a rut and had been ever since she'd fallen for the young man from Chicago? Because she'd come to believe that Lexie was frightened by the thought of ever falling for someone again?

Why couldn't she have just enjoyed Jeremy's company? Really, that was all she'd wanted Lexie to do. Jeremy was intelligent and charming, and Lexie simply needed to see that there were men like him out there. She needed to realize that not every man was like Avery or the young man from Chicago. What did she call him now? Mr. Renaissance? She tried to remember his name but knew that it wasn't important. What was important was Lexie, and Doris was worried about her.

Oh, she'd be all right in the long run, Doris knew. No doubt she would accept the reality of what had happened and find a way to move on. In time, she'd even convince herself it was a good thing. If she'd learned one thing about Lexie, it was that Lexie was a survivor.

Doris sighed. She knew Jeremy was smitten. If Lexie had fallen for him, he'd fallen even harder, and Lexie had learned the art of putting relationships behind her and living her life pretending they never happened.

Poor Jeremy, she thought. It wasn't fair to him.

Up at Cedar Creek Cemetery, Lexie stood in the thickening fog overlooking the spot where her parents had been buried. She knew that Jeremy and Alvin would be filming the trestle and Riker's Hill from the boardwalk, which meant that she could be alone with her thoughts tonight.

She didn't intend to stay long, but for some reason, she'd felt compelled to come. She'd done the same thing after her relationships with Avery and Mr. Renaissance had ended, and as she shone the flashlight on the inscribed names of her parents, she wished they would have been here to talk to her.

She knew she held a romanticized view of them, one that shifted with her moods. Sometimes she liked to think of them as fun-loving and chatty; other times she liked to believe they were quiet listeners. Right now she wanted to think of them as wise and strong, people who would give her the sort of advice that would make everything less confusing. She was tired of making mistakes in her life. That's all she'd ever done, she thought despondently, and right now she knew she was on the verge of making another, no matter what she did.

Across the river, only the lights from the paper mill were visible through the fog, and the town itself was lost in a dreamy haze. With the train approaching shortly—according to Jeremy's schedule, anyway—Alvin made one final check on the camera facing Riker's Hill. That was the tricky shot. The one on the trestle was easy, but because Riker's Hill was both distant and shrouded in mist, he wasn't absolutely certain the camera would work. It wasn't designed for long-range photography, which was exactly what was needed here. Though he'd brought along his best lens and high-speed film, he wished Jeremy had mentioned this little detail before he left New York.

Jeremy hadn't been thinking clearly for the last few days, so he supposed he could be forgiven. Normally, in a situation like this, Jeremy would have been talking and joking nonstop, but as it was, he hadn't said much of anything for the last couple of hours. Instead of being the easy, vacation-like shoot he thought it would be, the past couple of hours had begun to seem like work, especially with the chill. This wasn't what he'd signed on for, but whatever . . . he'd just raise his fee and send the bill to Nate.

Meanwhile, Jeremy was standing at the rail with his arms crossed, staring into a cloud bank.

"Did I mention that Nate called earlier?" Alvin asked, trying again to engage his friend.

"He did?"

"He woke me up from my nap," Alvin said, "and began screaming at me because you didn't have your cell phone on."

Despite his preoccupied mood, Jeremy smiled. "I've learned to keep it off as much as possible."

"Yeah, well . . . I wish you would have told me."

"What did he want?"

"The same thing. The latest update. But get this: he asked if you'd be able to get a sample."

"A sample of what?"

"I figured he was talking about the ghosts. If there was ooze or something. He had the thought that you could show it to the producers at the meeting next week."

"Ooze?"

Alvin raised his hands. "His word, not mine."

"But he knows it's just the light from the paper mill."

Alvin nodded. "Yeah, he knows. He just thought it might be a nice touch. You know, the big ta-da to really impress them."

Jeremy shook his head in disbelief. Nate had had a lot of crazy ideas over the years, but this one took the cake. He was like that, though. Anything that popped into his head came out of his mouth, and half the time, he wouldn't even remember saying it.

"He also said you should call," Alvin added.

"I would," Jeremy said, "but I left my cell phone back at Greenleaf." He paused. "You didn't tell him about the diary, did you?"

"I didn't even know about it then," Alvin said. "You didn't tell me until after he called. Like I said, he woke me up from my nap."

Jeremy nodded thoughtfully. "If he does call you again, just keep it to yourself for a while, okay?"

"You don't want him to know that the mayor's running a scam?"

"No," he said. "Not yet."

Alvin looked at him. "Not yet, or not ever?"

Jeremy didn't answer right away. That was the real question, wasn't it? "I haven't decided."

Alvin squinted through the lens once more. "It is a tough one," he said. "It might be enough to make the story, you know. I mean, the lights are one thing, but you have to realize that the solution isn't all that interesting."

"What do you mean?"

"For television. I'm not so sure they're going to be interested in the fact that a passing train causes the lights."

"It isn't just the passing train," Jeremy corrected. "It's the way the lights from the paper mill are reflected by the train onto Riker's Hill, and how the greater density of the fog in the sinking cemetery makes the lights appear."

Alvin feigned a yawn. "Sorry," he said. "You were saying?"

"It's not boring," Jeremy insisted. "Don't you realize how many things had to come together to create this phenomenon? How the quarries changed the water tables and made the cemetery sink?

The placement of the train trestle? The phases of the moon, since it's only dark enough to see the lights at certain times? The legend? The location of the paper mill and the train schedule?"

Alvin shrugged. "Trust me. It's boring with a capital B. To be honest, it would have been a lot more interesting if you hadn't found the solution. Television audiences love mysteries. Especially in places like New Orleans or Charleston or someplace cool and romantic. But reflected lights in Boone Creek, North Carolina? Do you really think people in New York or Los Angeles care?"

Jeremy opened his mouth to say something and suddenly remembered that Lexie had said exactly the same thing about the phenomenon, and she lived here. In the silence, Alvin looked at him.

"If you're serious about this television gig, you're going to need to spice it up somehow, and the diary you were telling me about just might be enough to do that. You can do the piece just like you researched it and spring the diary at the end. That might be enough to get the producers' attention if you did it right."

"You think I should throw the town to the wolves?"

Alvin shook his head. "I didn't say that. And to be honest, I'm not even sure that the diary will be enough. I'm just telling you that if you can't come up with some ooze, you'd better give using the diary some thought if you don't want to look like an idiot at the meeting."

Jeremy looked away. The train, he knew, would be coming in just a few minutes. "Lexie would never talk to me again if I did that," he said. He shrugged. "Assuming that she still wants to."

Alvin said nothing. In the silence, Jeremy looked his way.

"What do you think I should do?"

Alvin drew a long breath. "I think," Alvin said, "that it all comes down to what's most important to you, doesn't it?"

Nineteen

..... ❖ .....

Jeremy slept poorly on his last night at Greenleaf. He and Alvin had finished up filming—as the train passed, Riker's Hill only faintly registered the reflected light—and after viewing the film, both he and Alvin had decided it was good enough to prove Jeremy's theory, unless they were willing to arrange for better equipment.

Still, on their way back to Greenleaf, Jeremy's mind was barely on the mystery or even the drive. Instead, he began to once again replay the last few days in his head. He remembered the first time he'd seen Lexie in the cemetery, and their spirited exchange in the library. He thought of their lunch on Riker's Hill and their visit to the boardwalk, recalled his amazement at the extraordinary party in his honor, and how he'd felt when he first glimpsed the lights in the cemetery. But most of all, he remembered those moments when he first began to realize that he was falling in love with her.

Was it really possible for so much to have happened in only a couple of days? By the time he'd reached Greenleaf and entered his room, he was trying to pinpoint the exact moment when everything started going wrong. He wasn't quite sure, but it seemed to him now that she'd been trying to run away from her feelings, not simply from him. So when had she begun to realize that she had feelings for him? At the party, like him? At the cemetery? Earlier that afternoon?

He had no idea as to the answer. All he knew was that he loved her and that he couldn't imagine never seeing her again.

The hours passed slowly; with his flight leaving from Raleigh at noon, he would be leaving Greenleaf shortly. He rose before six, finished packing his things, and loaded them in his car. After making sure that he saw Alvin's light shining from his own room, he made his way through the chilly morning air to the office.

Jed, as he expected, scowled. His hair was even more unkempt than usual and his clothing wrinkled, so Jeremy figured he must have risen only a few minutes earlier. Jeremy set the key on his desk.

"Quite a place you have here," Jeremy said. "I'll make sure to recommend it to my friends."

If possible, Jed's expression grew even meaner, but Jeremy merely smiled ingratiatingly in return. On his way back to the room, he saw headlights bouncing in the fog as a car slowly made its way up the gravel drive. For an instant, he thought it was Lexie, and he felt a surge in his chest; when the car finally came into view, his hopes sank just as quickly.

Mayor Gherkin, bundled in a heavy jacket and scarf, emerged from the car. Showing none of the energy he had at their previous meetings, he groped his way toward Jeremy in the darkness.

"Packing up, I suppose," he called out.

"I just finished."

"Jed didn't slap you with the bill, did he?"

"No," Jeremy said. "Thanks for that, by the way."

"You're welcome. Like I said, it was the least we could do for you. I just hope you enjoyed your stay in our fine town."

Jeremy nodded, noting the worry on the mayor's face. "Yeah," he said, "I did."

For the first time since Jeremy had met him, Gherkin seemed at a loss for words. As the silence grew uncomfortable, he retucked the scarf into his jacket. "Well, I just wanted to drop by to tell you that the folks around here sure enjoyed meeting you. I know I'm speaking for the town here, but you've made quite an impression."

Jeremy put his hands in his pockets. "Why the ruse?" he asked.

Gherkin sighed. "About adding the cemetery to the tour?"

"No. I mean about the fact that your father recorded the answer in his diary and that you hid the answer from me."

A sad expression crossed Gherkin's features. "You're absolutely right," he said after a moment. His voice was hesitant. "My daddy did solve that mystery, but I suppose he was meant to." He met Jeremy's eyes. "Do you know why he became so interested in the history of our town?"

Jeremy shook his head.

"In World War II, my daddy was serving in the army with a man named Lloyd Shaumberg. He was a lieutenant, my daddy was a grunt. People these days don't seem to realize that during the war, it wasn't just soldiers out there on the front lines. Most of the people serving were just regular folks: bakers, butchers, mechanics. Shaumberg was a historian. At least that's how my daddy referred to him. Actually, he was just a history teacher at a high school in Delaware, but my daddy swore there was no finer officer in the army. He used to keep his men entertained by telling stories from the past, stories that hardly anybody knew, and it kept my daddy from being so scared about what was happening. Anyway, after the push up the boot in Italy, Shaumberg and my dad and the rest of the platoon were encircled by the Germans. Shaumberg told the men to retreat while he tried to provide cover for them. 'I don't have a choice,' he said. It was a suicide mission—everyone knew it, but that's who Shaumberg was." Gherkin paused. "Anyway, my daddy lived and Shaumberg died, and after my daddy came home from the war, he said that he'd become a historian, too, as a way to honor his friend."

When Gherkin didn't continue, Jeremy looked at him curiously. "Why are you telling me this?"

"Because," Gherkin replied, "as I see it, I didn't have much of a choice, either. Every town needs something to call its own, something to remind folks that their home is special. In New York, you don't have to worry about that. There's Broadway and Wall Street and the Empire State Building and the Statue of Liberty. But down here, after all the business closings, I looked around and realized that all we had was a legend. And legends . . . well, they're just relics from the past, and a town needs more than that to survive. That's all I was trying to do, searching for a way to keep this town alive, and then you came along."

Jeremy glanced away, thinking about the boarded storefronts he'd seen when he first arrived, remembering Lexie's comment about the closing of the textile mill and phosphorous mine.

"So you came by this morning to give me your side of the story?"

"No," Gherkin said. "I came by to let you know all this was my idea. It wasn't the town council's, it wasn't the folks' who live here. Maybe I was wrong to do what I did. Maybe you don't agree with it. But I did what I thought was right for this place and the people who live here. And all I ask is that when you do your story you keep in mind that no one else was involved. If you want to sacrifice me, I can live with that. And I think my daddy would understand."

Without waiting for a response, Gherkin went back to his car, and it soon vanished into the fog.

With dawn turning the sky an overcast gray, Jeremy was helping Alvin load the last of the equipment when Lexie arrived.

She emerged from the car looking much the same as she did the first time he'd seen her, her violet eyes unreadable even as she met his gaze. In her hand was Gherkin's diary. For a moment, they faced each other as if neither one knew what to say.

Alvin, standing near the open trunk, broke the silence.

"Good morning," he said.

She forced a smile. "Hey, Alvin."

"You're up early."

She shrugged, her eyes flashing back to Jeremy. Alvin looked from one to the other before motioning over his shoulder.

"I think I'll give the room one last check," he said, despite the fact that no one seemed to be paying attention.

When he was gone, Jeremy took a deep breath. "I didn't think you'd come by," he said.

"To be honest, I wasn't sure I would, either."

"I'm glad you did," he said. The gray light reminded him of their walk on the beach near the lighthouse, and he felt with a twisting arc of pain how much he'd come to love her. Though his first instinct was to close the gap between them, her stiff posture kept him at a distance.

She nodded toward his car. "You're packed up and ready to go, I see."

"Yeah," he said. "All packed up."

"And you finished filming the lights?"

He hesitated, hating the banality of their conversation. "Did you really come here to talk about my work or whether my car is packed?"

"No," she said. "I didn't."

"Why did you come, then?"

"To apologize for the way I treated you yesterday at the library. I shouldn't have acted the way I did. It wasn't fair to you."

He gave a half-smile. "It's okay," he said. "I'll get over it. And I'm sorry, too."

She held up the diary. "I brought this for you. In case you wanted it."

"I didn't think you'd want me to use it."

"I don't," she answered.

"Then why give it to me?"

"Because I should have told you about the diary passage and I don't want you to think that anyone here is engaged in some cover-up. I can see how you might have thought the town was up to something, and this is a peace offering. But I want to assure you that it wasn't some big scheme—"

"I know," Jeremy interrupted. "The mayor came by this morning."

She nodded, and her eyes dropped before rising to meet his again. In that instant, he thought she was going to say something, but whatever it was, she stopped herself. "Well, I guess that's it," she said, pushing her hands into her coat pockets. "I should probably let you finish up so you can be on your way. I've never been a fan of long good-byes."

"So this is a good-bye?" he asked, trying to hold her gaze.

She looked almost sad as she tilted her head to the side. "It has to be, doesn't it?"

"So that's it, then? You just came by to tell me it's over?" He ran his fingers roughly through his hair, frowning. "Don't I have any say in the matter?"

Her voice was quiet when she answered. "We've been through all of this, Jeremy. I didn't come here this morning to argue, and I didn't come here to make you angry. I came because I was sorry about the way I treated you yesterday. And because I didn't want you to think that the week meant nothing to me. It did."

Her words felt like physical blows, and he struggled to speak. "But you're intent on ending this."

"I'm intent on being realistic about it," she said.

"What if I told you that I love you?"

She stared at him for a long moment before turning away. "Don't say that."

He took a step toward her. "But I do," he said. "I love you. I can't help the way I feel."

"Jeremy . . . please . . ."

He moved more quickly, sensing that he was finally breaching her defenses, his courage building with every step. "I want to make this work."

"We can't," she said.

"Of course, we can," he said, rounding the car. "We can figure this out."

"No," she said, her voice growing more adamant. She took a step backward.

"Why not?"

"Because I'm going to marry Rodney, okay?"

Her words stopped him cold. "What are you talking about?"

"Last night after the dance, he came by and we talked. We talked for a long time. He's honest, he's hardworking, he loves me, and he's here. You're not."

He stared at her, stunned by her announcement. "I don't believe you."

She stared back, her face impassive. "Believe it," she said.

When Jeremy failed to say anything, she handed him the diary, then raised a hand in a brief wave and began to walk backward with him in her sights, much the way she had that day at the cemetery.

"Good-bye, Jeremy," she said before turning to get in her car.

Still frozen in shock, Jeremy heard the ignition turn over and saw her look over her shoulder as she began to back out. He strode forward to put his hand on the hood, trying to stop her. But as the car started to move, he let his fingers glide along the damp surface and finally took a small step back as the car slid into drive.

For an instant, Jeremy thought he caught the flash of tears in her eyes. But then he saw her look away, and he knew once and for all he wasn't going to see her again.

He wanted to shout out, telling her to stop. He wanted to tell her that he could stay, that he wanted to stay, that if leaving meant losing her, then going home wasn't worth it. But the words stayed trapped inside him, and ever so slowly, the car rolled by him, picking up speed as it made its way down the drive.

In the fog, Jeremy remained standing, watching until the car turned shadowlike and only the taillights were visible. And then it vanished completely, the sound of the engine fading into the woods.

Twenty

·····❖·····

The rest of the day passed as if he were watching it through someone else's eyes. Hurt and angry, he barely remembered following Alvin along the highway back toward Raleigh. More than once, he glanced in his rearview mirror, staring back over the black asphalt, watching the cars that followed in the distance, hoping that one of them was Lexie. She'd been perfectly clear in her desire to end the relationship, but even so, he felt a surge of adrenaline whenever he saw a car that resembled hers, and he would slow down to get a better look. Alvin, meanwhile, would move farther into the distance. Jeremy knew he should be paying attention to the road beyond the windshield; instead, he spent most of his time looking back.

After dropping off his rental car, he paced the terminal and made his way to the gate. Walking past crowded shops, veering around people who were scurrying his way, he wondered again why Lexie seemed so willing to give up everything they'd shared.

On the plane, his thoughts were interrupted when Alvin took a seat next to him.

"Thanks for making it so we could sit together," Alvin said, his voice dripping with sarcasm. He stored his bag in the overhead bin.

"Huh?" Jeremy said.

"The seats. I thought you were going to take care of them when you checked in. It's a good thing I asked when I got my boarding pass. I was supposed to sit in the last row."

"Sorry," Jeremy said. "I guess I forgot."

"Yeah, I guess so," Alvin said, dropping into the seat next to him. He glanced at Jeremy. "You want to talk about it yet?"

Jeremy hesitated. "I'm not sure there's anything to talk about."

"That's what you said earlier. But I've heard it's supposed to be good for you. Haven't you been keeping up with the talk shows lately? Express your feelings, purge your guilt, seek and ye shall find?"

"Maybe later," he mumbled.

"Suit yourself," Alvin said. "If you don't want to talk, fine. I'll just take a nap." He leaned back in his seat and closed his eyes.

Jeremy stared out the window as Alvin slept for most of the flight.

In the cab he took from La Guardia, Jeremy was bombarded with noise and the hectic pace of the city: businessmen rushing past carrying briefcases, mothers towing small children while attempting to manage shopping bags, the smell of car exhaust, horns honking, and police sirens blaring. It was perfectly normal, a world he'd grown up in and had taken for granted; what surprised him was that as he looked out the car window, trying to orient himself to the reality of his life, he thought of Greenleaf and the utter silence he'd experienced there.

Back at his apartment building, his mailbox was stuffed with advertisements and bills; he grabbed it all and trudged up the stairs. Inside the apartment, everything was the same as he'd left it. Magazines lay strewn around the living room, his office was as cluttered as always, and there were still three bottles of Heineken in the refrigerator. After stowing his suitcase in his room, he opened a bottle of beer and carried his computer and satchel to his desk.

He had all the information he'd accumulated in the past few days: his notes and copies of the articles, the digital camera containing the photographs he'd shot of the cemetery, the map, and the diary. As he began unpacking, a packet of postcards fell onto the desk, and it took him a moment to remember that he'd picked them up on his first day in town. The top postcard was a view of the town from the river. Removing the wrapper, he began to thumb through the rest of them. He found postcards depicting the town hall, a misty view of a blue heron standing in the shallows of Boone Creek, and sailboats congregating on a blustery afternoon. Halfway through the packet, he found himself pausing at a picture of the library.

He sat motionless, thinking of Lexie and realizing again that he loved her.

But that was over now, he reminded himself, and he continued shuffling through the postcards. He saw a strangely grainy photograph of Herbs and another of the town as viewed from Riker's Hill. The final postcard was a picture of the downtown area of Boone Creek, and here he found himself pausing once more.

The postcard, a reproduction of an old black-and-white photo, captured the town circa 1950. In the foreground was the theater with well-dressed patrons waiting near the ticket window; in the background stood a decorated Christmas tree in the small green area just off the main street. On the sidewalks, couples could be seen peeking in windows decorated with garlands and lights, or strolling hand in hand. As Jeremy studied the picture, he found himself imagining how the holidays were celebrated in Boone Creek fifty years earlier. In place of boarded storefronts, he saw sidewalks crowded with women wearing scarves and men wearing hats and children pointing upward at an icicle hanging from a signpost.

As he looked, Jeremy found himself thinking about Mayor Gherkin. The postcard depicted not only Boone Creek's way of life half a century before but also the way that Gherkin hoped the town could be again. It was a Norman Rockwell existence, albeit with a southern flair. He held the postcard for a long time, thinking about Lexie and wondering again what he was going to do about the story.

The meeting with the television producers was scheduled for Tuesday afternoon. Nate met Jeremy at his favorite steak house, Smith and Wollensky's, beforehand. Nate was his buoyant self, excited to see Jeremy and relieved to have him back in town under his watchful eye. As soon as he sat down, he began talking about the footage that Alvin had shot, describing the images as fantastic, like "that haunted house in Amityville, but real," and assuring him that the television executives would love them. For the most part, Jeremy sat in silence listening to Nate jabber on, but when he saw a dark-haired woman leaving the restaurant, her hair exactly the same length as Lexie's, he felt a lump in his throat and suddenly excused himself to go to the restroom.

When he got back, Nate was perusing the menu. Jeremy added sweetener to the iced tea he'd ordered. He, too, scanned the menu and mentioned that he was thinking of having the swordfish. Nate looked up.

"But this is a steak house," he protested.

"I know. I'm in the mood for something lighter, though."

Nate's hand absently traveled to his midsection, as if wondering whether to do the same thing. In the end, he frowned as he set the menu aside. "I gotta go with the strip steak," he said. "I've been thinking about it all morning. But where were we?"

"The meeting," Jeremy reminded him, and Nate leaned forward.

"So it's not ghosts, right?" Nate said. "You mentioned on the phone that you saw the lights but had a pretty good idea of what they were."

"No," Jeremy said. "It's not ghosts."

"What are they, then?"

Jeremy pulled out his notes and spent the next few minutes

telling Nate what he'd learned, beginning with the legend and describing in detail his process of discovery. Even he could hear the monotone in his voice. As Nate listened, he nodded continually, but when he finished, Jeremy could see wrinkles of concern forming on Nate's forehead.

"The paper mill?" he said. "I was hoping it was some sort of government tests or something like that. Like the military testing a new plane or something." He paused. "And you're sure it's not a military train? News folks love to expose anything about the military. Secret weapons programs, things like that. Or maybe you heard something out there that you couldn't explain."

"Sorry," Jeremy said, his voice flat, "it's just light that ricochets off the train. There weren't any noises."

Watching Nate, Jeremy could see the wheels turning. Nate, Jeremy had come to realize, had better instincts than his editors when it came to stories.

"It's not much," he said. "Did you find out which version of the legend was true? Maybe there's something you could do with the race angle."

Jeremy shook his head. "I haven't been able to confirm that Hettie Doubilet even existed. Aside from the legends, I couldn't find any record of her in any official documents. And Watts Landing is long gone."

"Look, I don't mean to be picky here, but you've got to pump up your delivery if you want this to work. If you're not enthusiastic, they're not going to be excited, either. Am I right or am I right? Of course, I'm right. But come on, be honest with me. You found something else, didn't you?"

"What are you talking about?"

"Alvin," Nate said. "When he dropped off the videos, I asked him about the story just to get his impression, and he mentioned that you found something else that was interesting."

Jeremy's expression didn't falter. "He did?"

"His words, not mine," Nate said, looking pleased with himself.

"He didn't tell me what it was, though. He said that was up to you. Which must mean that it's big."

Staring at Nate, he could practically feel the diary burning a hole through the fabric of his satchel. On the table, Nate fiddled with his fork, turning it over and back again, waiting.

"Well," Jeremy began, knowing his time to make his decision had finally run out.

When he didn't continue, Nate leaned forward. "Yes?"

That evening, after the meeting was concluded, Jeremy sat alone in his apartment, absently watching the world outside. It had begun to snow, and the flakes were a swirling, hypnotic mass under the glow of the streetlamp.

The meeting had started out well; Nate had revved the producers up to such an extent that they were transfixed by the images they saw. Nate had done the best he could. Afterward, Jeremy told them about the legend, noting their growing interest as he spoke of Hettie Doubilet, and the painstaking way he'd approached the investigation. He interspersed the story of Boone Creek with other investigations into the mysterious, and more than once, he saw the executives glance at each other, clearly trying to figure out how to work him into the show.

But as he sat alone later that night, the diary in his lap, he knew he wouldn't be working with them. His story—the mystery of Boone Creek's cemetery—was akin to an exciting novel that petered out at the end. The solution was too simple, too pat, and he'd sensed their disappointment by the time he said good-bye. Nate had promised to keep in touch, as they did, but Jeremy knew there would be no further calls.

As for the diary, he'd kept that to himself, as he had with Nate earlier.

Later, he made a phone call to Mayor Gherkin. Jeremy's proposal was simple: Boone Creek would no longer promise visitors on the Historic Homes Tour a chance to see ghosts in the cemetery.

The word "haunted" would be removed from the brochure, as would any claims that the lights had anything to do with the supernatural. Instead, the legend's history would be given full play, and visitors could be informed that they just might witness something spectacular. While some tourists might see the lights and wonder aloud if they were the ghosts from the legend, the volunteers who conducted the tours were told never to suggest as much. Finally, Jeremy asked the mayor to remove the T-shirts and cups from his department store downtown.

In exchange, Jeremy promised he would never mention anything about Cedar Creek Cemetery on television, in his column, or in an independent article. He wouldn't expose the mayor's plan to turn the town into a ghostly version of Roswell, New Mexico, nor would he tell anyone in the town that the mayor had known the truth all along.

Mayor Gherkin accepted the offer. After hanging up, Jeremy called Alvin, whom he swore to secrecy.

Twenty-one

......❖......

In the days following Jeremy's unsuccessful meeting with the producers, he focused his attention on trying to return to his previous routines. He spoke to his editor at *Scientific American*. Behind on his deadline and vaguely remembering something Nate had suggested to him, he agreed to do a column about the possible dangers of a low-carbohydrate diet. He spent hours on the Internet, scanning countless newspapers, looking for other stories that might be of interest. He was disappointed to learn that Clausen—with the help of a high-profile publicity firm in New York—had largely weathered the storm after Jeremy's appearance on *Primetime* and was still in negotiations for his own television show. The irony of the situation wasn't lost on Jeremy, and he spent the rest of the day bemoaning the gullibility of true believers.

Little by little, he was getting himself back on track. Or, at least, he thought he was. Though he still thought of Lexie frequently, wondering whether she was busy preparing for her marriage to Rodney, he did his best to force those thoughts out of his mind. They were just too painful. Instead, he tried to resume the life he'd been living before he met Lexie. On Friday night, he went out to a nightclub. It didn't go particularly well. Instead of mingling and trying to catch the attention of the women standing nearby, he sat at the bar nursing a single beer for most of the night, leaving long before he normally would have. The next day, he visited his family in Queens, but seeing his brothers and their wives playing with their kids only made him wish again for something that could never be.

By Monday noon, as another winter storm was settling in, he'd convinced himself that it was really over. She hadn't called and neither had he. At times, those few days with Lexie seemed like nothing more than the mirage he'd been investigating. It couldn't have been real, he told himself, but as he sat at his desk, he found himself thumbing through the postcards again, finally pinning the one of the library on the wall behind the desk.

He ordered lunch from the Chinese restaurant down the block for the third time in a week, then leaned back in his chair, wondering about the choices he'd made. For an instant, he wondered if Lexie would be eating at the same time he was, but the thought was interrupted by the buzz of the intercom.

He grabbed his wallet and headed toward the door. Through the static of the intercom, he heard a female voice.

"It's open. Come on up."

He riffled through his bills, pulled out a twenty, and reached for the door just as he heard the knock.

"That was fast," he said. "Usually it takes . . ."

His voice trailed off as the door opened and he saw who was standing before him.

In the silence, he and his visitor stared at each other before Doris finally smiled.

"Surprise," she said.

He blinked. "Doris?"

She stamped the snow off her shoes. "It's a blizzard out there," she said, "and it's so icy I wasn't sure I was going to make it. The taxi was sliding all over the road."

He continued to stare, trying to make sense of her sudden appearance.

She slipped her handbag from her shoulder and met his gaze. "Are you going to make me wait out in the hallway, or are you going to invite me in?"

"Yeah . . . of course. Please . . . ," he said, motioning her inside.

Doris moved past him and set her bag on the end table near the door. She glanced around his apartment and removed her jacket. "This is nice," she said, walking around the living room. "It's bigger than I thought it would be. But the stairs were a killer. You really need to get the elevator fixed."

"Yeah . . . I know."

She paused at the window. "But the city is beautiful, even in the storm. And so . . . busy. I can see why some people would want to live here."

"What are you doing here?"

"I came to talk to you, of course."

"About Lexie?"

She didn't answer right away. Instead, she sighed, then said evenly, "Among other things." When his brow furrowed, she shrugged. "You wouldn't happen to have any tea, would you? I'm still a little chilly."

"But . . ."

"We've got a lot to talk about," she said, her voice holding steady. "I know you have questions, but it's going to take a while. So how about some tea?"

Jeremy went into the small kitchen and heated a cup of water in the microwave. After adding a tea bag, he carried the cup back to the living room, where he found Doris sitting on the couch. He handed her the cup, and she took a sip almost immediately.

"I'm sorry that I didn't call. I know I should have. You must be pretty shocked. But I wanted to talk to you in person."

"How did you know where I live?"

"I talked to your friend Alvin. He told me."

"You talked to Alvin?"

"Yesterday," she said. "He had given his phone number to

Rachel, so I called him, and he was kind enough to give me your address. I wish I'd had the chance to meet him while he was in Boone Creek. He seemed like a perfect gentleman."

Jeremy sensed that the small talk was a sign of mounting nervousness and decided to say nothing. He knew she was simply trying to work up to whatever it was she was going to say.

The buzzer sounded again and Doris glanced toward the door. "That's my lunch," he said, annoyed by the distraction. "Give me a minute, okay?"

He rose from his seat, pressed the intercom, and unlocked his door; as he waited, he glimpsed Doris smoothing her blouse. A moment later, she fidgeted again, and for some reason, the fact that she was nervous helped to steady his own nerves. He drew a long breath and stepped out into the hallway, meeting the deliveryman as he emerged from the stairwell.

Jeremy came back in and was just about to set the bag of food on the kitchen counter when he heard Doris behind him.

"What did you order?"

"Beef with broccoli, pork fried rice."

"It smells good."

It was, perhaps, the way she said it that made him smile. "Would you like me to make up a couple of plates?"

"I wouldn't want to take your food."

"There's plenty," he said, reaching for some plates. "And besides, didn't you tell me that you like to talk over a good meal?"

He spooned out the food, then brought it to the table; Doris sat down next to him.

Again, he decided to let her begin, and they ate in silence for a few minutes.

"This is delicious," she finally said. "I didn't have any breakfast, and I guess I didn't realize how hungry I was. It's quite a trip to get here. I had to leave at crack of dawn, and my flight was delayed. The weather had everything backed up, and for a while there, I wasn't sure we'd even take off. I was nervous, too. It was the first time I've ever flown."

"Oh?"

"Never had a reason to. Lexie asked me to come up and visit her while she lived up here, but my husband wasn't in the best of health and I just never got around to it. Then she moved back. She was quite a wreck back then. I know you probably think she's tough and strong, but that's just what she wants others to believe. Underneath, she's like everyone else, and she was crushed by what happened with Avery." Doris hesitated. "She told you about him, right?"

"Yes."

"She suffered in silence, kept up the brave front, but I knew how upset she was. There was nothing I could do for her. She hid it by keeping busy, running from here to there, talking to everyone and trying to make sure they had the impression that she was okay. You can't imagine how helpless that made me feel."

"Why are you telling me this?"

"Because she's acting the same way now."

Jeremy moved his food around with his fork. "I wasn't the one who ended it, Doris."

"I know that, too."

"Then why talk to me?"

"Lexie won't listen."

Despite the tension, Jeremy laughed. "I guess that means you think I'm a pushover?"

"No," she said. "But what I'm hoping is that you're not as stubborn as she is."

"Even if I'm willing to try again, it's still up to her."

Doris watched him carefully. "Do you really believe that?"

"I tried to talk to her. I told her I wanted to find a way to make the relationship work."

Instead of responding to his comment, Doris asked, "You were married once, weren't you?"

"A long time ago. Did Lexie tell you that?"

"No," she said. "I've known it since our first conversation."

"Psychic abilities again?"

"No, nothing like that. It has more to do with the way you interact with women. You carry yourself with the sort of confidence that a lot of women find appealing. At the same time, I had the sense that you understand what women want, but that for some reason you're unwilling to give yourself completely."

"What's this got to do with anything?"

"Women want the fairy tale. Not all women, of course, but most women grow up dreaming about the kind of man who would risk everything for them, even knowing they might get hurt." She paused. "Kind of like the way you went to find Lexie at the beach. That's why she fell in love with you."

"She's not in love with me."

"Yes, she is."

Jeremy opened his mouth to deny it but couldn't. Instead, he shook his head. "It doesn't matter now, anyway. She's marrying Rodney."

Doris stared at him. "No, she isn't. But before you think it was her way of pushing you away, you should know that she only said it so that if you did leave, she wouldn't lie awake at night wondering why you never came back for her." She paused, letting that sink in. "And besides, you didn't really believe her, anyway, did you?"

It was the way Doris said this that made him remember his initial response when Lexie first told him about Rodney. No, he suddenly realized, he hadn't believed it then.

Doris reached across the table and took his hand.

"You're a good man, Jeremy. And you deserved the truth, which was why I came up here."

She stood from the table. "I've got a flight to catch. If I don't get back tonight, Lexie's going to know something's up. I'd rather she didn't know I came up here."

"That's quite a trip. You could have simply called."

"I know. But I had to see your face."

"Why?"

"I wanted to know if you were in love with her, too." She patted him on the shoulder before heading to the living room, where she picked up her handbag.

"Doris?" Jeremy called out.

She turned. "Yes?"

"Did you find the answer you were hoping for?"

She smiled. "The real question is, did you?"

Twenty-two

...◆....

Jeremy paced the length of the living room. He needed to think, to work through the options, so he would know what to do.

He ran his hand through his hair before shaking his head. There wasn't time for indecision. Not now, knowing what he knew. He had to go back. Get on the first plane he could and find her again. Talk to her, try to convince her that when he'd told her that he loved her, he'd never been more serious about anything in his life. Tell her that he couldn't imagine a life without her. Tell her that he would do whatever it took so they could be together.

Before Doris had even hailed a cab outside his building, he was reaching for the phone and calling the airline.

He was put on hold for what seemed like forever, growing more irate with every passing moment, until he finally got an agent to assist him.

The last flight to Raleigh was leaving in ninety minutes. Even in good weather, the cab ride could take half that long, but it was either make the flight or wait until tomorrow.

He had to move quickly. Grabbing a duffel bag from the closet, he tossed in two pairs of jeans, a couple of shirts, socks, and underwear. He threw on his jacket and stuffed his cell phone in his pocket. Took the charger from the top of the desk. Laptop? No, he wouldn't need it. What else?

Oh, yeah. He rushed to the bathroom and checked the contents of his dop kit. Remembered his razor and toothbrush and shoved them in. He turned out the lights, put his computer to sleep, and grabbed his wallet. Flipping through it, he saw that he had enough cash to get him to the airport—good enough for now. From the corner of his eye, he spied Owen Gherkin's diary half buried beneath a stack of papers. He tossed the diary and his dop kit into the duffel bag, tried to think if he needed anything else, then gave up. No time for that. He picked up the keys from the end table near the door, took one last look around, then locked the door before charging down the stairs.

He hailed a cab, told the driver he was in a hurry, and sat back with a sigh, hoping for the best. Doris had been right: due to the snow, traffic was bad, and as they came to a stop on the bridge crossing the East River, he cursed under his breath. To cut time at security, he removed his belt and threw it in the duffel bag, along with his keys. The driver glanced at him in the rearview mirror. His expression was one of boredom, and although he drove fast, it was without any sense of urgency. Jeremy bit his tongue, knowing it wouldn't do any good to irritate him.

Minutes passed. The flurries, which had temporarily stopped, started up again, reducing visibility even further. Forty-five minutes until his flight.

The traffic slowed again, and Jeremy sighed aloud as he looked at his watch once more. Thirty-five minutes before the flight. Ten minutes later, they reached the exit for the airport and headed toward the terminal.

Finally.

The moment the cab came to a stop, he opened the door and tossed two twenties to the driver. Inside the terminal, he hesitated for only an instant before the electronic departure board to figure out which gate he needed. He stood on a mercifully short line to get his electronic ticket, then headed toward security. He felt his heart sink when he saw how long the lines were, but caught a break as a new line suddenly opened. People who'd been waiting began drifting that way; Jeremy, on a run, cut three of them off.

The flight would close its doors in less than ten minutes, and once through security, Jeremy started to jog, then run. Weaving through the crowds, he reached for his driver's license, counting the gates.

He was breathing hard by the time he reached the gate and could feel himself beginning to perspire.

"Did I make it?" he panted.

"Only because of a brief delay," the woman at the counter said, typing into the computer. The attendant near the door glared at him.

After taking his ticket, the attendant closed the door after Jeremy had started down the ramp. He was still trying to catch his breath when he reached the plane.

"We'll be backing off the gate shortly. You're the last one, so you can take a seat anywhere," the flight attendant said as she made room for him to pass.

"Thanks."

He moved down the aisle, amazed that he'd made it, and spotted an open window seat halfway down. He was storing his duffel bag in the overhead bin when he caught sight of Doris, three rows behind him.

Returning his gaze, she said nothing; she simply smiled.

The plane touched down in Raleigh at half past three, and Jeremy walked with Doris through the terminal. Near the exit doors, he motioned over his shoulder.

"I've got to get a rental car," he said.

"I'll be happy to take you," she said. "I'm going that way."

When she saw him hesitate, she smiled. "And I'll let you drive," she added.

He never let the speed drop below eighty and shaved forty-five minutes from the three-hour drive; dusk was setting in as he approached the outskirts of town. With random images of Lexie floating through his mind, he didn't notice the passage of time, nor could he remember much of the drive. He tried to rehearse what he wanted to say or anticipate how she would respond, but he realized that he had no idea what was going to happen. It didn't matter. Even if he was flying by the seat of his pants, he couldn't imagine doing anything differently.

The streets of Boone Creek were quiet as he approached downtown. Doris turned toward him.

"Would you mind dropping me off at home?"

He glanced at her, realizing that they'd barely spoken since leaving the airport. With his mind fixed on Lexie, he hadn't even noticed.

"Don't you need your car?"

"Not until tomorrow. Besides, it's too cold to be walking around tonight."

Following Doris's directions, Jeremy pulled to a stop in front of her house. At the small white bungalow, he could see her newspaper propped against the door. The crescent moon hovered just above the roofline, and in the dim light, he glanced at himself in the rearview mirror. Knowing that he was only minutes from seeing Lexie, he ran his hand through his hair.

Doris noted his nervous gesture and patted him on the leg. "It's going to be okay," she said. "Trust me."

Jeremy forced a smile, trying to hide his doubts. "Any last-minute advice?"

"No," she said, shaking her head. "Besides, you already took whatever I had to give. You're here, aren't you?"

Jeremy nodded, and Doris leaned across the seat to kiss him on the cheek.

"Welcome home," she whispered.

Jeremy turned the car around, the tires screeching as he sped back toward the library. Lexie had mentioned keeping the library open for people who came in after work, hadn't she? In one of their conversations? Yes, he thought, he was sure of it, but for the life of him, he couldn't remember when. Was it the day they'd met? The next day? He sighed, recognizing that his compulsive need to review their history was simply an attempt to calm his nerves. Should he have come? Would she be glad to see him? Any confidence he had evaporated as he neared the library.

Downtown appeared in sharp focus, in contrast to the dreamy, misty images he remembered. He drove past Lookilu and saw half a dozen cars parked out front, saw another group of cars clustered near the pizza place. A group of teenagers was loitering on the corner, and while he initially thought they were smoking, he realized it was simply the warmth of their breath condensing in cold air.

He turned again; on the far side of the intersection, he saw the lights from the library blazing on both floors. He parked the car and stepped out into the cold night air. Taking a deep breath, he strode quickly to the front door and pulled it open.

With no one at the front desk, he stopped to peek through the glass doors that opened into the downstairs area. No sign of Lexie among the patrons. He swept his gaze around the room, making sure.

Figuring Lexie was either in her office or in the main room, he hurried down the corridor and up the stairs, where he glanced around before heading toward her office. From a distance, he noted that the door was closed, no light spilling out beneath it. Checking the door, he found it locked, then searched among the aisles as he made his way to the rare-book room.

Locked.

He cut a zigzag route through the main room, walking quickly, ignoring the stares of people who no doubt recognized him, then ran down the stairs. As he headed for the front door, he realized that he should have checked for Lexie's car and wondered why he hadn't.

Nerves, a voice inside his head answered.

No matter. If she wasn't here, she was probably at home.

One of the elderly volunteers was emerging with an armful of books, and her eyes lit up when she saw him approaching.

"Mr. Marsh?" she called out in a singsong voice. "I didn't expect to see you again! What on earth are you doing here?"

"I was looking for Lexie."

"She left about an hour ago. I think she was heading to Doris's to check on her. I know she called earlier, and Doris didn't answer."

Jeremy kept his expression steady. "Oh?"

"And Doris wasn't at Herbs, I know that much. I tried to tell Lexie that Doris was probably running some errands, but you know how Lexie worries. She's like a mother hen. Drives Doris crazy sometimes, but she knows that it's just Lexie's way of showing that she cares." She paused, suddenly realizing that Jeremy hadn't explained his reappearance. Before she could say another word, however, Jeremy cut her off.

"Listen, I'd love to stay and chat, but I've really got to talk to Lexie."

"About the story again? Maybe I could help. I have the key to the rare-book room, if you need it."

"No, that's not necessary. But thank you."

He was already past her when he heard her voice behind him.

"If she comes back, do you want me to tell her you came by?"

"No," he called out over his shoulder. "It's a surprise."

He shivered as he stepped into the cold and ran back to the car. He pulled onto the main road, followed the curve to the edge of town, watching as the sky grew even darker. Above the trees, he could see stars, thousands of them. Millions. For an instant, he wondered how they would look from the top of Riker's Hill.

He turned onto Lexie's street, saw her house, and felt something give way when he saw no lights shining from inside and no car in the drive. Reluctant to believe his eyes, he passed the house slowly, hoping he'd made a mistake.

If not at the library, if not at home, where was she?

Had she passed him on the way to Doris's? He tried to think. Had anyone passed him? Not that he remembered, but he really hadn't been paying attention. He was sure he would have recognized her car, anyway.

He decided to swing by Doris's just to make sure, and—driving too fast through town while watching for her car—he sped back to her white bungalow.

One look was all it took to see that Doris had already gone to bed.

Still, he paused in front of the house, trying to figure out where Lexie had gone. It wasn't that large of a town and the options were few. He thought immediately of Herbs, but remembered it wasn't open in the evening. He hadn't seen her car at Lookilu— or anywhere else downtown, for that matter. He supposed she could have been doing something mundane: grocery shopping or returning a video or picking up dry cleaning . . . or . . . or . . .

And with that, he suddenly realized where she was.

Jeremy gripped the steering wheel, trying to steel himself for the end of his journey. His chest was tight and he could feel himself breathing too quickly, just as he had earlier in the afternoon, as he'd taken his seat on the plane. It was hard to believe that he'd started his day in New York thinking he would never see Lexie again, and now here he was in Boone Creek, planning to do what he thought was impossible. He drove the darkened roads, still unnerved by the thought of what Lexie's reaction to his return might be.

Moonlight lent the cemetery an almost bluish color, and the

tombstones seemed to glow as if lit dimly from within. The wrought-iron fencing added a spooky touch to the ethereal setting. As Jeremy approached the cemetery's entrance, he saw Lexie's car parked near the gate.

He pulled up behind it. Climbing out of Doris's car, he could hear the ticking of the engine as it cooled. Leaves crackled underfoot and he took a deep breath. He placed his hand on the hood of Lexie's car and felt the warmth radiating through his palm. She hadn't been here long.

He passed through the gate and saw the magnolia, its leaves black and shiny, as if they'd been dipped in oil. He stepped over a branch and recalled groping his way through the cemetery on that foggy night with Lexie when he'd been unable to see anything. Halfway through the cemetery grounds, he heard an owl hoot from one of the trees.

Leaving the path, he moved around a crumbling crypt, walking slowly to keep the noise to a minimum, climbing the slight incline. Above him, the moon hung in the sky as if tacked to a blackened sheet. He thought he heard a low murmur, and when he stopped to listen, he felt an intense surge of adrenaline. He had come to find her, to find himself, and his body was readying him for whatever came next. He crested the small hill, knowing that Lexie's parents were buried on the other side.

It was almost time. He would see Lexie in just a moment and she would see him. He would settle it once and for all, here where it all began.

Lexie was standing just where he imagined she would be, bathed in silvery light. Her face had an open, almost mournful expression, and her eyes were a luminous violet. She was dressed for the weather—a scarf around her neck, black gloves that made her hands mere shadows.

She was speaking softly, but he couldn't make out the words. As he watched, she suddenly paused and looked up. For the longest moment, their eyes simply held one another.

Lexie seemed frozen in place as she stared back at him. Finally, she looked away. Her eyes focused down on the graves again, and Jeremy realized he had no idea what she was thinking. He suddenly felt that it had been a mistake to come here. She didn't want him here, she didn't want him at all. His throat tightened, and he was about to turn away when he noticed that Lexie wore the slightest smirk on her face.

"You know, you really shouldn't stare like that," she said. "Women like a man who knows how to be subtle."

Relief flooded his body, and he smiled as he took a step forward. When he came close enough to touch her, he reached out and placed his hand on her lower back. She didn't pull away; instead, she leaned into him. Doris had been right.

He was home.

"No," he whispered into her hair, "women like a man who will follow them to the ends of the earth, or even Boone Creek, if that's what it takes."

Pulling her close, he lifted her face and kissed her, knowing that he would never leave her again.

Epilogue

······❖······

J eremy and Lexie were sitting together, cuddled beneath a blanket, staring down at the town below. It was Thursday evening, three days after Jeremy's return to Boone Creek. The white and yellow lights of the town, interspersed with occasional reds and greens, seemed to be flickering, and Jeremy could see plumes of smoke rising from chimneys. The river flowed black like liquid coal, mirroring the sky above. Beyond it, the lights from the paper mill spread in all directions, illuminating the railroad trestle.

Over the past couple of days, he and Lexie had spent a lot of time talking. She apologized for lying about Rodney and confessed that driving away as Jeremy stood on the gravel road at Greenleaf had been the hardest thing she'd ever done. She described the misery of the week that they'd been apart, a sentiment that Jeremy echoed. For his part, he told her that while Nate wasn't thrilled with his move, his editor at *Scientific American* was willing to let him work from Boone Creek, provided he made it back to New York regularly.

Jeremy didn't mention that Doris had come to visit him in New York, however; on his second evening back in town, Lexie had brought him over to Doris's for dinner, and Doris had pulled him aside and asked him not to say anything.

"I don't want her thinking that I was interfering in her life," she said, her eyes shining. "Believe it or not, she thinks *I'm* pushy."

Sometimes he found it hard to believe that he was really here with her; on the other hand, it was hard to believe that he'd ever left in the first place. Being with Lexie felt natural, as if she were the home he'd been seeking. Although Lexie seemed to feel the same way, she wouldn't let him stay at her house, insisting, "I wouldn't want to give the folks around here something to gossip about." Nevertheless, he felt reasonably comfortable at Greenleaf, even if Jed still hadn't cracked a smile.

"So you think it's serious between Rodney and Rachel?" Jeremy asked.

"It seems that way," Lexie said. "They've been spending a lot of time together lately. She beams every time he shows up at Herbs, and I swear he *blushes*. I think they'll be really good for each other."

"I still can't believe you told me you were going to marry him."

She nudged her shoulder against his. "I don't want to go into that again. I've already apologized. And I'd rather you not remind me about it for the rest of my life, thank you very much."

"But it's such a good story."

"You think so because it makes you look good by making me look bad."

"I was good."

She kissed him on the cheek. "Yes, you were."

He pulled her closer, watching as a shooting star skimmed the sky. They sat in silence for a moment.

"Are you busy tomorrow?" he asked.

"That depends," she said. "What did you have in mind?"

"I called Mrs. Reynolds, and I'm going to check out some houses. I'd like it if you came along. In a place like this, I wouldn't want to find myself in the wrong sort of neighborhood."

She hugged him tighter. "I'd love to come."

"And I'd like to bring you to New York, too. Some time in the next couple of weeks. My mom's insisting that she have a chance to meet you."

"I'd like to meet her, too. Besides, I've always loved that city. Some of the nicest people I've ever met live there." Jeremy rolled his eyes.

Above them, thin strands of clouds floated past the moon, and on the horizon, Jeremy could see a storm approaching. In a few hours, the rains would come, but by then, he and Lexie would be sipping wine in her living room, listening as the raindrops pelted the rooftop.

In time, she turned toward him. "Thank you for coming back. For moving here . . . for everything."

"I had no choice. Love does funny things to people."

She smiled. "I love you, too, you know."

"Yeah, I know."

"What? You're not going to say it?"

"Do I have to?"

"You bet you do. And use the right tone, too. You have to say it like you mean it."

He grinned, wondering if she would guide his "tone" forever. "I love you, Lexie."

In the distance, a train whistle sounded, and Jeremy saw a pinprick of light in the darkened landscape. Had it been a foggy night, the lights would soon be appearing in the cemetery. Lexie seemed to follow his thoughts.

"So tell me, Mr. Science Journalist, do you still doubt the existence of miracles?"

"I just told you. You're my miracle."

She rested her head on his shoulder for a moment before reaching for his hand. "I'm talking about real miracles. When something happens that you never believed possible."

"No," he said. "I think there is always an explanation if one digs deep enough."

"Even if a miracle were to happen to us?"

Her voice was soft, almost a whisper, and he looked at her. He could see the reflection of the town lights flickering in her eyes.

"What are you talking about?"

She took a deep breath. "Doris shared some news with me earlier today."

Jeremy watched her face, unable to grasp what she was saying, even as her expression shifted from hesitant to animated to expectant. She gazed at him, waiting for him to say something, and still his mind refused to register her words.

There was science and then there was the unexplainable, and Jeremy had spent his life trying to reconcile the two. He dwelt in reality, scoffed at magic, and felt pity for the true believers. But as he gazed at Lexie, trying to make sense of what she was telling him, he found his old sense of surety slipping.

No, he couldn't explain it, and in the future, he never would. It defied the laws of biology, it shattered his assumptions about the man he knew himself to be. Quite simply, it was impossible, but when she gently placed his hand on her stomach, he believed with sudden, euphoric certainty the words he never thought he would hear.

"Here's our miracle," she whispered. "It's a girl."

Reading Group Guide

Discussion Questions

1. In the opening chapter of *True Believer*, science reporter Jeremy Marsh exposes the tricks of a famous psychic who claims to talk to the dead. Do you think it is possible to communicate with the dead? Why do so many people want to believe we can?

2. Also in the opening chapter, Jeremy, a New Yorker, says that Boone Creek, North Carolina, is "right between the *middle of nowhere* and '*where are we exactly?*'" It is the first of many "put-downs" of the small town. Is it common in America for urbanites to feel superior to those who live in small towns?

3. Like Boone Creek, many American towns and cities such as Gettysburg, Savannah, Charleston, New Orleans, and Boston have "ghost tours." Have you ever taken one? Have you or someone you know ever seen a ghost? Do you believe in them?

4. Lexie Darnell has been hurt in relationships and she admits she isn't a good judge of men. Why do you think she is attracted to men who are ultimately wrong for her?

5. Lexie is in a one-sided relationship with police officer Rodney Hopper, one-sided because he loves her and she doesn't feel the same. Do you think she is stringing him along? Why does Rodney keep pursuing Lexie when he knows his feelings aren't reciprocated? Have you ever been involved in a one-sided relationship and, if so, what role did you assume?

6. The reader finally learns that Jeremy's marriage failed not only because he traveled for his job, but because he was sterile. Do you think this would be a "deal-breaker" in most marriages?

7. Lexie and Jeremy's relationship has several obstacles to overcome. One of them is Lexie's determination that she isn't going to let "anyone or anything upset the balance" of her life. Do you think this is a positive or negative attitude? Can upsetting the balance ever be a good thing?

8. Jeremy pursues Lexie to the Outer Banks because he felt like he "didn't have a choice." Do you think that this kind of compelling desire is a component of "true love"? How does "true love" differ from a crush, a fling, or just sexual attraction?

9. Lexie's grandmother Doris says she has premonitions and presents some proof for this, but Jeremy remains a skeptic. Is Jeremy closed-minded? Do you think women are more likely than men to believe in the supernatural? Why or why not?

10. During one conversation, Jeremy talks about unfulfilled dreams. Lexie responds that "everyone has dreams that don't come true." Do you think it's important to have a dream, even if it isn't realized? Or does dreaming keep a person from facing life's realities?

11. Doris interferes, with good intentions, in Lexie's life. How much, or when, do you think a mother or grandmother should interfere in a daughter's life?

12. Doris says that Lexie "was a survivor" and would get over Jeremy faster than Jeremy would get over Lexie. Do you agree?

13. Lexie doesn't feel a long-distance relationship with Jeremy can work. Do you think they could have worked out a compromise? Why does Jeremy make the sacrifice and not Lexie?

14. The book ends with a miracle. Or is it something other than a miracle? What impact do you think this will have on Jeremy's skepticism? Is this miracle different from the paranormal events he rejects?

15. *True Believer* has a sequel entitled *At First Sight*. What do you think will happen in this story? What do you believe should happen?